THE BURIED SYMBOL

RUNES OF ISSALIA, BOOK I

JEFFREY L. KOHANEK

Jenny,
Follow your dreams.
Find your magic.

FALLBRANDT PRESS

Fifth Edition, 2019

ISBN: 978-1-949382-08-2
PUBLISHED BY JEFFREY L. KOHANEK and FALLBRANDT PRESS
www.JeffreyLKohanek.com

Print edition produced in the United States of America

This tale is dedicated to my family for their inspiration and support.
Believe…

ALSO BY JEFFREY L. KOHANEK

Fate of Wizardoms

Book One: Eye of Obscurance

Book Two: Balance of Magic

Book Three: Temple of the Oracle

Book Four: Objects of Power

Book Five: TBD

Book Six: TBD

* * *

Prequel: Legend of Shadowmar

Runes of Issalia

The Buried Symbol: Runes of Issalia 1

The Emblem Throne: Runes of Issalia 2

An Empire in Runes: Runes of Issalia 3

Rogue Legacy: Runes of Issalia Prequel

* * *

Runes of Issalia Boxed Set

Heroes of Issalia: Runes Series+Rogue Legacy

Wardens of Issalia

A Warden's Purpose: Wardens of Issalia 1

The Arcane Ward: Wardens of Issalia 2

An Imperial Gambit: Wardens of Issalia 3

A Kingdom Under Siege: Wardens of Issalia 4

ICON: A Wardens of Issalia Companion Tale

* * *

Wardens of Issalia Boxed Set

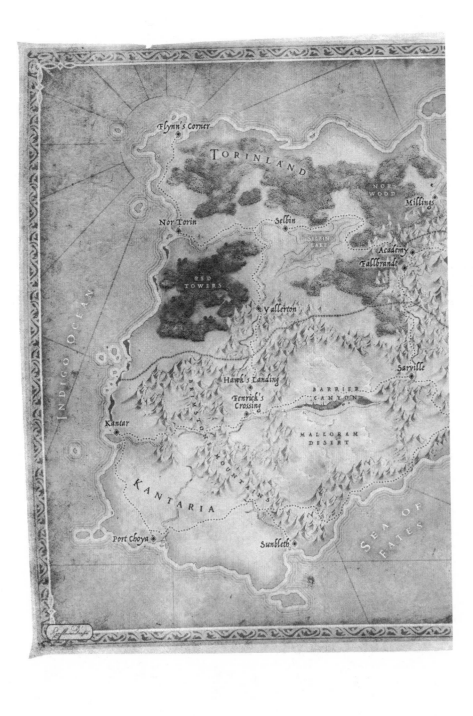

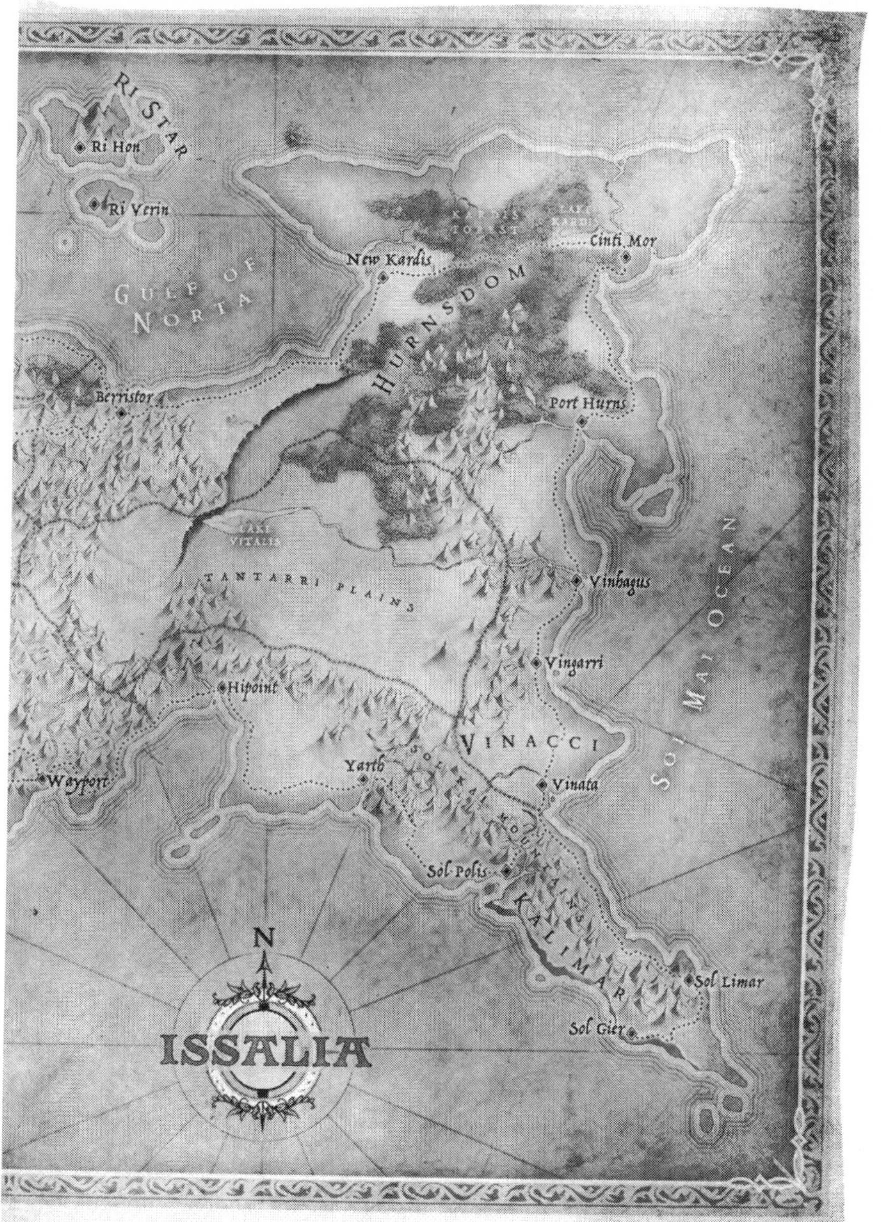
Ri Star
Ri Hon
Ri Verin
Gulf of Norta
New Kardis
Cinti Mor
Hurnsdom
Berristor
Port Hurns
Tantarri Plains
Vinhagus
Sol Mai Ocean
Vingarri
Hipoint
Vinacci
Yarth
Solkal Mountains
Vinata
Wayport
Sol Polis
Kalimar
Sol Limar
Sol Gier
N
Issalia

PART I

UNCHOSEN

1

Moisture from the mist left Brock's hair damp and the roof tiles slippery. He leaned against the brick chimney, ensuring his footing as he watched the shop across the street.

Now nearly midnight, the only light was the pale blue aura emitting from the glowlamps at nearby intersections. With the shop positioned midway between the lamps, the light barely reached it through the gloom. The effect of the blue glow upon the milky air gave an otherworldly feel to the quiet evening.

The door to the inn beneath him burst open, and two men stumbled out – the ruckus disturbing the tranquility of the setting. One man helped the other to his feet, and they set off down the street. Weaving as they walked, they bellowed a common tavern song, not caring that they were quite out of tune. Soon after the drunken men turned the corner their sorry song faded into the night.

When the street quieted, Brock heard another door open.

Through the fog, he could just make out the shop owner pulling the door shut. The man locked the deadbolt and hurried down the street, heading the opposite direction of the two drunks. He scurried past the glowlamp and was swallowed by the mist.

Stillness again loomed over the street and a tension as thick as the fog seeped in. Brock gathered his resolve and shimmied over the edge of the eave before dropping to the balcony below. He stepped over the railing and lowered himself with arms fully extended before he let go to lightly land on the wet cobblestones. With a furtive glance in each direction, Brock crossed the street and tested the handle, confirming that the door was locked. Reaching into a coat pocket, he withdrew a sheath containing a knife and bent needles. Skill and dexterity – combined with a childhood that danced at the edges of the law – took over. The deadbolt clicked open, and he slid inside.

After gently closing the door, Brock paused to listen for movement within the darkness. Deciding he was alone, he stowed the knife and needles in exchange for a glass tube from another pocket. After he gave the tube a couple good shakes it began to glow.

The light revealed the front section of the store, divided from the rest of the building by a long service desk. He circled the desk, observing shelves lined with jars and canisters filled with liquids and powders. It appeared to be a typical apothecary shop. After a week of spying, Brock knew otherwise.

He crept past the shelves with his gaze focused on the dark doorway at the back of the room. The soft light from the glowstick ate away at the darkness as he advanced, giving shape to the room beyond. Stopping before the doorway, Brock scanned the interior without crossing the threshold and considered the situation. *If there are traps set against thieves, they would be back here, beyond the area of normal business.*

Brock knelt to examine the floor beyond the doorway. From the low angle, he noticed one floorboard sticking above those around it and he frowned in thought. Perhaps the wood was swollen from moisture. Perhaps it was something else. Caution prompted inspiration as he reached into a coat pocket and removed a pouch filled with coins. He hefted the weight in his palm for a moment before tossing the pouch toward the floorboard and quickly spinning from the doorway.

The thump of the pouch landing was followed by a *twang* as two crossbow bolts flew through the doorway to impale the wooden shelf across from him. The *thud* from the impact of the bolts left Brock's heart pounding and his stomach twisting. He stared at the vibrating shafts and thanked Issal that they were embedded in the shelf and not in his chest.

Brock closed his eyes and took a calming breath. He hated this, but he had no choice. Once he found his resolve, he slid through the doorway, scooped up his coin purse, and paused to examine his surroundings.

Mounted on a stand atop a workbench was an empty dual crossbow, pointed toward the door. Two similar workbenches hugged the wall, each covered in bowls, vials, jars, papers, and hand tools. A wooden stool sat before each bench, and a large fireplace waited at the far end of the room.

Brock approached the nearest workbench and began searching for a hidden compartment. Finding nothing of note, he turned toward the next bench when the fireplace caught his attention. A stirring at the back of his mind made him think it an ideal location to hide items of value. He started toward the fireplace, stopping abruptly when that same stirring in his head erupted into a startling flash. Feeling a slight pressure against one shin, he leapt backward. A *swoosh* of air passed by his head, and a sharp pain stung him below his eye.

His hand went to his cheek as he looked up to see what had cut him.

Two spinning blades, set at a height to decapitate an average man, swung on a pole that had dropped from the ceiling. Brock's quick reaction upon feeling the tripwire had saved him from a grizzly death. Again, he thanked Issal for the luck that he still lived.

He grabbed a rag from the nearest bench and dabbed it on his wound, checking it to find that only a small streak of blood appeared on the cloth and that the cut was nothing of concern. After tossing the rag aside and ducking below the swinging blades, Brock warily advanced toward his goal at the end of the room.

Wider than Brock's arm span and stretching from floor to ceiling, the fireplace was constructed from irregular stones the size of a man's head. A large black kettle occupied an arched opening that stood eye level to Brock at its apex. He spit on the kettle to test if it was hot. When the saliva did not sizzle, he reached out and touched the cast-iron body, confirming that the kettle felt cold.

Brock held the glowstick inside the fireplace to inspect the interior. Looking up, he noticed one stone less soot-covered than the others. He nudged the stone with his hand and discovered that it was loose. Twisting his body to grab it with both hands, he wiggled and pulled until the stone came free. He set it down and reached into the opening, immediately feeling something hard and smooth. Grasping it, he withdrew a small jar, opened it, and sniffed to identify the contents. A bitter aroma attacked his senses, making his eyes water and leaving him lightheaded. It was Yellow Sky. The presence of the illegal drug confirmed his suspicions about the shop owner –

abusing his vocation by creating the addictive drug to sell on the streets of Kantar.

Holding the glowstick high, he peered into the hole to find a dark pouch among six similar jars. Brock replaced the jar and grabbed the pouch, which clinked with the sound of coins as he stepped from the fireplace. After loosening the drawstring at the top, Brock peeked inside and saw the glint of gold. A satisfied grin spread across his face as he examined his newfound wealth.

A startled yelp escaped from his lips when something moved within the sack. He quickly dumped the contents of the pouch onto the nearest workbench and coins spilled out, the gold and silver disks spreading on the benchtop, along with something else. Brock's alarmed eyes grew wide when a red scorpion emerged from the pile. He knew that the little critters were lethal – a single sting could send their victims into seizure, foaming at the mouth as paralysis set in, followed by a slow and painful death.

The upset scorpion scuttled across the bench and disappeared into a leather glove. Brock scooped the coins back into the pouch, wondering if the creature would sting the shop owner when he next used those gloves. If the man was willing to deal with a scorpion, Brock mused, it was at his own risk.

Retracing his steps through the store, he slid his glowstick into his coat and peeked out the window. With nobody in sight, he slipped out the door and faded into the foggy night.

2

Light from the rising sun crept westward across the continent, toward the province of Kantaria. For some time, the peaks of the Brimstone Mountains kept the capital city of Kantar in shadow, allowing the fog's embrace of the city to linger. Once the sun crested those peaks, the heat from its rays began to burn away the marine layer that had covered the city after nightfall. As if retreating in fear of the light, the wall of mist slowly faded back toward the ocean, revealing the world that had been hidden beneath its white blanket.

To the south, the dissipating fog revealed farmers already tending their crops. Water from the Alitus River flowed from the nearby mountains as it wound its way past the southern outskirts of the city. Sluice gates lining the banks of the river provided a steady flow for irrigation ducts that fed the fields and orchards that stretched toward the southern horizon.

The morning bell tolled, marking the start of a new day, and the gates of the city opened to welcome locals and travelers who had gathered in the early morning hours. Some had arrived from the east via Glowridge Pass, while those coming from the south had crossed the bridge over the Alitus River.

To the west was Kantar Bay, the largest harbor on the Indigo Ocean. Two ships drifted into port while dockworkers lined up with wagons, ready to unload the cargo and deliver the goods to the holding yard for distribution.

Other ships that had docked overnight were being loaded with fresh cargo to be delivered to distant ports for sale or trade. The slips closer to shore – where the smaller watercraft docked – sat empty, with the local fishermen already off in search of the day's catch.

Inside the walls of Kantar, the streets were coming alive. One such street housed businesses tucked along the eastern wall in the district of Lower Kantar. This particular street was the least desirable in the city, avoided by most citizens because of the pungent odors coming from the fisheries, tanneries, and metal smelters that operated there. The predominant west winds pushed the unpleasant smells away from the city and toward the mountains to the East. Someone with a flair for ironic humor had long ago named it Flower Street.

As the rising sun crested the eastern wall, a ray of sunlight streamed into the second story loft of a nondescript tannery. Sunlight crept down the wall until it shined on a pallet where a brown-haired teen slept. The warmth and light from the incoming sunbeam caused him to stir. Opening his eyes, he rubbed them to work the sleep away and sat up to look toward the pallid-skinned woman on the nearby bed.

He leaned over and gently shook her frail body. After a moment, her eyes flickered open. She blinked as she turned to face him. Although she had seen only twenty-nine summers, she appeared much older – worn and visibly ill.

Her heavy eyes gazed at him, focused on the intense green eyes staring back. His disheveled brown hair enhanced his engaging smile.

"G 'morning Ellie," he said softly. "How are you feeling?"

"Brock," Ellie mumbled, "I'm so tired…" Her weak breath emanated the fetid stench of the disease that racked her body.

Brock reached for a pewter cup resting on the nightstand. "Here. Drink some water."

He lifted her head with one hand while holding the cup to her mouth. She slowly took a sip, her gaze never leaving him. After swallowing, she spoke again.

"There is more for you, Brock. Your future remains open and the life of an Unchosen is no life to live," she pleaded. "I want so much more for you. Your mother did too."

"What choice do I have, Ellie? It's not like I have options," he replied.

Ellie began to cough, clutching her stomach in pain. When the coughing subsided, she spoke again.

"No, there's a way. My friend, Harriet knew the Unchosen whom the Ministry executed at Southgate last year. Before his capture, he told her about a man named Alonzo." She paused for a wheezing breath. "Apparently, he can be found at the Aspen Inn, near the Lower Wall gate. The price is steep, but he can help you start a new life."

She lifted her arm, her hand shaking as it reached out to touch his face. Her eyes locked on his, pleading.

"Promise me that when I'm gone, you'll do this."

Ellie's eyes remained on Brock, waiting for his response until another round of coughing spoiled the moment.

When she quieted, he responded, "Nothing's going to happen to you Ellie. I had a good night, and I now have enough money to pay a medicus to come see you."

Her eyes had fallen closed while he spoke. He tried to get her to take another drink but found her unresponsive. If not for the slight movement of her chest rising and falling, she could be a corpse.

Brock could see that she was getting worse every day, but he could save her. He now had the money he needed, but he didn't have much time. The thought of losing Ellie stirred memories of his mother and brought a pang of loss.

Deciding that he had best hurry, he kissed her forehead and began to dress.

Brock slipped into his worn brown trousers and his over-sized leather boots. He pulled a light-brown shirt with torn armpits over his head as he climbed to his feet. From a hook on the wall, he grabbed the thigh-length leather coat that held his knife, glowstick, and lock picks. He pulled the coat on as he ran to the stairwell.

When he descended into the tannery, Brock saw his father busy treating a hide. As usual, the man was well into his work before Brock woke. Despite the pungent smell filling the room, Brock was unaffected after living with it for seventeen years.

His father was of average height with a sparsely populated head of short brown hair. He wore heavy leather gloves and a tanner's smock to protect him from the harsh chemicals. The man glanced up from his work when he noticed Brock.

"It's about time you got up, boy." His father always called him boy. "I thought you were going to sleep the whole day away."

Brock knew enough not to be confrontational, instead focusing on what was important.

"She's not doing well, Father. She needs help."

His father glanced toward him again. His brow furrowed, distorting the *artifex humis* rune that marked his forehead. "Well, be that as it may, I've no means to help your aunt Ellie. If it's her time, hopefully she's done enough good in this life that Issal will bless her in the next."

The man turned back to the hide he was treating. Brock's lips pressed together, and he tried again.

"If you don't have anything pressing for me right now, I want to see if I can find someone to help her."

His father continued to work the hide as if he hadn't heard a word. After a minute, he sighed. "Go on and do what you think you need to do."

Brock hurried out the door before his father changed his mind.

Weaving through the crowd, Brock's feet moved as quickly as possible without attracting the attention of the city guards. How could he explain the gold in his purse?

He turned from Alistair Avenue onto Center Street and the foot traffic thickened, the smell from the bakery he passed causing his stomach to rumble and reminding him that he had yet to break his fast. Continuing upward as the street's slope increased, he passed numerous shops and vendors including farmers selling fruit and vegetables off the back of wagons, butchers offering their best cuts of meat, and tailors displaying garments for sale.

Melvin, who often purchased hides from Brock's father, was placing a pair of black leather boots in his shop window. Brock paused to stare through the glass, longing for a new pair of boots to replace the oversized pair he wore now.

A fast-approaching rumble broke him from his reverie. Turning, Brock saw a steam carriage roaring toward him. He dodged to the side as it sped past and continued down the hill toward Southgate.

Staring at the rear of the coach as it rolled on, he wondered what it would be like to ride in such an amazing contraption, knowing he could never afford one. He turned as a man barged into him, knocking him back.

"Watch where you're going, you filthy Unchosen," the man grumbled.

Not wanting to draw trouble, Brock gave a small bow. "Sorry, sir. It was my fault. Won't happen again."

The man sneered as he walked away. A frown rested upon Brock's face as he stared at the man's back. A moment later he turned and moved along, soon approaching the wall that separated Lower Kantar from Upper Kantar. As he passed through the gate, he glanced up at the brick barrier towering above him. The other side of the wall revealed a district far different from the one below.

The wide clean streets and elegant buildings of Upper Kantar were a stark contrast to the dirty streets and dilapidated buildings that prevailed in the lower portion of the city. Within Lower Kantar, only Center Street and Alistair Avenue largely escaped these issues.

His gaze landed on the Citadel, looming above the city. The bright sun made the stone towers appear like pale sentinels watching over the people of Kantar. Light reflected off the stained glass panels of the Citadel Temple's domed roof. With the backdrop of vertical rock walls behind the citadel, the image was impressive. The idea of living in Upper Kantar seemed like a dream, but the concept of living in the Citadel was unimaginable.

He passed a blacksmith shop and slowed to admire a beautiful longsword and dagger displayed in the window. Turning at the next intersection, he approached the second door on the right, knocked, and stepped back to wait. With a glance, he read the sign above the door, engraved with the words *Miguel Guyenne, Medicus*.

A young man, a few years older than Brock, opened the door. He was tall and thin with well-kempt black hair combed to one side. The bangs hanging on his forehead partly obscured the *medicus* rune that marked him for his vocation. Brock assumed the young man to be Guyenne's apprentice.

"I'm here with a commission for Medicus Guyenne," Brock said.

The apprentice looked him up and down with a doubtful expression. "Medicus Guyenne is far too busy for jokes. You should run along to wherever you came from, boy," he replied with a sneer.

Taking a breath to keep his cool, Brock reached into his coat and removed a leather pouch, the coins inside clinking distinctively.

"I met with the medicus last week and he told me he'd heal my aunt if I could pay the commission," Brock explained. "Inside this pouch are four gold Imperials, which is the rate he quoted. She's very ill and needs attention as soon as possible."

The apprentice grimaced, hesitating before retreating into the building.

Brock stepped into the same room he had waited in a week earlier, closing the door behind him. The waiting room had a glossy wooden floor, a high ceiling, and wood-paneled walls. Six chairs ran along two of the walls, between the two entrances to the room.

He soon heard footsteps approaching. The interior door opened and a man with silver-peppered black hair emerged, followed by the apprentice.

"I understand that you have funds for a commission." The man's heavy brow and piercing brown eyes gave a serious weight to his gaze.

"Yes, sir. I have the four gold Imperials you require to come heal my aunt."

He handed the pouch to Guyenne, waiting anxiously as the medicus examined the contents. Guyenne's eyebrows lifted in surprise as he looked at Brock in a moment of consideration. The medicus handed the pouch to his apprentice and then turned to Brock.

"Let me gather my supplies, and we'll be on our way."

Pushing past his apprentice, the man stepped through the interior doorway. The apprentice grimaced at Brock before turning to follow his master through the door.

Brock ignored the look of disgust that Guyenne's apprentice flashed toward him. He was used to others treating him with contempt. That is, if they bothered to acknowledge him at all. When they approached Flower Street, the apprentice pinched his face, further souring his disposition.

"What's that horrible smell? Do we really have to be here?" the young man complained.

Guyenne nodded. "That's the aroma of Flower Street. I'm sure you've heard of it. And, yes, we do have to be here. I promised this boy that I'd come and help his aunt if he paid the commission."

They turned onto Flower Street and approached the tannery. When Brock opened the door, holding it for Guyenne and his apprentice to enter, he couldn't help but smile after they passed him. If the apprentice didn't like the smell before, he really wasn't going to like the smell inside the tannery.

Brock's father glanced up from his work, visibly startled to see the well-dressed medicus and his apprentice. Dropping his tools, he removed his gloves and greeted the two men.

"Hello good sirs. I'm Milan Tannerson, owner of this shop. What can I do for you?" Brock's father extended his hand.

Guyenne ignored the man's hand. "I've accepted a commission to treat this young man's aunt. Where can I find her?"

Confusion crossed Milan's face. "You...I...well...she's upstairs." Milan's brow furrowed. "But I don't understand. Who paid the commission? Are you aware that she's Unchosen?"

With his apprentice in tow, Guyenne headed for the staircase. He turned his head to respond over his shoulder. "The boy paid the sum required."

The medicus ascended the stairs without looking back. Milan turned toward Brock, his face red with anger. Brock hesitated for a moment before bolting up the stairs.

Arriving in the loft, he noticed that his aunt hadn't moved since he had left. The medicus approached Ellie, setting his case down beside the bed. He pressed his fingers to the side of her neck and then bent to put his ear to her chest. After a moment, he picked up his bag and turned to Brock.

"I'm sorry, but I cannot help this woman." Guyenne's voice reflected regret.

Brock was stunned. "But sir, you promised you'd heal her if I paid you."

Guyenne retreated to the stairwell, pausing at the top to share a sympathetic look.

"I cannot heal the dead, young man. Nobody can. Not even the most skilled healer within the Ministry." The man and his apprentice quickly descended the stairwell.

Shock held Brock in a momentary stasis. *She was alive just an hour ago.* He rushed to her and knelt at the bedside. Calling her name, he shook the woman and tried desperately to wake her. He patted her cheek while tears tracked down his.

"Ellie! Ellie! Please wake up!" His voice croaked with pain, desperation. "The medicus is here to heal you! Ellie!"

Her skin felt cold and clammy. *How could she die when I was so close to saving her?* Something inside him broke. His cheek lowered to her forehead, and he sobbed.

"It was her time, boy." His father's voice came from behind him. "Like your mother, she's moved on from this life. We just have to pray that she lived well so Issal will bless her with a better station in the next life."

Through a blur of tears, Brock turned toward his father.

"Ellie filled the hole in my heart when mom died. What am I going to do without her?" Using his sleeve, he wiped the tears from his face.

After a moment, his father responded, "Here's what you're going to do. You will fill that hole with honest work, boy." His voice took on an edge of anger. "I don't know how you came up with the gold needed for a medicus to break the law and come to heal your aunt, but I do know it was nothing honest."

His voice rose to shouting. "First, you will take a batch of hides out in the yard and clean them up. Then you're going to march over to the stockyards for another batch. And that's only the beginning." He paused, pointing at Brock. "See, your hole will be filled with work because you won't have time for anything else."

His father turned and stormed down the stairs, leaving Brock with his dead aunt in his arms.

3

The days seemed a blur. Brock's father worked him relentlessly from dawn to well past sunset. Exhausted at the end of each day, Brock would drag himself up to the loft and fall into bed. His lone break came on the second day when he and Milan visited the seaside to attend Ellie's funeral. An hour later and he was right back to work.

Three weeks and two days into this grueling schedule, Milan relented and began to wrap up the day's work while the sun was still above the horizon. Brock ran out into the tannery yard and washed to remove the grime and smell from the day's efforts. Entering the rear apartment where his father lived, he quickly ate dinner before rushing up to the loft to change.

Once in his street clothes, he grabbed his coat and returned downstairs.

He stopped back in the apartment and grabbed two extra biscuits while his father was clearing the table. With a wave to Milan, he ran out the door with one biscuit in his mouth and the other in his pocket. When he emerged outside, he squinted in the sunlight. It was still warm, so he carried his coat under one arm, expecting that he would need it after the sun set.

Brock hurried down Alistair Avenue, turning south when he reached Center Street. Just prior to reaching Southgate, he spotted a teenage boy sitting on the ground, leaning against the outer wall of a butcher's shop. The boy had unkempt blond hair and a dirty face. A forlorn look reflected in his blue eyes as he begged passers-by for coin or food. The boy's long, thin fingers gripped a dented pewter cup held above the dirty gray blanket that covered his unmoving legs. It was a pitiful sight.

Brock walked up to the boy, who happened to be facing the other direction, and gave him a swift kick.

"Ouch!" The boy yelled as he grabbed his leg.

"I guess you *can* feel those legs," Brock said with a smile. "I'll try to be more careful."

"Brock!" the beggar exclaimed. "Where've you been? I was afraid you'd gotten yourself thrown into jail."

Brock smiled. "Sorry, Tipper. My father figured I'd been stealing again, and he set me to a grueling work schedule. I think he finally got tired of it himself after three weeks. I'm sure he thinks I've learned my lesson, so he let me off early today."

Tipper smiled. "You got here just in time. I was about to close up shop and head over to Sally's. That is, unless you've got other ideas."

Brock tossed the biscuit to Tipper, who snatched it with his free hand. "I'd rather sit and talk for a bit. How about up on the wall?"

Tipper put the biscuit in his mouth, grabbed his blanket, and stood to dust the dirt off of his pants. Standing a half-head taller than Brock, Tipper smiled down at his friend while he chewed. While Brock was thin, his short frame carried a fair amount of muscle from many hours of carrying hides. Tipper was just thin, with long wiry limbs.

Tipper darted down the adjacent alley as he yelled, "Let me put my stuff away, and we can head up there."

After a minute, Tipper re-appeared while stuffing the last bite of the biscuit into his mouth.

They headed toward Southgate and turned west just before the wall.

Looping around a guardhouse along the wall, they climbed onto an old crate. Tipper grunted as he hoisted Brock up until he could reach the eave of the guardhouse. Brock pulled himself onto the roof and then crossed to a ladder waiting beside the trap door to the guardhouse below. He lowered the ladder to the ground for Tipper to climb, and he then lifted it and placed the ladder back against the wall. Without hesitation, Brock scaled the ladder with Tipper following close behind.

The wall, which surrounded three sides of the city, was about four strides deep. The outer rim of the wall stood waist-high at the low points with merlons lining it such that the top of each stood just above Brock's head.

The two boys turned and walked down the wall, toward the bay. At the midpoint between the gate and the western wall, they each sat on neighboring merlons with their legs dangling three stories above the ground. Brock settled in and gazed at his surroundings.

Palms swayed in the wind, their movement synchronized as if dancing to the slow song of the ocean. The cool breeze ruffled Brock's hair, causing him to squint and blink as it dried his eyes. Looking to the west, he saw the last rays of the sun reflecting on the water at the distant horizon, the low evening sun casting a red hue on the clouds above. In mere minutes, the ocean would swallow the sun completely.

The last ship of the day was nearing the docks, its sails down as it drifted into port. Workers scurried around the docks in an effort to finish the day's business before the last remnants of light gave way to the black of night.

To the south was the majesty of the Southgate Bridge, rising over the Alitus River. The blue stone bridge appeared purple in the reddish hue of the fading sunlight. One lonely wagon rolled over the peak of the bridge before disappearing from sight on the downslope. The straight lines of farm fields stretched into the hazy distance, beyond the river.

Brock sat in quiet, relishing the peaceful view as the light of the setting sun continued to fade. He tried to internalize the tranquility of the moment, hoping to mend his broken heart. After ten minutes of silence, he finally spoke.

"Ellie died," he said without looking at Tipper.

Tipper knew how much Brock's aunt meant to him. He also knew she was quite ill.

"I'm sorry, Brock."

Brock turned to look at his friend. "Tip, I had the gold needed to pay a medicus to come help her. I got the last bit I needed from that dirty apothecary, and I went straight to the medicus the next morning." He looked down as emotion welled up inside. "But when we got back to my pa's place, she was already dead." He paused as a tear dropped off his cheek, carried away by the breeze. "Why couldn't she hang on a little longer? Why did she have to die?"

A quiet moment passed before Tipper spoke. "You did your best, Brock. She was very ill. What else could you do?"

He turned toward Tipper and shouted. "I could have saved her if I knew how!"

Tipper glanced around. "Quiet! Do you want them to catch us up here?"

Brock turned toward the ocean. His mind drifted back to his last conversation with Ellie. After a minute, he spoke again.

"I can't live this way, Tipper. I want to make a difference. I need to do something."

Tipper responded, "What can you do? We're stuck with the lot we're dealt. We just have to ride this life out and hope for a better one in the next life. That's what the Ministry tells us, right?"

Brock turned toward Tipper. "I've decided I won't accept that line of thinking any longer. I want to do something more. I need to try to make my own life, a better life. I don't want to live like this."

Tipper stared back intently, nodding. "Okay. I assume you have a plan. I know you don't do anything without a plan."

Spinning around, Brock jumped off the merlon onto the wall. He waved Tipper down as he started toward the gate.

"Let's go. We have to visit a man at the Aspen Inn."

Stars began appearing through the dim light of dusk as dockworkers and sailors streamed through the gate. Like two leaves caught in a swift stream, Brock and Tipper found themselves swept along with the crowd. The glowlamps lining Center Street provided an inviting path through the heart of the city. The further they walked, the thinner the crowd became as groups peeled off to their evening destination. By the time they neared the Lower Wall, only a few stragglers remained.

Brock continually scanned the signs of the shops and inns as they passed. Spotting a sign with a single tree carved into it, he and Tipper broke from the crowd and entered the inn.

The common room buzzed with loud conversation, while the air carried the aroma of spiced lamb. Most tables were full, the benches and stools occupied. A number of patrons were eagerly consuming bowls of stew, while others simply had a tankard of ale in hand.

Brock approached the bar and signaled for the barkeep, a man with a round face and bushy black mustache. With sleeves pushed up to his elbows, he wore a dirty apron around his portly mid-section. After handing a fresh ale to a patron, the barkeep slid over and gave them a stare.

"What do you boys want?" the man grumbled.

Brock addressed the large man. "We're looking for a fellow named Alonzo."

The barkeep snorted. "Is that so? Well, you're in luck 'cause he's right over there."

He nodded toward a man at the end of the bar, whose balding head sported less hair than his beard-covered face. The barkeep stepped away to help another customer.

Brock traversed the bar, claiming the stool next to the man as Tipper sat at the other open seat.

"I'm looking for Alonzo." Brock announced. "I hear he can help me with something. Are you the man I'm looking for?"

The man glanced over, squinting to assess Brock before responding. Brock noted the rune of *mercator* on the man's forehead, marking him as a trader.

"Might be. It depends on why you're asking," the man responded.

He took a long swig of his ale, his eyes remaining on Brock throughout the process.

Brock shrugged. "My aunt suggested I seek out Alonzo at this inn. She said he could help improve my situation."

Brock brought his hand up to his forehead to ensure Alonzo understood his meaning. Alonzo's eyes followed his hand, obviously noting the lack of a rune.

"Might be that I can be of assistance, but it ain't free." Alonzo took another drink, setting the mug back on the bar. "I'll be needin' five Imperials."

Brock sighed. He only had two Imperials and nine silver marks left.

The rest had gone to pay the medicus for Ellie.

Brock responded, "Okay, but I need a little time to pull that much together. Where can I find you?"

Alonzo smiled. "I'm right here every night. When you get the gold, come see me and we'll do business."

Brock slid off the barstool, motioning for Tipper to follow as he headed out the door. Once outside, he began walking back toward Southgate.

Tipper caught up to him. "What was that about? What did you mean when you said he has a way to improve your situation? What situation?"

"This life, Tipper," Brock said. "The situation of this dead-end life."

4

B rock needed more gold and only knew one way to get it.

Halfway to Southgate, he and Tipper ducked into a dark alley. Once beyond the mouth of the narrow corridor, they put their backs to a wall and watched the alley entrance. Confirming they weren't followed, Brock tugged on Tipper's sleeve and continued.

They crossed a dark intersection and circled around the trash and old barrels that had been discarded there. The alley soon terminated at a wall made of stones, creating a dead end. Brock put his hands on the wall and began feeling the stones. He could barely see the wall in the darkness, but that was irrelevant. Even in the light of day, you needed to feel with your hands to find the trigger. After a bit, he found a stone with a pattern of five shallow dimples.

When he leaned against the stone, it sank into the wall. A distinct click sounded as a section of the wall began to move, revealing a hidden door that slowly swung open. The rank stench of human waste wafted from the pitch-black space within.

Brock stepped inside and removed his glowstick. Once activated, the blue light illuminated the upper portion of a stairwell that led into inky darkness. Brock began his descent with Tipper close behind. In the dim light of the glowstick, he could barely see the far wall of the sewer tunnel, fifteen feet away. A thud sounded when the stone door behind them closed, echoing in the quiet tunnels.

Upon reaching the bottom of the stairs, they continued down the tunnel, carefully navigating the narrow brick ledge that ran along the wall. They soon heard a dull roar ahead, the noise growing louder as they drew closer. When they reached a recessed door in the side of the tunnel, Brock knocked five times. After a couple seconds, he opened the door and light poured into the tunnel.

The dull roar instantly transformed to the rumble of loud conversation. Big Ed nodded as they entered, setting his cudgel back on the floor and leaning it against the wall near his stool. The bouncer crossed his beefy arms and resumed monitoring the crowd.

Patrons occupied tables, chatting, eating, and drinking. A man in one corner celebrated a winning dice throw, hooting and jumping around. Two intoxicated men were harassing a pretty waitress as she deftly swatted groping hands. All were common traits found in any taproom in Lower Kantar. However, this was no ordinary taproom.

For one thing, nobody in the room was marked with a rune on his or her forehead. This place was a secret refuge for Unchosen – the one place in Kantar where they felt welcome and were treated as equals, treated like humans.

The second unique aspect of the taproom was Sally.

She was an attractive middle-aged woman with long brown hair. Although a bit plump, her weight was distributed in all the right places, giving her a voluptuous figure that the male patrons admired. However, those men soon learned that Sally was to be respected. Unwanted attention would likely earn them a cracked head and see them tossed into the sewer outside.

As Brock approached the bar, Sally's eyes met his. A smile spread across her face and he gave a broad smile in return. It was difficult not to smile when Sally smiled at you.

She finished pouring a tankard of ale, set it before a man at the bar, and pocketed his copper. Brock and Tipper grabbed two open stools as Sally walked over to greet them.

"Brock, Tipper. How are my favorite boys?" Her brow furrowed at Brock. "Where've you been? I haven't seen you for weeks."

Brock flashed a smile. "Hi, Sally. Sorry I haven't been around. I ran into a bit of trouble with my father and was on lockdown for a while." He paused and the smile slid off his face. "Ellie died, Sally. She's gone."

Sally's face clouded with sympathy. She reached across the bar and held her hand to Brock's cheek. "I'm so sorry to hear that, dear. She was a good woman. I know how much she meant to you after your momma died."

Tipper cleared his throat, breaking the somber moment. "Sally, can we get something to drink? I was on the street all day, and Brock has been running me around ever since. I'm parched."

Sally stepped away, returning a moment later with two mugs. "Here you go. It's on the house."

They both took a big drink of the cider. Brock set his mug on the bar and smacked his lips before speaking.

"Sally, I need another mark. Same rules apply. It needs to be someone who is shady. I'd rather not target someone who's honest, regardless of his or her station."

While she had looks, personality, and compassion, what made Sally special was her being the ultimate source of information within the city. People often ignored Unchosen, which allowed them to overhear things normally kept secret. Those secrets inevitably found their way to Sally.

She stared back a moment before releasing a sigh. "You seem determined. I suppose I do have a mark that suits your needs. If the rumor proves true, what he's doing is horrible. It might be particularly dangerous though."

She stepped away to help another customer.

Tipper leaned close. "I have a bad feeling about this. She wouldn't warn you unless there was a problem."

Brock turned toward Tipper, speaking with determination. "I have to do this, Tip. I'm willing to take a few risks."

"Okay, Brock." Tipper shrugged. "If you're sure you want to do this, I'm here to help."

Sally returned, holding a piece of paper toward Brock. He grabbed it, but she held it tight, looking him in the eye as she spoke. "Be careful."

Releasing the note, she stepped away to help another patron. He opened it and read the contents.

Tipper peeked at the paper. "What's it say?"

Like most Unchosen, Tipper couldn't read. Brock was a rare exception.

Brock took one last swig of cider and slid off the stool. "C'mon. I'll tell you after we're out of here."

5

After a long day of working hides, Brock headed out with concern occupying his mind as he passed through the streets of Lower Kantar. What he was planning was dangerous and held life-altering implications. Crimes against members of the Ministry were treated harshly in all cases. Being Unchosen only made it worse.

Brock turned the corner, leaving Center Street behind as he approached the temple near the Southgate guardhouse. He stopped when he spotted Tipper seated with his back against the temple wall, begging to those passing by. A score of people passed in and out of the temple over the next ten minutes, none offering Tipper a single copper.

Finally noticing Brock, Tipper gathered his things and crossed the street to where Brock waited. A moment later, he had settled on the ground and resumed his pose. Without looking at Brock, Tipper spoke.

"Samson's inside now. I followed him last night to a house along the West Wall. He seemed nervous and stopped to check if anyone followed, but I was careful to stay out of sight. I bet he goes there again tonight."

Brock listened to Tipper as he worked on a plan. After a moment, he responded, "When he leaves, you wait here for a bit. He may have noticed you by now, but he won't be looking for me, so I'll follow instead. After he's been gone for fifteen minutes, you head over to that house.

Let's meet across the street from it. If you don't see me within an hour, I'll meet you at Sally's."

"Will do," Tipper replied before calling out to someone walking past.

"Please ma'am. Can you spare a copper for a homeless Unchosen?" Without pause, the woman continued and entered the temple.

Brock chuckled as he pulled an apple from his pocket and tossed it to Tipper. He then strolled down the street until he found a spot on a low wall where he could sit and still see the temple entrance.

A half-hour later, the sky darkened as dusk set in. A junior minister emerged from the temple and grabbed the small glowlamp located near the door. After a few shakes, it came alive with soft blue light. He then placed it into the wall sconce and disappeared back inside.

Ten minutes later, a man in a dark cloak emerged from the temple, heading directly toward Brock. As the man walked past, Brock stared hard at him. Even in the fading light, the spiked blond hair made him easy to identify. It was Minister Samson.

Brock watched the back of the man's cloak as Samson continued westward. After a moment, he stood and followed along.

Samson turned north at an intersection just short of the West Wall. Brock quickened his pace until he was close to the intersection before slowing to a casual walk. As he crossed the opening, he glanced right and spotted a shadow near a glowlamp two buildings down, realizing that Samson had stopped with his back to the light and was watching for anyone following. Brock continued his casual pace until he was clear of the intersection and beyond Samson's vision.

Brock then leapt onto the rim of a full rain barrel. The extra height enabled him to jump and grab the edge of the second-story balcony. He pulled himself up and was soon standing on the balcony railing. With practiced balance, he leapt to grab the drainpipe anchored to the wall above the barrel and scaled the pipe until he could pull himself onto the second-story rooftop. He hurried across the tiled roof to the neighboring building, slowing once past the glowlamp below. Lying on his stomach, he pulled himself to the edge and saw Samson standing near the lamp, still looking toward the street corner.

Samson then turned and hurried down the street, passing directly below Brock's position. Brock stood and hurried along the rooftops as he followed the man.

Brock came to a gap where a narrow alley crossed the street below. He paused to check if Samson turned, but the man continued on. Backing up two steps, Brock leapt over the span to the next rooftop, hurrying to catch his prey. When he stopped to peek over the roof edge again, Brock spotted Samson turning left at the next intersection. Brock made his way across the roof until he was directly over that street and saw Samson passing below him, heading toward the West Wall.

Brock hurried along the roof edge, keeping Samson in sight until the Minister turned right onto the last street before the city wall. A stab of panic struck when Brock realized that there was no way he could jump to the next rooftop. He needed to get down to the street before he lost the man.

As he was searching for a way down, Brock saw Samson enter a building not far from the intersection and he discovered that he had successfully followed the man to his destination. Deciding that his current location was an ideal place to stage his lookout, he settled in to wait for Tipper.

The evening fog continued to thicken as Brock watched the house across the street from his rooftop perch. Located at the outer edge of town with no shops or inns nearby, the area was dark and quiet.

After a half-hour, he began to worry.

"Where is he? He should be here by now," Brock muttered to himself.

Hearing a noise below, he leaned over the edge and saw two men heading in his direction, one with a bundle over his shoulder. As they passed below him, he overheard their conversation.

"…was right. This one was even easier than the others."

The other man replied, "As long as he pays us the same, I don't care."

The first man made a suggestion: "You wanna head over to Drake's for a drink after this?"

The response was too muffled to hear as they passed beyond earshot and approached the same house that Samson had entered. The unburdened man knocked and waited. When the door opened, soft blue light bled into the street and the first man entered. As his partner neared the light, Brock noticed the bundle move. *There is a person wrapped in that bundle!*

The bundle began to squirm wildly, and the man swung the bundle against the doorframe, producing a *thud* that Brock heard from his perch. The bundle fell limp, and the door closed, leaving the street dark and quiet.

Brock swallowed hard. Sally had been correct. The note said that Minister Samson was involved with a slavery ring, kidnapping Unchosen. Seeing those men smuggle somebody into the house confirmed the rumor. Unchosen disappearing was nothing new, but Brock had always assumed it was due to them leaving the city or dying a natural death. Unchosen didn't have much in the way of rights, but at least they were free. The thought of a life of slavery appalled him.

Although there were three men in that house and he was alone, Brock felt that he had to do something to help. Steeling himself, he began looking for a way down.

When he spotted a balcony on the building next door, Brock crept across the damp roof until he was above it. He slid over the edge to hang by his hands before dropping feet-first onto the balcony. He climbed over the railing and hung from the edge again, landing on the street below.

Darting across the street, he hugged his back against the building next to the one the men had entered. He remained still, listening for a minute as he considered his next move.

Noise from a door opening startled him. Soft blue light poured into the street and the two thugs emerged, closing the door behind them.

They turned north, walking away from where Brock now stood. One man elbowed the other.

"You ready to grab that drink now?"

"You know it," the other man responded. "I hope that busty wench is working tonight. I think she likes me"

"I'm sure she does, Mick. I heard she goes for big smelly guys who're missing half their teeth."

Mick pushed the other man. "Funny, Wes. You're just jealous because she ignores..."

The sound of the two men faded and the street was again quiet.

With the two thugs out of the house, Samson and his victim might be the only two remaining. Brock considered his options and decided it was a chance he was willing to take.

Creeping to the front of the house, he tried to peer through the window but couldn't see beyond the closed drapes. He put his ear to the door and listened. Not hearing anything, he tested the door. It was unlocked so he turned the knob and stepped inside.

Light from the glowlamp near the door illuminated the first floor of the house. An empty sitting room with a brick fireplace was to his left, a small kitchen area with a dining table to his right. Other than the glowlamp, there was no sign of activity.

He climbed the stairwell across from the front door, finding the second story empty other than dusty furniture.

Brock crept back down to check the closet under the stairs. Finding it dark and completely empty, he returned to stand near the lamp.

I have inspected the entire house. Where are they? They hadn't left out the front door and he hadn't found any other exits.

Mentally retracing his steps, he tried to place anything odd and it occurred to him that the closet under the stairs was completely empty. Why is there *nothing* inside a closet?

Brock opened the closet door again and drew his glowstick, activating it. With the added light, he spotted a small knothole in the floorboards. He put two fingers in the knothole and lifted. A trap door swung upward to expose steep wooden stairs leading into the darkness below. He drew his knife and descended into the cellar.

Holding his glowstick high, he found the cellar empty until he turned and noticed a dark opening cut into the far wall. Two heavy posts and a crossbeam framed the opening, holding the earth in place around it. As Brock approached the doorway, the light from the glowstick revealed a tunnel just wide enough for two men. The tunnel sloped downward, likely going under the wall and out of the city. He crept down the tunnel, pausing when he heard noises ahead.

After stuffing the glowstick in his coat, Brock could see faint light coming from around the tunnel bend. He crept forward, peeking around the corner to find that the narrow tunnel opened to a larger gallery with another dark tunnel on the opposite end. A single glowlamp sat on the ground, lighting the cavern. Samson stood in the center of the cavern, his back to Brock as he spoke to his victim within the squirming bundle of cloth near his feet.

"...and don't worry. You won't have to wait long. My friends will be here soon, and you'll be safe on a ship before sunrise." The Minister reached down with a knife. "Now don't move or you might get cut."

The knife sliced the twine binding the blanket. Samson then grabbed one end of the blanket and gave it a hard yank. The person in the bundle rolled away from him, out of the blanket and onto the cave floor.

Brock could see the poor soul lying face-down, his hands tied behind his back and gag tied around his head. The minister stepped closer and used his foot to roll the person onto his back. That's when Brock realized it was Tipper.

Emotion welled up within Brock's chest. He charged the man, stabbing with his knife as he collided into the Minister's back. They flew over Tipper and tumbled to the cave floor, their momentum causing the Minister to roll on top of Brock and roll again to end with Brock on top and Samson beneath him face-down.

Brock regained his feet, ready to defend himself. When Samson didn't move, Brock noticed the knife sticking from the back of Samson's neck. The man was dead.

He spun and ran to Tipper, pulling the gag from his mouth, down to his neck.

Tipper spat and coughed. "Boy am I glad to see you. I thought I was done for."

"Are you okay?" Brock asked.

Tipper nodded. "I'll live. Just cut me loose so we can get out of here."

Brock ran over to the Minister to reclaim his knife. When reaching for the blade, he noticed something at the base of the man's hairline. Parting the hair with his fingers, he saw a mark in the shape of a hand.

Shaking his head to refocus, he gripped the knife to pull it from the man's neck, but it didn't move. Using both hands for a better grip, he pulled harder and it came loose. As the knife slid out, it made a nasty slurping sound and blood spurted from the deep wound. Brock gagged and his stomach cramped as he turned to vomit. After emptying his stomach, he wiped the knife on the dead man's cloak and ran back to cut Tipper loose, his hands shaking as he sliced the bonds.

With his wrists freed, Tipper sat up and rubbed them. He looked over at Samson's body on the cave floor. "That bastard planned to ship me off to work in a mine for the rest of my life. I don't know where, but it sounded horrible."

Tipper tried to stand, but stumbled. Brock leapt forward and grabbed his friend's arm to steady him.

"Are you sure you're OK? You have a nasty lump on your head," Brock said in concern.

Tipper nodded. "My head is pounding something fierce, alright. Whoever hauled me here must've knocked me out. I think I'll be okay though. Let's go. I just want to get out of here."

After helping Tipper to the tunnel leading back to the house, Brock patted his shoulder. "Wait here."

Brock ran to where Samson lay on the cavern floor and began searching through the dead man's clothes. He found a money pouch, cut it loose, and poured the contents into his palm, counting four gold imperials and seven silvers. It was more than enough.

After replacing the coins, he slid the pouch into his coat pocket and ran back to where Tipper waited. "I almost forgot what I came for." "I thought you came for me," Tipper gave a weak smile.

Brock grabbed his friend's arm and hooked it over his shoulder. "I didn't know it was you. I only knew it was some poor soul who needed help."

Tipper smiled again. "Well, it don't matter to me. I'm just glad you showed up."

Brock nodded. "Me too, Tip. Now let's go before Samson's friends arrive."

The two boys disappeared into the narrow tunnel, leaving the dead Minister behind.

6

A white-bearded man strummed on a lute, his lively tune attempting to battle the buzzing conversation while patrons periodically dropped coppers into the bowl at his feet. Approaching the bar, Brock spotted Alonzo on the same stool as their last meeting. The man was working on a bowl of potatoes and a half-eaten jackaroo leg. Claiming the stool beside Alonzo, Brock waved to the barkeep.

Brock smiled. "I'll have a cider."

The large man approached, raising an eyebrow until Brock placed a copper on the bar. Sweeping up the coin, the man filled a mug and set it on the bar before moving on. Brock took a long drink and turned to Alonzo.

"Mister Alonzo, I have the five Imperials. How soon can we do business?"

Without looking at Brock, Alonzo finished the poultry leg, set the bone down, and wiped his mouth with his sleeve. He took a swig of ale and set the tankard on the bar.

"The night's young, and I think we have an opening. If you've got the coin and the time, we can do it now." Alonzo scooped potatoes into his mouth, glancing toward Brock as he chewed, his piercing green eyes measuring Brock.

Brock was surprised. He hadn't expected it to happen tonight, and he wasn't even sure of what was coming. Regardless, he wasn't about to let this chance slip by.

Brock nodded. "I'm ready when you are."

Alonzo took one last swig of his ale, used his sleeve to wipe the bits of potato from his beard, and pushed away from the bar.

"Let's be off then." Alonzo headed toward the exit.

Brock took a drink of his cider and hurried to catch the big man.

Alonzo stepped outside and turned toward the Lower Wall Gate with Brock close behind. The streets were shadows now, the scattered clouds above showing a hint of red. They marched through the Lower Wall Gate into Upper Kantar. Shortly after passing through the gate, they turned onto a wide cross street. Alonzo turned again at the next intersection and entered a white stone building. As Brock climbed the stairs to the entrance, he read the plaque engraved above the door marked *Kantarian Art Institute*.

The interior was spacious, with a dark marble floor and rows of round alabaster pillars supporting the high ceiling. The walls formed a series of alcoves, each lit by a small glowlamp illuminating a work of art. Some contained paintings displaying historic figures, majestic landscapes, or static objects. Others displayed marble statues carved into the likeness of legendary heroes or shaped into fearsome beasts.

Alonzo approached the reception desk. "Hello. I have an appointment with Mr. Bennett."

The girl searched the schedule on her desk. Brock noticed how her long black hair flowed over her bare pale shoulders when she leaned forward. Her elegant hand scanned the paper until her finger stopped.

She looked up with large brown eyes. "Yes. He should be in the drawing studio at this time. It's on the second floor, third door on the left."

Alonzo thanked her and proceeded to the wide, curved stairwell.

Brock nodded to her, smiling when she smiled back at him. She had a nice smile that made his pulse race. Still looking at the girl as he walked toward the stairwell, he stubbed his toe on the first step and nearly fell. Recovering, he sped up the stairs to catch Alonzo.

When they reached the drawing studio, Brock counted eight people intensely sketching on large sheets of yellowed paper – some using charcoal while others used ink. In the center of the room, a man stood motionless, dressed in armor. The man had a sword in one hand and a fierce look upon his face. Glancing at the nearest artist's work, Brock noted that she had created a strong likeness of the subject.

Alonzo waved his hand to catch notice. A young man, with long brown hair tied in a tail, nodded and rolled his paper before sliding it into a tube. He snatched up his charcoal and headed to the door where Brock and Alonzo waited.

Alonzo apologized, "Sorry, Bennett. I know I'm a bit early."

"That's okay. I can always make time for someone with a commission," Bennett replied. "Let's head to my apartment, and we can discuss the job."

Bennett headed to the stairwell, descending to the first floor with Alonzo and Brock following. They walked out the back door of the gallery, crossed a wide alley, and entered a building located behind the institute.

They ascended the stairs to the second level and proceeded down a long hallway lined with doors. Bennett stopped at a door and opened it with a key tied to a cord around his neck. Brock followed him inside and surveyed the interior as Alonzo closed the door.

The small apartment contained a bed along one wall and a desk, a chest, and a variety of art supplies along the other walls. Two chairs sat in the middle of the room.

Bennett gestured for Brock to sit as he rifled through his art supplies.

Alonzo cleared his throat. "Now that we're here, there's a matter of the commission that was promised. You need to pay before we perform the job."

Brock removed a pouch from an inside coat pocket and jingled it. "Yes, I have the gold, but I still don't know what this gets me."

A laugh burst from Alonzo. "Silly boy. You came all this way with all that gold, and you don't know what you're buying?" Shaking his head, he chuckled again. "You said you wanted a new life. Well, there's only one way to get that as far as I know." He pointed a finger at Brock. "You, my boy, need a rune to mark you for your new vocation. You just need to choose one first. Of course, this won't please Issal much since the mark won't be from a true Choosing, but I figure you can't make your lot in life any worse. The way I see it, you've got nothing to lose except five gold coins."

Brock was dumbstruck. Being so focused on obtaining the gold needed to change his life, he hadn't considered what might be involved. Denied a rune in his Choosing ceremony as an infant, Brock had never considered another option.

He noticed Bennett preparing ink and a set of needles.

"Body art? But...but that's forbidden," Brock said. "The Ministry says it's profane, a crime punishable by death."

Now it was Bennett's turn to laugh. "It's funny how I can make so much more gold doing what's forbidden than trying to sell my art through the gallery."

Alonzo spoke next, his tone serious. "You aren't having second thoughts, are you boy?"

"No. It's just a lot to consider," Brock replied. "I can't just show up with a rune on my head. Everyone I know will know it's not real."

Alonzo leaned closer, looking Brock in the eyes. "You wanted a new life. That means leaving the old one behind. You need to start over somewhere else, somewhere far from Kantar. Just remember, if the Ministry catches you, they'll kill you. Turning us in will only result in harm coming to your family as well."

Brock looked down, his brain racing. Was he ready to start over? He hadn't been close to his father since his mother's death. Of the others he knew in the city, Tipper and Sally were the only ones he would miss.

What should he choose? At only seventeen summers, he was still young enough to apprentice for any vocation. However, he didn't want just any vocation. He wanted to make a difference. He wanted to achieve something special. He wanted to be able to save the next loved one when they needed him.

"Okay. Let's do this." He took a deep breath, turning toward Bennett. "I want the rune of Issal."

Bennett's brows rose up in surprise. He glanced at Alonzo, who whistled. "Wow, boy. You're a bold one. I'll give you that."

Bennett shrugged and sat in the chair across from Brock. "I guess one rune is the same as any other as long as you're paying. After all, you're the one who has to live with it." He held the inked needle to Brock's forehead. "Hold still. This will hurt."

Brock circled the crowd surrounding the farmer's wagon and continued down the busy street. As he walked, he reflected on his father's reaction upon seeing the bandage around his head. When Brock told him he had run into a tree while playing a game with his friends, Milan's only response was, *"You'd think you were smart enough to watch out for something as big as a tree."*

Rather than asking further questions, his father had set him to work like any other day. After finishing his work and eating, Brock set out to find Tipper.

With the sun dipping behind the rooflines, he approached The Whispering Wench, a popular stop for travelers due to its proximity to Southgate and the low price for a room. That's where he found Tipper, seated on a barrel near the front door.

Tipper was waving his cup at four sailors entering the inn. One man dropped a copper into the cup and then followed his shipmates inside. Tipper pocketed the coin, smiling when he spotted Brock.

"What happened to you? I was the one who got thumped on the head." Tipper's eyes narrowed at the bandage on Brock's head. "Is this a sympathy ploy? Are you trying to poach my turf?"

Smiling, Brock shook his head. "Not at all. Let's go someplace private, and I'll tell you about it."

"The wall?"

"Sounds good." Brock nodded, waving for his friend to follow. "If we hurry, we can catch the sunset."

By the time they were on the wall, the sun was touching the horizon, its long reflection stretching across the water.

"I'm going to miss this," Brock said with a sigh. "Watching the sunset is one of the most amazing things about living here."

"Why do you say that? Are you in trouble with your father again?" Tipper asked.

Brock turned toward Tipper, whose face was orange in the light of the setting sun.

"I'm leaving Kantar. I haven't told anybody else yet. I'm telling you because I'd like you to come with me."

"Leave Kantar?" Tipper stared down at the road below the wall. "I guess I've never thought about it. I've never been anywhere else."

"Neither have I." Brock became passionate. "Think of the wonders and possibilities of the world out there. What do we have here? Can you honestly tell me you want to spend your life living in crates and begging for your next meal?"

"No. I'd love to have another option." Tipper shrugged. "But what can I do?"

"Come with me. I have a plan. I think we can really start over, but I need your help." Brock spun, hopping off the merlon. He pointed toward his head. "Under this bandage is the mark of a new man, Tipper. I'll no longer be the poor Unchosen boy who lives in the tannery on Flower Street. Now, I can be something more. I can make a difference."

Tipper squinted at him. "I don't understand."

"Tip, I've got to tell you a secret, something to keep between just you and me."

"You know me, Brock," Tipper shook his head. "I ain't telling nobody."

"I know. That's why I'm telling only you."

Brock began to unwrap the bandage on his head. As it fell away, Tipper gasped.

"The man who did this told me it would need a couple days to heal. He also told me to keep it bandaged and to treat it with this ointment."

Brock pulled a small jar from his coat, opened it, and rubbed the ointment onto his forehead. It left his skin shiny, reflecting in setting sunlight. He then wrapped the bandage around his head, folding the trailing end under the tight wrap to keep it secured.

Tipper's eyes widened. "You have to leave Kantar. Nobody that knows you can see that," Tipper said, finally understanding. "But if you're leaving, I'm leaving too."

Brock smiled. "I am so happy to hear that, Tip. I don't want to go alone, and you've been my best friend for years."

Tipper smiled back. "When do we leave?"

"I'm going to buy some things for the trip. Meet me at Eastgate at sunrise the day after tomorrow." Brock began walking toward the ladder.

Tipper jumped off the merlon and followed along. "Where are we going anyway?"

Brock stopped and smiled. "Isn't it obvious? We go to Fallbrandt. If I want to become a master in the Ministry, I need to enroll in the Academy."

7

B rock stepped from behind the changing curtain to show the tailor the fit.

She nodded. "It seems I was right. Those fit you well, young man."

He smiled. "I'll take these, and I need another set like this for my friend. He's about this tall." Brock held his hand about a half-head higher than his own. "But he's a skinny one. His waist is even smaller than mine." He gestured with his hands to get his point across. "Also, do you have any inexpensive traveler's cloaks? We're going on a trip, and we'll need to stay warm and dry."

The woman nodded. "You're in luck. I bought some lightly-used wool cloaks from a man who was in yesterday. I'll be right back."

She ducked into the backroom, returning a minute later with another shirt, trousers, and two dark gray hooded cloaks. She tossed a cloak to Brock.

"I think that one will fit you," she said to him.

He held out the cloak to inspect it and then slipped it over his shoulders.

"This one does fit me. How much for the lot?" he asked as he admired himself in the mirror.

The woman scribbled notes on a sheet of paper while muttering to herself. She had a reputation as a fair business owner, which is why Brock had come to her.

After a moment, she replied, "Two silvers for the lot. And that's a fair price."

Brock nodded and handed the woman two silvers. He scooped up his old clothes, the new set for Tipper, and the two cloaks before thanking the woman.

His next stop was obvious. If he was going to travel, he needed good boots. After walking a bit further up Center Street, he entered a familiar cobbler shop. The shop owner raised an eyebrow upon seeing Brock's bandaged head.

"My, if it isn't young Tannerson. It looks like you banged your head. Did some young lass thump you for getting too frisky?" He laughed.

Brock smiled. "No, Melvin. It was a tree that apparently thought I was too frisky. It got me good though."

Melvin laughed again. "Right you are, boy. Trees tend to do that when your head runs into them. Now, what do I owe the pleasure of your presence today? I don't see any hides so it must be somethin' else."

Brock pointed down at his boots. "I'm ready for an upgrade. What do you have that's stylish, yet functional? More importantly, they need to fit and not be overly expensive."

Melvin put his finger to his cheek as his eyes stared-off at nothing. After a moment, his eyes lit up. "I've got it!"

He darted around the corner. Brock heard him digging through shelves before he emerged with black boots in hand.

"You're in luck, my boy. A jeweler was in here last week and traded his son's riding boots for a larger pair. I guess the boy outgrew them in a matter of weeks due to a growth spurt. I'm thinkin' they're your size."

Brock took the boots, sitting to try them on. Not only did they fit, they felt good. The normal stiffness of new leather was gone, so blisters wouldn't be much of an issue.

He walked around the shop to test the fit. "They feel great, Melvin. Please tell me there's a discount since they're used."

"Lightly-used, that is. However, you are correct." Melvin stepped up to his desk and opened a logbook. He backed up a couple pages, reading his notes. "Yes. Just as I thought. The man purchased them from me new for four silvers, but I can resell these to you for as little as two silvers and five coppers since they've been used."

Brock nodded "Done." He withdrew his pouch and handed the coins over.

Melvin pocketed the coins and pointed at Brock's old oversized boots. "Don't you want to sell those now?"

Brock shook his head. "No. I have a friend who needs them."

"Why, that's mighty kind of you, Brock. Are you needin' anything else today?"

"Nope. That's all I need. Thanks again, Melvin." He waved goodbye, carrying his growing pile of goods with him.

Brock stopped outside and counted through his remaining coins.

The journey to Fallbrandt was likely quite far, and he would need money for food and lodging along the way. Deciding that he wanted to know how long the trip would to take, he headed toward Upper Kantar for his next stop.

Brock approached the shop and pulled the door open, the bell on the door jingling as he stepped inside. An old man's voice called out from another room.

"I'll be right with you!"

"Okay!" Brock yelled back.

After setting his things on a chair, he began examining the various maps displayed on the walls, each depicting a different region. When the cartographer appeared, Brock was studying a map of the entire Issalian continent.

"She's a beauty, right? A true rendition of the whole Empire."

Brock turned to the see an old man with spectacles leaning against a service counter.

He nodded in response. "It's amazing. Kantar is so small on this map. It makes me wonder how big the Empire is."

"It's nearly three million square miles, of course," the man said, as if it were well known. He nodded, and his thin white bangs dropped over his *artifex altus* rune, causing him to push them back.

"Um...OK. That's big, I guess."

Brock wasn't sure how big one square mile was, so he couldn't fathom millions of square miles. He stepped closer to address the man.

"I need a map."

The cartographer cackled. "You wouldn't be in my shop if you didn't need a map." He cackled again and then pointed at Brock with his gnarled finger. "The question is, which map do you need?"

Brock shrugged. "I'm traveling from here to Fallbrandt, and I need a map to guide me."

"A traveler's map! Okay, then. Now, we're talking," the old man responded, rubbing his wrinkled hands together.

He turned and began searching through a wall of slotted shelving behind his desk. Various sizes of round tubes filled the slotted shelves. The man pulled a few tubes out, mumbling to himself as he read the labels before sliding each back into its slot. After a minute of searching, he held one of the tubes high.

"Here it is!" The old man cackled in laughter.

He slid a rolled paper map from the tube and then spread it out on the counter. Brock looked down at the map, trying to get his bearings. The man pointed to the lower left area of the map as he spoke.

"We are here in Kantar. When you leave, you follow the Great West Road heading east into the Brimstone Mountains." He slid his finger to the far corner of the map. "Fallbrandt is here, nestled among the Skyspike Mountains to the north. You take Greenway Road north to Fallbrandt from Sarville."

There were mountains to cross, but the trip didn't look that bad.

"How far would you say that is?" Brock asked

"Well, you see this here?" The cartographer pointed at a bar drawn at the bottom of the map. "This is the scale of the map. The length of this bar equals fifty miles."

Brock eyed the route. "So, the trip from Kantar to Fallbrandt is… about six of those bars?"

The man nodded. "I would say so. That makes the trip roughly three hundred miles."

Without a sound, Brock's mouth repeated the distance. Having never been away from the city, he had no idea how long it would take.

"Okay. How much for the map?" Brock asked.

"Let's see here." The man put a finger to his mouth as he considered the price. "One mid-size traveler's map. You can have it as-is for eight coppers. It's one silver if you want the storage tube."

"No tube needed. I'll just take the map."

After handing eight coppers to the man, Brock took the map and stepped outside.

He took a deep breath as he headed toward the next shop. The trip to

Fallbrandt was farther than he thought. He hoped he had the coin needed to get them there.

~

It was early evening when Brock returned to the tannery, lugging two heavy packs filled with supplies. Milan was cleaning up from the day's work when Brock arrived. Rather than interrupt, Brock ran upstairs to store the heavily loaded packs. When he returned, his father had gone into the apartment at the back of the shop.

As he entered the room, Brock found his father removing the soup kettle from the fireplace. Milan set the steaming pot on the end of the dining table and removed his thick leather gloves. Without glancing at Brock, he used a ladle to scoop soup into two bowls.

Following some unwritten script, they sat on opposite sides of the table and ate in silence. Ten minutes later, both bowls were empty and only crumbs remained from the half-loaf of bread that had accompanied the meal. Brock cleared his throat to steady his nerves before breaking the silence.

"Father, I have to tell you something."

His father said nothing, merely looking at Brock with one brow raised.

"I'm leaving Kantar, first thing in the morning." Brock considered what more he could say without lying. "I'm going to try to make something of myself, make a new life somewhere else."

His father nodded. "I expected this day would come. Since Ellie died, I figured it'd be coming soon." He sat back and looked Brock in the eye. "Whatever you do, make sure you do it honestly. Do right by Issal and you'll see yourself blessed in the next life."

That was it. No sadness. No begging him to stay. No emotion at all.

Brock knew he shouldn't feel surprised, but he was anyway. He didn't realize how much it would hurt – the indifference.

Brock kept his emotions under control as he asked, "What about the tannery? Will you be okay without me around to help? I feel bad leaving it all on you."

His father grunted. "Oh, no problem at all. It's time for me to get an apprentice anyway. Things will be fine here."

Milan pushed himself from the table and began to clear the remains of dinner as if nothing had happened. Feeling heartbroken, Brock stood and left the room.

⁓

The day felt full of possibilities. After a night of tossing and turning, Brock should have been exhausted. Instead, he had never felt more alive. Charged with anticipation, he was ready to begin his new life.

With a heavy pack and cloak over each shoulder, he strode down Flower Street toward Eastgate. Rounding the corner, he spotted Tipper among the small crowd waiting for the gate to open. Tipper noticed Brock and walked over to meet him.

"You look fancy in those clothes," Tipper said with toothy grin. "It's about time you showed up. I've been here for thirty minutes already."

"What are you talking about?" Brock smiled back. "The gate's not even open yet." He swung one of the packs around and tossed it. "Catch."

The pack hit Tipper. "Oof," he stumbled backward from the weight. "What's this?"

Brock threw him a cloak, which landed on Tipper's head. "That's for the journey. You'll find new clothes along with my old boots. I figured they'd fit you since they were always too big for me."

Tipper yanked the cloak off his head, leaving his hair even messier than normal. "Great. I'll be right back."

He disappeared into the nearest alley. Two minutes later, he strolled out wearing his new ensemble.

"How do I look?" Tipper asked, smiling as he sauntered over.

"Much better. You're almost not embarrassing now," Brock grinned.

"Very funny."

The loud peals of the gate bell shattered the stillness of morning. In the distance, the bell at Southgate returned the call. The guards cranked the gate open, and people began to trickle in and out of the city.

Brock tossed his pack over his shoulder. "That's our cue. Let's go. An adventure awaits."

Falling in line with the small crowd, they passed through the gate and out of the city.

PART II

AN ADVENTURE

8

From his vantage point atop the foothill, Brock's impression of Kantar felt completely different. It felt odd, seeing the only home he'd ever known from a distance. The city appeared so small beside the high rock walls of Jepson Peak to the North and the expanse of water that stretched across the western horizon. It occurred to him that he might never again see Kantar, but the twinge of loss at the thought quickly passed.

Brock took another bite of the hard roll and chewed vigorously as he stared to the west. From this height, he could clearly see the entire path they had traveled. From Eastgate, the Great West Road crossed the basin floor and climbed into the foothills of the Brimstone Mountains. A cloud of dust trailed a two-horse wagon heading their direction as it followed a snaking road bordered by the green and brown scrub that dotted the otherwise barren landscape.

Now some distance from the ocean, the air felt much hotter. They had stripped down to trousers and tunics with sleeves rolled up. The heat of the mid-day sun and the effort of climbing uphill left their shirts and brows damp with sweat. Brock was thankful to remove the sweaty bandages from his head and that Tipper had informed him that his rune seemed fully healed, now appearing natural.

Finishing his strip of dried meat, Brock washed it down with a drink from his water skin. He capped the skin, wiping his mouth with the back of his hand.

"I didn't realize how much hotter it would be out here away from the ocean. I hope we have enough water." Brock threw his pack over his shoulder and resumed walking. "Let's keep moving. We've a long way to go."

Tipper followed along, looking at what lay ahead.

"My legs are already numb. I can't imagine how they'll feel after we climb that." Tipper pointed toward the high pass between the peaks to the east.

The Brimstone Mountains were an imposing wall, towering over the smaller foothills around them. The mountains stretched in a line from the north to the south, looking as black as their namesake. Glowridge Pass was the lowest point along the dark wall of peaks, yet it was still a far higher altitude than where they currently stood.

"I guess it's the price you pay for adventure," Brock responded.

The rumble of the approaching wagon warned them to move aside. Moments later, the clopping of hooves filled the air as two horses eased past. When the wagon pulled even with them, the reins tightened, and the horses slowed to a walking pace.

A tanned man with dark hair and a wide-brimmed hat held the reins. A freckled boy with red hair, a couple years younger than Brock, sat beside him. Both were marked with the rune of *mercator*.

The man greeted them. "G'morning boys. How's life on the road?"

Keeping pace with the wagon, Brock glanced toward the man and replied, "It's going well, other than the heat."

The man snorted. "Yep. It's hot all right. However, what do you expect in early summer down here? Heck, if you guys plan to cross the Maloram Desert, it's going to get a lot warmer."

Brock remembered seeing Maloram Desert his map. "Yeah, we're heading that way."

The man nodded. "In that case, I assume you're going through Glowridge Pass?"

Brock nodded. "Yep. That's the only way through the Brimstone Mountains, right?"

The man snorted again. "Well, it's not the only way, but it's the easiest." He took his hat off, wiping his brow with a sleeve. "Even then, it's a tough climb up the mountain to get there. If you boys have some coin, we could give you a ride up to the pass."

Brock glanced back at Tipper, who nodded eagerly at the idea.

Wary of the price, Brock casually responded, "We might take you up on that, but we don't have much coin left. How much are you asking?"

"I'll give you boys a ride for five coppers each."

"That's one whole silver!" Brock exclaimed. It was still a long way to Fallbrandt, and he didn't know how much it'd cost to get there. "We're pretty small and light. Surely, you could find room for us for a couple coppers each?"

The man glanced toward his apprentice, then back to Brock. "I can do it for three coppers each, but that's as low as I go."

Brock stopped walking and the man stopped the wagon. Brock glanced at Tipper, whose eyes pleaded for Brock to accept the offer.

"Alright. Six coppers for the two of us to the top of the pass. It's a deal."

The man nodded. "Good. But you need to pay first." He lifted a loaded crossbow from the wagon seat. "And don't try anything funny, or you'll end up with one more hole in you. Got it?"

Brock nodded. "Got it."

He counted six coppers, handing them to the man.

"Thanks, boys." The man pocketed the coins. "My name is Hank, and this is my apprentice, Ren. Go ahead and climb into the wagon beside those crates." He set the crossbow down and grabbed the reins.

"Thanks, Hank. I'm Brock, this is Tipper," he responded.

They tossed their packs into the wagon and climbed on. Hank snapped the reins and the wagon lurched forward toward the mountain pass.

Brock and Tipper held their cloaks over their heads as cover from the hot sun, growing hotter as they descended into the valley. Though thankful to be riding rather than walking, their rears were sore from the abuse of the bumpy ride on the hard wagon bed.

Shortly after reaching level ground, the wagon crossed a small bridge over a creek that split the valley floor. They stopped near the bridge to let the horses drink and graze upon the grasses growing nearby. While Hank and

Ren tended to the horses, Brock and Tipper refilled their water skins and waited in the shade of the trees lining the creek.

Once the horses had their fill, they resumed their journey. The road angled south and was soon within sight of the Alitus River. As they began the steep ascent toward the pass, their pace slowed and the road became a series of switchbacks, twisting and turning as it wound its way around elevated obstacles and deep drops.

Facing backward in the wagon bed, Brock watched the landscape behind them shrink into the distance. The sun was sinking and with night fast approaching, he became nervous about reaching the pass before dark.

"It's almost nightfall, and we aren't to the top of the pass yet." Brock shouted over the clopping hooves and rumbling wheels. "Are we going to make it today?"

Hank turned his head and shouted, "We'll make it tonight. Should be there in two hours."

Brock grew even more nervous. He glanced to the side of the road, eyeing the cliff edge and the drop to the river, hundreds of feet below. The narrow road posed a constant threat of the wagon straying too close to the edge, sending them to a certain death.

Brock yelled to Hank again. "You'll bring us to the top like we agreed, right?"

"Don't worry, son. We'll get you there tonight."

Brock looked at Tipper, who shrugged. Brock shivered, picturing the wagon veering slightly off course in the darkness and tumbling over the edge.

The sun dipped below the horizon, showing a sliver of reflection on the distant ocean. The dark foothills below and red clouds above framed the bright slice of remaining sun, creating a stunning view. Moments later, the sun disappeared, leaving them in the dwindling light of dusk.

A faint blue glow caught Brock's attention, causing him to glance toward the rock wall beside the road. Light blue streaks marked the face of the black rock. Amazed, he turned forward as they rounded a bend. The entire cliff face above the pass was a pattern of glowing blue stripes that illuminated the road ahead.

Brock now realized how Hank was able to drive the wagon on the narrow road despite the loss of sunlight. The whole side of the mountain acted as a huge glowlamp. Glowridge Pass--the name now made sense.

A roar began to rise over the noise of the wagon and horses. The volume increased as they rounded a bend, exposing the source of the sound.

Hank turned his head and shouted, "Whitecap Falls. Beautiful, isn't it?"

Speechless, Brock just nodded.

The heavy flow of the Alitus River rushed over the cliff ahead, dropping into the dark canyon far below. Although not as wide as where the bridge crossed it south of Kantar, the river was still hundreds of feet across. The roar steadily increased as they passed over the falls, and the wagon rolled on into the night.

∾

The fire crackled, sending occasional sparks floating toward the starry sky. The air was cool in the high mountain pass, but the fire wasn't large enough to provide much heat. Armed with heavy cloaks and blankets, it wasn't necessary anyway.

Blue veins of glowstone in the cliff walls illuminated the alcove, giving an eerie feeling to the night. The tall cliffs surrounded them, leaving only the south side open, where the road passed just beyond. At the far side of the road was a steep drop to the river far below.

When they had first pulled into the alcove, Hank tended to the horses while the three boys went in search of scrub they could burn. After lighting the fire, the four broke out trail rations and ate while they got to know each other. Once Ren had become familiar with Brock and Tipper, he rarely stopped talking. The exuberant flow of words finally ended when his eyes lit up and he suggested that Hank tell a story. After some resistance, Hank relented to Ren's pleading. The three boys now listened in silence, hanging on every word.

Hank poked at the embers again, sending another wave of sparks into the sky as he continued his tale.

"And so, the horrible might of The Banished Horde swept over the lands, destroying everything in their wake. Cities were crushed, crops burned, and the individual armies of each nation they faced were easily defeated. Like a swarm of locusts in a field, they devoured everything in their path." Hank's arm swept before him in a flourish.

"The Horde was relentless and unforgiving as they killed any man, woman, or child they found. Their hearts were so dark and twisted that they even ate many of their victims."

Hank glared menacingly. In the red light of the fire, the image was effective. After a brief pause, he continued.

"The Banished Horde crushed one city at a time until a whole country was destroyed and then moved on to the next. In mere months, the eastern half of the continent was lost, and it appeared that all of mankind would fall victim to this plague."

Hank took a breath and resumed. "The Ministry sent a call out to the rulers of the western kingdoms, the King of Kantaria among them. The rulers and their armies gathered in a desperate attempt to stop the wave of destruction. It had become apparent that this fight was not about any one kingdom or people, but instead was about all people. They had to act fast or face extinction."

Again, Hank paused, his eyes reflecting the orange of the flames.

"Those rulers met and formed an alliance, the first inkling of a unified empire. Under this alliance, they would work as one and would meet The Banished Horde on a field of their choosing. They would defeat The Horde or die trying."

Hank stood and raised his arms. "The united Armies of Issal rode forward to meet The Horde on the Tantarri Plains. When the battle was finished, The Banished Horde was defeated and humanity survived. The lands east of the Skyspike Mountains had been destroyed, but they would heal over time." He reclaimed his seat on the rock. "Nobody knows how the Armies of Issal were able to defeat the might of this army of monsters who had ravaged all prior to that battle. Perhaps it was the will of Issal himself, for that's what the Ministry tells us. However, events from history become clouded by legend as the years pass, and this war occurred two hundred years ago. The only truths we know for certain are that mankind survived, the Empire thrives, and The Horde is nowhere to be found."

Hank quieted, stirring the fire again.

Like most, Brock had heard this story before, but not told so effectively. Through the telling, he imagined a grand battle of men fighting some faceless, gruesome enemy. His mind raced with unanswered questions. *Where did The Horde come from? Did the Armies of Issal completely wipe them out? How did they win if The Horde was so fearsome and powerful?* Questions kept spinning in his head as he stared into the flames.

"That was great, Hank!" Ren burst out, breaking the silence. "Can you tell another? Maybe the one about Fallbrandt the Great?" He waved his arms in excitement. "Oh! I know! Tell us one about the time of legends! You know, when men could fly. How they had swords that could cut through stone!"

Hank waved his hands. "Whoa. Slow down, boy." Ren stopped his torrent of words at Hank's interruption. "We have an early morning, with many miles to cover to reach Fenrick's by mid-day. A hot meal will be waiting for us. I certainly don't want to miss it, so it's time to sleep."

Ren didn't object, although his disappointment was obvious. He nodded and climbed under the wagon to lay down.

Hank turned toward Brock and Tipper. "It was nice meeting you boys. We'll be up and on the road at first light. I'm saying farewell now in case you're still asleep when we're gone. I'm exhausted and off to bed."

Tipper stood and stretched. "I hear you. I'm beat too. In addition, my rear is sore, and I just can't sit anymore. We appreciate the ride, but sitting in the back of the wagon all day is like taking a switch to the rump for getting caught stealing." He rubbed his backside as he winced. "I should know, since it happened to me more than once."

Brock laughed, stepping back from the fire. "Stop complaining. My rear hurts as much as yours." He turned to Hank. "It was great to meet you, Hank. Thanks for the ride and for the story."

Brock wrapped his cloak around himself and curled up on the ground, using his pack as a pillow.

"Tip, get some sleep. We have a lot of walking to do tomorrow." Closing his eyes, Brock was soon fast asleep.

9

B rock stood on the peak of an impossibly high mountain. He spun about to scan the horizon, drinking in the incredible vista. From his vantage point, it seemed as if he could see the entire continent.

He glanced down at his feet and at the hard gray rock that was beneath them. Odd that he couldn't feel it. The bare rock spread out around him in all directions, eventually giving way to drifts of white snow. Having lived his whole life by the ocean, Brock had never seen snow this close. He felt a child-like desire to go jump in it, but his feet were immobile.

His body felt chilled, but not a sharp, biting cold. It was the kind of cold that slowly seeped in after long exposure. He searched the sky, but he couldn't seem to locate the sun to determine the time of day. *Why can't I find the sun?*

The bright light of the sun suddenly burst into sight. He held his hand up to block it, squinting, and the intensity receded as his eyes adjusted.

A man stood before him, wearing an iridescent cloak that billowed in the breeze although Brock felt no wind. The glowing, shifting colors of the cloak were mesmerizing. Brock lowered his hand to get a look at the man's face. Where the man's head should be, he instead found a bright white light. *Who is this? Is it God? Is Issal himself standing before a lowly Unchosen?*

A powerful voice broke the tranquility of the mountaintop. "The time has come for that which was sleeping to awaken. Seek the truth. Follow its path.

The shadow lengthens. Mankind will soon fall to the shadow unless the light of the truth is set free."

Raising his arms high, the voice grew even more powerful. "I command what is inside you to awaken!"

The world began to shake, sending a high-pitched wail throughout the land. As the wailing grew louder, the bright white light morphed into a tangible shape. It was a rune—one that Brock had never seen before.

With even more intensity, the voice spoke. It seemed to shake the universe. "Awaken!"

The bright image of the glowing symbol roared toward Brock, searing his eyes. The wailing grew to a crescendo.

~

Brock woke, sweating despite the cold air around him. He blinked, trying to clear his vision. The negative image of the rune from his dream remained when he closed his eyes, as if it were burned into his eyelids. A horrifying high-pitched wail echoed through the alcove, causing his hair to stand on end.

Hank shouted as he ran to the wagon. "Get up! It's a banshee. Everyone up!" He reached into the wagon, grabbing his crossbow.

Brock scrambled to his feet, still trying to shake the odd feeling of his dream, trying to focus on what was happening. Tipper was standing beside him, also looking confused. Ren scrambled from beneath the wagon and stood beside Hank. The wagon shifted and rocked as the frightened horses stirred, the whites of their eyes showing in the pale light of the glowstone.

Brock noticed something moving at the mouth of the alcove.

Emerging from the roadway was a human-like creature standing nearly twice Brock's height. It had long, tangled black hair and ghostly white skin. The monster lumbered toward them, emitting an ear-piercing wail. Ice-cold fear gripped him, making it difficult to breathe. The horses backed away in fear, forcing the wagon backward.

As the banshee approached, Brock noticed that its eyes were glowing red, appearing as huge crimson pupils. Incredibly long arms stretched out, flexing fingers capped by sharp black talons. Tattered rags covered much of its body. A breeze carried the rotten stench of the beast toward them, causing the horses to panic.

Hank grabbed Ren by the shirt, yanking him away from the approaching nightmare and toward the wagon.

"Get on. I'm going to try to distract it. When I do, you start driving the team toward Fenrick's as fast as you can."

Ren climbed onto the wagon and grabbed the reins. His eyes were wide with fright, matching the horses.

"What about you, Hank?" Ren was sobbing. "You can't let it kill you. I need you."

Hank stepped sideways, edging away from the wagon while keeping his eyes on the banshee.

"Don't worry about me, boy. You just take care of the team and wagon. I'll catch up to you at Fenrick's." Hank lifted the crossbow, pointing it at the banshee.

During this entire affair, Brock remained dumbstruck. He couldn't believe it. Banshees were real. He had thought them to be a legend meant to scare children.

The banshee lumbered forward, approaching its prey. Tipper took a step backward and tripped over his pack, crying out as he fell. Tipper's scream diverted Brock's attention from the banshee, breaking through the shock and fear. He turned to find his friend on the ground, and he scrambled to help him.

The banshee broke into a run toward them. Hank pulled the crossbow trigger and the bolt struck the beast with a thud. The impact caused the monster to lurch back, its body twisting as the bolt pierced its shoulder. It blasted a horrifying wail and raw terror captured Brock's thoughts, seizing his faculties as if they were encapsulated in a block of ice.

The horses reared and bolted, pulling the wagon with them. The rapid acceleration sent Ren flipping over the driver's bench and into the wagon bed.

In two long strides, the banshee closed the distance and swung its long arm. Sharp talons struck Hank on the left side of the head, sending him spinning to land three strides away. The blow caused Hank's hat to fly off, flipping through the air to settle at Brock's feet. The crossbow smashed into the rock wall, bits of wood scattering into the air as it shattered.

The banshee turned to pursue the wagon, which was now almost to the road. Its long legs allowed it to cover ground quickly, despite its lumbering gait. Ren grabbed the reins just in time to avoid plunging over the cliff edge, and the wagon turned east before rounding a bend with the banshee following fast behind.

As the alcove fell still, Brock regained his faculties and ran over to help Hank.

The man lay on his stomach – his head twisted in an odd way. When he rolled Hank over, Brock's stomach turned. The entire left side of the man's face was gone, with raw pink and red flesh clinging to the man's skull. His left eye dangled from the socket and the man's body twitched twice before falling still.

Something inside Brock broke. This was not supposed to happen. He had to do something to make it right. He closed his eyes in frustration and found the rune from his dream hovering in his vision.

His eyes flashed open to stare at his hand, dark with Hank's blood. In an act of bizarre intuition, he began to draw the rune from his vision onto the remaining side of the man's forehead.

Horrified, Tipper screamed, "Brock, what are you doing? The man is dead! We have to get out of here!"

Brock ignored him, concentrating on the symbol, drawing it clean and exact.

He closed his eyes, focusing his mind on the rune he had drawn.

Filled with fear and anger, he felt another energy, a heat just beyond the grasp of his mind. He mentally reached for it, thinking it was Hank's life force. He pulled at it, feeling the heat grow. Suddenly, his body was flush with energy as a tempest raged within him. His body felt alive, but with too much life, as if he would explode. He opened his eyes and poured the energy into the rune he had drawn on Hank. The energy expelled as rapidly as it had come on, leaving him cold and tired.

Brock pulled his hand away, watching the rune as it glowed a bright, angry red. It pulsed before the glow began to fade.

"What?" Tipper mumbled as he stared at the glowing symbol.

A terrifying wail broke Brock's focus. A second wail followed, growing louder. The banshee was returning.

Brock scrambled to his feet. He and Tipper backed away from the entrance to the alcove, finding themselves trapped with no other way out.

Hank's body suddenly twitched and convulsed. In jerking motions, the torn and bloody remains of Hank began to rise. Swaying as he stood, Hank's remaining eye looked at Brock, the pupil now glowing red like the banshee's.

Bits and pieces of flesh hung from the other side of the man's face, his torn-out eye swinging as it dangled. The sight was even more horrifying than the banshee. Brock stepped backward, away from what was once Hank.

"What have you done?" Tipper whispered.

Brock just stared, shaking his head. This is not what he wanted. This is not what was supposed to happen.

Hank turned and shambled toward the road. The banshee reappeared and blasted another horrible wail. Hank attacked.

As Hank ran toward the monster, it swung its huge arm and caught the man in the shoulder, sending him spinning to the roadway and nearly over the cliff. The banshee wailed and lumbered forward. Hank stood to face the beast, his left arm hanging limply, his shoulder torn wide open.

Again, the banshee swung at Hank, but Hank's living corpse spun into the swing and latched onto the monster's arm.

The weight of a full-grown man at the end of the banshee's long arm pulled it off balance. It took a step, teetered for a second, and disappeared over the edge with Hank still latched on. A screeching wail followed, growing more faint as the distance grew…until it suddenly stopped.

Brock and Tipper ran to the edge to see what had become of the two horrifying creatures, but they could only see the dark water of the river far below.

Shocked by what had happened, they wandered back to the camp, each sitting on a rock near the dormant fire. After a few minutes of silence, Brock spoke.

"Tip, we can never speak of what happened here. I don't understand it myself, but I don't want to even think about it." Tipper's response was a weak nod.

Brock grabbed his pack and stood. "Let's leave this place. I can't sleep any longer anyway. I want to get as far from here as we can."

They walked out of the alcove and onto the road heading east. As he rounded the bend, Brock noticed dim light along the eastern horizon. It would be dawn soon. He ached for the daylight to come and wash away the horrors of this night.

10

"That must be Fenrick's Crossing." Brock pointed ahead. "We'll be there in time for dinner."

Tipper broke into a grin. "Just thinking of hot food is making my stomach growl. No offense, but these trail rations are getting old."

"Hot food sounds amazing right now," Brock agreed.

He took a drink from his nearly empty water skin, put the skin away, and forced his legs to move. At least it was all downhill from here. The weather had been hot, but not unbearably so with the high altitude helping to moderate the temperature.

Tipper fell into line beside Brock, quiet for the moment. He had talked more than usual today, rambling about this and that. Brock guessed that it helped him avoid thinking about what occurred the previous night.

The view of the valley revealed less than a dozen buildings nestled beside the river at the bottom. Trees and brush lined the banks of the river, creating a green stripe through the heart of the valley.

The incline leveled as they reached the floor of the valley and the air began to ring with the strikes of a hammer on iron. Following the sound, Brock spotted a smith working at the edge of the village. The man's hammer gleamed in the evening sun, reflecting a flash of light each time he raised it above his head. Delayed by the remaining distance, the clang from the smith's pounding reached them during each upswing.

A rhythmic rumble echoed from behind and Brock turned to see two horses approaching. A man and a woman soon rode past, stirring up dust as they swept by. He watched the two riders roll into the village, coming to a halt in front of what he assumed was the local inn. A man met the two riders, speaking with them before taking their horses as the riders ducked into the front door of the inn.

Tipper waved to the smith as they walked past his yard. The man waved with his hammer and returned to the horseshoe he was working. The metal of the shoe glowed orange, sending sparks into the air with each strike.

When the boys entered the village, Brock counted a row of five houses lining the south side of the road, while the smithy, the inn, and two other buildings lined the north side. Ahead, the road vanished from sight where it descended toward the river.

As they approached the inn, Brock read the words *Fenrick's Inn* carved into a door stained dark green. He stepped into the building with Tipper a step behind. Before his eyes could adjust to the dark interior, his nose caught the delightful scent of cooked beef.

The small dining room held ten tables and offered no bar. Three of the tables had patrons, including the man and woman who had just ridden into town. A loud squeal startled Brock as he led Tipper across the room.

"You're alive! Thank Issal!" Ren rushed over to hug them. As usual, a torrent of words came rolling out. "I can't believe it. I was hoping, but it seemed impossible. I got here, and waited, and waited, and was giving up hope. Then you showed up. You're here. I can't believe it. Where's Hank?" He smiled expectantly.

A glance toward Tipper revealed a haunted look as thoughts of Hank and the banshee resurfaced. Brock turned to Ren, putting his hand on the younger boy's shoulder.

"Hank didn't make it, Ren. I'm sorry," Brock said, sympathetic.

Ren glanced at Tipper and then back to Brock. "I don't understand. What happened? How did you guys make it then?"

With sadness in his voice, Brock replied, "Hank saved us. He was somehow able to push the monster off the cliff, but the beast pulled Hank over with him. They're both gone, Ren."

That quieted the talkative boy. He sat down as tears began to well up.

"What am I going to do? I can't do this alone. I need Hank," he sobbed.

Brock sat on the bench across from Ren, motioning for Tipper join him.

"Don't worry, Ren. It isn't something you need to solve this minute. Let's order some food and we'll see if we can help you figure out a plan."

Ren nodded and wiped his eyes with the back of his hand. He used his sleeve to wipe his nose and glanced up as a serving girl walked past. After delivering two ales and two bowls to the couple who had recently arrived, she turned and strolled over to greet the boys.

Long red hair framed a young face with large green eyes, lightly freckled pale skin, and a perky nose. The swooping neckline of her dress exposed more of her pale skin and revealed a fair bit of her curves.

The girl appeared to be about Brock's age, perhaps slightly older. Her full lips formed a smile as she approached the table. He smiled back, feeling a warm rush of desire for this pretty girl.

"Ren, I see you've found some friends." She looked them over as her hands rested on her rounded hips, her gaze landing on Brock's face. "What can I get for you boys? Maybe something to drink? We also have some beef stew on the fire."

Ren responded, "These are my friends, Meg. This is Brock, and that's Tipper. We met them on the road from Kantar." Ren paused, sadness apparent on his face. "Hank's dead, Meg. The banshee got him."

Showing concern, Meg's hand rested on Ren's shoulder as she spoke. "I'm so sorry, Ren. Hank was a good man. We'll all miss him." She pulled her hand away, placing both hands on the table to lean on them. "Don't worry; my father will still buy supplies from you. You still have our business."

As she leaned against the table, Brock found it difficult to look away from her exposed skin. His heart was racing.

Ren nodded. "Thanks Meg. I have the load of supplies he requested in the yard out back. When do you think Derrick can go over the delivery?"

Meg stood upright. "You'll have to wait 'til tomorrow. He had to make a run to Hawk's Landing and won't be back 'til late morning."

Looking the boys over, she smiled again. "In honor of Hank, you boys eat and drink for free tonight. I'll get you each a bowl of stew and some bread. Be right back." She turned and left, her hips swaying as she walked.

Ren asked, "Have you guys ever had ale?"

Tipper replied, "No. The owner of the tavern we frequent won't serve us ale. She says we don't need our brains addled until we're older. Although, she never did say how old we needed to be."

"Hank loved ale. He let me have a mug from time to time." Ren sat upright. "I want to order a mug of ale to toast to Hank. Will you guys join me?"

Without a glance at Tipper, Brock responded, "We'd be honored, Ren. We owe our lives to Hank."

The kitchen door swung open, and Meg emerged with three steaming bowls of stew, placing them on the table along with half a loaf of bread.

"Careful, boys. It's hot."

Meg stood back, flipping her hair over her shoulder and teasing it with her right hand as she spoke. The pale skin of her neck was making Brock's heart beat fast again.

She looked at Brock, sharing a coy smile. "So, what will it be, boys? Do you know what you want?"

Brock stammered, "Umm. What do you mean?"

"What do you want to drink?" Her smile grew larger. "I know the place isn't packed, but I don't have all day."

Ren saved him. "Three ales, please. We want to toast to Hank's memory, Meg."

She nodded. "Three ales, it is. Be right back." She shot another glance at Brock before heading back to the kitchen.

With Meg away from the table, Brock's brain began to function again. Remembering something, he reached into his pack.

"I saved this for you, Ren." Brock held the wide-brimmed hat toward Ren. "I think Hank would want you to have it."

Moisture reappeared in Ren's eyes as he accepted the hat. He put it on his head and wiped the tears away.

"Thanks guys. This means a lot to me. I'm so happy you brought it."

Meg returned from the kitchen, setting three ales on the table before sliding onto the bench beside Ren. She leaned forward, speaking in a low voice.

"We heard that a whole family was murdered by a banshee up near Hawk's Landing last fall. Their bodies were torn and mutilated. They say banshees are giants and have the strength of ten men. I guess few see one and live to tell about it. Until last fall, I thought they were only a myth."

Meg gazed into Brock's eyes. "How did you live to tell about it? What was it like?"

Brock's tongue was tied, her large green eyes affecting him as much as the rest of her.

Tipper saved him by responding. "It was horrible. It was huge and disgusting. The banshee wailed like nothing you've ever heard. It hurt our ears just to be near it." Holding his hands to his ears for affect, he then lifted his hand high above his head. "It was twice as tall as me and stunk like rotten meat. It had long claws on its hands, sharp as knives. It was a nightmare."

When he finished, Tipper's eyes glazed over as unbidden memories returned.

Brock picked up where Tipper left off. "Hank distracted the banshee by shooting it with his crossbow so Ren could flee with the wagon, but the crossbow barely slowed the monster. Somehow, Hank was able to lure it to the road and...they both went over the cliff." His voice quieted as he relived the moment. "We ran to the edge to look, but we saw nothing. It was so far down. Nothing could survive that fall."

The table was quiet. It was a somber moment.

Ren lifted his mug in the air. "To Hank. He was a fine man with a big heart."

Brock and Tipper lifted their mugs, clinking them together for the toast. "To Hank."

Bubbles tingled Brock's tongue and throat as the first drink went down, followed by a slightly bitter after-taste.

Meg stood and smoothed her skirts. "Sorry boys, but I do have other customers." She surveyed the room and looked back, directing a smile at Brock. "Don't worry though. I'll be back soon to attend to your needs." Meg left to wait on four men seated at a table across the room.

Ren took another drink, smiling afterward. "Ah. It's good stuff. I wasn't too fond of ale the first time I tried it, but it grows on you. What do you guys think?"

Brock swallowed a second drink from his mug, wiping foam from his lips as he responded, "I like it a lot already. If it gets better, I could be in trouble."

They all laughed. It felt good to laugh.

Brock opened his bleary eyes. A thin slice of sunlight was cutting through the room, lighting the wall near the bed. His head hurt something fierce and the bright bit of sun seemed to stab at his eyes, making the throbbing more intense.

He turned his head to find a mess of red hair resting on his chest. Realizing he had no shirt on, he felt around to find he still wore his smallclothes. At least he wasn't naked.

His movement caused Meg to stir. She lifted her head and looked up at him with heavy eyes, her long eyelashes sweeping the air as she blinked.

He thought she looked gorgeous.

"G'morning sweetie," she said. "How do you feel?"

Brock brought his hand to his head, covering his eyes. "It feels like my head is going to explode."

Meg laughed. "You boys were going through mugs of ale like you were on a mission to empty the whole keg." She reached toward the nightstand, her hand returning with a pewter mug. "Here, drink this. It should help."

He looked at the mug. "No thanks. I don't need any more ale," he groaned. "I don't think I'll ever drink that stuff again."

She laughed. "Silly. It's water. Drinking water is supposed to help after you've had too much ale."

Brock lifted his head and took the mug. "I am thirsty. Water sounds good."

He took a long drink and then another. After a breath, he took one last drink and emptied the mug.

Meg set the mug on the nightstand before resting her head on his chest, nestling up to his neck. He felt her warm breath on his skin as she lightly raked her fingers across the ripples of his stomach, drawing random shapes.

Brock enjoyed the attention and warmth Meg was sharing. It felt wonderful to have this pretty girl lying beside him. Her hair smelled good. Lying on a soft bed felt great. He decided if his head would stop pounding, this moment would be perfect.

His eyes closed as he tried to remember the events of the prior evening.

The three boys drank together, with Ren telling stories of Hank. The ale was good. The more he drank, the more he wanted. Meg kept coming to the table to join the conversation. Eventually, the other tables emptied, and Meg joined the boys for good. Somehow, she ended up on Brock's lap with her arm around his shoulders.

Things became foggy after that. He remembered kissing Meg, her lips feeling warm and soft. He vaguely recalled going upstairs, his hand in hers as she pulled him along. He couldn't remember anything else.

Meg lifted her head from his chest. His eyes opened to find her staring at him, smiling. She leaned close and kissed him, her soft lips lingering for a moment before pulling away.

Regret reflected in her eyes. "I have to get up now. Our guests need someone to serve them breakfast. The cook should have it prepared by now, but someone still has to serve it."

Brock opened his mouth, hesitating briefly before asking his question. "About last night…did we…um…you know?"

She laughed again. "No, sweetie. When you told me you'd never been with a girl, I decided it wouldn't be fair to take advantage of you… considering your condition."

Wearing only her cream-colored shift, Meg climbed out of bed and stepped over to the vanity. She then wet a cloth in a bowl of water and used some soap to wash her face, neck, and under her arms.

"This is your room?" Brock asked as he turned to observe the surroundings.

It was a small room with a single door and a window. The bed was barely large enough for two. A nightstand, vanity, and a wooden chest were the only other items of note.

"Yes," Meg replied. "If you're wondering about Tipper, he's sharing the room that Ren normally shared with Hank." She paused, considering something. "I think Ren was happy to have company last night. I don't think he was ready to be alone after what happened."

She set the cloth down, picked up a brush, and began to tame her wild mane of red hair. Brock found himself spellbound, his heart racing faster the longer he watched her go through her morning ritual.

Meg discarded the brush, reached into the wooden chest, and grabbed a dress. She put her legs through and pulled it up. After sliding her arms through, she stepped next to the bed with her back facing him.

"Will you button me up, please?"

Brock sat up, his head spinning as he did. He swung his legs off the bed with the blanket over his lap. When he secured her last button, she turned and cupped his cheeks while planting a kiss on his lips.

"I hope you weren't offended by my being so forward last night." Meg gazed into his eyes. "I don't see many boys my age and I feel…so lonely, sometimes."

"How could I possibly be offended?" Brock replied. "You're absolutely stunning. Any boy would be thrilled to have your attention."

Meg smiled. "You're so sweet. You flatter me." She leaned in and kissed him longer this time. It was like swimming in a dream. A sweet, sweet dream.

She stepped away from him and walked to the door. "I wish it weren't so, but I have to go. Feel free to wash up before you come down. I'll see you downstairs for breakfast."

The door closed and he found himself already missing her.

Brock descended the stairs, finding Ren and Tipper at the same table as the night before.

"G'morning, Brock." Tipper's hand rubbed his temple as he chewed. "I hope you're feeling better than I am."

"I don't know, Tip. I don't think I can eat right now," Brock replied. "The food smells good, but my stomach is rolling, and my head is pounding."

Ren nodded. "I know what you mean, Brock. I ain't ever had that much ale before. Now I know why Hank always said that you gotta count your ales. You lose count, and it all goes sideways." He laughed.

It was good to hear Ren laughing, although it hurt Brock's head. He sat next to Ren and put his head in his hands, resting his eyes until a soft touch caused him to stir. He looked up to see Meg standing beside him. "Try some hot tea. It's supposed to work wonders. I even squeezed a lemon into it for you." She stepped away to serve the couple seated nearby.

Brock stared at the steaming tea. Figuring that anything was worth a try, he lifted the cup and took a sip. It was hot, but not burning hot. The aroma loosened his sinuses, and the heat felt good on his throat.

As Ren continued to talk, Brock continued to sip tea. By the time the tea was gone, Tipper and Ren had finished their breakfast, and Brock began to feel better.

Meg approached their table. "Brock, are you able to eat anything yet?" she asked.

"Maybe a biscuit?" he replied.

Meg nodded and disappeared into the kitchen. She returned a minute later with a warm biscuit.

Tipper sighed. "I feel a bit better after eating. I should be ready to go soon."

Brock swallowed and responded, "Yeah. We should get going, but we need to restock before we hit the road."

Ren turned toward Brock. "Thank you, guys, for toasting to Hank with me last night. I know you have your own path to follow, but if you're ever back in these parts, will you look me up? Hank and I have a house...well, now I guess I have a house in Port Choya."

Tipper responded, "Ren, thanks for sharing your room. If we're ever in Port Choya, we'll be sure to look you up. We may even buy you an ale."

Brock groaned, "Please, no more ale."

Meg returned to the table. "Can I get anything else for you boys?" she asked as her gaze swept over them, landing on Brock.

His eyes locked onto hers and he responded, "Meg. Can we buy some trail rations from you before we go?"

She nodded. "Sure, Brock. Come into the kitchen, and we can figure it out."

Brock stood and followed Meg. When they stepped through the door, she pinned him against the wall and gave him a deep kiss. She pulled away and he stared at her, drinking in the sight of this wonderful girl.

The sound of someone clearing her throat broke him from his trance.

He turned to find an old woman shaking her head as she set a pan of biscuits on the counter.

"Sorry, Ferdie." Meg said. "This is Brock."

"Nice to meet you Ferdie," Brock said, smoothing his shirt. "I must say that the food you serve here is delightful."

That earned him a snort from the cook, but he also spotted a small smile before she turned to flip some sizzling eggs.

Meg pulled him through the kitchen until they were both outside behind the inn.

"I know you have to leave," she said. "I see the mark you have. I'm sure you're off to Fallbrandt."

Brock didn't know what to say. Apparently, his silence was enough.

"Yes. That's what I thought," Meg said, glancing at her feet before looking into Brock's eyes. "If you come this way again, stop by to say hello. Maybe we can pick up where we left off."

"Ah. You could come with me maybe?" Brock asked, hopeful.

She became serious again. "No. My place is here. My path was set when I was born." Her eyes searched his. "You're special, Brock. I can feel it. You're going to do great things. I cannot leave Fenrick's Crossing. My fate is tied to this inn and to this village. You can't stay. Your fate awaits you in Fallbrandt. We just have to live with what might have been." She kissed him again. "But, if you do return, and I'm still single, we'll have some fun."

She stepped away. "Now, you must be heading east across the Maloram Desert. You'll need some food and lots of water. Let's get you set."

She opened the door and stepped into the inn. Brock hesitated, wishing things could be different. He took a deep breath, releasing a sigh as he followed her inside.

11

I t was mid-afternoon when they cleared the pass to get their first view of the land east of the Brimstone Mountains.

Barren desert sands stretched for miles to the east and to the north. In the distance, far across the Maloram Desert, was the mountain range where their destination was located. The most impressive landmark in view was to the south.

A deep gorge, miles across, ran from the Brimstone Mountains to the distant Skyspike Mountains to the east. Various shades of tan and red rock lined the steep canyon walls, while the Alitus River snaked its way through the canyon floor, far below the desert.

"That must be Barrier Canyon," Brock said, looking at the map in his hands.

"That's a lot of desert to cross. Those mountains look far away," Tipper replied as he capped his water skin. "I just wish it wasn't so blasted hot."

Brock rolled the map and slid it into his pack. "Let's keep moving. We have to find a shady place to rest near the desert floor until nightfall."

They trudged down the east side of the mountain, finding scattered weeds and cacti as the only signs of life. There were no other travelers in sight. In fact, they hadn't seen anyone since the ferry landing across the river from Fenrick's Crossing.

After two hours of steady descent, the land began to level. They found shade on the east side of an outcropping of rocks, just north of the road.

Brock pulled out the food provided by Meg, making him think of her. He wished he were back in Meg's bed with her lying beside him. *Is this what it's like to be in love? Filled with excitement and passion when together, heartache and longing when apart?* He didn't know what it was, but he knew it hurt.

They ate in quiet, their bodies sore and tired from the hot trek over the mountain pass. After eating, they relaxed in the shade and watched the scattered clouds slowly floating by. It was a peaceful scene without even the wind making noise...until Tipper broke the silence.

"How do you feel?" he asked.

Brock shrugged. "Hot and tired, I guess."

Tipper shook his head. "No. I mean...I've never seen you with a girl before."

"Oh, that." He thought about Meg. He had tried to focus on other things during the day, with little success. "I don't know. I keep thinking about her. I know I just met her last night, but I miss her anyway." He reflected on how he felt. "Or maybe... I miss the idea of her. Regardless, now I know how it feels to connect with a girl. To be close. To feel her warmth. To share something." He was quiet for a moment. "What I can tell you is that I certainly could go for more of that."

Tipper laughed and nudged Brock's ribs. "Now you know what I've been telling you about. You've just gotta be confident and go for it. If the girl isn't interested, she'll let you know, and you can move on."

"Yeah. I guess you're right, Tip," Brock replied. "Maybe there'll be some pretty girls in Fallbrandt, just waiting for two jokers like us." They both chuckled at the thought.

After mentioning Fallbrandt, Brock decided to check on their progress. He sat up and spread the map on the dry ground, while Tipper leaned close. Brock put his finger where the Brimstone Mountains met the Maloram Desert, just north of Barrier Canyon.

"We're here. It took three days to get this far, but riding in the wagon likely saved another day."

His finger then ran along the map, tracing the route they were to follow.

"I guess it'll take two or three days to get to Sarville." Brock pointed at a city in the heart of the Skyspike Mountains. "From Sarville, we continue north through the mountains until we get to Fallbrandt. That looks like another two or three days."

"Ugh. We still have a long way to go," Tipper groaned. "I hope my feet don't fall off. They're killing me already."

"Mine too." Brock rolled the map and stuffed it in his pack. "We need to cross the desert at night when it's cool. Why don't you relax and get a little sleep before it gets dark? I'll wake you when it's time to go."

"You don't have to ask me twice. I'll take any sleep I can get right now." Tipper slid down, put his head on his pack, and covered his face with his cloak.

Brock chuckled when Tipper began to snore.

With only the light of the stars to guide them, Brock and Tipper could barely see the road as they hiked across the desert. The wind eventually picked up, forcing the boys to don their cloaks for protection. When the sky began to lighten, their vision gradually extended beyond the immediate surroundings. Brock shielded his eyes from the gusting wind as he surveyed the view.

Miles and miles of open flat ground lay to the north and to the east. Beyond Barrier Canyon to their south, the desert seemed to stretch on forever. Gusts of wind stirred the sand, blowing it into the air and obscuring his vision. The wind seemed to increase in intensity with each passing minute, with loose sand pelting them more and more frequently. Luckily, the wind blew from the northwest, hitting their backs and nudging them along as they walked. Their cloaks blocked most of the sand blown by the wind, but it stung any exposed skin.

They continued walking as the day dawned, and when the sun edged over the mountain peaks to the east they still hadn't found anything but dry, flat ground. It wouldn't be long before the dry desert air grew hot from the sunlight, far too hot for comfort.

The roadway became a series of small dunes, slowing them as they dragged their feet through the loose sand. As the wind continued to grow worse, Brock feared that it would soon become a full-blown sandstorm.

Stumbling, Brock fell into the sand. Tipper helped Brock to his feet as he wiped sand from his face and spit some out of his mouth. Tipper pulled Brock forward, but he resisted as something occurred to him.

"What is it? Why are you stopping?" Tipper shouted.

Brock yelled back. "Hold on a second. I need to look at something."

Keeping his back to the wind, he began walking backwards. As he expected, the first steps were downward before having to step up again. He looked to the south, recognizing the shallow ditch running toward the canyon.

Brock yelled again. "Let's go this way. We might be able to get out of the wind."

Holding his cloak up to shield his face, Brock followed the wash. He kept his head down, scanning the ground before his feet as walked. The depth of the wash steadily increased, lending hope that it ran deep enough for them to escape the wind.

Brock came to a sudden stop at the edge of a drop. As his eyes adjusted to the depth of the canyon floor, Tipper crashed into his back. Brock's arms whirled wildly as he struggled to regain his balance, but the momentum was too much, and he tumbled over the edge.

His throat constricted as he fell, unable to scream at the fear of falling to his death. He hit the ground hard, the impact blasting the wind from his lungs. Panicked as he struggled to breathe, he rolled over and his lungs regained their function, enabling him to gasp a rush of air. Breathing heavily, he realized he was still alive. He sat up and looked around to discover that he had fallen onto a shelf overlooking the canyon.

When he noticed Tipper above him, trying to block the blowing sand from his face, Brock moved aside and waved for Tipper to jump down. Tipper sat at the edge of the drop and pushed off. He landed on his feet, but his momentum kicked him toward the canyon opening. Brock lunged out and caught Tipper's cloak, yanking him back from the edge. Tipper landed on his rear, choking from the pressure the cloak had applied to his throat. Brock sat beside him, exhausted. Above them, the wind howled and sand occasionally fell onto their heads, but it was better than being in the open and getting hit directly.

Brock opened his water skin and took a drink, thankful that Meg had given them each a second skin, the first having been emptied an hour earlier.

Tipper was the first to speak. "That wind is scary. I wouldn't want to be out there if it blows any harder."

Brock nodded. "That's what I was afraid of. It appears we're safe here for now. That is, if it doesn't rain."

Tipper looked at him, his brow furrowed. "Why do you say that? Wouldn't rain be a good thing? We'd have more water, and this sand would stop blowing around."

Brock shook his head. "That was a wash we followed here. This shelf only exists because water has worn it away. When it rains, this basically becomes a waterfall." He pointed toward the gorge.

Tipper gazed at the canyon opening, swallowing hard. "Let's hope it doesn't rain, then."

Brock looked up toward the sky. Despite it being mid-morning, the sunlight was dim, obscured by the blowing sand. He wiped his weary eyes and suddenly realized that he had been awake since the prior morning.

Without a word, he laid his head on his pack, covered his face with his cloak, and was sleeping in seconds.

12

"**B**rock! Come down here!"

He scrambled to the stairs and ran down from the tannery loft. Reaching up, he twisted the knob to the apartment door and darted inside.

The scent of sweet apples greeted him. Ellie gave him a smile as she put the lid on a large canister and placed it on a shelf. Brock's mom was facing the fire. Hearing the door open, she spun around and flashed him a warm smile. She was young and pretty with long brown hair and intense green eyes.

"G'morning, dear. I have a surprise for you. But you only get it if I get a hug first."

He burst into a run, flying into her arms. She gave him a big hug and kissed him on top of the head. Her hugs felt good, so full of love.

She relaxed her arms and looked down at him. "We made your favorite for breakfast."

Her gesture toward the table revealed a steaming bowl.

Brock's eyes lit up. "Apple cobbler?"

"Yep. I know how you love it."

He climbed up onto the bench, sitting on his knees so he could reach the table.

His mom handed him a fork as she sat across from him. "You need to wait a minute for it to cool, dear. It's still hot."

Brock nodded. "Yes, Ma. Mmm mmm. It smells so good."

His mom stared at him with a serious look on her face. "I need to tell you something important, Brock. Something you need to remember always."

Again, he nodded. His expression was serious, matching hers. Whatever his mom had to tell him, it must be super important.

She reached across the table and took his hand. "Brock, your life belongs to only you. I know that the Ministry says we must live the life they've defined for us, but I don't believe that. I believe we make our own fate, and it's not something predetermined. Just because you have no rune doesn't mean you aren't special or that you cannot find happiness in this world. Look at me. Look at all I have. I've no rune, but I have a great life with a loving husband and a wonderful son."

Ellie spoke up, "Be careful, Emily. What you speak is heresy. If the Ministry heard that kind of talk, you'd be arrested or worse."

Emily looked toward her sister. "They may call it heresy, but it's the truth." She looked down at Brock again. "I believe that Issal loves us and rewards us for being good people, not for obeying the rules the Ministry has created. Be a good person, Brock, but be your own person. Be who and what you want to be, but always remain compassionate and willing to help others. Understand?" Brock nodded solemnly.

She added, "But you cannot repeat these words to anyone. You could get into big trouble."

Brock nodded again. "Okay, Mamma. I won't tell anybody. I swear."

She smiled again. "That's good, dear." She stood, pointing toward the bowl. "You can go ahead and eat your cobbler now."

Brock scooped a big bite into his mouth. It was still hot, but tasted delicious.

The door from the tannery burst open, startling him.

His father stood in the doorway. He pushed his long, thick hair back from his face as he surveyed the room.

"What's this?" He demanded. "Are you having a party without me?"

Milan closed the door and crossed the room, sweeping Emily into his arms as he bent to give her a long kiss. When the kiss ended, they stared into each other's eyes – Emily smiling up at him with his arms still around her. He let her go and scooped Brock up, spinning him around.

"Who let this ragamuffin in?" Milan asked before setting him back down on the bench.

"I let myself in," Brock giggled. "I live here."

"You do? Are you the one who's been creeping around my loft?" his father teased.

Giggling, Brock said, "Yep. That's me, Pa."

"Okay, but you need to earn your keep around here," Milan said with a serious expression. "And that means you have to pay in hugs every day."

Brock giggled again and stood on the bench to give his father a hug. He then knelt to eat his cobbler.

"It looks like apple cobbler. You must have done something special for that," Milan noted.

"Yep. Ma said I was special. Me just being me is special enough for cobbler I guess," Brock replied as he scooped a spoonful into his mouth.

Smiling, Milan put his arm around Emily again. "Yes, you are son." Brock smiled up at his parents. The love in the room felt so good. The room began to waver, the image before him transforming.

He sat at the same bench, staring at his mother as she stumbled and fell to floor. Ellie ran to her side to help her.

"What are you doing out of bed, Emily?" Ellie helped her sister to her feet. "You need to rest. We need you to get well."

She helped Emily across the room. As they reached the bed, Emily collapsed into it.

Tears ran down Emily's face. "Ellie, I feel so horrible. Everything hurts. I feel so weak."

Emily coughed. The hacking cough continued for a couple minutes before subsiding, leaving her gasping for breath.

Brock didn't understand what was happening, but he was concerned for his mother. He jumped off the bench, crossed the room, and sat on the side of the bed to give his mom a hug. Her arm wrapped around him limply, not any sort of squeeze like normal.

"I love you, mommy," Brock said. "I want you to get better. I don't like seeing you sick."

"I love you too, dear," Emily said. "Don't worry, though. Mommy's going to be okay."

He lay there, hugging her for another minute. When he sat up, she was fast asleep.

As he stared at his mother, the image warped and changed again.

Brock stood in the bright sun, holding Ellie's hand. The minister finished his prayer and held the candle out, the flame igniting the kindling and the fire rapidly growing into a raging inferno. The pyre cracked and sizzled as it burned.

The minister lit a small white lantern and held it up before the fire. He let it go and it floated toward the flame. Once over the pyre, it quickly rose into the sky. Moments later, it was but a white speck against the vast blue background. After some final words to the small group before him, the minister then turned to climb the stairs back to the city.

Brock turned toward the flames. They were hot and hurt his eyes. He looked up at his father. Tears ran down the man's face. He was in bad shape. Broken.

He turned the other way to look at Ellie, who also had tears on her face. She looked down at Brock and began crying in earnest, bending to give him a hug as she sobbed on his shoulder.

Eventually, the fire began to die down. Brock's father turned and ascended the stairs toward the city. Ellie followed behind, dragging Brock by the hand. Nobody said a word.

Brock took one last look back toward the dying fire. Silently, he waved goodbye to his mother. His toe hit the edge of a step and he stumbled. Falling face first, the stairs gave way to become a deep canyon. He was over the edge, and the bottom was racing toward him. Panic struck.

He tried to scream, but fear's grip only allowed a weak squeak.

Brock jerked awake and sat up, his body covered in sweat. Sand poured off his cloak. He blinked, trying to gather his bearings.

The dream had been so vivid. So real. It was as if he had relived those precious, yet difficult memories. They reminded him of how much he missed his mother. Now he missed Ellie as well. Thinking about the dream, he was surprised to find that he missed his father too. He missed the man his father used to be before his mother's death. Brock had forgotten the man his father had been, so loving and passionate – so different from the distant, bitter shell that remained.

Breaking from his reverie, he took in his surroundings. The sun was low, with long shadows cast along the canyon walls before him. It would be dark soon. The wind had stopped sometime while he was sleeping.

The sandstorm was over.

13

The view expanded as the road emerged from the narrow mountain pass. When the cliff walls fell away, the vista revealed sharp mountain peaks from horizon to horizon, as if the continent were reaching toward the sky. Although it was summer, bright white snow covered the north face of the taller peaks.

In contrast to the barren desert behind them, the valley was teeming with life. The deep green of the pines covered the lower ground, running up the mountains until they gave way to bare peaks of exposed grey rock and white snow. The Alitus River meandered along the valley floor until disappearing around a bend south of them, where the river turned westward.

The road they were following twisted its way down the mountainside until it came to a bridge that crossed the river far below. Beyond the bridge, the road split with one branch becoming a series of switchbacks leading to another pass between peaks to the east. The other branch turned south, down the center of the valley. Just north of the bridge, a town stretched along the riverbank, a thin strip of civilization cutting through a sea of green wilderness.

"It's amazing," Tipper said, interrupting the peaceful moment.

"Yeah. It's hard to believe we were in that desolate desert just hours ago." Brock remarked. "The weather on this side of the mountains must be quite different. It's like another world."

While enjoying the view, they broke out their water skins.

"That was the last of it. I'm out." Tipper capped his skin. "That river down there looks awfully good right now. I wish it were closer. I'm still thirsty"

"I'm empty too," Brock replied. "That town down there must be Sarville. We can drink our fill there. Let's go."

Motivated by the lure of water at the bottom, the boys broke into a run, letting gravity pull them down the mountainside. Pines and undergrowth enveloping the narrow road created the feeling of running down a tunnel. Birds and rodents scattered from the road as the boys sped past. Dust from the dry gravel flew from the rapid shuffle of their boots, leaving a trail in the air behind them.

As they neared the valley floor, the forest thinned and the ground leveled. The boys slowed to a walk, trying to regain their breath.

The area along the road had been cleared, leaving an open glade filled with long grass and flowers among a patch of stumps. Butterflies flitted about in the afternoon sun, while the buzz of bees traveling from flower to flower hummed in the air around them.

They rounded a bend, and the bridge again came into view, now less than a mile away. Energized by the idea of water ahead, they quickened their pace.

The open area south of the road revealed a few scattered farmhouses among fields of crops. Pines were still scattered here and there, but far less dense than in the forest behind them.

When the bridge was less than a quarter mile away, Tipper broke into a run. Brock laughed and ran after him, quickly passing the taller boy and running past the split in the road. Slowing when he reached the steep bank, he scrambled down until he was at the river's edge. He dropped to his knees and scooped water into his mouth, finding it cold and refreshing. Tipper scrambled down the bank and knelt beside him.

After a dozen scoops, Brock's thirst began to quench. He sat back to watch Tipper feverishly scooping water into his mouth. Looking down at his own shirt, he found the whole front wet. His knees were sunk a couple inches into the muddy riverbank. He began to laugh. Tipper stopped and looked at him in confusion, water dripping down his face, his tunic soaked. Brock laughed harder. Tipper broke into a grin, laughing.

They had made it to Sarville. Life was good.

∾

The boys paused inside the doorway, their eyes adjusting to the dark interior of the inn. The place was busy, and the air hummed with conversation. Followed by Tipper, Brock crossed the room and sat at an open table. A plump woman with curly blond hair slowed as she walked past them.

"I'll be right with you boys."

She deposited four full mugs on the table next to theirs and continued to a table further down.

Tipper sighed. "My feet are killing me. I can't wait to take my boots off. I say we get a quick dinner and go relax in our room."

"I couldn't agree more, Tip. I'm exhaust…"

Brock jumped when two meaty hands slammed down on their table. He looked up to find a large, burly man with curly black hair and a shaggy beard. The rune of *silvas* marked him as a woodsman, likely a lumberjack or a hunter. Looming over them, the large man seemed like a mountain about to become a rockslide.

"You need to leave," he said, glaring at Tipper. "We don't want your kind 'round these parts."

Tipper swallowed visibly with fear reflecting in his eyes.

Brock leaned forward. "Sir, he's with me. He won't trouble you, I promise. We just want some dinner and we'll be away, in our room for the night."

The large bear of a man turned his gaze on Brock, his demeanor softening when he saw the rune on Brock's forehead.

"Sorry, Minister." The man stood upright, removing his paws from the table. "We're good, god-fearing folk here in the Greenway. But we can't have the taint of Unchosen among us. Ain't right."

Brock had seen people avoid and ignore Unchosen. He had seen them belittled and treated as less than human. However, this level of outright hostility was uncommon.

"Surely, you have other Unchosen in town," Brock said to the man.

"No." The big man shook his head. "We're pure in Sarville. Ain't got no tainted Unchosen here. Heck, I ain't seen one in five years, and that was down in Wayport."

Brock didn't want a fight. Not only was this man huge, but he likely had friends in the room.

"I see. In that case, we'll be going."

The man nodded and stepped away. The boys grabbed their packs and left the inn.

It was darker outside than when they had entered, with the sun obscured by the tall peak to the west.

Brock turned to Tipper. "You'd better put your cloak on and use the hood to hide your face. We don't want more trouble."

Tipper nodded and donned his cloak as they walked through town. They passed numerous buildings before coming to another inn, but found it just as crowded as the last. Brock decided to find a quieter place to stay. When they came to a shop with a sign saying *Sarville General Goods*, Brock gestured toward the building.

"We need to restock. Give me your pack, and I'll go see if I can buy what we need."

Tipper handed him the pack, waiting with his hood up and face down. Brock emerged five minutes later with two full packs. He handed one to Tipper and they continued northward.

At the north edge of town, they came to an inn called The Horned Frog. Knowing that this was their last hope, Brock steeled himself and stepped inside.

Hoping to keep a low profile, Brock paid the woman working the bar and led Tipper upstairs. He used the key to open the door and slipped inside a small room with two small beds and a narrow table between them. A bucket of water, two towels, and a bar of soap lay on the table.

Brock sat on a bed and yanked his boots off, rubbing the soreness out of his feet with his hands.

"You go ahead and wash up first," he suggested to Tipper.

"Good idea," Tipper responded. "I hope our dinner shows up soon. I'm starving."

Tipper threw his cloak on a bed. After his boots were off, he removed the shirt from his thin frame and stepped to the bucket. While he was washing, there was a knock on the door.

Brock answered. A young woman handed him two mugs of cider and a steaming hot meat pie with two forks stuck into it. He thanked her and closed the door before setting the mugs and the pie on the table. Beneath the pie were two plates. He handed one to Tipper, who had finished drying off. Brock used a fork to scoop half of the pie onto his plate, the aroma making his stomach growl. Tipper flashed a grin and scooped the remaining pie onto his plate, not waiting for it to cool before he dug in.

The boys ate in silence until every bit was gone and both mugs were empty. Brock then took off his shirt and began to wash. Tipper sat in quiet for a moment before speaking.

"Brock, why do you think these people hate me so much?" He looked at Tipper as he dried his face.

"I've been thinking about that, Tip. It's not that they hate you. I think that maybe they're afraid of you, afraid of what they don't understand." Brock dried his arms and torso as he continued. "That big guy at the inn said there weren't any Unchosen around here, and he hadn't seen one in years. They aren't used to us and don't know any better. Instead, they've somehow twisted the doctrine the Ministry preaches and made it even worse."

Tipper shook his head. "That's something else I don't understand. There must be a hundred Unchosen in Kantar. Surely, there must be some who are born here."

Brock sat on the bed, frowning. "You're right. There would have to be some Unchosen born here. I wonder where they are now."

14

B rock stopped by the kitchen to purchase a couple sausages and a loaf of bread before leaving. He handed Tipper a sausage and stuffed the bread into his pack as they set off. With their early start, they were miles north of Sarville when the sun emerged between two peaks to the east.

By mid-day, clouds began to roll in, obscuring the sun. A few hours later, the clouds darkened and the wind increased, blowing from the north down the length of the valley.

No sooner did the boys don their cloaks than it began to pour. The wind drove the rain into their faces as they trudged north on the winding Greenway Road. Puddles pooled in dips dotting the road and washes crossing the road flowed into the river. Brock glanced toward the river, noting the heavy flow racing past them and imagining the horror of being swept into the raging waters.

It wasn't long before the road turned to mud, causing them to slip and slide while they walked. The mud would sometimes grab ahold of their feet and they would pull hard to break their boots from its grip, creating a "pop" sound when coming free. Now feeling cold and wet, the hot dry days marking the first half of their journey seemed a distant memory.

After an hour, the storm began to lighten, becoming a steady rain rather than a heavy torrent, but by that time, they were soaked through and through. With daylight failing and the rain persisting, Brock knew that they needed shelter so they could dry off and get some rest.

"Look for someplace dry we can stay for the night," Brock said to Tipper, who nodded in reply.

Ten minutes later, Tipper tapped Brock's shoulder and pointed toward a dark spot among an outcropping of rocks. It appeared to be a cave, but it was difficult to be sure in the dying light. They turned from the road, navigating through the brush toward the rock formation. As they drew close, he could tell that it was indeed a cave. He climbed up the stack of wet rocks, slipping a few times along the way. Stepping beneath the over-hanging rock, he thanked Issal when he pulled his hood down and felt no rain.

Brock removed his glowstick and activated it, finding a rock ceiling that was high enough that Tipper couldn't touch it. As he entered the dark opening, Brock judged the cave to be at least ten strides deep, with a width that was about half the depth. It was perfect.

The boys set their packs down and began wringing moisture from their clothes near the cave entrance. Once finished, they then moved farther in and sat to eat.

Still cold and damp, they soon settled in to get some sleep.

A noise woke Brock, who sat up to find his clothes still damp. He rubbed the crust from his eyes and blinked to shake the cobwebs from his brain.

Recognizing his surroundings, he remembered the cave they had found to escape the rain. Early morning light emanated from the entrance, giving shape to Tipper, who lay asleep beside him. In the dim light, Brock noticed something near his friend.

He leaned close to get a better look, finding bones he hadn't noticed in the dark of night. Near the bones, rows of four parallel lines marked the surface of the rock. His chest constricted as he realized that something lived here, something large.

A howl echoed in the forest outside the cave.

Brock urgently shook Tipper.

"What? What's happening?" Tipper blurted, sitting up in confusion.

"Shh." Brock whispered. "Be quiet. There's something out there."

Tipper rubbed his eyes. "Huh? What are you talking about?"

A shadow eclipsed the light at the mouth of the cave. As Brock turned toward the entrance, his breath caught in his throat.

Against the light of the morning sky, the silhouette of a massive four-legged creature blocked the opening. Whatever it was, they were in its home and it was angry.

A low growl rumbled, its ferocity reverberating within the small cave. The boys backed away, and Brock stumbled when he collided with a boulder. He scrambled to his feet as his mind raced. The beast blocked the only exit. Like the banshee attack at Glowridge Pass, they were trapped in a hopeless situation with no way out. His mind drifted back to that event and he reacted.

Brock scooped a bone from the cave floor and began scraping a symbol on the boulder – the same rune he had drawn on Hank.

The creature stepped forward, and Brock noticed the beast's eyes glowing an angry red. The smell of wet animal filled the cave, mixing with the smell of fear from Brock and Tipper.

Spurred by desperation, Brock closed his eyes and began pushing with his will. He felt the same force as last time, just beyond himself. Pushing harder, he latched onto it and his body grew flush with hot energy. A storm raged within, threatening to destroy him. He opened his eyes and poured the energy into the rune. It glowed bright red, pulsing as the boulder began to shake.

Brock backed from the advancing creature into the rear of the cave, against Tipper's cowering form.

The boulder suddenly burst. Bits of rock pelted him, cutting hands held up to protect his face from the beast. The creature leapt back from the blast, dozens of small shards hitting its face and body. It howled in rage as Brock lowered his throbbing hand to see what had happened.

The boulder moved toward the beast. The round headless body of the rock advanced on four legs made of stone, emitting crunching and grinding sounds with each movement.

The hairy beast attacked, swinging vicious swipes with its huge paws. Sharp claws scraped the hard surface of the living boulder and bounced off harmlessly. The beast backed away, but the boulder continued to advance.

The beast attacked again, with little result as the boulder relentlessly forced it backwards. Suddenly, the animal was outside, its red eyes squinting in the pale light of pre-dawn. It made one last swipe and then bolted.

The boulder turned the corner to give chase, one leg stepping over the edge, and it disappeared. The rumbling and crunching sound of a small rock-slide followed as it tumbled away.

The cave became silent.

"What in the blazes? Brock, what did you do?" Tipper shouted. "What was that thing? What's happening?"

"I don't know!" Brock yelled back. He was breathing heavily, trying to calm himself. "I don't know, Tipper. I had to do something, and it just came to me. I don't know what it is."

"It's like what happened with Hank. You did it again with that big rock," Tipper said.

"Yeah. I know," Brock replied. "I wish I knew what it was, but I don't."

Brock grabbed his pack and headed toward the entrance. "Let's get out of here before that thing comes back."

Stepping outside the cave, he looked down. The rock-thing lay at the bottom of the outcropping, its legs broken off with the pieces still twitching. A shiver wiggled down Brock's spine.

"That's creepy," Tipper said.

With a nod, Brock began to climb down as the first rays of morning sun streaked across the valley.

15

"It's definitely Fallbrandt. We made it, Tipper." Brock stored the map, now worn and crumpled from the harsh treatment of their travels.

"Well, not yet," Tipper replied. "It's still miles away."

Brock shrugged. "Okay. In another hour or so, we'll be there."

After the encounter with the huge animal at the cave, their journey had been event-free. In fact, it had been rather pleasant.

Compared to the lower lands to the west, the early summer weather in the Greenway Valley was mild. With the tall trees providing shade along the road, they were able to avoid direct sunlight for all but a small portion of the day. As they traveled north, the valley floor seemed to perpetually rise, slowly gaining altitude.

The boys had spent the previous night in a small clearing encircled with thick pines, not far from the road. After diligent effort, Tipper was able to start a small fire using his flint. The dead wood they had gathered burned hot and fast, giving the boys a sense of comfort as they talked until drifting to sleep.

Two and a half days after leaving Sarville, the gradual incline steepened as they passed over a low saddle. Cresting that rise offered their first view of Fallbrandt, nestled along the mirror-like lake bearing the same name.

Stuffing the map back into his pack, Brock led Tipper down the road, the first downhill slope they had encountered in days. He felt good. In fact, he felt better than he had felt in a long time. The majestic surroundings of the past day seemed to melt the wear of the miles away. Now within sight of his goal, his spirits had never been higher.

As they walked the last few miles, Brock's mind wandered to thoughts about the Academy. He had been focused on getting there but hadn't considered what was required to be accepted. Just being marked by the rune of Issal surely wasn't enough. The Academy was only so big, and if they let everyone in they would run out of space. Brock decided that it didn't matter. He was committed, and he was going to get in. Somehow, he would find a way.

A rumbling drew his attention to the road ahead. Rounding a bend, two horses pulling a wagon came into view. The wagon sped down the road followed by a trail of dust. Two bouncing bodies sat on the driver's seat, a man with a wide-brimmed hat holding the reins and a blond woman beside him. The woman flashed the boys a smile, while the sight of the man reminded Brock of Hank.

Over the next mile, Brock saw increasing signs of civilization as the trees gradually gave way to man-made dwellings. As they entered the city, he could see a lake between the buildings they passed. People milled about on the streets and shops were open, busily selling their wares. Men and women strolled purposefully, going about their business.

At random, Brock pointed to an inn beside the main road. The image of a headless woman was carved in the sign above the door – the woman's arms spread wide as if she were welcoming them. Tipper nodded and entered the inn with Brock a step behind.

Since it was mid-afternoon, the inn was quiet. Four women sat around the only occupied table. Giggles erupted in reaction to something said.

Brock smiled even though he had no idea why they had laughed.

"Can I help you boys?"

Turning toward the table, he saw one of the women approaching. She was a voluptuous middle-aged woman with long brown hair and blue eyes. She reminded him of Sally, despite the rune of *dominus* that marked her forehead.

"Hello." Brock flashed a smile. "We're looking for a place to room for a few nights."

"You don't say," she responded. "I assume you have the coin to pay for your stay."

"Yes." Brock dug into his coin purse, placing one silver on the table. "What will this buy us?"

A friendly smile spread across her face as she swept up the silver.

"That will buy you both full room and board for two nights." "That includes food and baths?" Brock asked.

She nodded. "Breakfast is served at sunrise, dinner at sunset. You're on your own for lunch," the woman replied. She smiled again and extended her hand. "My name is Adorya, but everyone calls me Dory. Welcome to The Quiet Woman."

PART III

THE QUIET WOMAN

16

After leaving their packs in a room upstairs, Brock and Tipper followed Dory to a back room on the main level of the inn. Inside the room were two large copper tubs, half-filled with water. A fire was burning in the brick fireplace on the far wall. Steam rose from a black kettle that Dory pulled off the fire and set on the hearth.

"The water in the tubs is cold. Add some hot water from the kettle until it's warm enough. There's a bar of soap for you to share." Dory walked to the door. "Would you like to have your clothes cleaned? We have a steam cleaner we bought from the Academy a few years back. We can get your clothes clean and dry in a few hours. It'll be another four coppers though."

Brock nodded. "Clean clothes would be great."

"Okay." She opened the door to leave. "I'll have the maid come by to grab your clothing. Enjoy your bath, boys."

She closed the door, leaving them alone. Brock used a hot-pad to lift the kettle and to pour steaming water into each tub while Tipper got undressed. A minute later, they were each soaking in a warm bath.

There was a knock on the door. Before they could respond, the handle turned, and a girl poked her head into the room.

"Sorry sirs, but I'm here to get your clothes for steam cleaning." Seeing them safely in the tubs, she entered the room.

At roughly the boys' age, the girl had straight black hair tied into a tail.

Large brown eyes complemented her olive complexion, and her clothes wore loose on her thin frame.

"You can wear these robes until your clothes are ready." She set some towels and robes on a bench near the wall.

Scooping up the dirty clothes from the floor, she hurried from the room, keeping her eyes downcast the entire time.

Tipper stared at the door after it closed. "At least I'm not the only Unchosen in this town."

Brock nodded. "Yes, I noticed that. It's interesting that Dory has an Unchosen working for her. That's...uncommon."

"She's also pretty," Tipper said, still staring at the door.

"Okay, lover boy." Brock splashed water at his friend. "Toss me that soap."

Brock proceeded to scrub the grime of their travels from his body. When he was finished, the bath water was decidedly darker, and it felt good to be clean again. He climbed out and toweled dry while Tipper scrubbed his own filth away.

As Brock tied the towel around his waist, he noticed a bowl of water, a bar of soap, and a razor resting on the vanity. Standing before the small mirror, he examined his reflection.

He had always been fit from working in his father's shop, but nine days of hard travel with little food had worn away any remaining softness. Brock could easily see the ripples beneath his otherwise flat stomach, and he found that his chest and arms appeared more defined. His gaze shifted to his face, appearing more tan and rugged behind a patchy layer of scruffy hair. Deciding it was time for a clean shave, he soaped up and took the blade to his face. Minutes later, he rinsed the soap from his cheeks and toweled dry. His face now felt smooth with just two small cuts, leaving red smears on the towel. He turned to find Tipper standing in his robe.

"Don't you want to shave?" Brock asked Tipper.

The response was a shrug. "It don't bother me. It's hard to see with my blond hair anyway."

"Okay. Let's go then," Brock said, walking out the door.

Brock's eyes fluttered open to see Tipper asleep on the other bed. He sat up and glanced out the window to find the street darkened by long shadows. It was nearly time for dinner.

A knock on the door made him jump. He pulled his robe closed before responding.

"Come in."

The door opened, and a head peeked around the corner.

"Sorry, sirs."

The maid they had met earlier entered, placing their folded clothes on a chair near the door.

"Your clothes are clean and dry." She absently tucked a loose lock of hair behind her ear. "Is there anything else you need?"

"Yes," Tipper replied. Brock hadn't realized that he was awake. "I believe a proper introduction is what I...I mean, we, need. This is Brock, and I'm Tipper," he said with a grin.

"Nice to meet you...um...Mr. Brock and Mr. Tipper," she said, shyly. "My name is Libby. I'm the maid here at the inn. If there's anything you need, let me know."

Tipper took two steps and grabbed her hand. She looked startled as he bent to kiss it, his face sporting an even wider grin after lifting his lips from the back of her hand.

"It's a pleasure to meet you, Libby. Please call me Tipper. No need to be formal." He smiled his best smile, locking eyes with the girl.

Her stoic face cracked, a smile blooming. Brock had to admit she had a nice smile. She pulled her hand back, breaking eye contact. Her eyes opened wide and her hand went to her mouth.

"Oh my!" She squeaked and darted out the door.

When Brock looked to where her eyes had gone before fleeing, he burst out laughing.

"Showing her all your best moves already, aren't you, lover boy?" he said with laughter.

Tipper's face showed his confusion as Brock collapsed on the bed with tears running down his face. Tipper finally looked down, noticing that his robe had fallen open.

"Oh no," Tipper moaned.

Brock laughed even harder.

17

The Quiet Woman was anything but quiet. Brock paused on the landing to survey the room below. He noticed four men sitting at a table in a corner. One man worked behind the bar and another was waiting on tables. The rest of the room was filled with women.

Completing their descent, he and Tipper weaved their way toward the bar. While crossing the room, Brock heard women chatting with sprinkles of laughter. Eyes turned toward them as they passed, some of the women openly appraising them. He felt a bit like livestock at the market with these women evaluating him for purchase. Whispers and giggles followed in their wake.

They sat at two open barstools and signaled for the bartender, a handsome man roughly ten years older than Brock. The man slid over to greet them, wiping his hands on his apron as he flashed a smile. His perfect teeth seemed to glow against his tanned face and short-trimmed brown beard. He had bright blue eyes, strong brown eyebrows, and light brown hair with long bangs partially covering the rune of *famulus*.

He pushed the bangs back with one hand and addressed the boys. "You must be our new guests. Dory said you would be down for dinner.

"I'm James." He flashed a big white smile. "What can I get you to drink?"

Tipper spoke first. "I'll take an ale, please."

James shook his head. "Sorry, but we don't serve ale. We do have a fine selection of wine, though."

Brock turned and glanced around the room to confirm James' statement. While most of the women had wine glasses, some drank from tan cups filled with steaming liquid.

He turned back to James. "What's in the small cups?"

"That's caffe, of course," James replied.

"Caffe? What's that?" Tipper asked. "It looks like it's served hot."

James leaned forward. "Yes, it's served hot. It's quite popular here in Fallbrandt. As for what it is, I think you have to try it to understand. Someone at the Academy invented it a few years back, and it soon became popular at the school. Dory likes it and adopted it as an alternative to wine." He stood upright, gesturing to himself. "However, I only drink it in the morning. I prefer wine with my dinner."

Brock glanced at Tipper, who shrugged. "I guess we'll each try one of those...what did you call it? A calf?"

James smiled. "Caffe. I'll be right back"

The man crossed to the other end of the bar and filled two small cups, steam rising from the liquid as he poured. Returning, he set them on the bar.

"Careful, this is hot. If it's too bitter, let me know, and I'll add a little sweet milk to it."

Brock nodded. "Thanks, James."

The man stepped away to help two women who were waving for his attention. He greeted the women with his engaging smile, holding one of their hands and oozing charm.

Brock picked up his cup, blowing to cool it. The drink had an interesting aroma. He took a small sip, the heat burning the tip of his tongue. Tipper laughed at the face Brock made after swallowing the bitter liquid.

Tipper also took a small sip and his face yielded similar results.

A minute later, James returned. "So, what do you think?"

"I think we'll accept your offer to add some of that milk. It is awfully bitter," Brock replied.

"That's what I figured." James left to fetch the milk.

When he returned, he poured a little milk into each cup and motioned for them to try it again. Brock took a sip and found the taste much better. It was still bitter, but only mildly so. After both boys nodded in approval, James left to wait on other customers.

Brock took another sip. While it wasn't great, he was determined to learn to drink it. He wanted to fit in at the Academy when he was admitted. Not if, when.

A burst of laughter erupted nearby, drawing Brock's attention. Six women sat at the table. Five of them covered their mouths in laughter as Dory spanked the waiter, who had his rear stuck up in the air and his back arched. When she finished, he turned and bowed to the women. Dory handed him two coppers, and he moved on to fill some glasses at another table.

Dory's eyes met Brock's. She smiled and stuck two fingers up, scooping them toward her. He picked up his cup and walked to the table as the laughter died down and all eyes turned toward him. Dory tapped the open chair beside hers, bidding him to sit. He smiled and gave a nod to the women as he took his seat.

Dory turned toward her guests. "This is Brock. He arrived today and is staying at the inn for a bit."

He smiled his best smile and greeted the group. "Hello ladies. I'm honored to be in the presence of such beauty."

His greeting scored him five glowing smiles. Dory was not so easily swayed, but she did give a nod as if he had done the right thing.

"Brock, I assume you came here to join the Academy. Am I correct?" Dory asked.

He finished his sip of caffe and nodded. "Yes. I'm planning on going there tomorrow to meet with admissions. I didn't see the Academy when I came into town today. I assume it's a big building, right?"

Dory laughed. "I would definitely categorize the Academy as a big building. However, you won't find it here. It's about an hour's walk north of here."

He nodded again. "Well, it makes sense I didn't see it, then."

Dory put her hand on his arm. "Brock, will you please have some wine with us? I know caffe is wonderful, but wine is much better with dinner."

Not wanting to offend anyone, he agreed. Dory waved and the waiter set a stemmed glass on the table near Brock, filling it with deep red liquid. He had heard of wine, of course, but he hadn't seen it before tonight. Wine was reserved for the finer inns in Kantar – places where Unchosen were unlikely to be welcome.

Dory lifted her glass for a toast. "To Brock. We wish him success on his quest for admission to the Academy."

Their glasses tapped together over the table before rising to their lips.

An explosion of flavor splashed into Brock's mouth, warming his throat on the way down, while leaving an aftertaste that was less bitter than caffe. The warmth in his throat felt good, so he took another drink.

A soft hand touched his arm. He turned toward the pretty woman who sat in the seat next to him. At about five years older than Brock, she was absently twisting her long black hair with two fingers.

"Brock, can you tell us where you come from? Did you have any adventures on your journey to Fallbrandt?" she asked, eagerness reflecting in her large brown eyes.

Dory touched his other arm. "Yes, Brock. Tell us of your journey."

Brock took another drink, the wine warming him inside. It was odd how each drink seemed to make him want more. He cleared his throat before speaking.

"I'm from Kantaria. It took the better part of two weeks for us to reach Fallbrandt." He paused, remembering Tipper's role in his charade. "My servant and I, that is."

He was feeling more confident, his head swimming from the wine. If these women wanted a story, he would tell one. "What began as a simple journey soon turned into one of adventure and peril."

Brock began with the wagon ride to the top of the eerie Glowridge pass, observing the awe-inspiring Whitecap Falls along the way. The ladies gasped in horror when he described the encounter with the banshee, a creature from nightmares. They cried out when he described Hank and the banshee falling to their deaths. Of course, he did not mention how Hank's corpse had risen to fight the creature.

He paused as the waiter refilled their glasses. After taking a drink, he resumed his tale.

The women cringed as he described the harsh desert crossing and escaping the deadly winds of the sandstorm. Nodding heads and knowing eyes met his gaze when he told them of the hostility against Unchosen in Sarville. A look of relief crossed their faces when he mentioned how they had found shelter in a cave from the torrential rain.

The look turned to horror when he told them of the beast that had attacked them in the cave.

Dory sat upright, her eyes wide. "Wait. What you describe is a bacabra. Few people see one and live to tell about it. How did you escape?"

Brock's mind raced. "Well, a boulder saved us," he said in truth, before twisting it to a story he could tell. "We were able to roll it down the slope of the cave. Luckily, it clipped the beast's shoulder and it left us to tend its wounds. Sensing our chance, we escaped from the cave and continued our journey."

"And now, here we sit in this lovely inn, two days after the encounter with the...bacabra." Brock concluded his story, capping it off by emptying his glass.

Dory began to clap, the other women following suit. When the applause receded, Dory spoke again.

"My, Brock. That was a wonderful tale. You must be favored by Issal to have survived such a perilous journey. Thank you for sharing it with us." Dory paused as the other women nodded in agreement. "Ah, I see dinner is being served. Please stay and eat with us, won't you?"

As James and the waiter began to set plates on the table, Brock decided he had no choice but to accept. He glanced toward Tipper, who was already busy eating his food at the bar.

The fish was light and delightful. The vegetables were warm and juicy, yet still crisp. Overall, the dinner was delicious. The table conversation was engaging and unguarded. It was a wonderful night.

It was a horrible morning. Brock felt dreadful. His head was pounding, and the room tilted when he moved, causing his stomach to churn. The sunlight coming through the window made it even worse.

He sipped water, wetting his dry mouth. Setting the glass back on the table, he resumed holding his head in his hands while sitting on the edge of the bed. He heard the door open, followed by Tipper's voice.

"It's good to see you're awake and alive." Tipper sat on the bed opposite from Brock.

"I'm kinda wishing I wasn't alive right now. I feel terrible." Brock's words sounded muffled as he held his face in pain.

Tipper laughed. "I'm not surprised. You seemed to enjoy the wine last night. I realized you'd had quite a bit when you started dancing on the table."

He looked up at Tipper. "What?" He blinked, trying to recall the evening.

"Now that you say it, I guess I vaguely remember that. I don't seem to remember much of last night though. I know it started well with pleasant conversation and some wonderful food. Then it becomes muddled, like trying to see through a thick fog."

Tipper smiled at him. "Yeah, James told me you'd likely feel like this and not remember a whole lot. He and I got along well, having more than a few laughs as we watched your antics. Lucky for me, I stuck to caffe. It's quite good you know..."

Brock moaned, "Tip, stop torturing me and tell me what happened."

Tipper leaned back on his elbows. "Well, everything seemed to start fine when you joined the ladies at Dory's table. You drank wine and chatted with them for a while. Then James and Garrett – he's the waiter – brought dinner out, and I stopped watching while I ate my food. The fish was delicious, and the vegetables were the best I'd ever had. James told me that they were steamed. I wonder how they do that. They were hot and juicy, but still had a lot of flavor. I need to ask James next..."

"Tip!" Brock pleaded. "Please, just tell me what happened."

"Oh, yeah. Sorry." Tipper smiled as he continued the story. "After dinner, you continued to pour wine down your throat. In between, you told stories and shared laughs with those ladies. Then, they began to clap in unison. In fact, everyone in the room was clapping. The next thing I know, you were up on their table, dancing to the beat. Then they started yelling for you to take your shirt off, and you obliged."

Brock groaned at this news.

"With your shirt off, you leapt from the table to the top of the bar. Your dancing continued until you did a handstand on the bar. You then began walking across the bar on your hands, making it about six or seven steps before your hand went off the edge, and you fell behind the bar, landing beside James."

"Oh no," Brock groaned again. "Well, now I know why my hip is killing me."

Tipper flashed a big grin. "When you fell, everyone gasped, and the room got quiet. Suddenly, you popped up with your hands raised high and gave a bow. Everyone clapped and cheered. You hopped over the bar, retrieved your shirt, and resumed drinking with the ladies. After your performance, women from the whole room were surrounding your table."

Tipper reclined, swinging his legs onto the bed as he rested his head on the pillow. "It was about two hours later when I convinced you to bid them goodnight. You kept turning and waving to the room as I helped you up the stairs. I dragged you in here and dumped you onto the bed. You were snoring less than a minute later."

Tipper turned toward Brock again. "You were in the exact same position when I woke this morning. You never even took your boots off." He smiled, clearly enjoying Brock's suffering.

Brock groaned at having already made a spectacle of himself on the very day he arrived in Fallbrandt. Even if his head didn't hurt so much, his behavior was warning enough that he had better watch his wine consumption.

Taking another drink of water, Brock emptied the glass. He set it on the table and glanced out the window, trying to judge the time. Now mid-morning, it was far too bright outside. He closed his eyes in pain. He had planned to visit the Academy in the morning, but now he would have to wait until after lunch. Even then, he needed to work on his recovery. He took a breath and stood. The room tilted, and his stomach tilted with it.

"You don't look so good, Brock," Tipper noted.

"I know. Anyone could probably guess that," Brock grumbled. "I plan to go to the Academy today, so I need to recover soon. I'm going downstairs to find someone who can help me."

Tipper replied, "Go ahead. I already had breakfast. It was quite good. Not as good as last night's dinner, but still quite good. The cook here has talent."

Brock washed his face in the bowl on the table and dried it with a clean towel. He dipped his fingers in the water, raking them through his hair in an attempt to tame it. When the image in the mirror looked presentable, he forced himself to walk out the door.

He found Dory alone in the dining room, seated at the same table as the night before. With papers spread out before her, she was busy writing numbers into a ledger.

Brock descended the stairs and walked toward the table. As he approached, Dory looked up and gave him a smile. "Good morning, Brock. I hope you're feeling well." "Well...actually, I feel awful," he replied.

Dory nodded. "Yes, I expected that might be the case. You certainly took to the wine last night. If you're not careful, it can sneak up on you and leave you in a bad way the next day."

"Well, it has done a good job on me," Brock replied, settling into the chair across from her. "I apologize for my behavior last night. If I offended anyone, I'm sorry."

"Don't be sorry. You were genuine, you were fun, and you were entertaining," Dory said with a smile. "With the Academy influencing the area, most of the men here believe that they must always be proper. It's even worse with those who work at the Academy itself. They treat maintaining personal decorum as a virtue. However, the women here find it dull and boring." Dory smiled again. "You, on the other hand, are not boring. You had a room full of women, many twice your age, wrapped around your finger last night. They listened, they laughed, and they had a good time. There's no apology needed. In fact, I'd like to thank you."

He nodded, not knowing what to say. Dory spoke so he didn't have to.

"Now, how about a cup of caffe to help nurse you back to health?" She stood and made her way to the end of the bar. "Do you like it with sweet milk?"

"Yes, please," Brock replied.

Dory returned, handing him the cup as she reclaimed her seat. They chatted as he sipped the hot drink. By the time he was on the second cup, he began to feel better.

18

It was refreshing to be on the road without the weight of a heavy travel pack. A cool mountain wind balanced the warmth of the sun, resulting in a beautiful afternoon. The breeze ruffled Brock's shirt and blew his hair back as he marched uphill toward the Academy.

The forest abruptly ended a mile beyond Fallbrandt, revealing a wide field of knee-length grass. Lines of pines, two miles apart, surrounded the field while more trees lined the road up the middle.

An immense building stretched across the far end of the field, near the head of the valley. The center section of the structure was large and blocky. Two long outer wings bent southward at an angle, stretching out from the main building until they ended with a circular tower at the end. Scattered trees among the lawn provided shade along walking paths lined with occasional benches near the building.

As Brock neared the main entrance to the Academy, he realized the structure was made of multiple connected buildings, giving it a disjointed appearance. Above the doors was a stone marquee that read *Academy for the Ministry of Issal, Established 1055*, making the Academy nearly four hundred years old.

He climbed the stairs and pulled on the heavy door. It groaned as it reluctantly swung outward. Brock stepped inside the Academy for what he hoped was the first time of many.

The sound of his boots on the marble floor disturbed the silence of the hall, echoing off walls standing over one hundred feet apart. Light streamed in from the windows above him. He glanced up at the high ceiling, supported by two rows of pillars that interrupted the otherwise open space. Closed doors lined the interior walls, and each of the upper two stories had dark wooden rails lining a terrace that overlooked the room below. At each corner, a stairwell connected one level to another. The main level had three wide hallways at the far end – one leading to the left, one to the right, and the third leading straight ahead.

Brock stood alone in the hall, gawking at his surroundings, when a bell tolled. Doors burst open and blue-cloaked students emerged from classrooms and connecting corridors to fill the hall. Some exited the building, some disappeared down hallways, and others entered another room within the hall. Minutes later, only a few stragglers remained. Another bell rang, and Brock found himself standing alone again, leaving the hall eerily quiet.

He crossed the room to stand where the three hallways met. Not knowing what else to do, he randomly picked a direction.

As Brock strolled down the quiet hallway, he passed numerous glowlamps lighting the corridor. He found a set of doors between each lamp and noticed a plaque inscribed *Hedgewick Knowledge Center* beside the doors.

The hallway connected to another open space, this one with a two-story ceiling. To his left was another set of doors to the knowledge center. The next wall had a set of doors that appeared to lead outside. Ahead, the hallway continued toward an outer wing.

Two sets of open doors waited to Brock's right, the nearest with a plaque labeled *Office of Admissions*. Somehow, he had found what he was seeking.

He stepped into a small room with four chairs to one side, a desk to the other, and a closed door at the back. The blond girl sitting at the desk glanced up from her writing. She pushed her spectacles in place as she addressed him.

"Can I help you?"

His whole mission hinged on the next few minutes. Ignoring his fluttering stomach, Brock put on his best smile and responded. "Hello. I'm here to be admitted to the Academy"

"Well, you've come to the right place. My name is Monica. I'm the admissions assistant," she replied with a nod and a smile. "First, what's your name?"

"My name is Brock." He paused, mind racing. He couldn't use Tannerson as his last name. No tanner would have a son entering the Academy.

Monica finished writing his first name and looked up at him. "And, your last name?"

"Sorry. Yes, my name is Brock Ta…" He cleared his throat and coughed, buying time as he thought about a last name. A plaque on the wall with the word *talent* inscribed on it inspired him. "Brock Talen…z. Talenz, with a z."

Monica nodded and recorded the name on a form before looking up expectantly.

"I need your papers as well."

Oh no. A surge of panic struck him, twisting his stomach.

Brock smiled again, trying to be engaging. "I'm sorry, but I don't have any papers."

"No papers? No official writ? I can't help you then." She shook her head, sitting back. "The rules are quite clear. You must have official documents in order to be admitted."

He wasn't about to give up. "Isn't there someone I can see to resolve this? I must be admitted."

Monica glanced toward the closed door at the back of the room. "You'll have to speak with the master of admissions." She stood, walking toward the door. "Let me see if he's available."

She knocked, cracking the door open. After a brief conversation, she opened the door wide and waved Brock inside.

It was a large room with beautiful wood-paneled walls, covered by a bookcase on one end and a row of windows along the back. A table with six chairs stood to Brock's left, a big wooden desk to his right. A man in a purple cloak waited behind the desk.

The man looked up at Brock, his brown bangs hanging over the rune on his forehead. He had a chiseled face framed by a short-cut beard below squinting blue eyes. A small block of wood on the desk displayed the man's name: *Ackerson.*

As Brock took a seat, the man spoke, "Mr. Talenz, is it?" Brock nodded and the man continued. "I hear that you're requesting admission without the proper papers."

"Yes…um…Master Ackerson," Brock replied.

"So, you expect us to just accept you without a recommendation from a master minister?" The man had a smug smile on his face.

Brock's mind raced. "Well, you see, the minister I was training with died before he could write the recommendation. I'm from a small town, and he was the only master in the area."

Ackerson's smugness softened, looking unsure. "I guess that makes sense. Where did you say you were from? Who was the minister?"

When he realized that these questions were coming, Brock's mind had been racing to prepare a response.

"I grew up in Port Choya, in south Kantaria. His name was Master Snod. He was old and died this past winter." Brock used the name of an old master minister who had visited Kantar the previous summer, remembering it because he thought the name was funny at the time.

Ackerson's confidence appeared to be waning. "Um, yes. Well, this is still highly irregular." He shook his head. "Even if your story checks out, I can only accept applicants with an official writ. I'm sorry."

Brock pleaded. "But I traveled all this way. I'm here and am ready. Isn't there something you can do?"

Ackerson sat back again, his arms crossed. "The rules are clear. No writ, no admission. I'm sorry."

With his brain racing, Brock struggled to come up with a solution. Having the mark of Issal was supposed to solve his problems. Requiring a writ was not in the plan. He had come all this way for nothing, dragging Tipper along with him.

Heartbroken, Brock stood and walked out.

Brock somehow found himself on a bench on the academy lawn. A solitary bird in a nearby tree chirped a lonely tune. The sad melody matched Brock's mood as he sulked, finding his spirit crushed.

Eventually the bird took flight, soaring in circles as it continued to rise on the mountain breeze. He watched the bird disappear into the woods at the western edge of the lawn, and he noticed the trees covered in the shadow of the mountains to the west. Deciding he should return to the inn before nightfall, he forced himself off the bench to begin his trek back to Fallbrandt.

When Brock entered The Quiet Woman, dinner was underway. Again, the place was packed, and the room buzzed with the conversation of the women who had gathered.

Brock spotted Tipper at the bar, speaking with James while an empty plate sat between them. As he approached, he noticed that Tipper's scruff was gone.

"I see you decided to shave," Brock noted as he claimed a stool.

Tipper grinned, rubbing his face with one hand. "Libby doesn't like the facial hair," he explained. "How was the trip to the Academy?"

Brock's head dropped in dejection. "It was a dead end, Tip. They require a written recommendation from a master minister. I don't have one, so they sent me away." He stared down at the bar, feeling hollow inside.

Tipper's smile slid away. He put his hand on Brock's shoulder and glanced at James, who shrugged.

"There has to be something you can do, Brock," Tipper said. "You've come this far. You can't give up now."

Brock looked at Tipper, his frustration boiling over. "I don't know what to do, Tip. I tried. I made my case, but they have rules." He stood and shouted. "I'm sorry I had to drag you here for nothing! I tried and I failed! Ackerson said there was nothing he could do!"

Angry, exhausted, and feeling empty, Brock sat and stared at the bar.

Moments later, he felt a tap on the shoulder. He looked up to find a pretty brunette waiting. He remembered her from the prior evening.

"Hi Annabelle." Brock smiled weakly. "What can I do for you?"

"Hi Brock." She smiled, her long eyelashes fluttering. "I'm so glad you remembered me. You were…um…entertaining last night. I want to thank you for the wonderful evening. Now I think there's something I can do for you."

Brock raised a brow, allowing her to continue.

"I heard you mention the name Ackerson. Are you talking about Abe Ackerson? A Minister with brown hair and a short-trimmed beard?"

Brock nodded. "Yes. I met with him today about admission to the Academy. He denied me, saying it wasn't possible because I don't have the necessary papers."

Annabelle nodded, twisting her hair with a finger while her other hand remained on his shoulder.

"That's what I thought. Well, Abe is my husband. When he gets home tonight, I'll set him straight. There has to be a way. There's always a way." Her face was firm, and she nodded again. "Return to the Academy in the morning, and the answer will be different. Get yourself ready. I'll worry about Abe."

Annabelle removed her hand from Brock's shoulder and walked away. She stopped to say something to Dory before departing, looking like a woman on a mission.

Brock turned to find Tipper flashing toothy a grin.

"See, Brock. There's always hope." Tipper hoisted his cup. "Would you care for some caffe? I love this stuff."

19

B rock waited in the Office of Admissions while Monica sat at her desk. Whenever he glanced at her, he would catch her looking at him. She would look down at the desk and shuffle papers in an attempt to look busy. Eventually, her eyes would shift back to him. He found himself feeling self-conscious, sensing the heat of her gaze as he tried not to look at her.

Approaching footsteps echoed in the hall outside. Ackerson strolled into the room and greeted Monica. He paused when he saw Brock waiting. With a grunt, he walked past and opened the door to his office.

"You can come in," Ackerson said from beyond the open doorway.

Brock scrambled to his feet and followed the man inside. Closing the door behind him, he took a seat in the same chair as the day prior.

Ackerson put his hands behind his head and leaned back in his chair with his squinty eyes fixed on Brock.

"You've apparently convinced my wife to offer support. While I find that utterly annoying, your resourcefulness does display promise." The man lowered his hands and leaned forward, elbows on the desk. "I've arranged for you to undergo some evaluations. They're a simple set of tests designed to measure your potential. If you truly were to be recommended for the Academy as you claim, there should be no issues."

Brock couldn't believe it. He had hoped that Annabelle might be able to help, but he hadn't dared to believe it.

Before he could respond, Ackerson spoke again.

"I stuck my neck out to make this happen, so I hope you don't embarrass yourself. On the other hand, if you succeed and show promise, it could be a boost for my career."

"Thank you, sir," Brock said. "I appreciate the consideration. I won't let you down."

"See that you don't." The man stood, walking toward the door. Brock stood to follow.

The man opened the door. "Monica, would you please escort Mister Talenz to Master Pretencia's classroom?"

Monica stood, pushing her spectacles up. "Yes, Master Ackerson."

She stepped into the hallway with Brock following along. His stomach began to flutter as anxiety set in. He walked beside Monica, whose blue cloak swished in time with her footsteps. She led him to the Main Hall and turned left into the center hallway. Too nervous to pay attention to details, Brock's surrounding seemed to flow past in a blur.

After turning down another hallway, Monica stopped outside a door and spoke for the first time since leaving Ackerson's office.

"This is Master Pretencia's classroom. I understand he's expecting you. Good luck."

She shared a brief smile before turning to leave. Moments later, he was alone in the hallway. He raised his knuckle to the door and gave a timid knock.

"Come in." Brock heard through the door.

He turned the knob and pushed the door open.

Morning light streaming through windows made the room much brighter than the hallway outside. Rows of tables, four chairs per table, faced the front of the room where a lone desk sat in the corner. Shelves filled with books lined one wall. A black sheet of some material unknown to Brock ran along the wall at the front of the room. Words and runes drawn in glowing blue streaks marked the otherwise black wall.

A man in a purple cloak sat at the desk, busy writing. Brock approached the desk, watching the feather on the man's pen wiggle to the rapid rhythm of the pen scratching on the paper. The man's black hair was slicked back from his forehead with every strand in place and the wrinkle-free skin of his pale face seemed almost made of porcelain.

The master finished his writing, set the pen down, and sat back in his chair. His dark eyes scanned Brock from head to toe, measuring him silently. Brock wanted to shuffle his feet and look away, but he forced himself to bear the uncomfortable scrutiny.

Pretencia let loose a grunt of disgust. "So, here is the young man who seeks to enter the holy Academy with no writ." The man stood, his eyes alight with anger. "You seek to circumvent the rules? You choose to dismiss the requirements that all students before you, for centuries, have had to endure?"

Brock didn't know what to say. Expecting a negative reaction regardless of the response, he opted not to respond at all.

After a moment, Pretencia spoke again. "Ackerson has convinced the others to offer you a chance to prove yourself. I disagree, but I am forced to do the same."

He snatched the paper off his desk, holding it out toward Brock. "You have a half-hour to formulate responses to the three questions on this paper. You will find a pen and jar of ink at that table. Once you are seated, I will start the timer."

Brock took the paper, walked to the table, and sat down. The man flipped the large hourglass on the corner of his desk and then began to look through a set of papers.

Focusing his attention on the paper before him, Brock found three questions on it and read the first question.

Two landholders of adjacent properties are in a dispute. A tree located near the property line has grown so that a major branch is now touching the stable of the neighboring property. When the wind blows, the branch scrapes against the stable and damages the roof, causing it to leak during rainfall. The man with the damaged stable demands that the tree be removed to prevent further damage. The other landholder demands that you preserve the tree, which his grandfather had planted many decades prior. The tree is a major source of shade for the man's house, greatly reducing the heat of the summer sun on his dwelling. You are the magistrate, and you must decide on the course of action. Do you require the tree removed to prevent further damage, or do you support the man who owns the tree and relies on it for shade?

He re-read the question, trying to make sense of it. Both men seemed to have valid claims. Removing the tree caused hardship for one man; keeping the tree was bad for the other.

After some thought, he opted to do neither. He responded by suggesting that the damaging limb be shortened to prevent further damage to the building. He would require the man with the damaged building pay for the removal of the branch, while the man who owned the tree would pay for the repair of the roof. Brock felt good about the resolution.

He read the next two questions, finding them both to be situations where he was a Magistrate who must rule in a dispute. Each situation became more sensitive and complex than the one prior. In fact, any resolution appeared to leave one party upset or destitute. It was also unclear how empire law affected each situation. He struggled to find solid resolutions but proceeded anyway. As he finished responding to the last question, Pretencia stood.

"Time is up. Hand the paper to me."

Brock held the paper out, glanced at the hourglass, and noticed the sand in a pile at the bottom. Pretencia snatched the paper and walked away, his eyes scanning it as he read Brock's responses.

When the man sat in his chair, a smirk spread across his face. "You are dismissed. I will submit my recommendation, and you will have your answer this afternoon."

Brock stood and walked toward the door, pausing before he opened it. "I don't know where I am to go next."

Pretencia looked up from the paper, letting the smirk drop. "Oh yes. You are next required in the Arena. Turn right outside the door and keep going until the hallway ends. It is a large building. I doubt that even you could miss it."

"Um...thank you." He slipped out the door.

After pulling the door closed, Brock leaned against it and took a deep breath to calm his nerves. His evaluation with Pretencia seemed to go poorly. For some reason, the man hated him before he had even walked into the room. He needed to do better with the others.

20

The Arena was massive, easily the largest indoor space Brock had ever seen. Standing inside the doorway, he surveyed his surroundings.

A dirt floor occupied the center of the building, three stories below where he stood. Ten-foot tall walls surrounded the floor, spaced a hundred feet apart on the shorter side, with a length that was twice the width. Shaped like a rectangular bowl, rows of benches encircled the floor below. Each bench was a foot lower than the one behind it, making it easy to see the Arena floor over people seated in front of you.

Brock's focus shifted higher, noting the four large pillars stretching from the stands to the high ceiling. The center glass section of the ceiling mirrored the rectangular shape of the floor below and sunlight poured through it to illuminate the interior of the building.

Pairs of students dressed in white vests sparred on the dirt floor. The clacking sound of wood striking wood echoed off the walls as training weapons and shields collided, the sound growing louder as he descended the stairs. When Brock reached the bottom of the stands, he took a second set of narrow stairs that led to the Arena floor.

As he stepped onto the dirt, a man strolled over to meet him. The man's bald head glistened with sweat, a long bead dripping from his heavy brow and onto his bold nose. A trimmed brown goatee framed his square jaw. He wore a vest like the others, but with purple trim bordering the white cloth and a purple symbol of Issal on his right breast, matching the rune on his forehead.

The man stopped before him, staring with his thick arms crossed over his massive chest. His eyes scanned Brock from head to toe, measuring him. Somehow, it didn't feel as uncomfortable as when Master Pretencia had performed a similar assessment.

"You are Mr. Talenz, I presume," the man said as he held out a meaty hand, which Brock shook in response. "I'm Master Budakis. I'll be evaluating your potential to be a Paladin." The man gestured toward a weapon rack filled with wooden training gear. "If you're familiar with any of these weapon types, you should take whichever you're most proficient at. If you have no weapons training, I suggest you try a quarterstaff as it seems the best match for your build."

Brock certainly had no weapon training. The most he had done is wave a stick around, pretending it was a sword. He stepped over to the rack, filled with wooden rods of various lengths. Budakis followed and grabbed a staff from the rack, setting the butt of the staff in the dirt.

"I suggest you select a staff that's the height of your brow. A longer staff may provide more reach but will be more difficult to manage."

Nodding in response, Brock chose the shortest staff, which seemed to be the suggested length for his height. It wasn't heavy but still felt solid, the thickness of the wood feeling good in his hands.

Budakis walked to an unoccupied area of the floor with Brock in tow. The man turned and stood with his feet apart and staff held firmly before him.

Butterflies fluttered within Brock's stomach and his armpits felt damp. "I don't think I'm ready for this. I have no training. I've never used anything but a knife before, and not even that in a fight."

"This isn't about your training." The man smiled. "This is about your potential. Now, get ready. Prepare to defend yourself. I'll try not to hurt you too badly."

With his heart racing, Brock held his staff up and mirrored the larger man's stance.

Budakis stepped forward, his staff snapping toward Brock. Brock swung his up to block. A loud clack sounded out. Budakis smiled. "Good. That's it."

The man flipped his staff and swept it low. Brock jumped, and the staff passed under him.

Budakis smiled again. "Okay. I think you're ready now. Here comes the good stuff."

Brock stared at the man's hands, trying to anticipate the next move. His nerves had settled, now replaced by adrenaline. Fear had become focus.

The master paladin snapped his staff at Brock's head. Brock ducked, feeling the air swish against the back of his neck as the rod swept by.

The man swung at his side. With a quick twist and bend of his wrists, Brock blocked the strike.

The man's staff snapped down at his shoulder. Brock twisted away, deftly dodging the blow.

Defending a quick flurry of left-right and up-down strikes had Brock panting. Focused on defending himself, he didn't even consider striking back.

Another set of strikes backed Brock up. He reset, and Budakis snapped the staff at his head, causing Brock to duck again. Budakis spun around in a tight rotation, sweeping his staff low. Like the last time, Brock leapt in the air, and the staff passed under him. Budakis brought his staff around, swinging it at Brock's head while he was still in the air.

In desperation, Brock brought his staff up to block the blow. He yelped in pain when the staff struck his finger. The blow affected his balance, causing him to stumble when he landed. Rolling backward with his momentum, he came to his feet a few strides away. His finger was numb with pain, but he didn't let down his guard.

Budakis smiled again. "Good. You can relax now." He shifted his staff to one hand, setting the butt on the ground. He then turned and shouted, "What are you slugs looking at? Get back to work!"

That's when Brock realized everyone had stopped to watch. After the scolding, they quickly resumed their sparring.

He took his hand off the staff, examining his finger. It was red and had already begun to swell. Stabs of pain throbbed to the rhythm of his racing heartbeat.

"Sorry about the finger. It's probably broken. It's a common injury with quarterstaff fighting. In fact, it's happened to me numerous times." Budakis stepped over to the weapons rack, replacing the staff he had used. "Lucky for you, we anticipated an injury to be likely. That's why your next stop is with the master ecclesiast."

21

The heavy door creaked as it opened, causing Brock to cringe at the echo that sounded throughout the empty temple.

The room was octagon-shaped with each wall roughly a hundred feet from the one opposite. Eight columns stretched from the base of the wall, up at an angle, to support the domed ceiling. Similar to the Arena, the floor of the temple sloped down toward the center, surrounded by descending rows of benches that faced the raised dais in the heart of the room. A glowstone altar stood upon the dais, appearing pale blue in the colored light shining through stained glass windows in the domed ceiling. A figure in a purple cloak stood near the altar, engaged in quiet conversation with a student.

While descending the slope toward the dais, Brock examined his throbbing finger. Now twice as thick as his thumb, the finger had turned an ugly purple.

He stopped before the dais and waited. Now that he was close, he realized that the master was a woman, her dark hair tied back in a bun. From this angle, he couldn't see her face or the face of the student and could only hear the murmurs of their muffled conversation.

After a minute, the student turned, descended the dais, and exited out of the far side of the temple. The master turned toward Brock, smiling when she saw him.

"Come on up. Don't be shy."

He circled the dais and climbed the four steps to the top.

Matching his height, the master had large brown eyes and olive skin. He guessed that she was perhaps thirty-five years old. She gave him a warm smile.

"You must be Brock." She extended her hand. "My name is Meryl Varius. I train academy novices in ecclesiastics. I'm pleased to meet you."

Brock reached his hand out to shake hers, wincing when she squeezed his broken finger.

"Oh, I'm sorry." She pulled his hand closer to examine. "It appears broken."

Brock nodded. "That's what Master Budakis said. It got smacked pretty hard by his quarterstaff."

Master Varius looked surprised. "You sparred against Budakis with staves, and your only injury is a broken finger?"

"Um, yeah," he replied, sounding unsure of himself.

"Allow me to heal that for you. Just stay still. You'll feel a bit of a chill."

She held Brock's wrist, not even touching his injured finger. Her eyes closed and a wave of icy cold washed over him, constricting his chest and making it hard to breathe. Moments later, it was gone. He sucked in a deep breath, gasping for air that had eluded him for mere moments. An involuntary chill shook his body and bumps arose on his arms. His stomach growled in hunger, demanding food.

Varius opened her eyes and smiled. "How does it feel?"

To his surprise, he felt no pain at all. He lifted his hand for examination and found that his finger looked healthy, the color and size back to normal. He flexed it tentatively.

"That's amazing." Brock stared at his finger. "It feels great."

Varius smiled. "The power of Order can do wondrous things."

She reached into her pocket, pulled out a hard roll, and handed it to him.

"What's this?" he asked.

"I believe it's a roll, Brock. You know, something you eat?" she replied with a smile.

"Um...I know. But why are you giving this to me?" he asked.

She lifted an eyebrow. "Aren't you hungry?"

"Well, I am starving. But, how did you know?"

"Healing requires energy from your own body. It leaves you hungry. You need food to replenish the energy that gets used," she replied. "And that's your first lesson in the arts of Order."

Brock nodded and took a bite of the roll, trying to chew quickly.

Varius turned and began pacing the dais. She clasped her hands behind her back, appearing to be in deep thought. As he finished the roll, she stopped and nodded as if she had made a decision.

She stepped close, looking into his eyes. "Brock, I want you to place your palm on my forehead."

He lifted his hand and put it on her forehead, covering the rune of Issal.

"Now, close your eyes and calm yourself. Try to find peace within." Brock nodded and closed his eyes. He was calm, relaxed.

She spoke again. "Try to absorb something from my mind through the connection of your palm on my forehead. Concentrate and try to discern what runes reside within my head. They will come to you as images. Remember them all, in order. You'll need to write them down when you're done."

Taking a breath, he closed his eyes and tried to relax. Just beyond, he could sense the hot energy that he had felt the night Hank died and again with the boulder in the cave. However, within himself, he felt a cool and calm peace.

He pushed his mind toward Varius and felt the calm cool peace within her. In his mind's eye, a rune began to coalesce. It was the rune of Issal. However, he sensed other runes beyond the first. Probing deeper, he saw the rune of *medicus* just beneath. Further down, he could make out the rune of *cognitio*. Further yet, two additional runes that he committed to memory.

Opening his eyes, he removed his hand. Varius gestured toward the altar where a piece of paper, a bottle of ink, and a feather pen lay waiting.

"Please write down what you saw, in order."

Brock stepped up to the altar, picked up the pen, and began recording the runes. When finished, five symbols marked the paper as had seen in his mind. He handed his notes to Varius.

She examined it far longer than he felt was comfortable.

Varius lowered the paper and smiled. "Thank you, Brock. You are dismissed. Please exit the way you came in. I've arranged for another student to guide you to your next evaluation."

Brock stepped out of the temple, still unsure of what had transpired. He had no idea if he had done well or failed miserably.

A figure in a blue cloak stepped from the shadows, startling him. It was a girl about his height. Her brown hair was tied back, a few stray curls dangling against her cheeks. She had a pretty face – not particularly delicate, but definitely female. The contrast of her bright blue eyes against her tawny skin made them particularly striking. Brock felt as if those eyes could see into his soul.

The girl looked him up and down before speaking. "I was asked to lead you to your next evaluation."

"Hello." He smiled. "I'm Brock. I'm pleased to meet you."

She glanced down at his extended hand before turning to walk away. Still holding his hand out, Brock hesitated a moment before he gathered his wits and followed.

They left the Ecclesiast Wing and crossed the main hallway that cut through the center of the school. Without pausing or turning, she continued down the opposite wing. After passing a number of doors, the hallway ended with two massive doors in the wall before them. She opened a man-sized door that was cut into one of the two larger doors, and she waved Brock inside.

Once he was through, the girl said, "Welcome to the Foundry. Master Nindlerod is waiting for you."

She closed the door, leaving him alone. Brock turned to examine the sight before him, trying to work it out in his head.

Pipes ran along the walls, twisting and turning in layers down the length of the building. Large vats boiled and bubbled. Fire burned in hot forges. A machine pumped out steam, its gears spinning and rods swinging up and down. Large tools leaned against the walls, while smaller tools littered benchtops. It seemed a mess, but a glorious mess.

Brock passed through the room as he searched for the master engineer. He noticed two boys looking at plans spread out upon a workbench. Another boy pounded a hot orange lump of metal, fresh from a nearby forge. A girl was blowing through a tube at a tiny piece of glass held over a flame. Two other students were connecting a heavy rope and hook to a pulley hanging from the ceiling. It all seemed quite amazing.

Finally, Brock spotted a man in a purple cloak working in a far corner. The master had a receding hairline surrounded by curly gray hair. A pair of metal tubes with glass lenses were strapped over his eyes – the strange spectacles making him look like an oversized bug. The man used metal tongs to hold a small copper tube over an open flame.

Brock approached and was about to address him when the man spoke.

"Don't just stand there. Use those tweezers to grab that ball from the casting."

As instructed, Brock grabbed the shiny metal tweezers and turned toward the metal block, finding a tiny metal ball half-buried in a small hole within the block. He carefully grabbed the ball with the tweezers and held it up.

"Good," the master said. "Now insert the ball into the heated end of this tube. Be gentle, because half of the ball must remain sticking out when we're done."

Brock held the metal ball to the hot end of the copper tube, still over the flame. He attempted to push the ball inside, but the hole was a bit small. He pushed harder, and the ball slid into the tube until half was sticking out.

Master Nindlerod removed the tube from the flame and began blowing on it.

"Okay." The master gestured to his side. "Now pick up that glass tube for me."

Brock grabbed the tube, holding it toward Nindlerod, who slipped the copper tube inside. The taper at the bottom of the glass tube stopped the copper tube from going all the way through, leaving the metal ball sticking out the bottom.

Nindlerod removed the strange spectacles and replaced them with common round spectacles before taking the tube from Brock. "There it is. Isn't it exquisite?" Brock nodded.

Nindlerod eyed him. "You don't know what it is, do you?"

Brock shook his head. "I've never seen anything quite like it, sir."

"Of course you haven't, you ninny," Nindlerod replied. "I've only just invented it." He held it closer for Brock to inspect. "Even though you haven't seen it before, perhaps you can guess what it does?"

Brock looked at the glass tube. It appeared to be a holder for the copper tube. He wet his finger in case the metal was still hot, using it to test the metal ball. It spun in the tube. In his mind, he tried to imagine it working. *What if liquid was in the tube?* The ball might block the end and prevent the liquid from leaking, especially if it was a thick liquid. However, a small bit would still coat the ball when rotated.

"I think this is an amazing invention." Brock nodded, smiling. "It'll be wonderful!"

Nindlerod smiled. "Thank you. I have the same feeling myself. Sometimes the smallest inventions yield the best…. Wait! You still haven't told me what you think it is."

"It's a new kind of pen, one that holds ink and lets a little out at a time." Brock gestured. "No need to dip into the ink well any longer."

Nindlerod nodded. "Good. Very good."

The master grabbed a dropper filled with black ink. He carefully squirted the ink into the copper tube and capped it with a small piece of cork. He then turned to a piece of paper on the workbench, eager to test his new toy.

The pen rolled across the paper but left no ink trail. Back and forth, he continued until black streaks began trailing the pen's path.

Nindlerod looked up with a grin. "Outstanding. Pretencia will have to eat his shoe, now."

Brock grinned. He didn't like Pretencia much. "Eat his shoe, sir?"

Nindlerod nodded emphatically. "Yes. He bet me that I couldn't come up with an invention that would make writing less tedious. He said he would eat his own shoe when I had an invention that did so." The man's head bobbed up and down as he cackled.

Brock smiled again. He liked this man.

Nindlerod waved him off. "You're done here. Go get some lunch and then return to the admissions office." He turned and walked to a nearby desk, cackling with laughter the whole way.

22

The bell rang as Brock stepped out of the Foundry. Doors opened, and students poured into the hallway, all flowing in the same direction. Like a feather caught in the wind, Brock was swept away with the crowd. As the mob of students neared the Main Hall, they slowed to funnel through a pair of double doors. He followed along and soon realized he was in the dining hall–a large room with long rows of tables stretching across it.

Not knowing what else to do, Brock worked his way across the room until he found an open seat. He felt self-conscious in his plain tan shirt while surrounded by a sea of blue cloaks.

"Are you following me?"

Brock stopped surveying the crowd and turned toward the voice. Bright blue eyes stared back at him. He smiled, recognizing the girl who had escorted him to the Foundry.

"Um...no," Brock said. "I just kind of ended up here. I was told to get lunch before I return to the admissions office, so I followed everyone and... here I am."

"Well, that's okay I guess," she said.

He pulled his hand from beneath the table and extended it toward the girl. "We didn't get a formal introduction earlier. I'm Brock. And you are..."

She glared at his hand, as if contemplating her options. Finally, she shook it.

"I'm Ashland."

"It's nice to meet you, Ashland."

He glanced side to side before asking her a question.

"Where did you get your food?"

"Well, see those students coming out that door?" She pointed across the room. "Those are the novices. Their job is to serve meals to the upper-level students before they eat."

He noticed that the students carrying trays of food wore cloaks that were slightly different. The blue cloaks of the older students had white piping around the edges. The novice cloaks were just solid blue. However, Ashland's cloak had no white piping.

"What about you? You're a novice too, right?"

Ashland shrugged. "I was here early and already served two others before I grabbed my own tray."

He leaned back as a student set a wooden tray before him. The wonderful smell of spiced lamb and potatoes wafted up from the plate. Brock took a bite and glanced toward Ashland, who was focused on her meal. Deciding that she was quite pretty and wanting to get to know her better, he asked her a question.

"So, what do you learn in Ecclesiastics?"

Ashland stopped chewing, her eyes flicking to Brock then back down to her plate. She swallowed before responding.

"I understand that you're applying for admission. Since you're being evaluated, I assume you don't have a writ." She appeared serious. "If and when you are admitted, I will be happy to answer questions regarding the Academy. However, students are not allowed to divulge what occurs here to outsiders. I'm sorry if I sound rude, but my path in life depends on my success here, and I won't risk that for you nor anyone else."

She looked down at her plate and resumed eating as if she was alone in the room.

Brock winced at the loud voices coming from Ackerson's office. The thick walls and heavy door muffled the words, making them not quite clear enough to understand. What began as a heated debate seemed to have devolved into an outright shouting match. At least, that's how it sounded from where he sat outside the door.

When everything quieted, he leaned closer and strained to hear what was happening. The door suddenly swung open and Master Pretencia stormed past, startling Brock. He could still hear the man's footsteps fading down the hall when Ackerson called out to him.

"Mr. Talenz, would you please join us?"

Brock entered the room and closed the door behind him. The master of admissions and the other instructors he had met that morning sat at the table.

Ackerson addressed Brock. "It appears that you do possess some potential after all. While clearly not a consensus, the majority of the evaluators believe that you would be a welcome addition to our school."

Brock scanned the faces in the room. Budakis sat with his bulging arms crossed, giving a firm nod when their eyes met. Varius gave him a warm smile. Nindlerod grinned and nodded, letting a cackling giggle escape. Brock was stunned. His gaze landed back on Ackerson, who continued speaking.

"The current school year ends tomorrow, followed by summer break. Please be back with your belongings in thirty days."

Seeds of happiness bloomed into a smile on Brock's face. It was happening. Then he thought about Tipper.

"Sir, what about my servant? Can he stay with me?"

Ackerson shook his head. "Sorry, son. Not even spouses of academy instructors are allowed to live here."

Realizing there was nothing to do about it, Brock just nodded.

Ackerson stood and opened the door. "Congratulations, young man. You are now a member of the Academy. What you do with this opportunity is up to you."

Brock turned toward the masters at the table. "Thank you all so much. You won't be disappointed."

Minutes later, he was outside and on the road to Fallbrandt. Whistling as he walked, Brock's spirits were high. Somehow, he had accomplished what had seemed like an impossible dream. Brock the Unchosen was a student at the Academy. It seemed unreal.

Before he knew it, he was back at The Quiet Woman. In the lull between lunch and dinner, the only person in the dining room was James, who waved and continued restocking the shelves behind the bar.

A shriek came from a room down the hallway. Brock followed the noise and discovered Tipper standing with his clothes soaking wet, the floor drenched in water. Libby's hand covered her mouth as she laughed, Tipper's eyes wide, his face slowly breaking into a grin.

"What happened?" Brock asked.

Tipper glanced from Brock to Libby, who was still laughing. His smile widened as he turned back to Brock. "I was trying to move a tub, and my hands slipped. I stumbled backwards and fell into the other tub."

Libby's laughter calmed. "You should've seen his face when he fell in. His arms were flailing around, splashing water." She laughed again with mirth in her eyes. "It was the funniest thing I've ever seen." Brock smiled. How could he not?

Tipper grabbed a towel and began drying himself. "So how did things go at the Academy?"

Brock opened his arms wide. "You're looking at the newest student of the Academy."

Tipper clapped Brock on the shoulder. "That's wonderful. When do you start?"

"I'm to return there in thirty days for the start of the new school year." As Brock said it, he remembered that Tipper wasn't allowed to come with him.

"Tip, I'm sorry but you can't come with me. We need to figure out where you'll stay."

Tipper glanced at Libby and then back to Brock. "I've got that figured out already. Dory thought that might be the case, and she told me that she could use another set of hands to help around here. She offered me a job, working for room and board."

Relieved, Brock smiled. "That's great, Tip."

Now recovered from her fit of laughter, Libby put her hands on her hips. "If you two are done congratulating each other, we have a mess to clean up here before the guests in room four come down for their bath."

Tipper nodded. "Right. Do you have a mop handy?"

The days passed slowly. Brock was anxious to move into the Academy, and the wait seemed torturous.

His extended stay at The Quiet Woman cost him most of his remaining coin, but he wouldn't need it once he was in the school. The accumulated wealth had not lasted long, but it had gotten him the new life he desired.

To make the time pass faster, Brock helped Tipper prepare his new accommodations. Dory couldn't afford to give up a guest room, needing those for income. Instead, the small storage room attached to the stable would become Tipper's home. The boys spent the better part of two weeks clearing the room out, repairing holes in the wall and floor, repairing the roof, and giving it a good cleaning. After adding a bed, a table, and a small chest of drawers, it seemed livable.

"What do you think, Tip?" Brock asked as they surveyed the fruits of their labor.

Tipper nodded. "This will do." A tear slid down his face. "My own room. I've never had a room of my own before."

Brock clapped his friend's shoulder. In the five years he had known Tipper, the homeless boy had never complained about living on the streets.

"You won't even have to beg for food." Brock grinned. "Although, the smell from the horses is likely to spoil your appetite anyway."

Tipper smiled as he wiped the tear away. "That ain't nothin'. I've had to sleep with worse smells." Tipper shrugged. "If I keep the stable clean, it won't smell that bad in here, anyway."

With Tipper moved out, Brock's last days at the inn felt lonelier. The eve before he was to leave, he tossed and turned, unable to sleep as he anticipated starting his new life. When the sky began to lighten, he had already bathed, shaved, packed, and headed to the kitchen to grab a quick bite for the road.

Saul, the inn's cook, was busy preparing breakfast. The portly man had a bald head and a short-cut black beard. Regardless of his appearance, the man was an artist in the kitchen.

"Good morning, Saul," Brock said as the man glanced up at him.

"You are up early, Brock," the big man replied. "So, my young friend, today is the day you leave us then?"

"Yes, Saul. I go to the Academy, where I will be relegated to far inferior meals. My tongue and stomach will miss you dearly."

Saul nodded, as if it were a matter of fact. "Well then, let Saul make you a parting gift. Come back in a few minutes, and Saul will have something ready for you to eat as you walk."

"Thanks, Saul." Brock walked out the back door of the kitchen.

He crossed the yard and knocked on the door to the room attached to the stable. With his blond hair a mess, a shirtless Tipper opened the door, holding his trousers up with one hand. He slid outside and pulled the door closed.

"Tip, is someone in there?" Brock asked.

Tipper grinned back.

"Libby?" Brock asked.

Tipper nodded.

"Well, you seem to be doing well here." Brock noted.

"Yeah. I've never been happier," Tipper said. "But I am going to miss you, Brock."

"I'll miss you too. I know it's early, but I wanted to see you before I left," Brock said. "I'll get every seventh day off, so I'll come visit when I'm able."

Tipper leaned close and gave him a hug. "Thank you, Brock." He let go, putting a hand on Brock's shoulder. "Thanks for everything. You've been my best friend for five years. You healed me back to health and you brought me food every time you saw me. You gave me clothes, you gave me friendship, and you gave me hope. Now, you've taken me from a life of begging on the streets to this." He gestured back at his room. "I have a roof and a room of my own. I'm fed amazing food every day. I've found a beautiful girl who I might even love." Tipper hugged him again. "You're the best, Brock. You know that if you need anything, anything at all, I'm here to help."

Brock was overwhelmed. He wiped a tear from his eye. "You'll always be my friend, Tip. This isn't goodbye, though. I'll see you soon and often."

With a nod and a smile, Tipper slipped back into his room. Brock stared at the door for a moment before returning to the kitchen. When he entered, Saul handed him a tube-shaped pastry filled with red sauce and berries. Steam poured from the middle, smelling delicious. Brock thanked him and left the kitchen, walking through the empty dining room and out the front door. His thoughts soon turned from sadness to anticipation.

When the Academy came into view, the first rays of the sun were lighting the upper floors of the massive building that was his new home.

PART IV

THE ACADEMY

23

New students crowded the Main Hall, standing in four lines. Those lines slowly advanced toward the check-in tables at the back of the hall, and Brock soon found himself at the front of his line.

The girl at the table smiled. "Welcome to the Academy. I need your name please."

"Brock. Um…Brock Talenz. T-A-L-E-N-Z." He spelled it out for her.

She flipped through a stack of papers. Her finger scanned the sheets until it neared the bottom of the last page.

"Here it is. It looks like you were a late addition." She turned to the boy behind her. "Boys' Wing, room 1099."

The boy turned and ran to a cart with rows of pegs, each holding a pair of keys.

She handed Brock a lightly-filled pack marked with the rune of Issal. "Here's your student pack. It has some information and supplies inside."

The boy returned with a key looped through a leather cord. He handed the key to Brock. "Here's your key. You'll find your room at the end of that hall." He pointed to Brock's right.

"Thank you." Brock looped the leather cord over his neck and shouldered the pack.

He headed down the corridor, following other boys heading the same direction. This was his first time down this particular hallway. Doors, glowlamps, and tapestries adorned the corridor walls. The hallway narrowed with doors on each side, set in regular intervals. Through an open door, he saw another student sitting on a bed, digging through his pack.

Brock continued down the long corridor, the traffic before him dwindling as other boys found their rooms. He soon found himself alone and nearing the end.

Just beyond his room, a set of double doors stood open. He peeked through and found that they led to a large, round lounge with a spiral stone stairwell in the center. Clusters of sofas, chairs, and tables dotted the room, hugging the curved walls. Brock turned back to his room, pulled the cord for his key over his head, unlocked the door, and stepped inside.

The small room contained two beds with a desk nestled between them at the far wall. Blue curtains were pulled open, allowing sunlight to illuminate the room through the window over the desk. Noticing a wardrobe beside the door, Brock set his two packs down and opened it. He found two blue cloaks inside and pulled the smaller cloak from its hook before securing it around his neck. The rumble of a deep voice startled him.

"Hello."

Brock turned to see a hulking figure blocking the doorway. The figure stepped forward and the light from the window revealed a blond-haired boy about Brock's age. Standing more than a head taller than Brock, the boy's shoulders were so wide that he had to twist to fit through the door. He held out a massive hand.

"Um. I'm Cameron." His blue eyes focused on the floor, flashing upward for brief moments. "People call me Cam."

Brock shook his hand, wincing at the larger boy's firm grip.

"I'm Brock. It's nice to you meet you, Cam," he replied. "I assume you're my new roommate then?"

"Um...Yeah. I guess," Cam replied.

Brock reached into the wardrobe and handed him the larger cloak. "Here's your cloak. Welcome to the Academy, Cam."

A grin stretched across Cam's face as he held the cloak up. "Thanks, Brock."

Cam grinned as he stared at the cloak. Brock felt the same way.

∾

The two boys settled into their new abode, each claiming a bed without contention. They were soon dressed in the Academy wear found in the drawers of their wardrobe.

Brock attempted conversations with Cameron a few times, but they soon died out. For such a large boy, Cam seemed shy and unsure of himself.

A few of those short discussions yielded information, allowing Brock to learn that Cam was from Nor Torin, the capital of the province north of Kantaria. Much like Brock's home city of Kantar, Nor Torin was a busy port city on the Indigo Ocean. He also discovered that Cam's father had been a paladin in the Holy Army and was retired, now acting as the captain of the guard for the prelate of Nor Torin.

It was late morning when a student popped his head through the open doorway. "Meet in the dining hall in fifteen minutes."

Brock felt thankful to have something to do after finding that waiting idly in his room felt agonizing.

They both stood and walked out into the corridor. Brock locked the door and looped the key back around his neck. At that moment, two boys exited the room across the hall. Brock gave them a nod in greeting.

"Hello."

The first boy was tall and thin, his dark hair combed back. He nodded in return before heading down the hall. The other boy locked the door and turned to greet them.

Standing a hair taller than Brock, the boy had a thick mop of dark hair, combed to one side. He had a thin, non-muscular frame and wore rectangular-shaped spectacles. Flashing a goofy smile, he put out a hand. Brock grabbed it, and the boy shook it vigorously.

"Hi guys. I'm Benedict. Benedict Hedgewick." The boy rocked his shoulders and jutted his elbows out as he spoke. "Everyone calls me Benny."

"I'm Brock, and this is Cam."

He shook Cam's hand. The larger boy nodded but didn't say anything.

Brock remembered hearing that name before. "Hedgewick? I know that name."

Benny nodded. "Yes indeed. You might know it from the Hedgewick Knowledge Center, the library here at the Academy. Or perhaps you know it from the histories."

Brock nodded and glanced at Cameron, who appeared confused. The three boys began walking toward the dining hall as Benny continued his story.

"My ancestor, Byland Hedgewick, was an influential figure," Benny said proudly. "He was an important leader at the Academy and was part of the very founding of the Empire."

Brock raised his eyebrows. "That's impressive, Benny. I assume you've had other relatives at the Academy then?"

"Oh, yes. While my father didn't come to the Academy, most generations of Hedgewicks since Byland had members who trained here." Benny's shoulders seemed to shrug involuntarily as he talked. "When my mother became pregnant, my father decided to remain in Selbin and serve the local temple rather than come here."

Brock took the opening to ask a question that was bugging him. "Speaking of age, I hope you don't mind if I ask, but how old are you, Benny?"

"I know, I know. I'm a bit old to be a student." Benny's face twitched a little as he talked. "You see, my mother died when I was sixteen summers, and I stayed to help my father. He was gravely injured in the same accident, and I stayed to care for him. It left him in a coma for months. The temple healer was able to do a lot for him, but he lost a leg in the accident and that will never come back. Otherwise, he's mostly recovered. That was five years ago."

"I'm sorry to hear about your mother, Benny. I lost mine when I was young," Brock said. "I know how hard it can be."

Benny nodded. "Thanks, Brock. It's hard. Sometimes I still think she's calling me, and I turn to look for her, but it's just my imagination I guess." He absently pushed his spectacles up as he spoke.

Cam's low voice came from behind, "I'm sorry too, guys. I miss my mother now, and she's not even dead. She's just back home in Nor Torin."

Brock slowed a step and reached up to clap Cam on the shoulder. "Since we've no family here, let's treat each other like family. You need someone to look out for you, right Cam?"

Cameron smiled. "Sure."

"That means you too, Benny," Brock said to the quirky boy.

Benny's goofy grin returned. "Thanks, guys." After a few more steps he added, "My father would be amazed. My first day and I already have more friends here than I had back in Selbin." Brock smiled. He liked Benny.

A crowd of students stood outside the dining hall doors, slowly funneling through. Brock and his friends merged with the others, shuffling their feet in small steps as the cluster inched forward. After a minute, they squeezed through the doors and into chaos.

Students milled about in search of an open seat. With the tables near the doors occupied, Brock and the others worked their way deeper into the room until they found a table with three open spots.

The loud peal of a bell caused many students to jump. All eyes turned toward the source of the noise as the roar of conversation dropped to a hushed whisper. A tall figure dressed in a silver cloak and dark gray clothing stood near the student holding the bell. The bald man smiled and raised his hands as he addressed the room.

"Welcome to the Academy," he said in a booming voice. "I'm Headmaster Vandermark. I am responsible for your training and well-being while you are here. You will find that we've assembled the finest minds in the Empire to instruct you as we identify how you can best serve the Ministry and, in turn, ensure that the Empire continues to thrive.

"Today is your orientation day. As a welcome gesture, apprentice-level students will serve you lunch. Enjoy the moment. After today, you'll be serving meals to the apprentice and adept students for the entirety of your first year," the man bellowed as he paced around the room.

After a brief pause, he continued. "Enjoy your meal but do not dally. When you are finished, find your way to the Academy Temple at the rear of the complex. You have one hour. At that time, we will begin your official orientation."

The man turned and exited the room with two students trailing close behind.

Students in white-trimmed navy cloaks began to filter out of the kitchen with trays of food. A female student placed a tray before Brock. He smiled when he noticed it was Ashland. She gave him a brief nod and the smallest of smiles before returning to the kitchen. He looked down at the tray to find a gravy-covered meat pie accompanied by a muffin and a glass of milk.

Empty plates and glasses soon occupied the table, the low hum of conversation replacing the sound of forks clinking on plates.

"That was delicious. I'm stuffed." Benny leaned back and rubbed his stomach.

"Yeah. The food here isn't bad," Brock replied. He turned toward

Cameron, who stared down at his empty plate. "What's wrong, Cam?"
"Well, I guess I'm still hungry," Cam replied.

Brock smiled and stood. "Let me see what I can do."

He looped around the perimeter of the room and headed for the kitchen. Approaching the long counter that separated him from the kitchen itself, he waved to an old woman with curly gray hair.

"Excuse me." Brock held his hand high over his head to get her attention. "I have a large friend who's still hungry. Do you by chance have some extra food I can bring to him?"

"Sure, dearie." The woman went to the rear counter and popped a muffin out of a metal cooking tray. "Here you go." She handed him a small plate holding the muffin.

"Thank you." Brock smiled. "I'm Brock. I'm new here."

She nodded. "It's nice to meet you, Brock. I figured you were new when I saw the novice cloak." She wiped her hands on her apron. "I'm Shirley, the head cook."

"It's nice to meet you, Shirley. Thanks again for the muffin."

He spun about and returned to the dining hall, where he set the muffin in front of Cameron and reclaimed his seat.

"Wow. Thanks, Brock." Cameron took a big bite of the warm pastry.

"I wonder what happens at orientation," Benny said.

Brock shrugged. "I don't know. But we're about to find out."

24

When Brock visited the temple during his evaluation, he had considered it impressive. Now that he sat in the real Academy Temple, the other seemed pitiful – a lake compared to an ocean.

While the smaller temple could seat a couple hundred people, this temple was large enough for thousands. Rows upon rows of benches ran in concentric circles, all facing the dais in the center. Sunlight streaming through the glass ceiling shined upon a teardrop-shaped object suspended below the center of its dome. Light reflecting from the mirrored panels on the teardrop caused prismatic shapes to dance around the huge space.

Brock's focus shifted to the dais, raised above the floor of the huge bowl. Five masters draped in purple sat in chairs arranged on the platform. Headmaster Vandermark stood before them, his hands leaning on the glowstone altar as he waited for the students to claim a seat. Vandermark raised his hands to quiet the crowd.

"Welcome to the Academy, novices."

Although Vandermark stood a good distance away, Brock could hear him clearly.

"Masters within the Ministry, all former academy students, hold critical positions throughout the Empire. They lead and guide other members of the Ministry, who guide citizens of the Empire. They build new devices to improve society. They protect our people and our lands by fighting in the Holy Army.

They gather, analyze, and share knowledge used to ensure a better future. They set us on our course in life, cure our sicknesses, and heal our wounded.

"When these masters leave the Academy, they are commissioned to seek out future students, but only those who exhibit the highest potential. You sit here today as the fruits of their labor." His arms swept wide in a flourish. "From across the Empire, you've journeyed to become the newest members of this illustrious institution. You are about to begin another journey--not one of physical distance, but one of academic, spiritual, and personal growth."

As the headmaster paused, Brock glanced around, finding all eyes directed toward the man on the dais.

"I realize that you know little of what is to come. This is expected. You see, what transpires here is to remain secret. By joining the Academy, you swear to an oath of secrecy. Stay true to your oath and you stay true to Issal."

His firm gaze scanned the room before continuing.

"The five masters sitting here," he gestured to the men and women seated behind him, "will take the active lead in your first year of education."

"Master Varius will be your guide in the ecclesiastic arts." Upon saying the woman's name, Varius stood and nodded to the crowd.

"Master Budakis will train you in the arts of the Paladin." The large man stood and thumped a meaty fist to his chest.

"Master Nindlerod instructs students in the arts of Engineering." The quirky old man stood and waved like a child.

"Master Pretencia is your expert in Hierarchal arts." The man stood and stared into the crowd with an intense gaze, as if seeking his prey.

"Master Mae will be your loremaster, instructing you on the history of our Empire." A small dark-haired woman stood and gave a quick bow.

Vandermark nodded to the masters before again addressing the students.

"When you return to your rooms, you'll each find your personal schedule. Not only will you be learning in the classroom, but you will also be required to conduct research, work on projects, and refine your skills outside of class. When your first year is complete, you'll have a basic knowledge of all five ministry arts."

Vandermark paused again, allowing this information to sink in.

"The potential and dedication you exhibit in the coming months are critical to your future. When the year is complete, most of you will be selected by one these masters to join his or her department to continue your training.

The remaining students will be assigned positions within temples throughout the Empire, their tenure at the Academy ending after just one year."

Brock considered the deceitful nature of his admission. A moment of doubt in himself and his abilities took hold of him and fed the fear of being discovered as Unchosen. Taking a deep breath, he focused on his resolve and buried the doubt. *I cannot think that way.*

Vandermark continued. "You've been presented an opportunity offered to but a few hundred young adults each year. Dedicate yourself to your training, and we will see you here next year and beyond. You have the rest of the day to yourself. Relish the freedom. Your training begins at sunup tomorrow."

~

It was a beautiful day, marked by the typically pleasant weather of late summer in the mountains. Like many of the students, Brock and his new friends opted to spend their last hours of freedom outdoors.

Brock lay on his back in the long grass of the lawn, watching the puffy clouds floating past. Benny lay a few feet away, describing what he saw in the shape of each cloud.

"That one looks like a big fish. Maybe a Sinnowfish. They spawn downriver from Lake Selbin and can grow to be three feet long, you know."

Cameron sat with his back against a large tree. "Fish sounds good. I'm hungry."

Brock laughed. "I think that's the fifth time you've told us, Cam. The schedule said dinner is at sunset. Well, it'll be sunset in less than an hour."

Cam grunted in response. He didn't seem to talk much unless he was hungry. Even then, it was only to state that he was hungry.

"What do you think Hierarchist training will involve?" Benny asked as he watched the clouds inch across the sky.

"I'm not sure, Benny," Brock replied. "From what I can tell, Hierarchy has something to do with the governing of people and dealing with laws."

"Ugh. That sounds dreadful," Benny complained. "I wish I could just focus on Engineering. It's going to be so amazing!" Benny sat upright, the energy level in his voice rising. "I'm excited to have access to the school resources. I plan to invent something spectacular, something that will make me famous."

"You must be good with numbers and that kind of stuff then?" Brock asked.

"Oh, yes," Benny replied. "To support my father, I worked as a clerk for a counting house. After less than a year, the owner told me I was the best clerk he'd ever seen. Some of the other clerks had been there over twenty years.

"Not long after I started, he realized I could do figures pretty well. He soon had me doing the analysis and proposals for business investments, working probability equations and forecast projections." Benny finished with a proud smile on his face.

Brock had no idea what Benny was talking about. "That's great, Benny," he replied, showing support for his new friend.

"You're lucky, Benny." The words came from Cam. "I wish I was smart like you."

Benny stared at Cam, an incredulous look on his face. "Are you kidding? Have you looked at yourself? You're tall, good looking, and you have those bulging muscles. I bet you could lift me over your head and toss me across a room. I wish I was like you."

Cam grunted but didn't argue. "I just wish people wouldn't treat me like I'm dumb."

Brock interjected, "Hey, look at me. I'm not big and strong, nor am I super smart. In fact, I don't know that I'm special at all." He stared up at the now reddening clouds. "But I'm not going to let it stop me."

Brock heard a faint scream coming from the woods at the edge of the lawn. He sat up, looking in that direction.

"Did you hear that?" he asked.

After a moment of consideration, he scrambled to his feet and ran in the direction of the scream.

"Hear what?" He heard Benny yell from behind.

Brock didn't reply. He just kept running, using his speed to close the distance quickly. As he neared the trees, he heard another scream, muffled this time. He angled toward the sound, bursting through the brush to find a dark-haired male student on top of another student. Not slowing, he lowered his shoulder and plowed into the student on top.

A shock of pain surged through Brock's shoulder. They tumbled across the ferns on the forest floor, rolling with the momentum. He scrambled to his feet, ready to defend himself.

Slowly rising, the other boy stood upright, matching Cameron in height, but lacking the thick bulging muscles that framed Cam's figure. Regardless, Brock didn't like his chances in a fight.

"You just made a big mistake, boy," the taller boy said. "You don't know who you're dealing with."

Hearing a whimper from behind the other boy, Brock glanced past him and saw a girl curled in a ball on the forest floor. Anger rose up within him.

"Oh, I know who I'm dealing with," Brock replied. "I'm dealing with an ugly toad who apparently can only get with a girl by forcing himself on her."

That triggered a reaction. The boy charged and took a swing at Brock, who deftly dodged. He cleared his attacker and spun around to find the boy holding a hand to his forehead. Apparently, he had run into a tree limb hanging above where Brock had been standing. When he removed his hand, blood dripped from a torn brow.

"You little bugger! Now I'm gonna kill you," the boy said as he advanced.

Brock backed away, keeping a safe distance. His foot caught on something and he stumbled, landing on his rear. It was the prone form of the girl, still curled up and crying. Looking up at the boy, fear finally struck.

The sound of breaking branches and trampled shrubs drew the other boy's attention, his look of anger changing to one of surprise.

"Come any closer, and you will know pain." Brock recognized Cam's voice coming from behind him.

The boy held his hands up and stepped backward. "I don't want any trouble, big guy."

"Leave." Cameron growled.

Looping around the clearing, the boy gave Brock one last hateful glare. "You'll regret this, you little peon." He turned and disappeared into the brush.

Benny burst through the trees at that moment. "What's happening? Is everyone okay?" he asked, breathing hard.

Brock knelt beside the crying girl, her blond hair full of pine needles.

"It's okay. He's gone. You're safe now."

She removed her hands, exposing blue eyes turned red and puffy from crying.

"Can I go back to the school now?" she asked timidly.

He smiled, trying to reassure the distraught girl. "Of course you can. We're here to help. My name is Brock. The big menacing guy there is Cam, and the other one is Benny. We'll walk you back to make sure you reach the Girls' Wing safely."

Nervous eyes darted between the three boys. Her hands came up to wipe tears away. She looked at Brock again and smiled. "Thank you. I'm so glad… so very glad that you showed up."

She took his extended hand and he pulled her to a stance. After he helped her brush pine needles from her hair and cloak, she gave him a weak smile.

"My name is Amber," she said, glancing toward the others. "You can't imagine how thankful I am that you're here."

"You're welcome, Amber." Concern reflected in Brock's eyes. "Are you sure you're okay?"

She looked down at the ground. "I…was so scared. I'm just a little shaken. I'll be fine."

Her eyes met Brock's and he smiled, hoping to reassure her.

They escorted Amber back to the Academy, entering the door closest to the Girls' Wing. Once inside, she thanked them again and retreated toward her room. They watched her walk down the hall until Cam broke the silence.

"Now can we eat?"

Brock and Benny laughed as they turned to head toward the dining hall.

25

It was the first day of Brock's official training. As he stepped into his Lore classroom, anticipation tickled his stomach. Other students filtered into the room with him, seeking empty chairs.

Five rows of tables faced the front of the room with an open aisle up the center. Brock sat in the third row, directly behind Benny. Within minutes, eager students occupied the room.

Master Mae sat at the desk in the front of the room. A bit younger than the other instructors, she had long dark hair, fair skin, and angular eyes. Her clothing drooped loosely on her petite figure.

The bell rang, and she stood to address them.

"Hello, students. I'm Master Mae, your Lore instructor. You might be wondering what Lore is. Quite simply, Lore is information. This includes facts about people, places, and events throughout history. Now, you're likely wondering why you need to learn about history. After all, why should we worry about something that happened dozens or hundreds of years ago?" She paused as many of the students nodded.

"Nearly a hundred years ago, a prelate decided to institute a law making it illegal to sell, buy, or consume ale or wine within the city. Over time, the prelate found the results were not what he had anticipated. Tax income decreased as the inns and taprooms had drastically fewer customers. At the same time, crime increased with the city watch busy trying to enforce the new law. In fact, an underground network of secret taprooms soon appeared. These illegal establishments made large sums of untaxed money, driven by their ability to meet a public demand for ale and wine. With this gold, the owners were able to pay for their own strong-arms to help them create crime gangs – gangs whose power soon surpassed that of the city government. Finally, the Empire had to intercede and squash the most powerful of these gangs as an example to the others. They removed the prelate and replaced him with a new ruler, who made ale and wine legal again. With their main source of income now public domain, the remaining gangs dwindled in power until crime returned to a normal level."

She walked down the center aisle until she was even with Brock's row, turning toward him with a question.

"Why did I tell this story, young man?"

Brock considered and responded, "Well, I guess you mean to point out how stupid it was for the Prelate to make this law. If we'd never heard this story and one of us was in a similar position in the future, we might make the same mistake."

"Exactly!" Master Mae responded. "Those who do not learn from history are likely to repeat the mistakes of others. This is a simple, yet powerful, example of why we study Lore."

She returned to the front of the classroom. "You may not find yourself in the position of prelate, but you'll still learn many things from the past. Only the future knows which of these things will prevent you from making mistakes like the prelate in this story."

Heads nodded as students began to understand why this instruction mattered. Satisfied, Mae continued.

"For today's lesson, we'll focus on how the Issalian Empire came to be. I'm sure that most of you have heard this story before, but likely an inaccurate version."

The loremaster paced around the room, her fingers tapping the tables she passed.

"Hundreds of years ago, the continent was divided into seven individual kingdoms. Each kingdom was ruled by its own king or queen, had its own citizens, its own lands, and its own agenda. Never-ending contention between these kingdoms resulted in frequent wars over borders, trade disputes, and other trivial issues."

Everyone in the class listened closely. Knowledge of anything prior to the existence of the Empire was scant at best.

"Roughly two hundred years ago, an event happened. Some say the sun darkened for days. Others say something strange appeared in the sky. Regardless, the event was a portent of something sinister."

The room seemed to darken. Brock glanced at the windows, trying to determine if it was his imagination.

"An invading army had found its way to the shores of our continent. A force known as The Banished Horde appeared on the Kalimar peninsula. Within weeks of first sighting The Horde, Kalimar was overrun by this evil army.

"The Banished Horde did not stop there. Northward they swept. One by one, they met the eastern kingdoms and obliterated them. Even worse, The Horde was made of evil beasts from some unknown origin, feasting on the bodies and souls of man."

Again, the room seemed to darken as she spoke of The Horde and the horrors they inflicted.

"As The Horde destroyed one country after another, it became apparent to the Ministry that they needed to take action. They requested that the rulers of the western kingdoms form an alliance. The King of Kantar and King of Torinland journeyed to Fallbrandt with their full armies in tow. Here at the Academy, they joined with the Tantarri head clansman to meet with the Ministry. The Queen of Ri Star, a tiny island nation, was the only western ruler who did not make the journey. She instead sent a message that she would have her naval fleet police the Gulf of Norta to ensure that The Horde could not bypass the armies of man.

"These rulers met with the leaders of the Ministry in a room not far from where you now sit. For days they met, discussing their options and laying out plans to stop The Horde in hopes of preventing the obliteration of mankind."

"After three days of deliberation, they agreed to follow the leadership of the Ministry. The combined forces of Kantaria, Torinland, and Tantarri would join with the Ministry's Holy Army of Paladins to create the largest single armed force in history."

Master Mae tapped her finger on a map tacked to the wall. Starting at Fallbrandt, she traced through the mountains as she spoke.

"On a spring morning in the year 1252, the unified might of the armies of man rode eastward to meet the armies of darkness, hoping to gain a position of tactical advantage prior to the arrival of the enemy. Upon the western steppes of the Tantarri plains, the clans of the Tantarri joined the army where it reached its full force.

"The armies of man arrived on the upper plateau first, forming a line of resistance at the narrow mouth to the lower plains. There, they prepared and waited for The Horde to arrive." Her finger stopped and tapped on the map, indicating a location where two cliffs came together on the plains.

"They didn't have to wait long. A few hours past nightfall, The Horde attacked. Much like our knowledge of The Banished Horde, the details of this battle are scarce. Suffice to say, it was like no other battle in history. After two days filled with death and destruction, The Horde was thoroughly defeated. The survivors gathered their wounded and began a slow march west. Sixteen days after departing from Fallbrandt, the armies returned victorious, but with less than a quarter of their original numbers."

"As the armies camped on the lawn outside the Academy, the remaining rulers met with Ministry officials. They reluctantly agreed to form what is now the Empire. They combined the bodies of church and state, with the leaders accepting roles as prelates within the Ministry. The idea was that the unification of all lands on the continent would provide a stronger, single entity that would be more resistant to invading forces. In addition, the structure and guidance provided by the Ministry would ensure that the Empire thrived."

She walked to the front of the aisle, her eyes scanning the room. "Your very existence was made possible by the sacrifices made during these events. The safe and productive lives of the the Empire's citizens are the result of the efforts of these forefathers."

After a pause, she addressed the class again. "There are many events and topics we will cover over the course of the year. In addition, I want each of you to visit the library and research empire history. Be ready to suggest a topic of interest for classroom discussion over the coming months."

Brock's mind was thinking about The Horde. Intrigued by this mysterious enemy from the past, he decided to seek out more information about them in the library.

As he stepped onto the Arena floor, a student in a white vest greeted Brock and directed him to the changing room at the far end.

Shelves lined the changing room walls, while rows of benches occupied the center of the space. Brock crossed the room, glancing through an open doorway and noticing pools of water cut into the rock of the neighboring room. He stared in curiosity at the steam rising from the water, wondering how they heated it.

Remembering that class was soon starting, Brock pulled his white sparring vest and tan breeches from his pack before stuffing the pack into an empty shelf. He stripped to his smallclothes and slipped into his training gear. While tucking the bottom of his breeches into his boots, he glanced sideways and spotted Cameron, leaving him glad to see someone he knew.

The bell rang, followed by a bellow coming from the Arena.

"What's wrong with you lazy dogs? Get out here now!"

Everyone scrambled in response, hastily dressing and running out the door.

"Get in a line, facing me!" Budakis shouted, pointing toward the floor.

Students began to line up side by side. Brock looked to his right to see girls scrambling from the other changing room and falling into line. With everyone in place, Budakis strolled down the line, his eyes scanning each student. Reaching the end, he returned to take a firm stance before the group. He crossed his arms and stared at them.

"Somehow, each group of novices seems more pathetic than the last. You students have done an admirable job of supporting that tradition," he grumbled. "In the future, I expect you dressed and on this line before the bell rings. In addition, you will not slouch. You are to stand at attention with your feet shoulder-width apart, eyes forward, chest out."

Budakis posed to show the students how it looked. Brock could feel others down the line making adjustments to mirror the master's stance.

The grimace on Budakis' face twisted into a grin. "Much better. Perhaps there's hope for you yet." His smile took on a sadistic edge. "Before we begin, I'll give you some insight into what you can expect from this class.

"My assistants, Mister Graves and Miss Harrister," he gestured toward the couple standing past the end of the line, "will be helping me get the sorry lot of you into shape. By mid-year, you'll be able to run for miles without stopping, do a hundred push-ups, climb a rope to the ceiling above, and defend yourself."

He paced before the line while he spoke. "For those who are eager to get a sword in your hand, you can forget that right now. It will be weeks before you touch a weapon and will be years before it is made of anything but wood. You see, being a paladin is a bloody business. It's a job filled with severed limbs, spilled guts, and many sleepless nights. I think you can wait a bit before you lose any appendages." Budakis stopped and grinned. "Sorry to squash your romantic thoughts of being some grand hero with a shiny sword. The reality is not glamorous like in the storybooks. Yes, there's a level of personal satisfaction, but in the end, paladins do the jobs nobody else wants to touch."

He paced the other direction as he continued. "It's not a calling for everyone. You cannot just be good at fighting – you must be among the best. Not just physically, but you need to have a good heart. The killing that Paladins do should be done by those who wish they didn't have to kill. Some of you might be among the next to join the ranks of apprentice paladin. My job is two-fold: first, I'll have you trained to at least defend yourself; second, I'll attempt to find a few diamonds amid a field of broken glass."

Budakis stopped in the center and smiled. "Are you ready to begin?"

Students up and down the line nodded, while Brock alone shouted, "Yes, Sir!"

Budakis stepped uncomfortably close, the smell of his morning caffe wafting up Brock's nose. Brock remained still, trying not to shake as his stomach fluttered.

"Mister Talenz. It appears that you already know the proper response when I ask a question." The master paladin smiled and stepped away. "In that case, you should lead us in our first workout. Please come up and face the group."

Budakis pointed toward a spot on the floor beside him. Brock stepped forward as Budakis addressed the class.

"Mister Talenz will lead us in push-ups. He will count as he does them. You will mimic him, matching his count and will continue until he is done." He then turned to Brock. "Do as many push-ups as you can."

Brock groaned. It wasn't that he hated doing push-ups. He was quite good at them and most of the others would be unable to keep up. They were going to hate him.

Having no choice, Brock crouched down and stretched out until he was on his hands and toes. He lowered himself to the ground and pushed up.

"One."

He did it again and again, many more times.

~

Brock soon realized that he was in better shape than most of his classmates. If he felt sore and tired, then the others were really hurting. Worked beyond their capacity, two students vomited and a third fainted.

While the workout was torturous, the hot baths afterward were glorious. He still didn't know how they heated them, but he appreciated it. When the bell rang, he reluctantly climbed from the pool and toweled dry. Minutes later, he was dressed and off to lunch.

His path took him directly to the kitchens to deliver a tray to a senior student. After making a second trip for another student, he claimed a tray for himself.

Brock, Benny, and Cam sat together. They were ravenous, consuming their meals without pause. With plates empty, the three sat back and discussed their morning classes until the bell rang.

Brock headed to the Ecclesiastics' Wing in search of his next class. Much like the other classrooms he had seen, an aisle down the center split the rows of tables crossing the room. He picked an open chair in the front row and watched other students filter in, but he didn't recognize anyone. A door at the front of the room opened, drawing his attention.

Master Varius entered, followed by another familiar face. He waved to get Ashland's attention as he flashed a hopeful smile. She saw him and gave a small smile as she took position along the wall behind Varius. The bell rang, and the students quieted.

With her hands clasped at her waist, Master Varius stood before the class. "Good afternoon. I'm sure you're wondering *What is an ecclesiast?*

You are thinking *What are we going to learn? What are we going to study?*" Nodding heads and murmurs confirmed her suspicions.

"An ecclesiast is a human conduit to the core life force of the universe: Order. Using the power of Order, an ecclesiast can perform amazing feats.

"You've all been marked by Issal, chosen to help guide the citizens of the Empire." Varius spread her arms wide in a welcoming gesture. "However, some of you have been chosen for something even more important. Some of you have the inherent ability to channel Order. You have an untapped potential to use this power to divine, to heal, and, perhaps, to perform other skills even less common."

Hearing her mention channeling a hidden power, Brock thought of what had happened with Hank and with the boulder in the cave. *Was that what I did?*

"The focus of this class is to discover any abilities you have with Order and to cultivate those abilities to the greatest extent possible. You are to make every effort and are not to give up, no matter how futile it seems. Sometimes it takes months for a breakthrough. You see, of all the arts within the Ministry, ecclesiasts are rarest and the most precious. The ability to heal using Order is worth more than any amount of gold. It's priceless.

"My assistant, Ashland," Varius gestured toward the girl, "and I are going to guide you in this effort. In fact, we will start today with some simple meditation exercises. This will be the first of many similar sessions over the coming weeks. The goal is to teach you to connect to your own sense of Order."

Varius approached the front of the room, pointing at a tapestry displaying the rune of Issal. She tapped on the tapestry as she addressed the class.

"You know what this is, or you think you do. It is not just the mark of Issal, but this symbol represents Order. Order is in every tree, every animal, and every one of us. It is the life force tied to all living things."

"I need you to clear your mind. Ignore the noise and concerns of your day." She tapped on the symbol on the wall. "Relax and think of nothing but this symbol. Focus on it. Feel connected to it."

She paused, allowing the class to stare at the symbol. With a softer voice, she continued. "Breathe slowly. Relax. With this symbol in your mind, close your eyes and feel the calm of the symbol. Feel the cool peacefulness deep within yourself."

With his eyes closed, Brock felt a tranquility. The rune of Issal, the symbol of Order, remained firm in his mind's eye and glowed with a cool, pale-blue light.

Varius' voice spoke from somewhere distant. "Feel the calmness of Order. It's like a comforting blanket wrapped around your soul."

Brock began to feel connected to everything around him. The rune's pale blue light sang to him. It was glorious. However, something felt off, something behind him and to his right. He felt it pulsing, an ugly red glow in the calm blue of his mind's eye.

He opened his eyes, turning in the direction of the wrongness. A male student sat with eyes closed, clutching his arm to his chest.

"Why are your eyes open, young man?"

Brock turned to find Varius standing over him. He glanced back at the male student who still had his eyes closed.

"Well...um...I don't know exactly," Brock responded.

Varius focused on the other student, a grimace crossing her face as her eyes narrowed. She looped around Brock's table and passed behind him to stand before the other boy. She placed her hand on his head and his eyes opened in surprise. Varius closed her eyes. They were both still for a moment until he visibly shivered and gasped for air. He stared down at his arm, his eyes wide.

"What...what did you do to me?" he asked.

Varius removed her hand and stepped back. "I just healed your broken arm. You're welcome." She pulled an apple from her pocket and handed it to him. "Here, eat this. I'm sure you're hungry."

The boy thanked her, biting into the apple as she returned to the front of the room. Varius stopped and stared at Brock with an inquisitive look on her face. After a moment, she shook her head and addressed the class.

"Work on this meditation technique at least once a day. Train yourself to seek the calm at your center. This will be our focus for the next few weeks. When I believe you're ready, we'll begin attempting to channel Order and things will get really interest..."

The bell rang, interrupting her speech. Brock wondered how class was over already. *How long were my eyes closed while meditating?*

Varius shouted to the students as they began to rise. "Remember to practice your meditation! Class dismissed!"

Brock stood and followed the cluster of students funneling out the door.

"Mister Talenz." He heard Varius say from behind. "Please stay. I would like to speak with you."

He set his pack on a table and approached the master's desk.

"Why did you break from your meditation and open your eyes earlier?" she asked him.

Brock glanced toward Ashland. Her striking blue eyes locked on his for a moment before she gave him a nod. He responded to the question, attempting to explain.

"The meditation exercise seemed to be going well. It felt so peaceful, so calm and cool. Then, I felt something wrong, as if something nearby didn't belong. That's why I opened my eyes and looked over at that boy, the one you healed."

"Thank you, Brock." Varius stepped close, looking him in the eye. "You must never be afraid to tell me the truth. I can't help you if you aren't straight with me. If you trust me and dedicate yourself, you might become something exceptional."

Brock nodded. "Okay. I'll do as you say," he replied. Then he smiled. "It did feel wonderful though: The harmony of Order."

It was Master Varius' turn to smile. "I like that. That's a good description."

~

The corridor walls sped past Brock as he ran, racing the clock but clearly losing. The bell finished ringing before he could even see the door. He stopped outside the door, pausing to catch his breath before opening the door and stepping inside.

He scanned the room, finding that the only open seat was in the front row. Making his way toward the chair, he glanced toward the instructor's desk and the pair of angry eyes staring back.

"Apparently, my class isn't important enough for you to be on time, Mister Talenz," Pretencia growled.

Brock groaned inwardly. The man had already made it clear that he didn't like Brock during the evaluation.

"Sorry, Master Pretencia," Brock replied as he took his seat. "Master Varius asked me to stay late after my ecclesiast class, and I didn't have enough time to get here before the bell."

Pretencia stood and placed his hands on his desk while staring down at Brock. "Do I look like I care what happens in your other classes?" Brock was wise enough to not reply. The master's voice rose as he continued. "I expect you to be here *on time*, ready to contribute to *this* class. If you cannot handle that responsibility, you will be visiting the headmaster." Brock swallowed hard. He certainly didn't want that. "Yes sir." Pretencia stared at him for a moment before addressing the class.

"Hello, novices. I trust that you're enjoying your first day at our illustrious institution." He stepped before the center aisle. "Welcome to your first Hierarchist class. I expect some of you are aware of what this class entails while others have no clue." His eyes had scanned the room until they landed on Brock as he finished the last sentence.

"Hierarchists are the glue that holds the Empire together. Members of the Hierarchy include everyone from city clerks to magistrates, prelates, and even the Archon himself." He clasped his hands behind his back as walked down the center aisle. "This class will introduce you to the structure and functions of our government and how the Ministry plays an intricate role in it all. You will learn the laws that citizens must follow and why those laws are critical to our civilized empire."

Pretencia reversed direction as he continued. "In addition, you'll be tested for your ability to reason and interpret the law. Someday, you may find yourself in the position of magistrate or city prelate."

He smiled, as if at a private joke. His slicked-back black hair glistened in the light of the afternoon sun. Pretencia's eyes lit up, and he spoke again.

"I must also mention that we have someone special in this class. The son of the Archon of the Empire sits among you." He held his hands out in a welcoming gesture. "Corbin, will you please stand and greet your classmates?"

Heads turned to see this prized student. Like the others, Brock looked back as a tall dark-haired boy stood and nodded to the class. The familiar face had a bandage above one brow.

"Oh, no," Brock groaned, recognizing the boy from the confrontation in the woods. On his first day at the Academy, Brock had assaulted the son of the most powerful man in the empire.

26

M aster Nindlerod's head bobbed as he cackled, laughing at his own joke. The students in the room looked to each other in confusion, not understanding the humor. Brock shrugged at Cameron's questioning look. Only Benny smiled and nodded. Brock wasn't sure if Benny understood the joke or if he was just playing along.

Nindlerod waved to his assistant. The heavy-set boy hauled a bag over, setting it on the worktable at the front of the room. Unlike other classrooms, this one had workbenches lined in rows from the back of the room to the front. Each row had two workbenches back-to-back with three stools at each bench. Brock, Benny, and Cam shared a workbench.

The Engineering master reached into the bag before removing a black metal ball that fit in the palm of his hand. Next, he pulled out a pillow. He placed both on the workbench and smiled.

"Now, we are going to talk about density. I assume that everyone here knows about weight." He scanned the room through his rounded spectacles before continuing. "Weight is pretty obvious. When something is difficult to lift, it is heavy. When something is easy to lift, it's light."

Nindlerod stepped in front of the bench, his eyes scanning the classroom again.

"How do you know if something's heavy? Lars?" He pointed to a big, muscular boy with curly black hair sitting near the front of the room. "Um. Cause it's big? You know, like a building?" Lars responded.

"Really?" Nindlerod replied. "What about a cloud then? Those are even bigger than a building. Are clouds heavy?"

The boy's nervous eyes glanced around the room before he replied, "No. I guess not. If they were heavy, they wouldn't be up in the sky."

"Correct!" Nindlerod said in excitement. "You see, the size of something is not what determines its weight. The density of something is the true measure."

Nindlerod pointed at the two objects he had placed on his workbench as he addressed a female sitting near Brock.

"Salina, can you tell me which of these two items is heavier?"

The dark-skinned girl brushed her black bangs from her forehead, tucking the hair behind an ear. "Well, the metal ball is surely heavier than a pillow. Everyone knows that."

"I see," Nindlerod said. "Is there anyone in the classroom that disagrees with this statement?"

Two hands in the class lifted high. Nindlerod raised one eyebrow and addressed Benny.

"Mister Hedgewick. You don't agree with this young woman's assessment?"

"Well, I would agree that the density of the ball is a lot higher than the pillow. But it doesn't mean that it's heavier."

The old man nodded. "Interesting. Perhaps we should weigh the two objects to find out."

He stepped to a large balance scale resting upon his workbench. After setting the metal ball on one tray, he placed the pillow on the other tray. The arms of the scale bounced a few times before settling at the same height.

"It appears that these two items are the same weight," the old master said to the class. "As Mister Hedgewick so eloquently stated, while these two objects weigh the same, their density is far from equal. The metal sphere is the same weight although it is far smaller than the pillow, and thus, has a far higher density."

The students in the room nodded, now understanding the concept. Brock wondered why they needed to know this. It seemed like simple logic.

"Density is just one of numerous topics we will cover over the coming months." Master Nindlerod stated. "In addition, you will undergo hands-on training with forging and casting metals, cutting and shaping wood, and many other skills that are essential to a good Engineer.

"To spice things up, we are also going to have a little competition that will enable you to put what you've learned to the test." Nindlerod strolled back to the scale, facing the class. "In a few weeks, you will have an opportunity to form teams of five students. Each team will have full access to Foundry materials and resources. Your objective will be to create your own catapult and enter our annual Catapult Challenge. For this event, you'll be launching a metal ball much like this one." Nindlerod picked up the metal ball off the scale, holding it up in the air. "But much larger and far heavier. The catapult that launches the ball the farthest, wins." Nindlerod smiled as he surveyed the students in the room. "Members of the winning team will no longer have to serve meals to the upperclassmen. That means you'll be served by other novices, among the first to eat every day."

The reward caused a buzz in the room. Nindlerod shouted to reclaim everyone's attention.

"The winning team will also receive twenty-five gold Imperials!"

The room fell silent. Nindlerod smiled a goofy grin at the looks of shock. Suddenly the buzz returned far louder as exclamations of excitement ran through the room.

It would take a lifetime of working as a tanner for Brock's father to earn twenty-five Imperials. Benny tugged on Brock's arm in excitement.

"We can win this, Brock!" Benny whispered. "I'll come up with an awesome design. You and Cam can help me build it. We can win!"

Brock looked at Cam, who smiled back. They would have to come up with something special. The competition was sure to be fierce.

Exhausted after a long first day of school, Brock finished dinner and headed to his room to relax. His thoughts wandered as he traversed the quiet hallway, still reflecting on the day's events when he reached his room and unlocked the door. "Hi, Brock."

He turned as a blond girl stepped out from the lounge, his gaze connecting with her large blue eyes.

"Amber. Um...I didn't expect you."

"Aren't you glad to see me?" she asked, her eyes searching his.

"Oh, yeah. Of course I am. I mean...I'm glad you're okay," he stammered.

Amber smiled, glancing down before her eyes rose to meet his again. "I'd like to speak with you in private. May I come in?" she asked.

"Um...sure." He stared at her, his mind numb. With her crying and distraught, he hadn't noticed that she was so pretty when they first met.

Her eyes flicked toward the room then back to him. "Aren't you going to move so I can get through the door?"

"Oh, sorry." He stepped back, waving her inside.

The sweet scent of her perfume teased Brock as she swept past. He watched her as she sat on his bed, feeling flustered by her beauty, as he had been when with Meg.

"Will you please close the door?" she asked.

"Oh, yeah. Sure."

He pushed the door closed and sat across from the pretty girl.

Amber leaned forward and grabbed Brock's hand, holding it in hers. "Thank you again for helping me yesterday. I was so scared, and I fear what would've happened if you hadn't come." She gave his hand a squeeze before letting go.

Before he could respond, she continued. "I've decided it's my responsibility to ensure it never happens again, to me or to some other innocent girl. That's why I plan to step forward and bring charges against Corbin. He can't be allowed to get away with something like that."

Her eyes reflected determination, but he knew what this meant. "Amber, you know who Corbin is, right?"

"Yes," she replied. "But that doesn't give him the right to violate me or anyone else against their will. He can't get away with it. He may have been stopped this time, but what about the next time...the next girl?"

"You're right." Brock agreed with her. "But it will be difficult. You need to approach it just right. It will require proof, or he'll just deny it and it will be your word against his."

"I know." She leaned close to take his hand while batting her long lashes, her eyes pleading. "That's why I need you to testify as a witness. I need your help, Brock. You're the only one who saw what happened."

Brock stared at the girl. Her lower lip quivered as she bit it, waiting for his response. He wanted to help her, but it was sure to be difficult. Even with a witness, accusing the Archon's son of attempted rape was likely to get messy. Just being involved could risk Brock's career at the Academy. He found his heart and his mind on different sides. His heart won out.

"Fine." He had barely gotten the word out when she leapt forward to wrap her arms around him.

"Oh, thank you. Thank you so much, Brock." She hugged him tightly.

He felt her body tight against his chest, and the blood in his veins surged as his heart pounded harder. After a bit, she released her arms and sat back on the bed.

"I was afraid you'd say no." She wiped tears from her cheeks with her sleeve.

"How could I say no? You asked for my help." He smiled. "I guess I'm a sucker for a damsel in distress."

Amber laughed and the sound warmed his heart.

She gave him one last smile before standing and stepping toward the door. Brock stood to open it for her, but she stopped him, gripping the front of his shirt as she stepped close. Her breath tickled his neck as she whispered.

"Stop by my room at sunset the day after tomorrow. It's room 1034. That will give me time to get my thoughts on paper. When we meet, we can go over my statement to make sure I worded it correctly. I want to make sure I get it just right."

She closed the last bit of distance between them, putting her lips on his. He responded, his lips intertwining with the softness of hers. With eyes closed, his head swam with the pleasure of the moment. She pulled away and his eyes opened to gaze into hers.

"Sunset, the day after tomorrow then," she said, slipping out the door.

The door closed, leaving Brock alone with the sound of his heart pounding in his ears. With her out of sight, his brain regained full function and he realized what he had done. *What have I gotten myself into?*

27

During dinner, Brock had little attention to spare. While others traded stories of their day, his mind floated back to thoughts of Amber. She seemed to consume his attention on a frequent basis the past two days, wavering between concern about her situation and the memory of their kiss.

After contributing little to the dinner conversation, Brock grabbed his empty plate and made his way to the kitchen. He slowed when his eyes landed on Corbin Ringholdt, sitting among the group of boys from Sol Polis. Brock found it irritating that they followed Corbin around like servants, fawning over him. Benny's roommate, Parker, was among them.

After a moment, Corbin's gaze met Brock's. Corbin stopped talking and glared back in response. He then smiled and made a cutting motion across his neck. A message. Brock already didn't like Corbin for what he had done to Amber. The feeling of dislike was becoming stronger.

"Brock, are you going to the library tonight?"

He turned to see Benny a step behind, giving him a smile as he pushed his spectacles back in place. With the tense moment between him and Corbin disrupted, Brock resumed his trek to the kitchen with Benny in tow.

"I guess I should. Mae wants us to have history topics to discuss soon," Brock replied. Then he thought about Amber. He was to meet her at sunset, giving him less than two hours. "But I can only go until sundown."

Benny nodded. "I'll go with you then. I need to find some history topics too." He raised one eyebrow. "Why only until sundown, though? Do you have a date or something?"

He turned sharply toward Benny, blushing as he thought of Amber.

"You do!" Benny's head bounced side to side, sporting a grin. "You sure work fast, Brock."

Brock shrugged. "Well, it's not really a date. I'm just meeting a girl about...a project."

"Sounds like a date to me," Benny replied.

They left the dining hall and followed the corridor to the knowledge center. Brock gripped the cool metal door handle and pulled hard. The heavy wooden door swung open, and they stepped inside.

Brock prided himself on his ability to read. However, most of his reading experience involved the small collection of books his mother had gathered before she died. He had read and re-read those fifteen books numerous times. Now, standing inside the academy library, he was in total awe at the sight of seemingly endless shelves of books. Prior to this moment, he would have doubted this many books existed in the whole world. To see them in a single building was astounding. He doubted he could read them all in a single lifetime.

The two boys walked down a wide aisle toward the heart of the building. After passing a dozen rows of bookshelves, the middle of the room opened to reveal desks arranged in a circle around a spiral staircase. Brock's eyes drifted up the staircase, where he noticed a catwalk leading to terrace levels at the second and third floor. The ceiling above the third floor held glass panels with light streaming through to illuminate the open center of the room. As his eyes drifted back down, he noticed another set of stairs located along the far wall, heading to the upper levels.

"Can I help you?"

Brock's gaze returned to the circle of desks, most occupied by students who were busy writing. A rail-thin girl with short brown hair stared at him with one eyebrow raised in question.

"Um. Yes." Brock approached the girl while turning on a smile. "Can you please direct me to a section covering details of The Banished Horde?"

"That would be late pre-empire era." The girl squinted as she considered the question. "We don't have many books from that period, but you can try looking in shelving rows 2236 through 2242. You'll find them on the second floor, southeast corner."

Brock had stopped listening, distracted. "Excuse me, miss. Can you tell me what's down there?" he asked, pointing at a trap door beneath the spiral stairwell. The girl glanced at the door before turning back to him.

"That's the archives. It's where we store books too old and brittle to handle. That way, the originals remain safe and secure." She pointed toward the nearby desks. "These students are working as scribes, copying books that will soon be in the same condition. It allows access to the information without risking damage to the original works, some that are hundreds of years old."

"Um. Okay," Brock said. "Thank you for your assistance." He turned to follow Benny toward the stairwell located near the south wall.

The girl called out, "I think you'll want one of these."

Brock turned to find a glowlamp swinging beneath the handle in her hand.

"Yes. Can we get a second lamp as well?" Brock asked as he returned to fetch the lamp. The girl nodded and handed him two lamps.

"Thanks again," he said as he retreated.

They crossed the room to the stairs. When reaching the second floor, they walked toward the east side. After a little searching, they found the shelves matching the numbers suggested. Brock stepped into an aisle and held his glowlamp up for light. Thousands of books filled this single aisle.

"This is going to take a while," Brock muttered.

"Yeah. You take that side, and I'll take this side," Benny replied. "There has to be something about The Horde in here."

Judging by the darkening room, it was nearly sunset. After more than an hour of searching, they had scanned the shelves of two of the six suggested aisles. In that time, they had collected twelve books that showed potential.

Brock and Benny each grabbed a pile of books and descended the stairs, heading back to the desk to return the lamps.

"I see that you found a few books to check out," said the girl at the desk.

"Yes," Brock replied. "Here are the lamps as well."

"Hold a minute while I record the books you're taking." She read the binding of each book, noting it in a ledger. "I need your name and room number, as well."

"Sure. Brock Talenz. Room 1099," he replied.

The girl recorded his name and pushed the two stacks of books toward them. Since Brock had other plans, he piled the books into Benny's arms to carry back to their rooms. Benny grunted under the weight of the volumes stacked to his chin. Brock held the door as Benny stepped out and scurried down the hall, weaving under the heavy load. As Benny reached the Main Hall, Brock turned and headed the other direction, toward Amber's room.

During his stroll down the hallway, Brock thought about the pretty girl. The memory of her embrace quickened his heart again. She also seemed quite taken with him since his heroic entrance into her life. In other circumstances, she might not have given him a second look. However, he wasn't going to worry about it now. He had enough to worry about in supporting her claims against Corbin.

When he entered the narrow hall leading to her room, he saw a crowd of people ahead. A purple cloak was among the blue of novice cloaks. As he neared the crowd, he heard frantic, anxious voices.

"Calm down and go back to your rooms." The large female in purple told the students.

In groups of twos and threes, girls began to peel away. They were holding each other, clearly distraught. As Brock passed the girls, he noted their blotchy, tear-streaked faces.

With thick arms crossed over her chest, the woman blocked the hall before him.

"What are you doing here?"

"I'm meeting someone about a project," he replied. "Her room is just ahead."

"Which room? What's her name?" the woman asked.

"Her name is Amber. Room 1034."

The woman's stern features softened. She glanced backward and Brock craned his neck to see what she was looking at, noticing that the open door was labeled 1034. Master Varius stepped from the room with her eyes downcast. She looked up and shook her head with sadness in her eyes.

Shock struck Brock so hard, he stumbled backward a step. He then darted forward, passing both women as he ran into Amber's room. The scene was one he would never forget.

The room was a mirror image of his own room, but with a chair in place of the second bed. On the floor, an open jar lay on its side with pale yellow powder spilling out on the stone tile. Amber lay still on her bed – too still.

He ran to her side, falling to his knees as he grabbed her hand. It was cold and limp. Her skin was pale and felt clammy, her lips blue. His view blurred as tears emerged and began tracking down his cheeks. He looked at Varius, who stood in the doorway.

"You need to help her. Please do something!" he pleaded.

She shook her head. "I cannot. It's not possible to heal the dead. I'm so sorry, Brock."

He held the girl's cold hand to his cheek as he struggled with the loss of a new friend. A deeper feeling of despair began to creep in. A feeling that any woman who got close to him was destined to die.

"How could this happen?" Brock asked, sobbing.

He heard Varius' voice from the doorway. "She apparently took too much yellow sky. It's been years since I've seen the drug here at all, let alone an overdose."

"Yellow sky?" he asked. "That doesn't make sense. She was to meet me tonight. We were to work on something important to her. Why would she do that?"

"I'm not sure, Brock. Perhaps she didn't mean to take so much," Varius replied. "While this appears to be an accident, we do need to investigate. That means I must ask you to leave. Again, I'm sorry for your loss."

Feeling numb, Brock stood and stumbled from the room.

28

A cloud of depression hovered over Brock. He attended his classes and did the work assigned, but his heart wasn't in it. If asked, he couldn't tell you what lessons were taught during that time. His friends tried to console him but to no avail. He just had to work through it himself.

On the ninth day after Amber's death, Brock woke to a bird singing outside his window. He sat at the edge of his bed and rubbed the sleep from his eyes. Reaching over the desk, he pulled the curtain back to see an orange starfetch serenading the breaking dawn. He stared at the little bird who had interrupted his sleep, singing as if it had no care in the world. He envied the bird.

But why? To not have a care, I would need to have nothing to care about. He realized that he would rather lose someone he cared about than never care at all. Suddenly, everything seemed better. He was still sad about Amber's death, but he no longer felt it should affect his own life.

He opened the wardrobe, dressed, and was out the door before Cameron even woke. When he stepped into the hallway, he noticed a soft blue glow coming from the lounge. Peeking in, he found Benny sprawled on a sofa with a book on his chest. The dim light of a glowlamp beside him told Brock that it hadn't been activated in hours. He chuckled as a loud snore came from Benny.

Walking over, he tapped Benny's shoulder.

"What?" Benny sat up, his spectacles askew. "What's that? Oh, Brock. I must've fallen asleep." He straightened his eyewear. "What time is it?"

Brock smiled at his confused friend. "The sun's about to rise. Were you here all night?"

"Um…yeah. I guess. I was working on our research late last night, and I must've dozed off." Benny set the book next to the fading glowlamp.

Brock suddenly felt guilty for not helping Benny with their research while he worked through the loss of Amber. The poor guy apparently stayed up late working on it alone.

"Sorry that I haven't been much help. I'll do better now, I promise," Brock said sincerely.

Benny looked at him, concerned at first and then a smile bloomed.

"You're feeling better, then?"

"Yeah." Brock nodded. "What have you found so far?"

Benny's smile faded, replaced by frustration. "Basically, nothing. They refer to it as the Wailing War, but nothing tells me why. The details about the war are vague at best, as are references to The Banished Horde. It's as if they don't want anyone to know anything about The Horde."

Brock's brow furrowed. "Strange. How many of the books have you gone through?"

"This is the last one."

Brock stared at the book. "I guess we should make another trip to the library."

Benny stood and nodded. "That's what I was thinking. But right now, I need to get changed and then get some breakfast."

Brock grabbed the glowlamp. "We can go to the library tomorrow, then."

"What about tonight?" Benny asked as he walked toward his room.

"Since we have tomorrow off, I thought you and Cam might want to join me for a little fun."

Benny smiled, his head bobbing up and down. "That sounds awesome. Where are we going?"

Brock flashed a smile. "We're going to visit an inn in Fallbrandt. We will leave tonight after class and should make it in time for dinner. The food is amazing. You're going to love it."

Brock felt in good spirits as he strolled down the road toward Fallbrandt. It was a beautiful late-summer day with strips of clouds overhead glowing orange in the evening sun. A mountain breeze cooled the heat of the day, making the weather perfect for travel. Brock was animated, waving his arms around as he relayed events from paladin training to Benny.

"...and when Cam stood over Lars, staring down at his bloody face, Budakis steps in and shouts down at Lars, '*You're not supposed to use your face to hit him you buffoon! You're supposed to use your fists!*'"

Benny squealed in laughter and reached up to slap Cam on the shoulder. Cam grinned sheepishly.

After a moment, Benny calmed enough to speak. "That must have been a sight. I bet nobody ever knocked big ol' Lars on his rump before."

Brock looked up at Cam, still smiling. "I bet he never faced anyone like Cam before. He's downright scary, and we don't even have weapons yet."

Cam shrugged. "I'm just doing my best to learn what I can to be a paladin. If Budakis wants me to fight, that's what I do."

Brock looked at Cam again, serious this time. "You'll be a frighteningly awesome paladin, Cam. I can't believe someone your size can move that fast. It's not fair."

"It doesn't have to be fair, does it?" Cam asked.

Brock laughed. "No. No it does not."

Benny jumped in front, walking backward to face them. "Okay, now let's talk about the Catapult Challenge." He grinned, rocking his shoulders side to side. "Nindlerod said that we'll soon need to have a team of five for the contest. You guys will help me, right? I mean, I couldn't do it without you."

Brock glanced at Cam, who nodded, and then back at Benny. "Of course, Benny. Neither of us has the faintest idea how to build a catapult, but we're happy to help."

A grin split Benny's face and his eyes were alight with excitement. "I'm telling you that we're going to build the best catapult ever!" The smile slid away, and his eyes unfocused. "Most of all, I plan to beat that Karl Jarlish. He thinks he's so special because his father invented the steam engine."

Brock had not seen this side of Benny before and found the boy's spirit surprising.

"Don't we need two more in order to have a team, Benny?" Cameron asked.

As Benny glanced up at Cam, he stumbled over his own feet and almost fell before recovering. He turned to walk forward before responding.

"Yeah," Benny said before his expression brightened. "Hey, maybe Parker will join us."

Brock was a little surprised at the suggestion. "Benny, I get the feeling your roommate doesn't like us much. He hangs around with Corbin and the other jerks from Sol Polis. Corbin certainly doesn't like us, and he leads that group of cronies."

"Oh, Parker's okay," Benny said. "You just have to get to know him."

He's not bad when he's not around Corbin." "If you say so," Brock replied.

The forest around them opened to reveal buildings clustered along the shore of a large lake. They walked past the buildings at the edge of town and a smile broke across Brock's face.

"There she is." Brock pointed as he walked. "The Quiet Woman. You guys are going to love her."

When they entered, Brock stepped aside and watched their reaction upon seeing a dining room filled with women. He wasn't disappointed when their dropped jaws transformed to smiles and nods.

"This was unexpected," Benny said over the loud buzz of conversation in the room.

"Brock!" A woman's voice shouted over the noise.

He turned to see Dory weaving her way between tables, her arms open in greeting. When she reached Brock, she gave him a hug.

"I'm glad you came back. I know it has only been two weeks, but the ladies miss you. I miss you." She turned her attention toward Cam and Benny. "And who are these two young gentlemen?"

"Dory, this is Benny." Brock introduced them. "The mountain standing beside me is Cam. They're my friends from the Academy."

Dory smiled and greeted the two new boys. "Welcome to The Quiet Woman. Any friends of Brock are friends of mine." She clapped her hands and shouted out. "Tipper!"

A mop of blond hair popped up near the bar as Tipper looked toward the doorway. Noticing Brock, he rushed over to give his friend a hug and a friendly thump on the back.

"I'm glad you came back, Brock," Tipper said as he released him. "How's life at the Academy?"

Brock smiled, happy to see his friend. "It's good to see you, too, Tip. Things are good at the school. I've made a couple friends and decided to introduce them to my friends here at the inn. Tipper, please say hello to Benny and my roommate, Cam."

Tipper reached out and shook their hands. "Nice to meet you."

Dory spoke to Tipper. "I thought you might like to share a table with your friend. Since we're full tonight, you and James will need to dig an extra table from under the stairs."

Tipper nodded and sped off to get James and a table.

Dory turned toward Brock. "Before you join your friends, would you please come say hello to the ladies?"

"Sure, Dory," he replied and then turned to Benny and Cameron. "You two go ahead and sit with Tipper. I'll be only a few minutes."

They nodded, and Brock turned to follow Dory. Smiles lit the familiar faces when the women saw him. They stood and hugged him as if he had been gone for years, not just for weeks. By the time he made his way around the table, Dory had a chair waiting. When he took his seat, Garrett was ready with a glass and a carafe of wine. The waiter then slowly circled the table, refilling glasses as needed.

Dory lifted her glass to toast. "Here's to our scholar, Brock."

"To Brock." They chimed as they tapped glasses together and took a drink.

The wine was as wonderful as he remembered. Recalling how bad he felt after consuming too much, he planned to pace himself.

Annabelle leaned closer, putting her hand on his. "I'm so glad you're doing well at the Academy. I told Abe he wouldn't be disappointed."

"Yes. I'm still thankful he gave me the chance I needed," Brock replied. "I'm even more thankful to you for convincing him to help me."

She smiled and gave his hand a squeeze. "It was my pleasure, Brock. I'm happy for you."

Dory squeezed his other hand. He turned to the owner of the inn, who smiled as she addressed him. "Brock, would you please entertain us with a story from your time at the Academy?"

"Well, the Academy is a secretive place," he replied. "However, I do have a story to share."

Struggling to keep his emotions under control, Brock told them about Amber. He relayed the tale of their brief relationship, from his timely rescue to her untimely death. Upon hearing the end of his story, the ladies expressed cries of shock followed by words of consolation.

Shortly after the story, dinner was served, and Brock excused himself to sit with his friends. As he headed to the other table, he realized that he felt better after telling the story, as if a weight had been lifted, reducing the sting of her loss.

Dinner consisted of pasta, poultry, and vegetables, in a creamy sauce. It was delicious. In a few short minutes, all four boys sat back with drinks in hand, their plates cleared.

"You were right, Brock. The food is amazing. I'm stuffed," Cam said, patting his stomach.

"Wow. We finally found a way to fill you up then?" Benny flashed a smile. Cam grinned in reply.

"Tip, where's Libby?" Brock asked.

Tipper glanced toward the kitchen with longing in his eyes. "She's helping Saul tonight. She should be done in an hour or so."

Brock smiled at his friend's expression. "You're totally smitten with her, aren't you?"

Tipper shrugged.

"Do you love her then?" Brock asked.

"Yeah. I think so," Tipper replied.

"That's great, Tip!" Brock reached across the table and shook his friend's shoulder. "I'm happy for you."

Benny sat forward, changing the subject. "Brock, Tipper was telling us about your journey to Fallbrandt. It sounds like you guys are lucky to be alive."

"Yeah. We had a couple close calls, but we're still here."

"What was the banshee like? And what about the bacabra?" Benny stared in anticipation.

Brock did his best to describe their encounters with the ferocious beasts without revealing the animation of Hank's corpse or the boulder in the cave. Benny listened intently and asked some good questions, his fascination by these otherworldly creatures evident.

As the evening wore on, they continued to drink and tell stories. Libby joined them but said little as she clung to Tipper's arm. Eventually, the room began to clear. Dory was kind enough to offer a free room for the night, asking Tipper to help haul a pallet in for Benny to sleep on while Brock and Cam took the two beds.

As he lay on the bed in his old room, Brock decided he felt better than he had in a while.

~

When he woke, Brock felt terrible. Again. Not quite as bad as his first experience with wine, but worse than he had hoped. Thankfully, a big glass of water and a single cup of caffe took the edge off his headache. Soon after breakfast, he bid Tipper and the crew of the inn farewell, promising to visit again soon.

Feeling the effects of the prior evening, the three boys walked back toward the Academy in quiet. The building was well within sight when Benny finally broke the silence.

"Brock, can I ask you a personal question?"

"Sure, Benny."

"How did you become friends with an Unchosen?" Benny turned toward Brock with concern in his eyes. "It's not that there's anything wrong with that. I just haven't seen many people treat Unchosen like they matter."

Brock nodded. "That's okay, Benny. I see how people treat Unchosen." After considering his response, he explained, "I fail to see how you can measure a person by a mark on their forehead. I would rather judge people by their actions and by how they treat others. Tipper may not have a rune, but he has a better heart than anyone I know. It may not be popular to befriend an Unchosen, but I'd rather call Tipper my friend than many others who do have a rune."

Benny glanced toward Cameron, who nodded in agreement.

Benny smiled. "You're a good person, Brock. A rare person. I'm glad I met you."

Cam chimed in. "Me too."

Feeling a bit embarrassed, Brock didn't know how to respond. He looked forward and found the school less than a quarter-mile away.

"When we get back, let's get cleaned up and grab some food before we head to the library. Would you like to join us, Cam?"

Cam gave his usual shrug as a response, seemingly content to follow along.

They returned to their rooms and grabbed clean clothes before they headed to the baths in the cellar beneath the lounge. Being nearly midday, the baths were quiet. Brock had discovered that the Academy was built above a series of hot springs, which not only fed the baths, but also heated the buildings by pumping hot water down pipes running throughout the complex.

The steamy water of the bath felt great, leaving the boys refreshed and hungry. They dressed and found their way to the dining hall for a quick meal before heading to the library. Again, the halls were quiet. The library was even quieter.

Brock and Benny dropped their books off at the empty desk, grabbed two glowlamps, and led Cam to the second floor. Within the designated aisles, they began searching for books that might include details of the Wailing War or the Banished Horde.

After an hour, they heard a squeaky hinge echo through the building. Footsteps and muffled conversation followed. Since it had been quiet until now, the three boys instinctively froze, careful not to make any noise. Brock motioned for Benny and Cam to stay put as he set his lamp down and crept down the aisle to the balcony.

He observed Headmaster Vandermark and two other masters--a gray-haired man and a woman–walk behind the circle of desks as they each removed a cord from their neck. Taking turns, each master bent to insert a key into a trap-door lock. When the third lock was released, Vandermark opened the door and made a waving motion with his hand. Holding a glowlamp, the woman descended the stairs, followed by Vandermark. The gray-haired master trailed the other two, holding a glowlamp in one hand as he pulled the trap door closed. The room fell silent.

Brock crept back to where Cam and Benny waited. He gave them a gesture with his finger to his lips, scooped up his lamp, and waved for them to follow.

The amount of noise from Benny made Brock wince, making it clear that he had no experience in sneaking. Cam, on the other hand, was surprisingly quiet as they crept down the stairs, returned the lamps, and snuck out of the library the way they had entered.

Without a word, Brock headed toward their rooms. Confused, Benny hustled to catch him, nearly dropping the books he held in the process.

"What's going on, Brock?" Benny asked. "Why all the sneaking?"

"Hush," he responded. "Wait until we get to my room."

Brock walked purposefully to the Boys' Wing and down the long corridor to their rooms. After unlocking the door, he led Benny and Cameron inside and closed the door behind them.

"Okay, Brock. Now explain what's going on," Benny said, exasperated.

Brock smiled in response. "I'm pretty sure we were not supposed to be in the library today. I also witnessed something I wasn't supposed to see."

Benny's brow furrowed in confusion. "Wouldn't the door have been locked if the library was closed?"

Brock shook his head. "It should've been locked, but someone messed up."

Still looking confused, Benny sat on Brock's bed. "I need you to explain, Brock. I'm not understanding your math yet." Brock sat across from Benny. Cam sat beside him.

"There are numerous sets of doors to the library. However, only one set has an external lock on it," Brock explained. "The others are bolted from the inside. This is something I noticed on our first visit as I thought it was interesting."

Benny nodded. "Okay. I'm with you so far."

"The door we used today wasn't the door with the external lock, and the bolt was certainly not secured when we entered." Brock grinned, holding his finger in the air. "The door with the lock also happens to have a squeaky hinge."

Benny's eyes lit up. "That's the squeak we heard when the others entered the library!"

Brock nodded. "Yes. They unlocked that door with their key and came into what they thought was an empty building. They didn't know we were there."

Benny looked confused again. "Why do you say that?"

Brock smiled. "Because, anyone with a brain would've realized that they have something secret or something valuable hiding there."

Benny shook his head. "You lost me again."

Brock stood and began pacing as he explained, "During our first visit to the library, I noticed a trap door under the stairwell behind the desks. The girl working there said it was just a place where they stored old books. While it seemed innocent enough, I thought it was odd that the door also had three heavy-duty locks."

He paused to make sure they were digesting what he was saying. When they nodded, he continued.

"Today, I found out why there are three locks. I saw Vandermark and two other masters, each possessing a key and each key unlocking only one of the locks. Once all locks were unlocked, the three descended and pulled the door closed behind them."

A grin broke across Benny's face. Cam, however, looked confused.

"I don't understand," the big blond boy muttered.

Brock explained, "Think about it. Why have a door with three heavy locks? Why have each lock opened only by a key owned by a different person? That's overkill for anything trivial or even mildly important. Clearly, requiring three individuals to enter the Archives means that they don't trust one person to have access, or they have three keys as a safeguard against one key landing in the wrong hands. Perhaps it's both reasons. Regardless, there's something down there they want to protect.

The Archives are more than just a place to store old copies of books."

Cameron nodded. "That makes sense. But, so what?"

Brock shrugged. "Beyond personal curiosity, that's a good question. Let me think on it. Something tells me that this secret, and whatever's down there, only leads to more secrets being kept by the Ministry."

29

"Maintain physical contact. Close your eyes, picture the rune for Order, and find your center." Master Varius instructed the class. "Feel the calm pureness of Order within. Then, extend your awareness, seeking that same sense of Order within your patient."

Varius waved Ashland over as she continued. "You should sense something that feels wrong or does not belong. Everyone will perceive this differently, so this is where things get difficult. You need to seek out this wrongness and then draw upon the Order within your patient, using that energy to correct the wrong that ails them."

Brock looked around the room and noticed confusion on the faces of his classmates.

"I told you that this is the difficult part," Varius said, smiling. "Trying to explain how to heal is like trying to explain a beautiful sunset to someone who has spent their whole life blind."

She reached out and held Ashland's hand as she continued. "The unfortunate truth is that performing healing is the best way to learn it. That's why it's such a rare and special talent. It can only be learned by doing it, but if you never do it, you aren't aware that it's possible."

With her free hand, Varius drew a dagger from behind her back and swiped the blade across Ashland's open hand. The girl tried to withdraw, but Varius had a firm grip on her wrist. Blood quickly filled Ashland's palm, dripping to the floor. To her credit, her only reaction was a clenching of her jaw.

"Now watch." Varius closed her eyes.

Ashland shivered, as if chilled. A collective gasp came from the class as they watched the gaping wound on her hand close.

Varius opened her eyes and pulled a white cloth from her pocket. She wiped the blood from the girl's palm and held her hand up for the class to see. Other than dried blood in the creases of her palm, there was no trace of the wound.

"This demonstration is a bit dramatic, but you can imagine how valuable this ability is to the welfare of the Empire." She let the girl's wrist drop. "That's why you must attempt to harness any ability you have with Order and focus on learning to heal."

Nodding heads from the class confirmed they understood.

"To heal, you need patients. We happen to have another class that naturally generates patients." Varius walked down the center aisle. "You'll be broken up into six groups with each group spending one day a week attending paladin training rather than coming here. A student guide who is skilled in healing will lead each group. Sparring injuries happen on a daily basis. This will give each of you a chance to practice healing. If you're unsuccessful, the student guide will take over." She smiled. "We can't leave our paladin students suffering with their wounds for too long."

She returned to the front of the room and opened a drawer. Gripping a hard roll, she held it up for all to see before tossing the roll to Ashland, who caught it and took a bite.

"You must also know that healing requires energy. That energy comes from the person being healed, which makes them hungry. Food helps to replenish that energy. The greater the wound, the more energy required."

Varius stepped closer to the class. "A common false belief about healing is that it comes from the healer. That's not really what's happening. You are a facilitator, guiding resources that exist within the patient to reestablish the Order that was present prior to the injury or illness."

Varius stopped to scan the room, ensuring that she had everyone's attention.

"However, there are limits to what healing can do. First and foremost, you cannot heal the dead. Healing requires energy. It requires life to feed it. The dead have nothing left to work with, thus it's impossible."

"Second, severed appendages cannot be healed. There's not enough energy in a person's body to regrow a missing limb or even a finger. The best you can do is heal the wound closed, but the appendage will remain incomplete. In fact, injuries involving large broken bones must be properly set prior to healing. If you heal bones that are broken at an odd angle, they will heal at that angle, leaving the person crippled."

"Third, you cannot heal yourself. Try as you might, you will find it a fruitless pursuit."

"Lastly, a broken mind cannot be healed."

Confused, Brock raised his hand. "What do you mean when you say a broken mind?"

Varius spoke directly to him. "It means you cannot heal someone who has become depressed, mentally unstable, or completely insane. Nobody knows why. We only know that it cannot be done."

The bell rang, and Varius held her hands up, indicating for the class to wait.

"When you come to class tomorrow, the healing schedule will be posted. On the days you are in this classroom, you will be learning about the human body. In order to heal, you must understand what you're healing. Class dismissed."

As the others filtered through the door, Brock approached Varius at her desk.

"Master Varius?" Brock began, "It's been two weeks since Amber's death. Can you share anything from your investigation?"

"Well, Brock. The only thing of interest we have found is that a male student was seen in the hall earlier that evening. However, we've no evidence of who he was or that he was in her room." Brock couldn't hold back any longer.

"I need to tell you something." He glanced around the room, verifying that they were alone. "On the eve of the first day of school, Corbin Ringholdt assaulted Amber in the woods near the lawn, but I showed up in time to stop him," Brock said. "Amber approached me the next day, asking for support. She planned to press charges. Before she could do so, she was dead."

Varius sat back with fingers tented, held to her lips. After a moment, she responded, "Brock, what you're insinuating is quite serious. I'm sure you're aware of who Corbin is? Who his father is?"

He nodded. "Yes. I cautioned Amber for that very reason. She knew it would be difficult, but I don't think she considered her life might be in danger."

Varius sat upright, placing her hands on the desk. "Do you have proof for any of this?"

Feeling his bubble of hope deflating, he shook his head.

"Without proof, this can go nowhere. It would just be your word against Corbin's. Even if you were able to convict him with the attempted rape, it doesn't prove he had anything to do with Amber's death. It would only prove motive. You cannot convict someone purely on motive, even if he wasn't the son of the most powerful man in the Empire."

Brock was crestfallen, foreseeing her response.

Varius stood and placed a hand on his shoulder. "I'm going to have to stick with the findings of our investigation. We will officially rule Amber's death as an accidental overdose. I'm sorry."

She lowered her hand. Brock nodded and turned to leave as the bell rang. His stomach twisted in a knot as he realized he was late for his Hierarchist class. Again.

With a swipe of his forearm, Brock wiped sweat from his forehead. He grabbed the next dirty pot and gave the pump three good strokes, filling it with hot spring water. After rubbing soap onto the scrub brush, he scrubbed away the baked-on food. He then dumped the soapy water into the floor drain, rinsed the pot, and held it to the glowlamp for examination. Deciding it was clean, he placed it on the dumbwaiter. That was the last one.

After a quick rinse of the scrub brush, he set it and the soap on a shelf and ran up the stairs. He arrived in the kitchen, gripped the rope, and began pulling, hand-over-hand. The pulley at the top squeaked with each pull, protesting at the weight loaded on the dumbwaiter. When the platform cleared the opening, he tied off the rope, grabbed a dry towel, and began unloading the platform, drying each piece as he placed it on the shelf where it belonged.

Pretencia had the right to issue punishment for Brock's repeated tardiness, and the man didn't hold back. He likely figured that two weeks of scrubbing pots would teach Brock a lesson, maybe even break him. He didn't know Brock grew up working in a tannery. Compared to tanning hides, cleaning pots was a pleasant diversion. Still, he wished he could be spending his time elsewhere.

Once finished, he looped the damp towel over a hook and walked to the kitchen office. The door stood open a crack with blue light sneaking through. He knocked before pushing it open. The woman at the desk looked up at him with spectacles resting low on her nose.

"Sorry to interrupt, Shirley," Brock said. "I wanted to let you know I'm finished."

She gave him a smile. "Thank you, Brock. I'll miss your help around here. If it didn't mean you'd gotten into trouble, I'd be wishing for you to come work for me again soon."

He flashed her a smile. "Sorry, Shirley, but my job right now is being a student. Working here doesn't give me enough time to keep up with my studies."

"I know, Dearie," Shirley said. "But you do such a good job. It will be difficult to go back to sorry old Lonnie doing the wash." A twinkling laugh followed.

Brock smiled again. She was a sweet woman. "Well, good luck with that. Good night, Shirley."

"Good night, Brock."

Whistling as he strolled through the dining hall, his body was tired, but his heart felt light, happy to be done with his time in the kitchens.

When he opened the door to his room, Cam sat up and blinked at Brock from his bed.

"Good. You're awake." Brock removed the cover from the glowlamp on the wall.

"Yeah. I just went to bed." Cam sounded tired. "Benny and I poured through the last of the books we pulled from the library." "Find anything?" Brock asked.

"Nope. It seems we're at a dead end," Cam said.

Brock sat on his bed to pull his boots off. "Oh, that feels good," he said, wiggling his toes. "I'm not going to give up yet. I think there are answers, they're just hiding."

Cameron stared at him. "The Archives?"

Brock smiled. "Yep."

"How are you going to get into that? It has three locks with three keys held by different masters. You said it yourself."

"I've been working on that," Brock replied, pulling his shirt off. "Scrubbing pots requires effort, but mostly physical effort. It gives you time for your mind to work on other things. I'm going to make one more trip to the library, and then I'll tell you the plan."

Cameron laid back down, letting out a sigh. "Why do I get the feeling that this is trouble?"

Brock laughed as he covered the lamp. "You just need to trust me."

30

The sweet, pleasant scent of Ashland's hair tantalized Brock as a stray curl tickled his nose. However, the warmth of her hand on his leg had most of his attention. She finished speaking with the student seated in front of him and sat back, removing her hand. He stared down at his leg, still feeling the lingering affect.

A shout echoed, followed by the loud clacking of wood on wood filling the air. On the Arena floor below, students swung, dodged, and struck back at their opponents. Brock's attention settled on a skilled pair dueling in the center of the floor. A large male student armed with a sword and shield was dueling a female student who was nearly the same height. From the back of her sparring helmet, a tail of red hair trailed as she fluidly dodged, parried, and attacked her opponent. Brock noticed that she wielded her two short swords with speed and precision.

"Who is she?" he asked Ashland, pointing toward the red-haired girl.

"Her name is Tegan. She is quite good and was a finalist in last year's Arena Championship despite being just a novice." Brock nodded as he watched her spar.

Tegan ducked under a wide swing, spinning and striking. Her opponent struggled to block her assault. Blows slid off his shield, struck hard against his sword, and connected with glancing blows off his shoulders and legs.

Tegan paused and smiled, standing straight with her weapons at her side.

The boy reacted, striking at her with a wide swing meant to finish her. He overstepped when his sword met no resistance. The girl had dipped beneath his swing to spin under the strike. Using her momentum, she rose up as she spun, striking with both blades at his open side. Brock heard bones cracking when her swords smashed into the boy's ribs. He arched his back with a cry of pain and collapsed to the floor. The master paladin jumped forward and called the match.

Tegan squatted and spoke to her downed opponent before helping him to his feet. He appeared to be fighting for air as his face contorted in pain.

Ashland nudged Brock's leg.

"This is your chance, Brock. They're heading over for healing. I have no doubt she broke his ribs, maybe worse. "

Brock took a breath and stood. He slid a flask over his shoulder and lifted the bread-filled basket.

"Brock." He turned back toward Ashland. When his eyes locked onto hers, he felt the intensity of her gaze. "You can do this."

He nodded again, feeling more confident. Stepping into the aisle, he began descending the stairs

During their first two sessions as healing support crew, he had watched the nine classmates in his group attempt to heal injured combatants. One by one, they had tried. One by one, they had failed. Each time, Ashland had to step in and heal the wounded. She continued to encourage them not to give up, that it often took weeks or months for a breakthrough. In the back of everyone's mind was the fact that the ability was exceptionally rare.

Now it was Brock's turn to try.

When he reached the Arena floor, Tegan and the wounded boy were waiting. His thickly muscled arm was over her shoulder – hers was around his waist, supporting him.

"Hi. I'm Brock," he said to the pair. "I'm here to heal you."

"Funny. I thought you were the baker trying to sell me day-old bread," Tegan said with a grin.

Brock ignored her and focused on his patient, whose face appeared pale as he struggled for air.

After placing his hand on the boy's bare arm, Brock closed his eyes.

He pictured the symbol for Order in his mind as he tried to relax, searching for calmness.

In the classroom, Master Varius had only been able to teach the principles of healing. She stated numerous times that the actual method was different for everyone, that the visualization was a matter of personal perspective. You had to figure it out yourself, so Brock was trying to figure it out.

After a minute, he relaxed and found the calm, blue-tinted presence of Order within himself. Extending his awareness, he found the sense of Order within his patient. He also felt something else. Something that felt wrong, out of place.

Searching with his mind, he sought the cause of the wrongness. In his mind's eye, he found what looked like symbols, pulsing with a red energy in the surrounding blue calmness.

Repulsed, Brock pulled at the Order within his patient, using it to smother the red symbols. He encountered the pressure of resistance, so he pushed harder. The symbols started to unravel as if made of cloth woven from wisps of thin red threads that began to fall away. The effect accelerated as the symbols unwound until they were gone.

When Brock opened his eyes, he felt the arm in his grip shudder. His patient's eyes were wide as he gasped for air. A fountain of blood blasted from his mouth, drenching Brock.

Brock let go, jumping backward in surprise. He looked down at his shirt, covered in red splotches and sticking to his torso. He looked at the boy, who was now gasping deep breaths. His color had already returned to normal. Tegan stared at Brock in shock.

Hearing laughter from behind, Brock turned to find Ashland standing on the stairs a few steps away. Despite the laughter, she got a few words out.

"Good job, Brock."

He then heard laughter from the other direction. It was Tegan.

"Um. Sorry," the boy said to Brock. "Do you have something to eat? I'm starving."

Still in shock, Brock nodded and bent to scoop the basket from the second step. He held it out to the boy, who grabbed a chunk of bread and took a bite.

Brock pulled the water flask off his shoulder, noting the streaks of blood on the strap as he handed it over.

Ashland's laughter had calmed enough to allow her to speak. "It's a difficult way to learn, but you should have guessed he had a punctured lung."

Brock looked at her, confused. "Okay. So what?"

"Punctured lungs can fill with blood. When you restore Order to the body, that blood has to go," she replied, chuckling again. "Apparently, all over you."

Ashland spun, returning to her seat. Brock didn't see what was so funny. He was still amazed. He had healed someone. *I did it.* A smile crept onto his face. He felt thrilled at his accomplishment.

A hand clapped onto his shoulder, and Brock turned to see his patient smiling at him.

"Again, sorry about the blood." He handed the water skin back. "And thanks for the healing. My ribs feel great now." He turned and walked away.

Tegan was still chuckling as she turned to follow her sparring partner.

31

As usual, Master Nindlerod cackled away, laughing at his own joke. As usual, his humor was lost on almost everyone in the class. Benny smiled and nodded, seeming to understand the humor. Karl Jarlish, the other brainiac in the class, chuckled as well. Everyone else appeared confused.

Two weeks earlier, they had moved from the classroom into the Foundry. Today, Nindlerod was conducting a demonstration of yesterday's lesson on casting steel. The master engineer walked them through the process, heating thin metal rods in the forge until they were red-hot. He then poured the liquefied metal into the casting block. The block was set into a shallow tub of water, which hissed and steamed. Nindlerod grabbed a pair of tongs and lifted the top half of the casting away.

"Behold our creation." Using the tongs, he held up a large bolt with a blob of metal on the end. "Now, we just need to clean it up."

The man stepped to a large stone wheel, pumping a foot pedal that caused the wheel to spin. He held the blob end of the bolt to the wheel, and sparks began to fly. A minute later, he stopped and held the bolt up for everyone to see. The blob was gone, leaving a clean, flat end.

"Isn't it wonderful?" the old man asked, cackling again.

He dipped it into the tub of water for a few seconds before flipping it toward Brock.

By instinct, Brock snatched the bolt out of the air. Realizing what he had done, he was surprised to find that he hadn't been burned. While it was still warm, it wasn't too hot to hold.

"Got you, sonny!" Nindlerod cackled again. "You see, the heat from the bolt dissipates when it's removed from the heat source. First, it cools as heat is conducted into the casting, then through the casting into the tub of water. Finally, it cools even faster when placed directly in water." He held up a finger. "However, the rate of cooling should be managed for best results to prevent it from becoming brittle." Brock stepped closer to hand him the bolt.

"No, you keep it. You might use it for what's next," Nindlerod said, cackling again before he addressed the class. "We've covered the basics of physics, woodworking, metalsmithing, and casting. You're now ready for the Catapult Challenge!" He ended the last sentence with a finger pointed high in the air.

Nindlerod waved for them to follow. Like a herd of cattle, the group of sixty students trailed along as he strode toward the huge double doors at the end of the building. Nindlerod's chunky assistant flipped the lock open and began pushing on one of the doors, the small wheel that supported the door squeaking as it rolled. As the door opened, sunlight streamed in. Nindlerod swept through the open doorway with his herd of students in tow.

They emerged in a holding yard filled with materials stacked in the shade of slanted awnings. Nindlerod stopped and waited for the group to filter into the yard with the students fanning around the small master engineer. Satisfied that everyone was present, he addressed the class.

"This is the Foundry yard. Here, you will find the raw materials you need to construct your catapults. Treated wooden beams over there." He paused and pointed to the side. "Wheels of different types and sizes over there. Metal rods, ropes, pulleys, and more." He pointed again.

"In addition, you have access to the casting blocks and tools I showed you in the forge area. This will allow you to cast bolts, nuts, hooks, levers, gears, and other components you might need, depending on your design."

Nindelrod paused a moment, scanning the faces before him. "You may be wondering what the Catapult Challenge is all about." He stepped over to a large cart loaded with metal balls, each about a foot in diameter. "These will be your projectiles, each weighing as much as I do. Your objective is to launch one of these balls as far as you can. Each team only gets two attempts, so make them count. The team who builds the machine that launches a ball the farthest, wins."

He paused again, rubbing his palms together in anticipation. "I'm so excited! I can't wait to see what you come up with this year!"

The crowd of students parted to create a path as Nindlerod headed back toward the Foundry. Just before entering the dark building, he turned to face them.

"Don't forget that the winning team gets twenty-five gold Imperials!" He smiled. "Form groups of five students and get to work. The challenge is four weeks from today."

The man pushed his round spectacles into place, nodded to the class, and disappeared into the dark building with his cackling laughter fading into the distance.

Students began to mill about, forming into teams. Brock was already standing next to Benny when Cam made his way over to join them.

Brock noticed Corbin grab Karl Jarlish, pulling him into his little clique. However, they now had six and someone would be excluded. Corbin spoke with Parker, who stepped away from the group and noticed Benny waving him over. When Parker approached, Benny greeted him.

"You can be on our team, Parker. We could use the help and would be happy to have you."

Parker nodded. "Um…Thanks," he said, not sounding thrilled.

Realizing that they needed one more member, Brock went in search of a student who still needed a team. That's when he spotted Lars standing by himself. Weaving his way through clusters of students, Brock headed toward the huge kid with black curly hair. As he approached, Lars glared at him.

"Hi, Lars." Brock nodded. "If you aren't on a team yet, we'd be happy to have you join us."

"You think you're funny, don't you?" Lars replied, crossing his arms on his massive chest.

Brock was confused. "What do you mean?"

"Nobody wants me on their team. I have no idea what's going on in this class. Clearly, I'm too dumb." His eyes looked down, and his voice quieted. "You don't want a big dummy messing things up."

Brock realized that Lars was feeling insecure. "We all have talents and weaknesses, Lars. I think that's why teams work. If we get a bunch of different talents together, we each contribute in some way. It makes a team more effective than someone working alone. If we all brought the same talents and weaknesses, the team might excel in some areas but would fail in others."

The large boy's brow furrowed. "What are you saying?"

"I'm saying that we already have one person who's amazing at this engineering stuff. You don't have to be good at it and neither do I. We just need to band together and contribute with our own skills, the best we can," Brock replied. "I'm saying that we want you on our team. Please join us, Lars."

Lars squinted at Brock, studying him for a bit before giving a nod. Brock smiled and waved for him to follow.

Brock crossed the yard to rejoin the group. "Lars is joining us to make five," he said, thumbing toward the big kid grinning over his shoulder before putting a hand on Benny's shoulder. "In this effort, I think we can agree that Benny is the lead."

Everyone nodded as a grin spread across Benny's face.

Brock pointed at Benny. "Now you know what we have to work with and what we need to achieve. How long will it take to draw up plans for our catapult?"

A look of concentration clouded Benny's face. His head bobbed and lips moved, but no sound came out. After a moment, he broke into a grin.

"Give me five days and I'll have it figured out."

Brock nodded. "Okay. Let's meet in the novice lounge after dinner five days from now. After that, things will get busy for a while."

Everyone nodded in agreement. Their team was set. Step one of their plan was in place. In four weeks, they had a contest to win.

Brock's gaze drifted across the crowded yard, locking onto eyes that burned with cold hatred. Corbin's clenched jaw loosened, and a smile spread across his face, taunting Brock with its smug arrogance.

Brock remained stoic, not responding to Corbin's smug grin.

Now fifteen minutes into the mock trial, Brock had meticulously stated his case. Master Pretencia, acting as magistrate, nodded and took notes the entire time.

Representing the plaintiff, Brock had one chance to state his case before relinquishing the floor to the state defense. Unfortunately, that person was Corbin Ringholdt. Brock regained focus and made his closing statement.

"As you can see, my client is innocent. The state, as I have proven without a doubt, has violated this man's rights," Brock stated confidentially. "I move for him to be cleared of all charges and to be issued the sum of eight gold Imperials to replace his destroyed property."

Brock bowed to Pretencia and retreated to his seat after building a strong case for his mythical client. He imagined how the man would thank him profusely for reclaiming his property and for convincing the Magistrate to award the gold needed to replace the building. Brock smiled, appreciating the reward of helping a person in need.

Corbin's voice disturbed him from his reverie.

"I must commend my opponent for his comprehensive and compelling argument," Corbin said as he took the floor. "If circumstances were different, I have no doubt that his case would be sufficient to sway the magistrate in his client's favor."

Corbin paused, looking back with a smirk.

"However, in this case, my opponent's argument is irrelevant." Corbin spread his hands out. "You see, when the plaintiff was described to us prior to these proceedings, there was one glaring omission."

Corbin pointed at his own forehead. "The man was never described to have a rune. That would make the defendant an Unchosen, which leaves him with no official rights and unprotected by empire law." Corbin slammed his hand down on the table as he ended the statement, the sound echoing in the room.

"I move for the state to retain this man's property. In addition, I move for the plaintiff to be jailed for thirty days, working slave labor to repay the state for the cost of these proceedings."

Corbin bowed to Pretencia and turned to face the audience, smiling as he retreated to his seat. Brock hated the pompous jerk.

Pretencia stood to address the courtroom. "I have come to my decision." His voice boomed with authority. "In the case of Dane Baskins versus the state, I find the state innocent in all regards. As the state defender noted, Dane Baskins is, indeed, Unchosen. Per empire law, he's not a protected citizen and has no official rights to property." Pretencia paused, changing his tone to one less official. "Very good, Mister Ringholdt. You've won again." He shifted his gaze to Brock. "You, Mister Talenz, have improved. However, you once again find yourself on the wrong side of the decision. Keep trying. Perhaps you will win a proceeding one day."

Brock had lost again. Three times, he had been matched against Corbin in a mock trial. Three times, he had lost.

"Better luck next time, peon," Corbin muttered as he passed Brock.

Brock's eyes narrowed as Corbin took a seat in the audience. Yes, he hated Corbin Ringholdt quite strongly right now. He still believed that Corbin was the cause of Amber's death, further fueling his hatred.

As Brock stepped into the audience, Pretencia announced the next case. Brock plopped down on a chair to wait for class to end. Frustrated, he ignored the remaining trials. He needed to focus on something else, anything else. His mind drifted to his plan to visit the library archives.

32

Lying still, Brock attempted to relax on the hard surface. He tried to ignore that his cloak was now filthy. He should have anticipated that nobody bothered to dust the tops of the bookshelves. It appeared to have been years, perhaps decades, since they had been cleaned.

In the distance, he heard Benny's voice.

"We'll take these."

"You're just in time. We're about to close." It was the girl working the checkout desk. "Name, please."

"Benny Hedgewick."

"Oh yeah. I remember. Like the guy that the library was named after."

"Yep. He's my ancestor," Benny replied.

After a minute, she spoke again. "Okay. Take care of these and return them in three weeks." She paused. "Weren't there three of you? I'm pretty sure your cute friend came in with you."

"What? Oh...Um..." He heard Benny stammer.

Come on, Benny. Don't mess this up, Brock thought.

"Yeah. That's Brock. He left about a half-hour ago." Cam's low voice rumbled. "He left to meet a girl to practice his meditation. You know, for ecclesiastics?"

"Oh. Okay then," the girl replied.

"Good night," Benny said.

The sound of a door opening and clicking closed informed Brock that Cam and Benny were gone, leaving just him and library workers within the building.

Minutes ticked by slowly. The hard surface of the shelf became quite uncomfortable, making it difficult for him to lie still.

He heard footsteps ascending the stairs, the steps growing louder as they approached his location on the second floor. The blue light of a glowlamp passed by and the footsteps began to fade, growing more distant.

Moments later, the footsteps ascended to the third level. After a minute, they again descended, returning to the main floor.

"Okay, Master Tennison. I updated the ledgers and cleared the library. It's empty except for us. I'm leaving," the girl said.

An old man's voice responded, "Thank you, Sandra. Have a good day off."

"Thank you. Good night."

A door opened and clicked closed.

Quiet minutes slowly ticked by until he heard distant footsteps followed by the thump of a deadbolt slamming closed. Three more deadbolts slammed closed and another door opened, this one squeaking on its hinge. The squeak repeated as the door clicked closed. The click of a lock sounded, followed by silence.

Patience. Brock knew a thief's greatest ally was patience.

A full quarter-hour of silence passed before he rolled off the shelf. He lowered himself until he was hanging by his hands, arms outstretched. Letting go, he dropped to the floor and cringed at the noise caused by his landing. He hoped he was alone.

Creeping to the edge of the terrace, he scanned the floor below. A dozen glowlamps rested on the desks, casting long shadows in every direction. Nobody was in sight.

Brock crept across the floor and down the stairs, grabbing a glowlamp as he passed the desks. He set the lamp on the floor near the trap door before reaching behind his back to remove his sheath. After withdrawing his knife and three bent needles from the sheath, he set to work on the first lock.

Again, patience was required. He had gotten a good look at the keys used for the locks. They were more complex than most, each lock containing three tumblers. After a few minutes of intense concentration, he was able to get the lock to turn. His relief was brief with two locks remaining.

By the time all three locks were released, his brow was covered in sweat, and he felt the sting of thirst. He should have brought water, but there was no help for it now. Sliding his knife and picks back into the sheath, he replaced it in his waistband at the small of his back.

He crouched low, pulled the trapdoor open, and scooped the lamp up as he began his descent. Almost as an afterthought, he lowered the door behind him.

Like the stairwell above, this one was curved. As he rounded the bend, the stairs ended to reveal a large room. Shockingly, it was another entire level filled with shelves of books like the floors above. *Where do I begin to search?*

He walked down the first row of books, scanning titles to discern their subjects and stopped when he heard a noise from above. The moment stretched, completely silent until he heard a key sliding into a trap door lock. Panic struck.

Brock scrambled out the other end of the aisle, seeking a place to hide. He noticed another stairwell under the one he had just descended. In a snap decision, he darted down those stairs. Arriving at the next level, he ran down the main aisle, putting distance between himself and whoever was entering the archives.

When he reached the far wall, he turned down a side aisle and spotted a table in the corner. He ducked under the table and pulled the chairs in tight around him. Using his cloak, he covered the glowlamp, and the room plunged into darkness.

Brock heard muffled voices, growing louder as they descended the stairs. The words became audible as they reached the level where he was hiding.

"...telling you that the way those students keep digging for information about The Horde is going to cause trouble. They must have gone through every book in that section of the library by now. The lack of detail is bound to increase their curiosity." It was the voice of Master Tennison, the librarian.

"What would you have me do, Frederick?" It was a female's voice. "We teach Lore for a reason. Curiosity is a positive trait for a student of Lore. Besides, the answers they seek are down here, safe and secure.

They will eventually tire of their search and will move on." They stopped one aisle from where Brock was hiding.

"Just make sure that Mae keeps them in line when they come asking the tough questions," he replied. "I'll handle it if they decide to pursue the issue here at the library."

Another voice broke in. "I'm sure it will be fine, Fred." It was Vandermark. "It's not the first time we've had curious students asking questions we choose to not answer. It's the way of the world. People feel they need to seek truth. It's our job to ensure they find the truth we have defined and nothing more. That's the only truth they need."

Brock heard shuffling as books were pulled from shelves. Tennison's voice followed.

"Here's what I have on the Tantarri. Let's go."

Feet shuffled, followed by footsteps retreating toward the stairwell.

"Good. Perhaps we can find something that will give us an edge," Vandermark responded as the footsteps and voices began to fade. "They've been a thorn in our side for too long. If we can find a means to destroy them, Archon Ringholdt would be in our debt. I might even..." His words faded.

Brock remained still for a few minutes. When his senses began to numb to the black silence surrounding him, he opened his cloak and blue light streamed out. He pushed a chair aside and crawled from under the table.

After creeping to the aisle where the masters had been standing, Brock found gaping openings where books had been removed from the shelf. A thick book near one of the gaps caught his attention. The binding read *The Wailing War*.

He lifted the heavy tome and began paging through it, immediately finding references to The Horde. Lowering his pack, he slid the book inside as a dusty volume on the bottom row caught his eye. The cover had an odd rune, one he didn't recognize. On impulse, he grabbed the book and stuffed it into his pack.

Moments later, he was at the top of the stairwell. Not hearing anyone above, he twisted each of the internal locks and pushed the door open.

He climbed out, lowered the trap door, and made for the exit. Sliding the bolt to unlock it, Brock peeked out to find the hallway empty. He slipped out and headed back to his room.

PART V

DISCOVERIES

33

With Benny off finalizing the design for their catapult, Brock began reading the book he had taken from the library archives. It was interesting and included far more detail than expected, but it contained so many pages. It was going to take a while to get through the whole thing.

After five hours of reading, Brock closed the thick book and rubbed his tired eyes. He stored the book safely in a desk drawer before stepping out into the hall and locking the door behind him. His stomach growled in protest, reminding him that he hadn't eaten since breakfast.

As he headed toward the dining hall, he reflected on something he had read in the early pages of the book. The volume's timeline began by noting something that had appeared in the sky a few months prior to the invasion. What it was hadn't been determined. The book also included information on the seven kingdoms that occupied the continent at the time, providing background on the structure and agenda of each kingdom.

Passing through the empty dining hall, he entered the kitchen and found Shirley giving dinner preparation instructing to her assistants. When she spotted Brock, she told the workers to get to work and then rushed over to greet him.

"Hello, Brock. It's nice to see you. Did you need something?"

"Hello, Shirley. What do you have to eat? I never made it in for lunch."

"I have just the thing."

She headed to the back of the kitchen, returning moments later with a bowl in hand. Brock eagerly accepted the bowl, which was steaming with the aroma of cooked beef.

"I kept the left-over stew from lunch simmering in case anyone came in late." She handed a spoon to him. "Would you like a hard roll to go with it?"

"That sounds wonderful," Brock replied.

She sped off again, returning with a small towel wrapped into a ball. It felt warm in his hand.

"There are two rolls in there, Dearie." She winked at him. "I was keeping a few warm in case someone special showed up. Good thing, too."

"Thanks again, Shirley," he said. "You're the best."

"Why thank you, Brock." She gave him a wide smile. "Are you sure you don't want to work in the kitchens again?"

He shook his head. "Sorry, but my path leads elsewhere. I'll be sure to stop by often, though."

Rather than sit alone in the dining hall, Brock decided to head outdoors and enjoy the weather. He hadn't seen much of the sun recently.

When he stepped outside, he was greeted by a distinct briskness in the air. The sun's rays were enough to make it comfortable, but it would cool significantly after sunset. Cold nights had become a common occurrence recently. The result was an amazing sight he hadn't experienced before.

Scanning the valley before him, Brock's eyes drank in a view spiced by a variety of color. While the pines still sported their deep green needles, the leaf trees had transformed. Reds, oranges, and yellows now mixed in with the greens. He was told that those leaves would soon abandon their trees, drifting to the ground to leave the branches bare until spring. For now, the color depth of the valley was gorgeous.

A voice interrupted the serenity of the moment.

"Beautiful, isn't it?"

He turned to find Ashland beside him. For a second, he didn't recognize her, having never seen her with her hair down. With the late afternoon sun shining upon her, she almost glowed. The curls of her long brown hair perfectly complemented her tawny skin. Her striking blue eyes squinted in the sunlight as she looked out across the colorful valley.

Still staring at her, Brock replied, "Yes. Quite beautiful."

She glanced toward him and smiled at the compliment, the expression increasing her beauty exponentially. Brock's heart began to thump.

"What have you got there?" she asked.

He had forgotten about the food he was holding.

"Oh. Just some rolls and a bowl of stew. I missed lunch, so Shirley helped me out."

"Would you like to sit and eat?" she asked.

He nodded. "That's a good idea."

"Come on then."

She descended the stairs with Brock close behind. They crossed the lawn with her in the lead. Ashland took a seat on a bench near a large leaf tree, patting on the spot beside her. He sat and scooped a spoonful of stew into his mouth. The taste was good, but the stew had grown cold.

As he chewed, he unwrapped the rolls.

"Would you like a roll?"

She nodded, tearing off a small piece and popping it in her mouth.

They sat in quiet, enjoying each other's presence. He found himself thinking that this was something special, enjoying this amazing sight with Ashland beside him.

She cleared her throat, breaking the silence. "This is only my second autumn here, but I can't imagine growing tired of this sight."

"It is beautiful," Brock said. "Did the leaves change colors and fall off where you grew up?"

"Yes...and no," she replied. After a moment, she explained, "When I lived with my parents, we were in a place where the leaves did change colors. When the leaves fell, my father would push them into piles so I could jump in them. It's one of my fondest memories."

Sensing she was sharing something, he remained silent.

"When I was ten summers, my parents sent me to the coast to live with an uncle. That's where I began my education, preparing for the Academy. There, the leaves did not change. I was no longer allowed to play in the fallen leaves. Actually, I was no longer allowed to play at all." Her demeanor became somber as she fell silent. She looked out at the horizon when she next spoke. "But I guess it was worth it. I did it. I'm now an apprentice at the Academy."

Brock nodded. He understood. "I believe there are a few students who've made sacrifices to be here. I also believe those students appreciate the opportunity far more than those who've had everything handed to them."

Ashland turned toward him. Her blue eyes studied his intently.

"I'm sorry, Brock," she said.

He was confused. "You're sorry?"

"Yes." She put her hand on his, staring down at the long grass. "I'm sorry I was rude to you when you first came here. As you are now aware, I had to make some sacrifices to be here. I seem to ignore that there are others who appreciate the opportunity."

Her eyes met his, drifting closer. Feeling an intense draw, a desire that began with his brain and extended to his body, Brock closed the distance. They were almost touching, holding still as if locked in an invisible state of tension. The tension increased, their breath quickening, and then it broke.

The kiss was warm, deep, and urgent. It seemed as if the kiss had always been there, waiting for months to happen. When it finally did, the release was wonderful. He felt like he had never felt before. He didn't just connect with this girl. In this kiss, Brock knew he could be more, was more, than he ever knew.

The thump and clang of the bowl and spoon tumbling to the ground disturbed the perfect moment. They pulled away, glancing down at the bowl as it rocked on its side in the grass.

When his eyes met hers again, a chuckle burst out from his lips. Another followed. By the third, she had joined him. They laughed for a bit until she suddenly leaned close and hugged him. Reciprocating the hug, he squeezed her as tight as he dared. With her face buried in his shoulder, it took a moment before he realized she was crying. He just held her, enjoying the contact, yet concerned at the same time.

After a bit, he spoke. "What is it? Can I help?"

She pulled away, wiping tears from her face. "I've just been so lonely. I...I haven't let anyone get close since I came here." She looked into his eyes. "I've been fighting it for some time, but you interest me, Brock Talenz. I...I like you."

He smiled. Hearing those words from this girl lit a flame of pure joy in his heart. "I like you, too. I really like you. I just didn't think you liked me. In fact, I had no idea how you felt."

She nodded. "I know." She smiled. "But now you know."

Brock smiled. "Now I know."

They sat in silence for bit, with Ashland's hand gripping his as if he would disappear if she let go.

"Did you love her?" she asked in a quiet voice.

"What? Who?" Brock asked before his mind cleared. "Do you mean Amber?"

Without looking at him, she replied, "I heard that you two were...close."

He thought for a moment. How did he honestly feel about Amber? In reality, he barely knew her.

"I wouldn't say that I loved her." He considered how to describe what he felt. "I...was attracted to her, I guess. We met by chance, and... she expressed interest in me. However, we never had time to see where it would go. In reality, I only knew her a few days...and then...she was gone."

He was surprised by how little of the sting of Amber's death remained. His connection with Ashland seemed to make the loss of Amber seem less painful. He realized that his relationship with Amber was superficial, never getting the chance to be anything more than physical. With Ashland, there was something profound between them before they had even kissed.

He turned toward her, cupping her cheek in his hand as he stared into her eyes.

"I can tell you that I feel something different with you. Something... special. Something I've never felt before...about anyone."

Her eyes were fixed on his, shifting as if to search out the truth of his words. A tear slid down her cheek. Her face drew close until her cheek touched his. He felt her breath on his neck. Their heads slowly turned until their lips met. He melted into the kiss. The world swam. It was glorious.

When he pulled away, her eyes remained closed, his hand still cupping her cheek. He swiped his thumb, wiping the tear away.

Her eyes opened, and she smiled. It was as if the sun had suddenly appeared in the sky.

She pulled back, wiping her eyes. "I should get going. I have a few things to prepare for class tomorrow. Master Varius has high expectations."

"I understand," Brock replied. "However, you need to understand that I plan to miss you until I see you again. I hope you can handle that."

She smiled. "I think I can handle that."

Brock bent and retrieved his bowl and spoon. "I better return these, or Shirley will have my hide for sure."

When they stood, Ashland kept her arm around his. The weight of her bumping into him as they walked was pleasant. They angled across the lawn to enter the doors closest to the Girls' Wing. Brock walked her to the stairwell leading to her floor. The hallway was empty except for the two of them.

"Goodnight, Brock," she said, stepping away.

Rather than release her, he pulled her close for one last kiss.

"Goodnight," she said, retreating.

"Goodnight, Ashland," he replied, smiling.

Even after she disappeared around the stairwell landing, his heart was singing. This girl. He felt something special for this girl. More than ever before, Brock thought that life was beautiful.

Life was filled with pain. It seemed as if every inch of Brock's body hurt. He closed his eyes, willing the hot water to soak his aches away.

Four weeks had passed since he and the other novices moved from hand combat to weapons in their Paladin training. During those weeks, the students had been sparring with wooden swords, short and long, as well as quarterstaffs. Brock had fared well, getting the better of every foe he faced until today.

After the forms practice, Budakis had pulled him aside for a private conversation.

"I'm sorry to do this to you, but I have no choice." The large man stared into Brock's eyes. "Your roommate has been thumping every opponent he's faced." He glanced toward Cam, who was practicing his sword stances. "I try to match sparring partners so they're similar in size or strength. Unfortunately, Cameron DeSanus has made that impossible. No other student over six feet can match his quickness. In fact, only a few students in the whole school have any hope." He turned back to Brock. "Only one of those students is in this class."

Brock stared into the man's eyes as the words began to sink in. "You want me to spar with Cam?" He glanced toward his mountain of a roommate. "He's twice my size. He'll crush me."

"Perhaps. However, he cannot crush you if he can't hit you." He patted Brock's shoulder. "Don't let him hit you, and you'll be fine."

The man walked away and announced the first six pairings. The twelve students, in groups of two, spread out to find their own space on the floor. The other students waited on the benches, with Brock sitting beside Cam. His massive roommate leaned over to whisper to him.

"I wonder who Budakis will match me with today."

Brock snorted. "I wonder."

While staring at the floor before him, Brock's mind raced. *How am I going to spar with Cam and not get killed?* He saw how the other students had fared. Broken bones were a regular occurrence. Two students were injured badly enough that they required a week of rest even after being healed. Despite wearing a helmet when sparring, one boy was hit in the head so hard that he still couldn't walk straight. That was two weeks ago.

When the matches ended, Budakis called out the next six pairings. Although he knew it was coming, Brock winced when his name was called right after Cam's. At least the big guy had the grace to look surprised before his expression became a grin. As they strolled to an open area, Brock pleaded to Cam.

"You can at least have the courtesy to stop smiling. I know you're going to kill me."

Brock slipped his helmet on. He didn't want his brains to leak out when he was thumped in the head.

Cam shook his head. "No. You don't understand. I was smiling because I think you're the one person in the class who will provide a challenge. You're quick, Brock. Really quick."

"Um...thanks. Somehow, I don't feel better."

Brock stepped back, holding his quarterstaff in a ready position. Cam adjusted his shield before raising his wooden sword. They both nodded, and a flurry of action ensued.

The rapid clacking of the wooden weapons colliding filled Brock's ears. He concentrated, blocking the fast strokes of Cameron's sword. Each offensive strike from Brock resulted in his having to dodge or block a counterstrike. Block, attack, block, dodge. Block, dodge, attack, dodge. The pair traded volleys repeatedly, leaving them both breathing heavily. Neither had experienced a match lasting nearly this long, and this match was exceptional not only in duration, but also in the sheer fury of the exchanges.

As he began to tire, Brock decided to attempt to end the duel. After blocking an overhead strike, he swiped at Cam's legs. The staff only nicked one boot. Cam had jumped, which would have been fine if he hadn't jumped forward. Thrusting his wooden shield at Brock as he descended, Cam's full weight slammed into Brock's head and shoulder. Air blasted from Brock's lungs as he was driven into the dirt floor. His vision blurred to white. *Am I going blind?*

As Cam rolled off him, pain rushed in. Brock tried to breathe, but air wouldn't come. Panicking, he rolled to his side and air finally filled his lungs.

Brock's ears rang and his head pounded. He sat up, realizing that his whole body hurt. As his vision began to clear, he saw Budakis staring at him with Cam looking over the man's shoulder. Next to Budakis was Jestin, the healer on duty. Jestin put his hand on Brock, closing his eyes briefly before opening them, shaking his head, and stepping away. Budakis smiled and gripped Brock's hand, pulling him to his feet.

Budakis clapped him on the shoulder, causing him to wince. "Wonderful match, Brock. I knew you could challenge the big guy."

Budakis turned to address the others. "Now that you jokers got to watch the big match, it's your turn. Pair up and get to work."

Cam put his meaty hand on Brock's shoulder, walking him toward the changing room. "Are you okay? I became so caught up in the match that I forgot whom I was fighting. I didn't mean to land on you like that.

It just...sort of happened."

Despite the pain he felt, Brock couldn't help but smile. That was the longest flow of words he had ever heard from Cam.

"I'm fine...I think," Brock replied. "Jestin didn't find anything serious enough to require healing. I just...hurt."

With a look of concern, Cam asked, "Where do you hurt?"

"Everywhere."

"Come on, we're done here." Cam put his arm around Brock. "It might help if you got a good long soak before lunch." He nodded as Cam ushered him to the baths.

That's where Brock remained, letting the heat of the water ease the pain from his sore body. Other boys eventually came through the baths, getting a quick rinse before returning to the changing room to dress for lunch. He relaxed and let the hot water do its work. When the bell rang, Cam popped his head through the doorway.

"Are you feeling any better? It's time for lunch."

"Yeah. I know." Brock waded to the side of the pool where his towel waited. He felt better, but would be sore tomorrow. He grabbed his towel and stepped out of the pool.

"Just give me two minutes to get dressed and we can go eat." Cameron nodded, smiling. He did love to eat.

34

B rock held the bolt and brace in place while Parker used a large wrench to tighten the nut. As he lay under the catapult, Brock reflected on how their creation had evolved.

For the past three weeks, the five boys had worked hard to build the perfect siege engine. It began with long nights and every Seventh Day spent in the Foundry. Guided by Benny, they crafted components for the catapult – cutting, drilling and shaping wooden beams for the frame and the launch arm. Using various casting forms, they poured steel to create all sorts of hardware. After two weeks of creating components, they moved to the massive outbuilding behind the Engineering Yard. The building contained fifty stalls, each large enough for a horse and wagon. Thirty of those stalls had been cleared to provide each team a space to construct and store their catapult.

For the past five days, the group of boys had worked late into the night, assembling Benny's work of art. As the machine began to take shape, their excitement grew. Other than Benny, nobody on the team knew how to assemble an axle and wheels. Only Benny understood why the stop rail had to be in a certain location in relation to the launch arm fulcrum. None but Benny would have considered reinforcing the launch arm with steel bands. They just listened to Benny and did as directed.

Brock had suggested that Cam, Lars, and Benny stop for the night while he and Parker stayed and assembled the last brace. With the brace in place, Brock crawled out from beneath the catapult, stood, and clapped a hand on Parker's shoulder.

"It's looking good, don't you think?"

Parker finished tightening the nut and stood upright, wiping sweat off his brow with his sleeve.

"I've never built anything before." He stared at the catapult. "The ability to take a bunch of raw materials and turn them into something useful is pretty amazing."

Brock nodded. "You're right about that. Thanks for the help." Parker smiled, which seemed a rare thing.

"Let's stop for tonight," Brock said. "Benny and I will come back for the final touches tomorrow."

He grabbed their cloaks from the wall hook and tossed one to Parker. It was cold outside, and they would want the cloaks for cover. Heck, it was cold inside the stall, and the boys would be shivering if they hadn't been exerting so much energy with the assembly.

As Parker secured his cloak, his eyes were on Brock. "He hates you, you know."

Brock looked up at Parker. "Corbin?" A nod confirmed his guess. "I expected that was the case. I'm not too fond of him either."

"I think you underestimate what I'm trying to say." Parker stepped closer, lowering his voice. "He hates you with a passion. He's making it a personal mission to destroy you in any and every way he can. I've known Corbin for ten years. I've never seen him like this."

"Okay. So he hates me in a special way," Brock replied. "I'm touched."

Parker looked down at the dirt floor. "When I first joined your team, he was upset, thinking I had betrayed him. Later, he decided on his own that I had made some clever move and was in position to make sure you fail." Parker paused briefly. "He wanted me to sabotage your catapult."

"What did you do?"

Parker's head snapped up, his eyes meeting Brock's. "Nothing. I told him that I know nothing about Engineering, which is true. I told him that I'm never alone with the catapult, which is also true. I told him I'd do my best, but couldn't promise anything, which is a lie."

Brock stared into Parker's eyes, searching for the truth. "How can I be sure? I want to believe you, Parker, but I need to be sure."

Parker sighed. "I grew up with Corbin. I've known him for most of my life. However, I never felt like I could call him a friend. He's not a good person. His father dotes on him and always let him do as he pleased, regardless of how it affects others. If he weren't being groomed to be the next Archon, I'd gladly be done with him forever." He paused, looking pained. "My father, who is Archon Ringholdt's chief advisor, has made clear what I must do. You see, since I'm also bound for the Hierarchy, I have to bow to the whims of Corbin Ringholdt and follow him around like he is a god. I need him to see me as an asset, not as a threat."

Brock's eyes narrowed. "So, you can't stand the pompous jerk, either. You pretend to abide by his rules, hanging out in his little clique, so you can ensure your career?" Parker nodded.

"Okay." Brock nodded back. "I can buy that. But how does it prove you're not out to destroy our chances in this competition?"

"That's simple. It's because I think you can win." Parker grinned. "Your winning this competition would infuriate Corbin. I'd love to see him knocked down a notch. As long as I'm not culpable or seen as working against him, it's perfect."

Brock smiled. "Well, winning is what we plan to do. If you want, I can spread rumors that you weren't any help at all. I'll get Cam and Benny to do the same. Those rumors should get to Corbin and keep him from thinking you were part of our success."

Parker smiled again. "Thanks, Brock. That would help a ton."

Brock grabbed the glowlamp off the hook and flipped the latch on the stall door. The big door creaked as it swung open. They stepped outside and Brock closed the door, using the key to secure the lock. As they crossed the dark grounds behind the Academy, Brock noticed his breath steaming in the evening air.

Parker spoke again. "Brock, I know you're doing your best to beat Corbin in those mock trials. However, he's been groomed for that stuff his whole life. He knows every Empire law and how to manipulate the system when it suits his needs." Parker paused before continuing. "What I'm trying to say is that you shouldn't get down on yourself for losing to Corbin when it comes to Hierarchy. That's his domain. I suggest you focus your efforts elsewhere. I just wish I knew why you continue to get matched against Corbin in that class. It's as if Pretencia has it out for you, too."

Brock looked at Parker, raising an eyebrow.

"Oh, he does, doesn't he?" Parker shook his head. "For such a nice guy, you sure know how to get under people's skin."

"Thanks," Brock said sarcastically. He reached out and pulled the Foundry utility door open. "It's a talent I was born with, I guess."

~

A knock on the door woke Brock, his eyes fluttering open. He glanced over at Cameron, who was still sleeping. A slice of morning light streamed through the curtain onto the pillow covering Cam's head.

Brock slid out of bed, padded across the room, and opened the door a crack.

"G'morning Brock." Benny whispered. "I stopped by to see if you were awake."

"I am now." Brock whispered back. "It's Seventh Day, Benny. Why are you awake so early?"

"I couldn't sleep. I'm too anxious about the catapult. I also wanted to give you the book back." Benny held *The Wailing War* up so Brock could read the binding.

Opening the door wider, he waved Benny inside.

"How far did you get?" Brock whispered as he dressed.

"I'm caught up to you. There's still a lot to read, though. It's a big book," Benny replied.

"You've got that right."

Brock took the heavy book from Benny and opened his desk drawer, spotting the other book he had taken from the archives. He placed one book in the drawer and grabbed the second book, holding it in his hands to examine the rune on the cover.

"What is it?" Benny whispered.

Brock's hand slid over the embossed rune. "I don't know for sure. It's...something I took from the library."

Curious, Benny sat beside him, inspecting the book. "Open it and see what it says."

Brock opened the book, looking up at Benny.

Benny squinted at the inside in confusion.

"What language is that?"

Brock smiled. "I have no idea."

Benny looked confused. "If you have no idea, why take the book?"

Closing the book, Brock looked at the cover. "I don't know. There's something about it, something about this symbol."

Benny leaned in, staring hard at the rune. "I don't know that one. I have a super good memory. I know I've never seen that rune before."

"I agree," Brock said. "But, it's still special to me. I can't explain it."

"Are you two going to blabber all day, or can I get some sleep?" Cam peeked from under his pillow.

"Sorry Cam." Benny stood. "We were just about to leave." Stuffing the book in the drawer, Brock followed Benny out.

Once in the hallway, Benny squirmed in anticipation. "Let's get some food, and then we can go finish the catapult."

Brock smiled at how Benny thrived on the catapult project, making it clear why his friend wanted to be an Engineer so badly. It was certainly Benny's passion.

They grabbed a quick breakfast of porridge and fruit before making the trek out to the catapult. A layer of frost covered the ground, their footsteps crunching as they crossed the yard behind the Foundry. When they neared the outbuilding, Brock noticed footprints in the frost leading to their stall. Recalling his conversation with Parker, anxiety began to twist his stomach. He pulled on the door and it opened to reveal an empty stall other than the catapult and a few tools.

Benny looked at Brock. "Didn't you guys lock the door last night?" Brock pulled the other door open and more light bled into the stall. "Oh, I locked it alright. But locks are beatable, Benny." He held the key up for Benny to see, the only key that existed for this lock. "This is an easy lock to pick, a single tumbler."

Benny stared at his precious catapult, concern showing on his face. "Why would somebody break in here? Do you think they want to steal my ideas? The competition is tomorrow. That doesn't leave much time."

Although Parker's confiding in Brock was meant to be private, Benny needed to know. He told Benny of how Corbin wanted Parker to sabotage their catapult but left out other details.

Benny put his palm on the catapult as if to feel for a pulse. "I was awake when Parker came into our room last night. I put out the light, and we both went to sleep. When I woke today, he was still in bed. I don't think he left the room."

Brock nodded. That's what he wanted to hear, not wanting to believe Parker would betray them.

"Okay. For now, let's not worry about who was in here. Let's figure out what they did."

They spent the next few hours tightening nuts and bolts. Some were completely missing, two so critical that the launch arm would have torn off when tension was applied.

It was past noon by the time they finished. However, they weren't about to leave their precious catapult untended. Instead, they decided to take turns sitting with their creation to keep it safe from further tampering. Brock told Benny to go eat and then to find Cam. When Cam came to relieve Brock, he would go get food.

Benny left with Brock pacing outside the stall, lost in thought. He soon spotted a group crossing the yard as they headed toward the far end of the outbuilding. At the front of the group was Corbin Ringholdt. As he waited for Karl to unlock the stall, Corbin stared at Brock. A smile crossed Corbin's face when their eyes met. While Brock remained stoic, he felt the heat of anger bubbling within.

The door swung open, and the five boys disappeared inside. Brock stared in their direction for another minute with his emotions storming. He walked back into his own stall and put his hand on the catapult. A spark of inspiration struck him. He picked up a chisel and began carving the wood frame. He dug and scraped at the wood, shaping it to meet the image in his mind.

He stared at the symbol he had carved, running his fingers over the grooves. It was a perfect replica of the symbol from the book cover. He still didn't know what it was, but it spoke to him. It was something special. He could feel it.

With the catapult under Cam's watch, Brock hastened to the dining hall. It was late afternoon, and he hadn't eaten since sunup. Shirley, as friendly as ever, heated some leftovers from lunch for him. He stayed and listened to her chatting as he ate, chasing the food with a glass of milk. When he was finished, he thanked the kind old woman before leaving in search of Ashland.

He knocked on the door to her room, but when there was no response, he descended the stairs and headed outside.

Squinting in the late afternoon sun, he scanned the lawn from the top of the stone stairs, finding students scattered in small clusters throughout the wide space. After a bit of searching, he became anxious. He desperately wanted to see her.

Brock's heart leapt when he spotted her rounding the bend on the road that looped around the back of the complex. He hurried down the stairs and cut across the lawn to intercept her. She smiled when she saw him, quickening her step.

Just before meeting, they both stopped, looking into each other's eyes. Ashland's smile ignited a sense of joy inside of him.

"I'm glad I found you. I was beginning to worry," Brock said.

"Sorry. I decided to take a walk, so I made the loop around the backside," Ashland replied as she glanced down at her hands clasped with his. *When did that happen?* Her eyes flipped back up, their gazes locking. "I happened to see Cameron when I passed the Engineering outbuilding. He told me that you left to get food. I was hoping you'd be out here by the time I circled around."

"Really?" he said, smiling. "You were hoping I'd be here. I find that interesting."

"Are you mocking me?"

He pulled her close and her eyes drifted closed when their lips intertwined. Brock's head spun in the rush of the kiss. His body reacted to the passion building up inside, causing his pulse to race. Reluctantly, he pulled away, still holding her with his hands on the small of her back.

"I'm happy to see you, too." He gazed into her eyes.

She smiled and backed away, grabbing his hand in hers.

"Let's go for a walk." She pulled him along.

They walked hand-in-hand down the road that led to Fallbrandt. The leaf trees they passed stood bare other than a few rogue leaves, refusing to give in.

"I'm sorry that I haven't spent much time with you recently," he said. "It just took so much time to construct our catapult."

"Don't worry. I understand." She leaned over, hugging his arm close. "Remember that I was in your shoes a year ago, working with a team to build one of our own."

"Oh yeah. I forget about that," he said. "So, how did you do?"

"We ended up third." She then turned and smiled. "They kept our catapult, though. They keep the top three each year and tear down the rest for parts. Who knows, maybe they'll use it for something important someday."

He smiled back. "That's pretty amazing."

They walked in quiet for a while, just enjoying each other's company until Ashland finally broke the silence.

"Brock, I don't really know much about you. I like you, and I like who I see in you, but I don't know anything about you."

He thought about what to tell her. "I'm from a port city in Kantaria, on the Indigo Ocean. I had…a difficult childhood. I was close to my mother, but she died during my sixth summer."

Ashland stopped and put a hand on his cheek. "I'm sorry, Brock. I can't imagine how difficult it must have been to lose her when you were so young."

Feeling vulnerable around this girl, he shed a tear at his mother's loss for the first time in years. She wiped his tear away and leaned in for a kiss, her lips tenderly brushing his before pulling away. She flashed a smile, and he immediately felt better.

As they resumed walking, he continued his story. "Prior to my mother's death, my father seemed to love me a lot. After she died, he changed. In the years after, he became cold and distant. It's as if he forgot how to find joy in life. Luckily, I had my mother's sister to take care of me until she got sick this past spring. She died a few weeks later. I…I tried to save her. I was so close…"

Ashland stopped again, meeting his eyes. "Wasn't there a master healer at the city temple?"

"Yeah. But he wouldn't come to heal her." Brock's frustration at the situation resurfaced. "I couldn't even get a medicus to help. When I finally convinced one, the price was quite steep, and then it was too late."

Ashland was confused. "I don't understand."

He took a breath and answered. "My aunt was Unchosen."

Ashland stared at him for a moment and then nodded. "I understand."

She leaned in for a deep, long kiss. When the kiss ended, she gazed into his eyes as if searching for something within.

"Thank you, Brock. You just confirmed everything I thought I knew about you."

"And what is it that you know about me?" he asked.

Ashland's eyes lowered. "I know you're a good person and you have a good heart. I know you care about people and you'll do anything to support your friends." She paused, her eyes rising to meet his. "And now I know you see Unchosen as people who matter. You realize that they deserve to live full lives and have hopes and dreams like anyone else."

Not knowing what to say, Brock nodded silently. Something was happening. Somewhere along the way, something had changed. He now couldn't imagine living without this girl. He considered telling her that he was Unchosen. Just as the words began to form on his lips, she spoke.

"That's where it happens." She nodded toward the southeast.

Brock turned to look in the direction indicated. There was a half-circle mound near the base of the mountain, just north of the woods. Noting the horizontal lines crossing the mound, he realized it was seating for an outdoor arena.

"That's where the Catapult Challenge will be held tomorrow," she said.

Brock glanced back toward the Academy. "I didn't realize it would be so far from the school."

"You'll have to push your catapult all the way down here in the morning." She smiled. "That's not the worst of it, though. You have to push it all the way back after the competition."

He glanced back at the Academy again. It had to be two miles away and at least a hundred feet uphill. "Well, I'm glad we have Cam and Lars, then."

Ashland laughed. "That will help."

"Will you come down to watch?"

She nudged him. "You're silly to think I might miss it. It's one of the biggest events of the year. Don't you know that they close the school for the afternoon? Everyone will be there."

35

E veryone was there. Blue-cloaked students and purple-cloaked masters filled the benches along the slopes of the mound. Humming chatter filled the air as the spectators waited for the event to begin.

An engineering assistant came around with water flasks, handing one to each team. Feeling parched after an hour of pushing their catapult to the competition area, Brock took a swig from the flask before handing it to Cameron, who took a big drink before passing it to Parker.

Brock gazed across the academy lawn and found himself dreading pushing the contraption back up to the school. He glanced toward Benny, who rocked his shoulders while watching the last few competing catapults roll in. Consumed with anxiety about the competition, Benny had relieved Cam shortly after sunset the prior evening. When Brock opened the stall door in the morning, he found Benny sleeping under a blanket against a catapult wheel.

A count of the catapults lining the side of the field yielded 29 machines, including the two still rolling in. That meant one remained. Brock looked toward the main road, partially obstructed by the trees beside it. The last catapult slowly emerged, turning onto the narrow road that lead to the field where the teams waited.

"Oh no," Benny mumbled.

Noticing that Benny was staring at the last catapult, Brock looked harder at the contraption. Something about it seemed odd. After a moment, he realized how small the students pushing it appeared. The catapult was huge, easily twice the size of theirs. The launch arm of the machine wasn't made of one timber like most, but of three timbers bolted together with the middle timber offset so half of it extended beyond the other two. The basket on the launch arm bobbed high in the air as the machine rumbled along.

When the huge catapult came to a rest at the end of the line, the students pushing it began clapping each other on the back. That's when Brock realized it was Corbin's team. Led by Karl Jarlish, Corbin and his cronies had constructed a massive catapult.

A mixture of emotions stirred within as Brock watched Corbin and the others stroll to the judging tables for check-in. Soon after, the lottery would take place to determine the launch order.

Headmaster Vandermark stepped onto the field to face the stands as Master Nindlerod and another master engineer joined him. Vandermark waved his hands to quiet the crowd. When the chatter subsided, he addressed the audience.

"Students and colleagues, I welcome you to our annual Catapult Challenge. This is where our first-year students display their ingenuity and engineering prowess.

"Since most of you are familiar with the rules, I'll not dwell on them today. Instead, I urge you to cheer on the contestants and their amazing creations. If we're lucky, one of these teams will surpass the longstanding record of 1087 feet." He paused briefly. "Introducing one of the members of the record-holding team, please welcome Master Pherran Nindlerod."

The small man waved to the crowd as Vandermark continued.

"Master Nindlerod and Master Shim join me as the judges of today's event." Vandermark turned to the two engineering masters. "Master engineers, will you please announce the first team?"

As Vandermark returned to the judging table, Nindlerod stepped forward, holding a cone-shaped device to his mouth.

"Students and faculty, I thank you for joining us. I see some serious promise in the designs before you. It appears that my long-standing record is, indeed, in jeopardy today. You don't want to miss this."

He paused and announced, "Our first catapult team includes Salina Alridge, Jonnis Farkle, Herry Dangst, Merrick Tandlehoff, and Barton Hinks."

Nindlerod and his co-judge retreated to the judging table as the first team pushed their catapult forward. An engineering assistant stood at the launch line, explaining the process to the team as they rolled the catapult into position.

Jonnis waited beside the wagon that held the large metal spheres that they were to launch. Merrick and Herry cranked the launch arm back, locking it into position. When it was ready, Jonnis lifted a big metal ball, grunting as he shuffled to the catapult and dumped the ball into the launch basket.

Salina stepped up to the catapult as her team members backed away.

She looked toward the judges' table, waiting.

Nindlerod held the cone up to his mouth and shouted, "Fire!"

The girl pulled the release and the launch arm shot forward. The dark metal ball sailed into the air, arcing high before it fell and landed midway between the first and second line of stakes posted across the field. A female student ran onto the field with a thin rope, sliding a loop around the nearest post before running to the spot where the ball landed. After taking a quick measure, she unhooked the rope and ran back to the edge, where four other students waited. The students shuffled around until three of them stood side by side, each holding a sign with a number on it.

Nindlerod put the cone to his mouth and shouted. "Their first attempt is two hundred thirty-two feet!"

Some in the crowd cheered, while others booed.

Brock found the process informative. He now understood that the arcing lines of stakes were distance markers, the first line being 200 feet out and additional lines posted every 100 feet.

After a second launch that was slightly farther, the first team was finished. While they pushed their machine to the side, Nindlerod announced the next team and students with wheelbarrows retrieved the two metal balls.

The process continued repeatedly over the next hour, yielding mixed results, with none of the first ten teams launching a projectile beyond the 800-foot line. The eleventh team called was Corbin's.

Due to the sheer mass of their catapult, it took twice as long to push the machine into launch position. Two students cranked the huge launch arm back and Corbin dumped the metal ball into the launch basket.

Everyone but Karl backed away as he readied for launch.

Nindlerod shouted, "Fire!"

Karl pulled the release and the arm snapped forward, launching the ball high into the air. As Brock watched the ball sailing through the sky, he realized that the crowd was quiet. A low thump sounded from far across the field, a half-second after the ball landed. This time, it took the girl much longer to run out and measure the distance. When the measure came in, it took four students holding signs to score the launch.

Nindlerod shouted. "First launch, one thousand one hundred and twenty feet. A new record!"

The crowd erupted. Cheers and screams echoed above the applause. Corbin ate it up, facing them as he pounded both fists into the air, as if he had done it by himself. Brock glared at his enemy with loathing.

The next launch fell a bit short of the first, but it didn't matter. The record had been broken and Corbin had won. Frustration began to well up inside of Brock. He couldn't lose to Corbin again, not to that hateful jerk. His hand rested on the frame of the catapult, his fingers feeling the grooves of the rune he had carved. Without considering what he was doing, Brock seized his anger and frustration. He closed his eyes, drawing in the angry red storm around him until he could no longer contain it. His eyes flashed open and he poured the energy into the rune, which glowed red and pulsed briefly before fading. With the storm of emotion spent, Brock suddenly felt numb and exhausted.

"Brock, what are you doing?" Lars asked. "You need to move so we can push this thing into launch position."

"What?"

Brock stepped aside as the others pushed the catapult to the line. He hadn't even heard his team called. He followed the catapult, his mind distracted.

Once in position, Cam cranked the launch arm back, winding it as far as possible before Lars rolled the metal ball into the launch basket. With the catapult loaded, they backed away.

Benny had declined the honor of launching the machine, stating that he wanted to stand back and watch their creation. Parker wanted nothing to do with it because of Corbin. Cam and Lars both suggested that it should be Brock, who now took position.

Nindlerod held the cone to his mouth and shouted, "Fire!" Brock nodded and pulled the release.

Brock had always been quick, and Paladin training had honed that natural quickness to the point of lethality. In this case, that quickness saved his life.

When he pulled the release, the whole catapult launched fifteen feet into the air. After diving out of the way, Brock stood to watch the heavy catapult smash into the ground right where he had been standing. It held together, despite bouncing a few times before settling.

With his heart racing, he searched the field for the projectile but saw and heard nothing. In fact, it was dead quiet.

"Ha!" A voice burst out, breaking the silence. Brock turned toward the sideline where Corbin stood pointing at him. "Ha, ha! What a failure!"

Anger and frustration began to resurface. All that time spent only to have the ball not go anywhere.

Wait. Brock thought. It had to go somewhere. As he scanned the field again, searching for a sign of the ball landing, a puff of gray dust erupted from the tower at the far end of the Academy. A second later, the terrible sound of the impact reached him. Brock froze in shock as he tried to comprehend the scene.

As he and everyone else realized what had happened, pandemonium erupted.

Many people cheered. Others yelled that he had cheated. Some even began to proclaim it was some dark magic. A number of scuffles broke out in the crowd, requiring the academy enforcers to break up the fights. Corbin and members from other competing teams ran to the judges table to protest.

Brock ignored it all. He just kept staring at the settling cloud of dust, over two miles away.

~

"What a mess," Parker shook his head as he stepped over a pile of debris.

"It's impressive, isn't it?" Benny replied. "Just think – a projectile a foot in diameter can do this kind of damage. The hole in that wall must be twenty feet wide."

Brock didn't respond, feeling both amazed and depressed by the damage the catapult had rendered. Broken stone blocks were everywhere he looked. Splintered wood and torn cloth from crushed furniture stuck up from piles of debris. Everything was covered in dust. He stepped around the hole in the floor, perhaps four strides across. Glancing down, he saw broken sections of flooring floating on the surface of the girls' baths. He stopped near the huge hole in the wall and stared out across the lawn. In the fading evening light, he could barely see the competition grounds across the open expanse. If the trees had still been covered with leaves, he wouldn't be able to see it at all.

He couldn't fathom how their catapult launched the heavy metal ball more than ten times the record launch. It was bewildering.

"This will take us days, even weeks, to clean up," Parker grumbled, kicking a small chunk of stone that splashed into the pool below.

"Worse, it will be far longer before it's repaired," Benny replied. "And we're on the cusp of winter."

Without comment or complaint, both Cam and Lars began picking up large stone chunks, carrying them to the opening and tossing them out onto the lawn. Soon, they were all tossing debris through the opening, careful to avoid the hole in the floor.

Brock resigned himself to the task, knowing that the cost of the repairs would come from the twenty-five gold Imperials they had won. When offered the opportunity to reduce the cost by helping with the repairs, the boys agreed in hopes of salvaging some of the winnings. Unfortunately, there was still a chance of further discipline. If the masters decided the damage had been intentional, the boys could end up expelled.

While performing the mind-numbing labor of tossing debris onto the lawn, Brock's attention drifted to thoughts of Ashland. His heart began to ache upon realizing that he wouldn't be seeing much of her for a while.

Distracted by those thoughts, he lost his balance when tossing a large chunk of stone. He twisted and grabbed the edge of the broken wall. With half of his body hanging outside, his face ended buried in the gap between the two layers of the outer wall. As he began to pull himself back into the room, he noticed an object wedged between the bricks. Reaching in with his free hand, his fingers scrambled for purchase. Once he got a grip on it, he pulled his discovery from the wall.

Using both hands, he lifted the thick book and expelled a deep breath, sending a cloud of debris into the air. When the dust cleared, it revealed a gold starburst-shaped rune embossed on a dark red cover.

Brock's finger traced the indentations of the symbol. It enthralled him.

"Brock, what do you have there?" Benny asked as he stepped close.

"It's a book." Brock stared it. "It was stuck in the wall. I think it's old."

Curious, Benny flipped the cover open to reveal a message written on the inside of the cover and on the opposing page. Brock tried to read the note on the left and found it to be an unfamiliar language consisting of strange symbols. On the opposing page, he found something he could read.

Master Arcanist,

As I saw in my vision, you have found this book. If my vision holds true, you are the one who will sow the seeds of Chaos, the catalyst of change, destined to send shockwaves throughout the Empire.

I chose to risk my life and store this volume away, for I do not agree with the path they have chosen. Their fear and shame have driven them to this end. The memory of the destruction wrought during the war is too powerful to soon forget, and thus, they have deemed it evil and have erased it from the histories. With The Horde exterminated, they see no need for this weapon. They choose to ignore that without it, man would have lost and would be extinct. They fail to acknowledge that evil does not exist within power itself, but resides in the brittle hearts of men and by how they use power.

I leave this book to guide you and hope that it is enough. Unfortunately, it was the only one I could rescue from the fires. There may be others, but that is for you to determine. Use the knowledge contained within to prepare, for the survival of man may depend on it.

I foresee dark days ahead. The past will return to haunt the Ministry. The time for change is imminent. Seek out the light of truth, for it is your only hope.

May your heart remain light under the heavy yoke you bear.

To the distant member of my lineage,

Know that the words I speak above are true. Do your best to support the Arcanist. While he appears to be the pivot point of the struggle ahead, he is but a spark to ignite the inferno required and he cannot do this alone. The minds of man will be as important as the muscle in the dark times to come.

Issal's Blessings,

Master Byland Hedgewick

Brock turned the page to get a hint of what secrets lay inside the thick volume. He flipped through more pages, jumping to later sections of the tome. It was all the same. The entire book was written in the same odd language as the note inside the front cover – a language neither of them knew.

While he wasn't sure what to make of the message, Brock sensed that it was important to keep the book a secret. As he stuffed it into his pack, he noticed the wonder he felt reflected in Benny's eyes.

36

With few idle moments to spare, the weeks passed quickly. Between attending classes, working on assigned projects, and rebuilding the Girls' Tower, Brock's days were full. Unfortunately, that left no time to spend deciphering the book he had found.

In a race against impending winter weather, the boys and the hired masons worked past sunset every evening. With the days growing shorter, the weather also became increasingly colder. As if it were orchestrated, the first snowfall hit as they sealed the last stone block into the outer wall. While the work crew was relieved, clapping each other on the back, Brock found himself mesmerized. He faced the sky as the shower of white flakes drifted down, holding his mouth open as falling snow tingled his tongue. It was wonderful.

The next day, they moved inside and began repairing the damaged floor. The baths below had remained closed since the incident, forcing the girls to bathe in the Arena changing room. During the cleanup, the boys had removed all fallen debris from the pools. By the time they attempted to remove the metal sphere from the bath, it had absorbed a great deal of heat and was difficult to touch for more than a few seconds. After hours of cooling on the stone floor, they were able to haul the ball from the cellar and submit it to the master engineers for analysis.

The now-famed siege engine had been confiscated as well. The Academy faculty expressed a great deal of interest in the catapult as they attempted to understand how it had launched the heavy ball many times further than the previous record.

Thankfully, Headmaster Vandermark had determined that the destruction was unintentional and required no further punishment. However, the repair bill would consume the bulk of their winnings, leaving them each with two gold imperials from the five that they had won.

On the third Seventh Day after the Catapult Challenge, they completed the last of the repairs. After almost a month of dedicated effort, the boys were free from this extra labor. Brock made a visit to the baths, relishing the heat on his weary muscles. He then changed into clean clothes before going in search of Ashland.

During the past month, they had seen little of each other. They found time for short interludes in between classes, but it wasn't enough. On the days she wasn't having lunch with Master Varius, they sat and ate together. It still wasn't enough. Ashland deserved more attention than that.

After checking her room, the library, and the dining hall, anxiety began to churn inside. He really wanted to see her. He needed to see her. Stepping outside, he scanned the lawn, squinting at the brightness of the snow-covered ground. Scattered evergreens and bare gray trees were dark towers among the white fields. Small light flakes drifted from the pale gray skies above, but Brock ignored the snow. His focus was on finding Ashland.

With a mixture of inspiration and desperation, he headed toward the Ecclesiastic's wing. He stepped into the training temple, and his anxiety evaporated instantly when he saw Ashland standing on the dais, speaking with Varius.

Brock took a seat near the door and waited. Varius turned to descend the dais, walking up the sloped aisle and smiling at Brock as she passed him to exit the building. Sitting alone, he watched Ashland prepare the dais as Varius directed. When she finished, she glanced in his direction and a smile lit her face. Despite the distance, her smile made his heart sing.

Rising, he approached the dais as Ashland descended the stairs to meet him. His arms wrapped around her waist, pulling her in tight as he kissed her. Her arms hugged him, squeezing tightly. When their lips parted, he stared into the depths of her blue eyes.

"I've missed you," she said.

"I've missed you too," Brock replied with a grin. "Just for you, I'll try not to destroy any parts of the school for a while."

Ashland smiled. "Just for me? I do feel special now. In fact, I believe that the Academy owes me for preventing its certain destruction."

"Well, I owe you as well," he said. "I owe you some personal attention. Which reminds me: have you eaten dinner yet? I'm starving, and I thought we could eat together."

"No, I haven't."

She released her embrace and hooked her arm in his before walking him toward the exit. "Let's get some food. I'm sure my Master of Destruction is famished from his hard work."

Brock screamed as Budakis reset the break. The pain was intense, almost too much to handle. Tears and sweat streaked down his face as the healer stepped in to take over. Placing her hand on Brock's arm, she closed her eyes.

Glancing at the grotesque wound where the bone had broken through the skin of his arm, Brock longed for the healing to take the pain away. A violent chill shook him when the icy wave swept through his body. The air expelled from his lungs, leaving him gasping to reclaim it. He lifted his arm, marveling at the lack of pain. Even after being healed a half dozen times and acting as the healer another half dozen times, he remained amazed by the process. That it was even possible seemed beyond reality.

"Thank you, Fion," Brock said as she removed her hand from his arm. "I appreciate it. You're a wonderful healer."

A shy smile crossed the girl's face as her eyes flicked up at him, then away again. "You're welcome, Brock."

She bent over, her black hair dangling as she retrieved her basket. "Would you like some bread?" She held the basket out to him, her eyes not meeting his.

"Yes, thank you." He grabbed two chunks. With lunch soon approaching, he had been hungry prior to the injury. The healing left him famished.

The girl gave him a small bow and retreated to the stands. Brock tore a bite, chewing vigorously as he watched her depart.

"I'm sorry, Brock."

He turned toward Cameron, who held his sparring helmet under one arm.

"Trust me, if anyone is sorry, it's me." Brock smiled when confusion clouded Cam's face. "I'm sorry that I got stuck with you as my sparring partner."

Cam smiled. "Well, you did get me pretty good last week."

Brock bit into the bread and bent to retrieve his helmet, which he had tossed aside after the injury.

"I was able to fracture your leg once in what, seven weeks?" They began walking toward the changing room. "In the meantime, you've smashed me to the ground, broken four fingers, two ribs, and now my arm. That doesn't even count dozens of bruises and one throbbing headache. Thank Issal that we only spar once a week."

"I can ask Budakis to pair me with someone else," Cam offered.

"No." Brock shook his head. "Even if I thought he'd listen, it would send the wrong message. He says that we need to be ready to fight the best because you never know who you might face in battle. If I avoid fighting you, he'll think less of me. I don't want to let him down like that."

He chewed on the second piece of bread as he led Cam into the changing room.

Cam set his helmet on a shelf and unstrapped his shield. "We have another week before we next spar. Maybe you'll learn a move that'll put you on top again."

"Again? What are you talking about?" Brock said incredulously. "Every week, you've got me on the run for the whole bout, barely surviving and rarely even touching you. It usually ends when I slip up and you whack me a good one. I got lucky one time and that was because you stumbled."

"Well, you did get me," Cam said with a smile.

Brock rolled his eyes as he pulled his vest over his head and stuffed it into his laundry bag.

"In addition to not sparring with you, I'm looking forward to the battle tactics session tomorrow. It's become quite interesting." Brock sat on the bench to remove his boots. "At first, I didn't understand the dynamics, but it's grown on me. It's like a puzzle. It seems like a jumbled mess at first, but when you understand how the pieces fit together, it's beautiful."

Cam snorted. "Well, maybe you can help me because I'm still struggling with that stuff."

"Like what?" Brock asked, pulling his other boot off. "Do you mean terrain advantages? Or maybe the strengths and weaknesses of different military units? Or about field feints and positioning?"

Cam shrugged, "All of it, I guess."

Brock began to remove his breeches. "I'll make you a deal. I'll help you with tactics if you don't end up killing me when we spar." He flashed a smile at his large roommate.

"That works for me," Cam replied, his face serious. "I won't kill you, then."

It was growing late. While the sun set much earlier in the winter, it had been down for hours. Brock and Benny sat in the otherwise empty lounge, each hunched over a thick tome.

Brock stared at the gibberish scrawled on the pages of the book he had found. Between the symbols and the foreign text, he had no idea what he was looking at, the characters so fundamentally different, he had no idea where to begin.

A sigh escaped as he sat back in his chair. He took a sip of his caffe, which had gone cold while he focused on the translation. After looking over his pointless notes, he crumpled the paper into a ball in frustration.

"Why, why, why?" Brock slammed the book closed. "Why would he leave this for me if there's no way to understand it?"

"I don't know, Brock." Benny sat up, stretching his neck. "The book was put there hundreds of years ago. Maybe the language that's used was common back then."

Brock rubbed his weary eyes. They had been at this for a few nights. While Benny made progress in his research on The Banished Horde, Brock struggled. Benny offered to take over, but Brock told him that he felt a connection to the message and that it was something he needed to do.

"At least you're making progress." Brock pointed at Benny's notes. "What've you found tonight?"

Benny started, as if his mind had been elsewhere. "What? Oh, right." He picked up his paper, looking at the notes. "Well, I've pinned down the first recorded sighting of The Horde."

Brock's brow raised. "That's interesting."

Benny nodded. "There was a woodsman hunting in the mountains of southern Kalimar who stumbled upon a group of perhaps a hundred of The Horde. He was careful to remain hidden until they moved on. The next day, he reported the sighting to the Duke of a nearby coastal city. Of course, the Duke called the man's story about such monsters '*Either a fantastical tale intended to frighten children or the ravings of a lunatic.*' Because the story had been reported during an official court session, a court scribe duly recorded it. It wasn't until years later, in the rubble of this destroyed city, that the records were found."

"Amazing." Brock observed. "Such an early warning, completely ignored. Who knows how things could have gone if the Duke had sent a squad to investigate?"

Benny nodded. "The author of this book gathered similar records over the period of eight years following the war. The fact that he was able to gather these pieces and pull together a somewhat cohesive story is amazing."

Brock's eyes narrowed. "If that was the first sighting of The Horde, how did they get inland without someone seeing them land along the coast?"

Benny shrugged. "I don't know. In fact, the author asks the same question. He confirmed that after all of his research, he could never determine where The Horde came from."

Brock frowned. He had hoped to have that question answered.

"Well, you keep reading and taking notes," he said. "We'll take what we can get from this book and then look for more answers elsewhere."

Looking down at his book, Brock traced his finger around the starburst symbol on the cover. He flipped it open and gazed at the messages written inside. One note was gibberish, the other he had read a dozen times over.

"Why would he leave this for us to find without some way to understand it?"

As Brock's mind drifted, his tired eyes stared at the pages before him, losing focus in his weariness. The letters blurred until each word became a block of text. He stared at the rows of blurry blocks lined across the page. Two blocks in the first row, fourteen in the second, fourteen in the third, and nine in the fourth. He glanced over at the other page, seeing the same rows of blurry blocks. He sat upright, leaning closer when he noticed that the number of words in each row was identical from one message to the other.

Excited, he grabbed a clean sheet of paper and began copying the gibberish from the first message. After recording the first paragraph, he did the same from the message that he could read, directly above the one he had just written.

"What is it, Brock?" Benny asked.

Feeling thrilled, Brock's pulse quickened with excitement. He considered what he had written, recognizing one of the symbols. He now knew what it meant.

"Brock? Aren't you going to answer me?"

Brock grinned in excitement. "I've got it, Benny. It was right in front of me the whole time. He did leave us the key." He tapped on the open book before him.

"What are you talking about? Did you figure out one of the symbols?" Benny asked.

Brock nodded. "Yes, and a lot more. I found the key, Benny. Both of these messages are the same. They're *exactly* the same. If you understand one of them, you can figure the other one out. It's the translation." A goofy grin crossed Benny's face.

"I now know what the book is about." Brock closed the book, tapping on the symbol engraved in cover. "This symbol is the title, Benny. The book is about Chaos."

PART VI

CHAOS

37

"I still don't understand," Benny said. "What is Chaos?"

Brock leaned across the table. "Hush. Not so loud."

He glanced around, thankful that nobody but Cam was paying attention. Spotting a novice bringing a tray of food over, he waited to respond. The student with the tray was Hamish, the same boy who had the broken arm healed on the first day of school.

Brock thanked Hamish as he set the tray on the table. Parker was among the other novices delivering trays to students sitting nearby. When Parker's eyes met Brock's, he gave a brief nod before returning to the kitchen. Hoping to remain in political favor, Parker had opted to continue sitting with Corbin rather than accepting the privilege of eating early as part of the winning team.

Left alone again, Brock leaned toward Benny. "I don't know what *it* is. However, I hope we can find out soon. Regardless, I suggest we keep *it* a secret until we know more. Got it?"

Benny nodded. "Got it." He picked up his fork, holding it above his food. "But I wish I knew what *it* was and what *it* means to us. The note makes it seem...important. Important but dangerous."

"That's even more reason to keep quiet," Brock replied.

He looked at Cameron, who nodded while scooping food into his mouth.

"Stay quiet like Cam, here. He's a good example."

Benny snorted. "If I were to be like him, the only words you'd hear from me would be *I'm hungry.*" He spoke in a low voice, sitting tall as he mimicked Cam. "That is until after I finish my meal and then it's *I'm still hungry.*"

When Benny did his imitation of Cam, Lars burst out laughing.

"That was good, Benny." Lars pointed across the table. "He's got you figured out, Cam."

Brock chuckled. Cam shrugged.

Swallowing his food, Brock shifted to another subject.

"Winter Break starts the day after tomorrow. What are you guys planning for your time off?"

As usual, Benny responded first. "I'm staying here and doing some serious reading." He winked at Brock, causing his spectacles to twitch.

Brock looked toward Cam, whose plate was mostly empty. He held a fork full of food before his mouth as he paused to respond.

"I'm just hanging here, I guess. I need to study those books on tactics we found at the library." Cam shrugged. "I'll work on my sword forms, too."

"I should've guessed. What about you, Lars?" Brock asked the newest member of the group.

Lars shrugged. "Pretty much the same as Cam, here. I recently started using the great sword. It's a lot different than the longsword I had been using. I'm still getting used to having no shield for blocking."

Again, Brock nodded. None of those responses surprised him.

"What about you, Brock?" Benny asked. "What are you doing with your time off?"

He swallowed before replying. "I'm heading to Fallbrandt for a couple days. I haven't seen Tipper for about three months." He smiled as he thought about his long-time friend. "I'm going to ask Ashland if she wants to come with me." His grin grew larger.

"Oh, Brock. You sly devil!" Benny chuckled. The other two boys joined him at Brock's expense.

Out of the group, Brock was the only one who had a girlfriend. He had kept it secret for a while, but keeping relationships secret at the Academy was difficult at best. Some would say impossible.

"Yes. I know. You guys just wait until some girl finds her way into your heart." Brock quieted, his demeanor changing. "It's amazing. You find yourself longing to be with her as if you're missing a limb and aren't whole unless she's with you."

The three boys listened intently, remaining quiet until Benny spoke.

"Wait. You're saying that being in love is like you've been through an amputation?" Benny shook his head. "No, thank you."

The others stared at Benny as he shook his head seriously. A burst of laughter came from Lars, who gave Benny a friendly slap on the back. The smaller boy's spectacles flew off, landing in his potatoes and gravy. Brock and Cameron joined Lars, all three laughing heartily. Benny looked up with his hair disheveled and began to chuckle along with the others.

As often happens in the low mountains, the snow melted after a few consecutive days of sun, leaving the road to Fallbrandt a brown stripe running through the white fields before the Academy. Even the snow pack of the fields had dwindled, with brown grass poking through everywhere.

While Brock and Ashland traveled the gravel roadway, their path meandered in an effort to avoid puddles and muddy spots. Even then, their boots were filthy, and splatters of mud streaked the lower half of their trousers.

The ground became far less muddy where the road cut through the forest, since the nearly constant shade of the thick evergreens kept the road mostly frozen. They were thankful for the cleaner road section until they reached the edge of the woods.

As they emerged from the thick trees outside of town, Brock's boot slipped on an icy patch and he tumbled. With Ashland's arm looped in his, he pulled her down with him and landed on his back with her on top. He hit the ground hard, the air blasting from his lungs. His back stung, but he focused on Ashland. She stared down at him in surprise and then began to giggle. He smiled, chuckling to himself. She snuck a quick kiss and rolled off him.

Brock sat upright and realized they were both sitting in mud. He turned to find a horrified look on her face, and he began laughing again. "Now I'm a filthy mess!" she complained. "I don't have anything else to wear!"

She slapped him on the leg as he laughed harder.

Pushing off on a dry spot on the road, he stood. Once upright, he held his hand toward her. She eyed him warily.

"Don't worry. Dory will find something for you to wear. I promise," he replied.

After a moment, she relented. "If you promise."

He pulled Ashland to her feet, and she circled the mud as she continued into town. Seeing her backside gave him an idea of how muddy he was. He would need a change of clothes, himself.

When he caught up to her, he offered his arm.

"Oh, no. I'm not letting you pull me into the mud again," she said.

He laughed. "You do know that wasn't intentional, right?"

She glanced toward him with a small smile tugging the corner of her mouth. "So you say."

"Okay. Now you're just teasing me," he said, smiling back.

"Perhaps. Or, maybe I'm just a mystery to you."

"I wouldn't use the word *just* in any description about you," Brock replied. "But there's no doubt you're a mystery to me. It's a mystery how you make me love you so much."

His throat tightened. He hadn't meant to say it. It wasn't that he didn't love her; he just didn't think he should say it. Not yet. He was terrified she might not feel the same way.

Ashland stopped walking. Brock took two more steps then stopped, glancing back at her.

"What is it?" he asked in an innocent tone.

"You love me?"

"What?"

"You said that you love me," she persisted.

"Well, I guess I did say that."

She took a step to close the distance. Quietly, she asked, "Did you mean it? Is that how you feel? Please don't lie to me, Brock."

He swallowed hard as he stared into her eyes. "Yes," he replied, exposing how he felt. "I love you. I love you more than anything. I wouldn't say it if I didn't mean it."

There it was, out in the open. No turning back. A quiet moment of incredible tension stretched out as he waited for her response.

A lone tear streaked down her cheek. She grabbed him, hugging him hard with her head buried in his shoulder. He held her, far more gently than she squeezed him. While he enjoyed the hug, he still wasn't sure of what was happening.

She released her grip and lifted her head to gaze at him with moist eyes.

"I love you too, Brock." A smile blossomed on her face. "You make me so happy."

They kissed for a long moment, right in the middle of the road. It was even sweeter than normal as their emotion enhanced the moment. Lost in the kiss, they were oblivious to the world around them, to the roaring thunder of horses approaching.

"Look out!"

Brock turned in the direction of the shout and saw a carriage speeding toward them, the driver waving his arms wildly. He grabbed Ashland and jumped to the side, pulling her with him. The carriage roared past and they watched it race through Fallbrandt.

"I wonder what the hurry is. That guy almost killed us," he said.

"Who knows?" she replied. "I noticed that it was a Ministry carriage, though."

Brock took her hand. "Come on. Let's go get cleaned up. I can't wait for you to meet Tipper."

He led her into the inn. Still covered in mud, Brock stopped just inside the door. The bartender looked up from the bar upon hearing them enter.

"Brock!" James smiled. "It's good to see you. It's been what? Two months?"

Brock waved. "Hiya, James. It's been over three months now."

James walked to the end of the bar. "More than three months, huh? I guess time goes fast when life is good." He poked his head into the kitchen. "Dory! Your favorite boy is back!"

Dory strolled through the door a moment later, looking as elegant as ever.

"Brock!" She smiled as she crossed the room. "My, how we've missed you. I'm so glad you decided to visit. Now come here and give me a hug."

"Um....Well." He pointed at his filthy boots and spun so to show the extent of the mud on his backside. "We had a little incident."

"Oh my. You sure did. In that case, stay there for now." Her eyes shifted to Ashland, scanning her from head to toe. "And who's this pretty thing?"

"Oh, I'm sorry." Brock replied. "This is Ashland. She's my girlfriend."

Ashland smiled at him before addressing Dory. "Dory, it's so wonderful to meet you. Brock clearly thinks the world of you, and I happen to believe he's an excellent judge of character."

Dory stepped forward to take Ashland's hands in hers. "My, aren't you precious?" She looked Ashland up and down again. "This won't do. Tsk, tsk. This won't do at all. We need to get you cleaned up." Dory turned her head and shouted. "Libby, get the bath ready!"

Brock pointed at his backside. "What about me? I need to get cleaned up too."

Dory glanced at him before refocusing on Ashland. "Oh, please. You can bathe later. For now, go around back and tell Tipper that you need his robe. Give him those dirty boots to clean and your clothes for Libby to launder. You can wear the robe until it's your turn for the bath."

Dory dropped one of Ashland's hands, holding tight to the other as she led her toward the baths. Ashland glanced back, her eyes locking with Brock's before she disappeared through the doorway.

Brock sighed and stepped outside to find the sun obscured behind a layer of gray winter clouds, leaving a chill in the air. He tracked through the ankle-high snow around the side of the inn. When he reached the stable yard, he circled the building and knocked. The door opened a crack, a familiar set of eyes peeking out.

"Brock!" Tipper opened the door wide to give him a hug.

"I'm glad to see you, Tip," he said. "Sorry it's been so long."

38

B rock sat at Dory's table, accompanying the women he had eaten with numerous times before. Despite the heavy-falling snow outside, the dining room was full. Dory explained that when word had spread that Brock was back in town, women opted to brave the weather for a chance to see him. He asked how they had heard so quickly, and Dory confessed that she was the one who initiated the message. When he asked about Ashland, Dory told him that she was preparing for dinner, and he would have to wait until she was ready.

As if they had been going through withdrawal, the ladies around the table begged Brock to tell a story. After some feminine coaxing, he agreed. Dory called for the room to quiet and made him stand so everyone could hear.

While he was aware that the Academy kept many things secret, he expected that everyone had heard of the yearly Catapult Challenge. When he began his story, nods about the room confirmed his assumption.

Brock relayed his tale, building up to the moment of the big launch. He paused for a breath but the words he had prepared never left his lips. Instead, his jaw dropped as he stared toward the stairwell. Heads in the room turned to see what had captured his attention.

Ashland smiled from the landing with brown curls tumbling to her shoulders, perfectly framing her beautiful face. The black dress she wore had sleeves that wrapped around her upper arm and exposed her shoulders. The dress fit tight in the waist and accentuated her curves in a way that Brock greatly appreciated. Exposed to just above the knee, her well-toned legs mesmerized him as she descended the stairs.

When she reached the floor, he stepped forward to meet her, grinning as his eyes scanned the length of her body. She glanced down at herself, giving him a shy shrug when their gaze met again.

Brock took her hands in his. "You look gorgeous." He wanted to pull her close for a kiss, but somehow resisted the urge.

"Thank you, Brock. You look quite handsome yourself," she replied.

"Thanks. I borrowed some clothes from Garrett." Summoning the will to break his focus from Ashland, he turned toward the room. "Everyone, this is Ashland. She's quite special to me. I would appreciate it if you'd show her the same hospitality you've shown me."

He turned to face her. "Ashland, please meet my good friends, the customers of The Quiet Woman."

Ashland flashed a smile to the crowd and waved. Everyone clapped, shouting greetings to the newcomer. Brock led Ashland to her chair at Dory's table, pulling it out for her to sit. As Ashland took her seat, Dory stood and spoke.

"Now that our guests of honor are here, dinner will soon be served." She waved her hand in the air. "Garrett, please pour this young lady a glass of wine. Also, do fill the other glasses, as well."

With glasses filled, Dory lifted hers high. "To Brock and his young love: May Issal guide them to happiness." The women mimicked her words as glasses connected.

After the toast, he leaned in and whispered in Ashland's ear. "You look stunning. By the way, have you had wine before?"

Ashland whispered back. "No. It's…interesting. Not too bad, though."

He smiled. "Warms you on the inside, right?" She nodded, smiling at him.

"Brock." Dory spoke over the buzz of conversation. "I believe you have a story to finish."

"Yeah, right," he replied as he stood.

The room quieted, and he resumed his telling.

"After my rival's team broke the school launch record, it was my team's turn. We wheeled our much smaller catapult to the launch line. My teammates cranked the launch arm and set the heavy projectile into the launch basket. The metal ball," he held his hands a foot apart, "weighed about the same as I do."

"Everyone stepped back, leaving me alone with the loaded catapult. The judge yelled, 'Fire!' I pulled the release and something crazy happened. The coiled energy in the catapult caused it to jump off the ground, higher than the ceiling above you. I dove out of the way and rolled to my feet as the catapult landed right where I had been standing." Brock paused for the buzz that ran through the room.

"Luckily, I was fine. However, it was now dead quiet, and the heavy metal ball was nowhere to be seen. I scanned the field, looking for a sign of the projectile, but saw nothing. A feeling of frustration began to grip my insides until a cloud of gray dust suddenly billowed into the air. The heavy ball had finally landed, blasting a huge hole in the wall of the Academy, over two miles away."

The room erupted in amazement. It continued for a while before Dory could calm the room. Once quiet, Brock continued.

"Having launched the heavy ball such an amazing distance resulted in our team winning the event. However, we were also required to clean the mess we had created and pay for the repairs. The effort consumed my life for almost a month, which left little time to spend with Ashland."

He ended the sentence looking down at his radiant girlfriend. Her smile beamed back up at him. Heartfelt sighs echoed from the women in the room.

"I'm still trying to make it up to her." He returned to his chair.

Applause rumbled through the crowded room, followed by the hum of chatter as the women discussed the story.

Annabelle leaned toward him, putting her hand on his arm. "My Brock. As usual, your stories are incredible, yet ring of truth. I heard of the damage that struck the girls' tower from Abe, but he never told me what caused it."

Tina chimed in, "Yes. I heard about it from Marcus Sprill and his crew of masons. He described the damage and how lucrative the job was for him. He even mentioned a helpful group of boys assisting with the repairs."

Dory nodded. "As you can see, while Brock tells some amazing tales, they're neither works of his imagination nor embellishments." She turned toward Ashland as she spoke. "I'm sure you're aware that Brock is special. He lives a charmed life, on a path that will surely lead to greatness. He could use the support of a strong, beautiful woman at his side."

Their conversation was interrupted as Garrett and Saul began setting plates on the table. The aroma rising from the steak and steamed vegetables made Brock's mouth water.

"This looks delicious." Ashland noted.

"I'm sure it will taste as good as it looks," Brock replied. "Saul is the most talented cook I've ever known."

~

Shortly after dinner, Brock and Ashland excused themselves to join Tipper and Libby at their table in the back of the room.

Brock introduced Ashland, whom Tipper greeted with a hug. Libby informed him that she already met Ashland while helping her with the bath and getting her prepared for dinner. After the greetings, they engaged in conversation over a glass of wine.

As usual, Libby was quiet. Brock noted that her reserved nature was a fair contrast to Tipper's friendly chatter. She eventually interjected, asking Brock a question that had apparently been on her mind.

"Is it true that your catapult launched a big metal ball over two miles?" Libby asked, tucking her long black hair behind an ear.

Before he could respond, Ashland spoke.

"I was there and saw the whole thing. The story Brock told earlier, if anything, was understated. When the catapult launched, jumping in the air like that, I feared for his life. I stood as tall as I could, trying to see if he was okay. After seeing him standing with his friends, I turned toward the field to see where the steel ball landed. When it hit the tower and everyone realized what happened, things got crazy." She smiled as she spoke. "Students still talk about it in the halls. The engineering masters are out of their minds about it, trying to understand how it was possible. They even confiscated the catapult and the ball. Despite dozens of repeated attempts, I hear that it barely launches more than 1000 feet. The other masters seem amused by their persistence over the whole thing." Tipper nodded, turning toward Libby. "That's what Brock told me earlier today, when he first described the incident. The story is true."

"But that still doesn't explain how it happened," Libby protested.

"Libby, I don't understand it myself," Brock replied. "The engineering masters' inability to reproduce the results using the same catapult and ball makes it even more bewildering."

The conversation grew quiet with nothing more to say on the subject. Ashland asked a question in another direction.

"Brock, how did you and Tipper...become friends?" Ashland asked before turning toward Tipper. "Please take no offense, but it is exceedingly rare for an Unchosen...to be held in such high regard by someone with a rune, especially if that someone has the mark of Issal."

Brock turned toward Tipper, the one person who knew the truth about his past. Having never lied to Ashland, he didn't want to start now. He cleared his throat, about to speak when Tipper interrupted.

"I never met my father," Tipper began. "As you might expect, my mother was Unchosen. When I was a baby, she decided that selling her body was the only way to support the two of us. She and I lived in a brothel in Lower Kantar for years. It wasn't so bad. I had chores, of course, but I had food and a roof over my head. Men came and went – none ever seeing her as more than a piece of meat. Some beat her. Others fled after the coupling, refusing to pay for what she had to endure. As I grew older, I began to realize that it was tearing her apart, but we never spoke of it. She had no other solution given her limited options."

Tipper's eyes were unfocused, distant as he spoke of the past. "When I was eleven, she became ill. At first, it was just strange behavior, but it soon became far more than that. It was as if her brain was coming apart. She had delusions, ranting and raving about this or that. In a matter of weeks, she became a psychotic animal. We were kicked out of the brothel, left to live on the streets. Two days later, I woke in an alley next to my mother's cold, dead body."

Clearly feeling old emotions returning, tears began to cloud Tipper's eyes.

"I learned to survive on my own, often the hard way. I slept in crates, scavenged food where I could, and somehow made it on my own for six months without ending up dead or in jail. Then a steady round of cold winter rain hit the coast. For days it rained. Try as I might, I couldn't stay dry. Being wet on those cold nights must've been too much for my under-nourished body. I became ill, coughing so hard that I would spit blood. Soon, the fever became too much. Weak and alone, I curled up in a crate to die."

Tipper looked down, a tear tracking down his face.

"That's when Brock found me. I was too far out of it to remember myself, but he took me in to nurse me back to health. I woke two days later with the fever gone and only a heavy cough remaining. Given a steady diet of soup and other liquids, I was soon healthy. That's when Brock's father found me hiding in their loft. Brock and his Aunt Ellie had kept it a secret as long as they could. His father told him I couldn't stay and had to be out by sunset. However, by that time, I was healthy. Since then, Brock has been my best friend, always watching out for me. He somehow got me out of jail both times I was caught for stealing food. He would bring me something to eat every time he saw me, whatever morsel he could take without his father noticing. He gave me clothes. He gave me his friendship. Thanks to his annoyingly positive attitude, he even gave me hope when I had no right to hope. This past summer he brought me here." Tipper gestured to the room around them. "Now I have a job. I have a room of my own with hot meals every day. Best of all, I have a beautiful girlfriend." He squeezed Libby close as she rested her head on his shoulder.

Ashland wiped her eyes dry as her other hand squeezed Brock's.

"Thank you for sharing your story, Tipper." Ashland told him sincerely. "I'm glad your life has taken a better turn. Take care of Libby. She's a nice girl."

Tipper nodded back, smiling as Libby snuggled against him.

Ashland turned to Brock. "I know I've said this before, but I'm sorry for how coldly I treated you when we first met." She looked down at their clasped hands as she spoke. "I...I guess I thought you'd be pretentious like others at the Academy. Many have had everything in life handed to them. They lack compassion and perspective." She looked into his eyes. "As I grow to know you, I realize I was wrong. I realize that you're exactly the kind of person I was looking for. After tonight, I realize it more than ever. I love you with all my heart, Brock Talenz." "I love you too, Ashland Pym." Brock gave her a quick kiss.

Ashland turned to Tipper and Libby. "Well, it's late. We've had a long day. It's time to say goodnight." She stood, looking at Brock expectantly.

"Goodnight Tip, Libby." Brock stood. "We'll see you at breakfast."

Brock followed Ashland toward the stairwell, hesitating when he remembered something. "Oh, wait. I haven't gotten a room yet." Ashland took his hand. "Don't worry about it. I have a room." She continued up the stairs with an anxious Brock in tow.

39

They woke as one the next morning --Ashland's shifting causing Brock to stir. Glancing out the window, he could only see white through the frosted panes. He gave her a kiss and slid out of bed. She remained under the sheets as he got dressed.

"Are you coming down for breakfast?" he asked as he pulled his trousers up.

"I will in a bit. I need some time to clean up," she replied. "A girl needs to be presentable, you know."

"I think you look great right now," he replied, flashing a devious smile.

She laughed and threw a pillow at him. "You're horrible."

He caught the pillow and sat on the bed, leaning in for a kiss. Before it got too far, she pushed him away.

"You'd better go before we get started again," she said.

He sighed before scooping his tunic off the floor, pulling it over his head, and lacing the collar. After sliding his feet into his boots, he walked to the door and turned to face her before he opened it.

"I'll see you soon."

She nodded, and he slipped out of the room.

As Brock descended the stairs, the front door opened, blowing snow into the entryway. Tipper followed behind, stamping snow off his feet.

"It looks like it's coming down pretty hard out there." Brock remarked.

Tipper looked up at him. "G'morning, Brock. Yeah, it's more snow than I thought I'd ever see. I know that's not saying much since the first time I touched snow was only a few weeks back, but it's crazy out there. It's already well past my knees. I just finished shoveling a path to the road. Dory says if it keeps coming down like this, I'll have to shovel the roof. Can you believe that? Shoveling snow off a two-story roof?" Tipper shook his head. "I never thought it was a thing, let alone that I'd be doing it myself."

Brock reached the bottom of the stairs and glanced at the empty room.

"I'm pretty sure that Ashland and I are the only ones in the rooms upstairs. The weather will likely keep everyone else home, so it'll be a quiet morning. Do you want to eat with us?"

Tipper nodded, clumps of snow falling on the floor. "Yes, definitely. Let me get the snow off and I'll join you. I'll see if Libby is free as well."

"Sounds great," Brock replied before heading to the kitchen.

He stepped inside to find Saul taking pastries out of the oven. They smelled wonderful.

"G'morning, Saul," Brock said. "What's for breakfast?"

Saul turned toward the door. "Brock. You kitchen thief. Are you here to steal some of Saul's treats before they're ready to serve?"

Brock held up his hands. "Oh no. Not this time, at least."

Saul set the hot pan on the counter and began scooping the pastries into a basket.

"That's good. Saul has made a special treat for you today. Saul promises you're gonna like it," he replied in his odd third-person manner.

"Well, I can promise that I like the smell already," Brock replied.

"You go on out and have a seat. Saul will bring it out shortly."

Brock backed through the door into the dining room and spotted James walking in.

"Hi James. Can I get four cups of caffe? Tip and Libby are going to join Ashland and me for breakfast."

"Sure, Brock," James replied, walking behind the bar. "They'll be right up, with a little milk."

Shortly after Brock found a seat at a table, James set four cups upon it. Just minutes after that, Tipper and Libby joined him as Ashland was descending the stairs.

After enjoying Saul's cheese and pepper pastry, the two couples spent the morning chatting in the empty dining room. It was nearly noon when Dory strolled in and declared that the roof did indeed need to be shoveled because of the snow piling up outside. Tipper went off to find Garrett to help with the effort, while Libby excused herself to get the baths ready in case anyone wanted to use them.

That left Brock alone with Ashland. They talked for a bit and then Ashland put her hand on Brock's leg. It only took moments before it affected him. He suggested that they retreat to their room for some time alone. She smiled, grabbing his hand and pulling him up the stairs.

~

Brock was lying on the bed with his arms around Ashland when they heard a noise on the roof. The sound of footsteps was followed by a loud scraping sound going across the ceiling.

"Good grief," Ashland said. "It sounds like he's going to fall right into the room."

He laughed. "That would be very much like Tipper."

Again, footsteps climbed toward the apex of the roof, followed by the scraping sound of the shovel pushing snow. The footsteps began the third ascent, followed by a loud thud, a rapid scraping sound, and a trailing cry.

Brock glanced toward the window as the dark shape fell past.

He bolted out of bed, running to the window. He flipped the latch, yanked it open, and stuck his upper body outside.

Through the thickly falling flakes, Brock saw Tipper buried in snow. He was curled up on his side, holding his leg as Garrett trounced through the snow toward his co-worker.

Brock retreated into the room and slammed the window shut. He ran to the pile of clothes on the floor and began to dress.

"What are you doing? What happened?" Ashland sat upright in the bed.

He glanced up at her. "Tipper fell. I think he's hurt."

Brock grabbed his trousers, quickly sliding his legs in. He secured them at the waist and glanced toward Ashland as his reached for the door handle.

"I really hate to say this, but you might want to cover up."

She hastily pulled the blanket up to her neck before he ripped the door open and shot out into the hallway.

Brock ran down the stairs as Garrett dragged Tipper and a lot of snow into the inn. A grimace of pain twisted Tipper's face. Brock scrambled over to Tipper, ignoring the cold snow beneath his bare feet.

"Where are you hurt?" Brock asked.

With a clenched jaw, Tipper groaned, "My leg."

Garrett was frantic. "He hit his leg on the hitching post when he fell. I think it's bad."

Brock lifted the leg of Tipper's trousers. The blood on the outside couldn't prepare him for what was underneath. Just above the boot, Tipper lower leg dangled at an unnatural angle with two white bones jutting out. Blood seeped down the leg from the wound.

Garrett's face went white and he backed away.

Brock glanced up at Garrett. "Get him some food."

Confusion reflected on Garrett's pale face. "What? Food?"

Brock spoke louder, his voice firm. "Do it. Anything Saul has. Go."

As Garrett scrambled off to the kitchen, Brock focused on Tipper's wound. Needing contact with exposed skin, he placed his hand on his friend's forehead and closed his eyes.

From behind, he distantly heard Ashland's voice. "Brock! No!"

Ignoring her, he quickly found his center in the calmness of Order, finding it easier every time he did it. Extending his awareness, he found the source of Order within Tipper, disturbed by the angry red tempest of his wound.

Brock reached out with his mind, diving into the fury of red symbols swirling about. He pulled hard at the Order within Tipper, using it to surround and squeeze the massive mess of red symbols. The swirling storm of runes sped up and then began to unravel, the red threads dissipating into the blue until they were gone.

His eyes opened to find Tipper's eyes wide as he struggled for air. Tipper gasped and his body shivered violently. Brock looked down at his friend's leg, now appearing normal other than the dried-on blood.

Tipper was still trying to catch his breath when Brock heard Ashland descending the stairs. Garret burst into the room with a half a loaf of bread and a chunk of cheese, running to where Tipper lay.

Ashland knelt next to Tipper. "Are you okay?" she asked.

Tipper sat up, looking down at his leg. "Yeah. I'm fine now. Except I feel like I could eat a whole cow."

Garrett held the bread and cheese toward Tipper. "Food," he said, his face still white.

Tipper grabbed the bread and bit off a big chunk, chewing heartily.

Ashland looked at Brock. "How did you do that?"

He shrugged. "What do you mean? I healed him like anyone else would."

Pausing his chewing, Tipper chimed in, "That was amazing, Brock. I was afraid it would have to be cut off, but now it's good as new. It's a miracle." Tipper looked at Ashland. "You can do this too?"

She glanced at Tipper before focusing back on Brock. "Yes, but I'm not this strong. In fact, I don't think anyone is."

Brock looked at her. "What are you talking about? You're the best healer at the school, except for Varius I guess."

Ashland shook her head. "You don't know what you did, do you?"

Brock looked at Tipper, who was taking a bite of cheese, and then back to Ashland. "No, I guess not."

"Brock." She stared into his eyes. "You forgot to set his leg."

A stab of panic hit as the realization set in. She was right. In his desire to help his friend, he had forgotten to set Tipper's leg before healing it. By all rights, it should have healed at an ugly angle below the knee. Even if the bones had fused back together, at that angle Tipper would have barely been able to put any weight on it. Brock could have crippled his friend.

As he stepped into the lounge, Brock scanned the room. A few boys rested on sofas and lounge chairs, while others sat at tables. He crossed the room, heading toward a table near the back. Two familiar faces sat there, staring down at thick books and scattered papers filled with notations.

"Hi guys. I'm back," Brock announced.

Benny looked up, smiling. "Brock, it's good to see you. We were beginning to wonder if the snow had trapped you until spring." Cam nodded at Benny's statement.

"For a while, it seemed that way. I don't know if you guys have been out there, but the snow is chest high." Brock shook his head in wonder. "After two days of steady snow, it finally stopped. By then, Fallbrandt was buried. Everyone took turns shoveling, making paths so people could at least get around. That worked for a few days, but it was still impossible to get into or out of town.

"Late yesterday, the academy trailblazer came through town, opening a wide path. Unfortunately, it also left tall piles of snow, burying the paths to the houses and businesses all over again. Around mid-morning today, we finished clearing those paths. And now, here I am." Brock held his arms wide open.

"Trailblazer? That must be the big steam carriage that was making all that noise outside the other day." Benny remarked.

Brock nodded. "That sounds right. It's like a steam carriage with spiked wheels and some sort of snow grinder on the front. It's pretty amazing."

Benny nodded. "Yeah. It was pretty cool to watch." Then he asked, "What did you do with all that time when you were stuck in Fallbrandt? It must have been boring."

Brock smiled as he recalled the wonderful time he had with Ashland. "Somehow, we survived." Changing subjects, he asked, "What about you, did you make any progress?"

Benny started. "What? Oh, Yes. Let me see here."

Grabbing a chair, Brock sat as Benny dug through his notes.

"Ah, here it is," Benny said, turning to address him. "First, I've confirmed that you were correct. The notes from Byland Hedgewick are definitely the key to translating the book. While the two messages don't cover every word and symbol, they cover enough that much of the rest can be deduced."

He tapped on his notes, excited. "The first thing I've learned is that Chaos is a natural force. It has something to do with change and destruction. It sounds a lot like Order, but the opposite, if you know what I mean."

Brock nodded. That made sense and felt right. "Okay. That's a start. Then what?"

Benny continued. "Well, like Order, there's a small part of the population that can, or could back then, manipulate it."

Brock nodded again, feeling excited by the progress. "I'm still with you. What else?"

Benny shrugged. "That's all I've got so far."

"That's it? In...how many days?"

Benny shrugged again. "Well, five days, I guess."

Brock realized he sounded ungrateful. "I know you're doing your best. I bet it'll go faster as more words and symbols get translated."

Benny shrugged. "That's true."

"See if you can find out how it works. Find out how Chaos can be used. We'll see where things go from there."

Benny nodded. "I'll do my best. However, there's only one day left before classes start again."

Brock smiled. "Yeah, but now I'm here to help you."

40

"Healing will remain your primary objective throughout the year. It's still the single most important resource the Academy can provide," Master Varius explained to the class. "However, healing isn't the only ability involving the use of Order. While you'll continue to spend one day a week as healers for Paladin training, it's time to cover something new."

"I'm aware that most of you have been unable to successfully heal. I expected as much, for it is a rare talent. However, this next ability is far more common."

She turned and tapped on a tapestry depicting a pyramid of twenty-one symbols with the rune representing Order at the top.

"These are symbols you've seen your whole life. The citizens of the Empire are marked with these runes, determining their vocation. They define who they are and how they can best serve the Empire."

She stepped forward and continued. "Divining is the talent of looking inside a person to identify their potential. Similar to healing, you must reach a state of meditation and locate your own force of Order within."

Varius clasped her hands together at her waist. "When divining, you must place your hand on the subject's forehead. You then extend yourself and seek their sense of Order in search of one of these runes." She pointed at the pyramid of runes on the wall.

"A rune will be seen in your mind's eye. When this happens, there will be no doubt," she said with confidence. "Those of you who have a stronger affinity with Order may see other runes behind the first, aligned in layers. While the first is the strongest, you may be able to dive deeper and see one or two others. These other runes reflect lesser potential vocations that are inherent in your subject, each a weaker natural ability than the one prior."

Brock thought back to his academy evaluation. Without knowing what he was doing, he had performed divining on Varius, finding five runes.

"Find a partner and pair up for your first session in divining. Take turns attempting this ability until the bell rings."

Brock's first thought was to take Ashland as a partner. He waved to get her attention, but she shook her head, so he searched for a different partner, eventually seeing Hamish alone. Standing from the table, Brock walked over to him.

"Hi, Hamish. It looks like you need a partner."

Hamish nodded. "Yes, Mister Brock. Will you be my partner?"

Brock smiled. "Of course, Hamish. Would you like to go first?"

Hamish nodded. "I'd be honored, Mister Brock."

He slid his chair closer as Hamish put his hand in place. Brock felt the warmth of the palm on his forehead. Hamish closed his eyes and began to meditate.

Relaxing as Hamish did his thing, Brock thought about how it felt when divining Varius. He thought about what Hamish might see. That's when he remembered he was Unchosen. A wave of fear struck. What would Hamish see? Would he be undone and cast out of the Academy?

Brock's stomach rolled with anxiety as the minutes slowly passed. Finally, Varius called for partners to switch places. Hamish removed his hand, shaking his head.

"I have failed again," the odd boy said.

"Don't worry, Hamish. This was just your first try."

"No. I have failed repeatedly," Hamish replied. "I seem to fail at every-thing I try in this class and all others. The exception is my passion for Lore."

Brock realized the boy was a bit odder than he had thought.

"Just relax, and I'll take a turn," Brock said to him.

Placing his palm on Hamish's forehead, Brock closed his eyes and dropped into meditation. The cool blue calmness of Order was soothing. He reached toward Hamish, and a rune filled his mind's eye. It was the rune of Order. Behind it, he found *cognitio*, the rune of knowledge. Even further back, he could make out the rune of *mercator*. Not giving up, he pushed harder, sensing an additional three runes hidden in the depths of his mind. He opened his eyes to look at Hamish.

"Did you see anything?" Hamish asked. "I really hope you saw something interesting."

"I definitely saw something," Brock replied. He scribbled down the symbols he had seen on a sheet of paper. Once finished, he showed it to Hamish.

"Oh my! I knew I had potential for knowledge!" he exclaimed. "I don't care about these other things, but the knowledge symbol is so exciting!"

Brock was a little overwhelmed by the odd boy's reaction. "That's nice. I'm happy for you, Hamish."

Hamish leaned forward, hugging him. Brock looked toward Ashland for help, but she just giggled at his dilemma. Thankfully, the bell rang.

The sheer amount of snow brought by the blizzard swayed things in winter's favor, giving it a firm grip on the valley. Brock knew that spring would come eventually, but the initial thrill he had felt from seeing snow was long forgotten. Like the other students, he now remained in the warmth and shelter of the Academy rather than venturing outside.

Due to their busy schedules, he and Ashland had to steal what moments they could to spend together. While trapped within the Academy, those moments were rarely private. Brock cherished every meeting, meal, and conversation, but he found himself longing for the time they had spent at The Quiet Woman.

Like any other student, his classes and studies consumed most of his time.

In Lore, they studied the history and details of each of the major Empire provinces. As always, the timeline started after the Empire had been formed. It seemed as if the kingdoms that had existed prior to the Empire were forgotten.

In Hierarchist class, they had begun operating as an imaginary city court. Each student was assigned a position found within city government. Unfortunately, Corbin had the privilege of being the city prelate while Brock was relegated the role of clerk. Corbin relished his position of power, running their government with practiced precision while assigning impossible tasks to Brock, berating him publicly at any misstep.

Frustrated with the situation, Brock approached Pretencia with his complaint. The master hierarchist told him that Corbin was within his rights as prelate and that Brock needed to adapt if he were to survive within the Hierarchy. In hindsight, Brock realized that he should've expected such a response. Pretencia seemed to hate him almost as much as Corbin did.

Thankfully, things proceeded far better in his other classes.

Paladin class continued on course, further honing Brock's speed, strength, and flexibility with a vigorous training program augmented by the mental and physical precision required to perfect weapon combat forms. The most intense day of the week was always sparring day, where Brock was faring better of late and rarely required healing.

In ecclesiastics, divining had proven to be far easier than healing. In fact, Brock could easily discern five or more runes in every subject he read. Unfortunately, he continually had to manipulate the situation to prevent being discovered as Unchosen. He tried to pair with students who had never displayed any ability with Order. When that didn't work, he made sure the other person never had the chance to perform divining on him. He felt relieved to escape the situation on the days he had healing duty. Not only did it allow him to be close to Ashland, but he also found that he felt stronger whenever they were together.

Engineering class had transitioned to new concepts. As usual, Nindlerod started with theory in the classroom, presenting the basic principles involved. As usual, most of the class failed to grasp the instruction. When they moved into the Foundry, he used demonstrations that helped them better understand the concept. As always, Benny embraced every new subject with excitement and enthusiasm.

When Nindlerod announced another competition coming in the spring, Benny was thrilled. This contest was wide open, allowing any student interested to present an invention of his or her choosing. Each creation would be judged for its potential uses and ingenuity with gold awarded for the winning design.

At dinner that evening, Benny informed the others that he was working on an invention that would win and make him famous. When Brock asked for details, Benny stated that he needed to finish his design before he revealed anything.

Brock and Benny later met in the boys' lounge to discuss the progress they had made in their research. Each with a cup of caffe in hand, the two boys sat alone at a table, away from the other students in the lounge. Benny brought the notes from his research on the Wailing War. Brock did the same on his translation of the book on Chaos.

"I'm over halfway through the book now," Benny said. "I've found a few interesting things of note about The Horde. First, they attack exclusively at night. In fact, fighting during the day seems to be a weakness of some sort. Thus far, they have crushed every city and kingdom force they faced, so that weakness hasn't come into play. In a matter of months, they had completely overrun the eastern kingdoms. I'm now at the part where the kingdoms of the west have acknowledged that they have to do something. However, they refused the first overture to band together under the Ministry's leadership. It seems they were distrustful of the others."

Brock nodded. "That pretty much aligns with the stories we've been told. Only the note about The Horde attacking at night seems to be something new. I wonder what it means."

Benny shrugged again. "I've no idea."

As Brock reflected on the information, Benny slipped his notes into his thick book. He then turned to Brock with an eyebrow raised.

"Did you hear about Salina?"

"Salina? The girl in our Engineering class?" Brock asked.

Benny nodded. "Yeah. She disappeared during winter break and hasn't been seen since."

Brock's brow furrowed. "Disappeared?"

"Yeah. I thought it was odd too, but I was told that one or two students disappear every year," Benny said. "I guess they give up and go home or something. Still seems weird to me."

Brock nodded. He couldn't imagine quitting on his dream.

Benny poked Brock. "Okay. It's your turn. What have you found?"

Pulling his notes out, Brock glanced at them before he spoke. "Well, I can tell you that it's slow going. Translating one word at a time and only having the key for one word in four is difficult, as you know." He tapped on the thick book with one finger. "I've made some progress, though. It appears that this book was intended to help others understand Chaos and instruct them on how to use it."

Benny nodded. "Good. I'd hoped as much."

"Many of the sentences contain nothing of note, only framing the subject or providing unnecessary details. Of course, there are many words that I can't translate at all. More importantly, as I progress, I've been able to use deduction to fill in some gaps. The list of translated words and symbols is now twice what it was when we started."

Benny grew excited. "That's great, Brock. It'll take a while, but we should eventually be able to translate most of the words."

Brock nodded. "Yes, but we're still many days from reaching that point." He opened the book. "We still have a few hours before we need to sleep. You get to reading, and I'll see if I can get another page or two translated."

Benny nodded. "Good idea."

The two boys ended up working late into the night, far later than they had planned.

~

Master Budakis nodded. "Good! Very good." He walked the floor, watching students going through their forms. "Okay, now stop and assemble at attention."

The students formed a line stretching across the Arena floor. Budakis examined the stance of each student, nodding in satisfaction as he paced down the line.

"We're now well past the mid-point of the school year. I've watched you transform since your first day." He stood before them with his hands clasped behind his back and his barrel-like chest thrust out. "From a pathetic beginning, you've grown fit and strong. While some will always be better than others in combat, you can at least defend yourself against an unskilled opponent. A few of you might even present a challenge to a master paladin."

Budakis continued as he again paced along the line. "Thus far, you've only sparred against the students in this group and you have a feel for how your skills compare against those who stand beside you. I'm happy to tell you that will soon change." He smiled before continuing.

"In three weeks, we will hold a three-day tournament, marking the end of the winter season. In this competition, some of you will have the chance to measure your skills against the best the Academy has to offer. The winner of the tournament will be crowned this year's Arena Champion."

He paused again, letting these words sink in. "However, we cannot let everyone into this tournament. Your weekly sparring matches have helped me determine which of you have the skills to compete. When I call your name, please step forward."

Reaching into his waistband, he pulled out a sheet of paper. Unfolding it, he began reading names off. As Brock expected, Cameron and Lars were both among those listed. As he feared, his own name was also on the list. When Budakis was finished, only eight of the sixty students had been called.

He folded the paper and addressed the class. "Everyone who hasn't been called is excused."

Budakis watched the students shuffle toward the changing rooms, while Brock and the others, including five boys and two girls, waited for what came next. Once the floor cleared, Budakis addressed them.

"Congratulations. You've been selected to participate in this year's Arena Championship. This is your chance to prove your skills to the whole school." His arms spread wide, his body rotating as he spoke. "These stands will be filled with fellow students and masters, cheering you on. You'll feel an energy in this building like never before. When you stand victorious over an opponent, backed by the roar of the crowd, it's a high like no other."

He lowered his arms and flashed a big grin. "Of course, for every winner, there's also a loser. It isn't grand to be publicly embarrassed in front of your peers. That's why you should focus on your training for the next three weeks." He stared hard at the small group of students. "As a little incentive, each student will also earn one silver for every victory. If you advance to the finals, you get a bonus of one gold Imperial. If you somehow find yourself crowned Arena Champion, not only does your name join the names of past champions, but you'll be also awarded an additional three gold Imperials."

Brock glanced at Cameron, whose face appeared stoic, focused.

Budakis grinned again. "Now that you know what to expect and why you need to prepare, you are dismissed."

41

B rock stepped from the changing room to the roar of the crowd. As the shortest, he was the first boy to exit. Corbin Ringholdt was the last, since he stood a hair taller than Cam.

With his helmet under one arm and quarterstaff clutched in the other hand, Brock led the group onto the Arena floor. He glanced up at the stands, packed with clumps of purple cloaks among a sea of blue. His eyes settled on one student in the front row.

Ashland told him that she had volunteered for healing duty, knowing he would be competing. While she explained that it was a way to guarantee a premium seat, he suspected that she was sure he would be injured and wanted to be there to heal him.

He came to a stop, turning to face the crowd. The thirty-one other novice contestants lined up with him down the center of the floor. He stood at one end of the line; the seven girls among the group at the other end, past where Corbin stood waving to the crowd. A prickle of anger began to simmer as Brock watched his rival bask in the applause, as if it were all for him.

Master Budakis and Master Kardan, who trained the apprentice and adept-level students, marched in and stopped between the contestants and the crowd. The masters made a motion for the crowd to be still. As the building quieted, the headmaster stepped forward to stand between them.

Vandermark raised his arms to greet the audience. "Welcome to our annual Arena Championship. Over the next three days, you will be treated to a series of duels involving the fiercest fighters at the Academy. For safety purposes, only wooden weapons will be used. However, I assure you that each bout will be filled with action and intensity, as if the fighters were battling for their very lives."

He gestured to the two men standing with him. "Master Budakis and Master Kardan will be the officials for this year's tournament." He turned to Budakis. "Master Paladin, the floor is yours."

As Vandermark departed, Budakis raised his arms and shouted.

"Listen up! I'm only going to explain the rules once." He glanced back at the contestants before turning to face the crowd. "This event will feature sixty-four of the best fighters at the Academy. Behind me are the first thirty-two entrants, all novice-level students. However, do not let their inexperience fool you. Trust me when I say that there is a high level of skill among this group, perhaps enough to win it all.

"Pairings for each round will be assigned by way of lottery. Once a pairing is set, the contestants will duel for the right to advance. Duels will continue until one of the following occurs:" Budakis held up a single finger. "A combatant is rendered unconscious." He raised a second finger. "A contestant has had a major bone broken." A third finger joined the others. "An official calls out a contestant due to his or her inability to mount a reasonable defense. The winner of each bout will advance to the next round."

Pausing briefly, Budakis continued. "Today will feature four rounds of intense duels to determine the top two novice-level warriors. Tomorrow's contest will involve the apprentice-level and adept-level contestants. Day three will pit the top two warriors from each day in the climatic finals, where the winner will be awarded the title of Arena Champion."

The crowd cheered in anticipation as Budakis waved the contestants to the benches near the changing rooms. Brock sat on a bench next to Cameron, trying to relax despite his fluttering stomach.

Vandermark stepped to the center of the floor and waved his arms to quiet the crowd. He called out the names of eight contestants, both Cam and Lars among those called. Brock watched his friends and six others cluster near Vandermark before splitting off in twos. Each pair settled into position at the four outer circles painted on the Arena floor. Three other circles were spaced along the center of the floor, remaining empty until later rounds.

The four pairs stood ready, waiting for the signal to begin. Budakis stood on one end of the floor, prepared to monitor the two nearest duels. Kardan stood on the other end, prepared to do the same. Vandermark nodded, and his assistant began to swing a bell, the sound ringing throughout the building. The contestants sprang into action and the crowd roared.

Brock focused on Cam, curious to see how others would fare against his massive roommate. Cam's opponent danced around, waving his short sword as he held his shield high and ready. In contrast, Cam held his longsword low and steady as he calmly moved with his opponent. Brock judged Cam to be five or six inches taller than the other boy, which increased the extended reach his longsword had over his opponent's short sword.

Cam's foe stepped forward with a playful swipe. Brock assumed he was testing Cam, which was a major mistake.

As soon as the move was initiated, Cam made a lunge to close the gap even further. He swatted the sword aside with his shield. With blinding speed, he made a low swing with his longsword, the tip rotating up as it came around. Brock noticed that Cam's opponent held his shield too high. Before he could lower it, the blunt tip of Cam's sword slammed into the boy's midsection. The boy collapsed in agony, and the crowd went wild.

Budakis called the bout. A healer descended the stairs as Cam helped his opponent to his feet.

Brock shifted his attention to Lars, who was having a bit of trouble getting a clean hit on the girl he was facing. Much like Brock, she used a quarterstaff and relied on quickness. Dodging the slow strokes of Lars' great sword, she would strike when he overextended. She hit him hard on the leg, but he held. She thumped him in the gut, forcing Lars to double over, but he recovered.

Taking another shot to his midsection, Lars clutched his stomach while breathing heavily. She stepped forward to finish him when Lars lunged with a wide arcing strike at her midsection. She twisted her staff to block the strike, but both of her hands were above the point of contact. Like a stick trying to stop a rolling boulder, the great sword hammered the staff aside as it rotated in her hands. The sword smashed into the girl's hip, launching her sideways to land two strides away.

Again, the crowd erupted at the display of violence. The bout was called, and Lars bent to check on his downed foe. Rather than helping her up, he waved for a healer. Having already descended the stairs, Ashland came running over. A minute later, they helped the girl to her feet and walked her off the floor.

By that time, the other two bouts had finished with one student rendered unconscious and carried away, while another required a broken arm to be healed.

Cam reclaimed his seat beside Brock.

"Nice job, Cam," Brock said. "I hope you didn't break a sweat out there."

Cam flashed a smile as he yanked his helmet from his head. "I doubt my other matches will be that easy. I got lucky."

Brock snorted. "Yeah. It's funny how you seem to get lucky every time you have a sword in your hand. You'd think it was a coincidence or something."

Cam shrugged and turned toward the center of the Arena. Brock noticed Vandermark waving to quiet the crowd before calling out eight more names. Corbin's was among them.

Brock had never seen Corbin fight, so he planned to watch his fight closely. Even if he didn't face Corbin in the tournament, they might clash in the future.

The four pairs took ready positions, waiting for the signal. When the bell rang, they sprang into action.

Corbin held his longsword with ease as it clacked repeatedly against his opponent's two short swords. The other boy was slightly taller than Brock but with a stockier frame. He had thick arms, twitching as his swords flicked at his taller opponent. The steady clacking of his strikes hitting Corbin's shield and sword filled the air. However, for all his effort, each swing was easily blocked or parried.

With a look of concentration on his face, Corbin continued to defend himself against his dual-armed opponent. The shorter boy pressed forward and made a low lunge. Corbin dodged and chopped down hard with his longsword, striking his opponent on the top of the helmet. The clang of the blow rang through the Arena as the stocky boy collapsed.

A healer ran in to check on Corbin's opponent, who lay unconscious. Corbin ignored his downed foe, instead removing his helmet to hold it and his sword high as he faced the roaring crowd. One of Budakis' assistants ran to help the healer haul the unconscious boy away. Corbin strolled back to the bench without a glance at his injured opponent. Brock wasn't surprised.

Corbin had proven that he lacked any sense of compassion. That trait alone would have made Brock despise him.

With the other bouts decided and the floor cleared, Vandermark again stepped to the center of the Arena and called the next group of eight. Not hearing his name called, Brock realized that he would be in the last group of the first round.

The eight selected took the floor, pairing up as directed and waiting for the signal. Rather than watching the matches, Brock leaned back and closed his eyes to calm his nerves. He opened them as the last match called.

Not waiting for his name to be announced, Brock stood and crossed the floor. Vandermark quieted the crowd and announced the names on his list. Brock stepped beside him as the headmaster announced his name, causing Vandermark to pause and glance at him before calling the last three names. When they had all gathered, Vandermark read out the pairings.

Brock was matched with a boy named Talvin. The two crossed the floor to the circle closest to the benches where Cam and the others sat watching. They studied one another from across the circle while waiting for the bell.

As expected, Talvin was taller than Brock, which gave him a reach advantage. He held a short sword in one hand and had a small shield strapped to the other arm. The boy was lean and muscular. His equipment and build showed that he, like Brock, relied on quickness. As Brock waited for the signal, he thought about the next match. If he advanced, he would have little time to rest since his first-round duel was among the last. A long, drawn-out duel would drain him, so he decided to be aggressive and end it quickly, one way or another.

The bell rang, the crowd cheered, and Brock sprang into action.

Advancing, he made a lunge to the shield side of his opponent, which was easily blocked. When Brock felt the staff strike the shield, he pulled back hard. Seeing Brock's backside open, Talvin swung wide, aiming at the small of his back. The wooden sword sped through the air but failed to connect.

Expecting that exact counter attack, Brock had dropped as low as he could. The other boy's swing left him open and vulnerable when his sword passed over Brock. In a reverse jab, Brock drove the butt of his staff upward, into his opponent's exposed ribs. He felt the crack of bones through the staff, the crunch making his stomach twist and threaten to revolt. Yanking his staff back, Brock spun away to get beyond the reach of his opponent's sword.

When he saw Talvin down on one knee, he knew the match was over. Budakis stopped the duel and declared Brock the victor.

Ignoring the thunder of the crowd, Brock bent down to check on Talvin. "Are you okay? Can you breathe?"

Talvin's face was in a grimace of pain. "It hurts. I feel like I can't get enough air."

Brock had seen this before. He glanced toward the stairs and spotted Ashland descending.

He gripped Talvin's arm and closed his eyes. Finding his center, he mentally reached out toward Talvin. A small storm of red symbols roiled within. He pulled hard on the Order within Talvin, causing the symbols to rapidly dissipate. Brock opened his eyes and stepped aside.

A shudder racked Talvin's body as a spray of blood launched from his mouth, splattering on the dirt floor. Brock glanced up as Ashland arrived.

"Decided you couldn't wait for me, huh?" she noted.

"Sorry, I realized his lung might be filling with blood, so I reacted. I figured the sooner he was healed, the better."

"Well, at least you didn't get covered in it this time," she said with a smile.

Brock chuckled as he helped Talvin to his feet. Ashland held out a big chunk of bread, which Talvin gladly accepted.

Talvin smiled. "Thanks for the bread." He looked at Brock. "Thanks for the help. Not being able to get enough air is pretty scary."

"No problem," he replied. "Sorry I caused the injury in the first place."

Talvin shrugged. "Someone was going to do it. May as well be you." He then turned and headed toward the changing room.

Brock walked Ashland back to the stairwell.

"That was a quick fight," she said.

"I took a chance and got lucky. I planned to end it quickly."

She stopped at the bottom step. "I'm glad you're okay. Please try to stay that way." She spun and hustled up the stairs.

Brock returned to the bench, reclaiming his spot next to Cam.

Cam leaned over. "Nice match."

Brock nodded. "Thanks."

Cam leaned over again. "You got lucky, you know. If he'd gone for your legs, you would've been pummeled."

Brock nodded again. "I know. I took a chance, guessing he'd go high with that counter."

Cam smiled. "You know that ploy won't work again. We all saw it."

"I know. I wanted to use as little energy as possible for the first round. I realize the others won't be this easy."

~

The second round was even easier than the first.

After a thirty-minute intermission, the contest resumed with two duels featured at a time. In this round, Brock's name was the first called, pairing him with a boy named Ulric. Like Cam, his opponent used a longsword and shield. Like Cam, Ulric was much taller and far stronger than Brock. Unlike Cam, he was also far slower.

After dodging a clumsy opening strike, Brock swept his staff low to take the legs out from under Ulric, who landed hard on his side. His wooden sword popped out of his hand and tumbled to the ground. Brock was standing over Ulric with the butt of his staff held above his face when Kardan called the match.

Ulric scrambled to his feet and began to protest, stating that he could have fought back. Kardan wouldn't have it. He sent the frustrated boy to the changing room and awarded the match to Brock.

Brock took a seat on the bench to watch the other matches as the round proceeded. An hour after it began, round two was complete. Eight contestants remained with Brock, Cameron, and Lars among them. Unfortunately, Corbin also remained.

Vandermark addressed the crowd. "The first two rounds of today's contest are complete. We will now break for lunch. Please enjoy your meal, but be back in two hours for the third round of duels."

Brock and the other remaining fighters returned to the changing room to store their gear before heading to lunch.

Even though Brock was hungry, he was careful not to eat too much. A full stomach might slow him and cost him a match. That thought didn't seem to occur to Cam, who ate as much or more than usual. During lunch, Benny rattled on about the skills of the other three. He also revealed a secret betting pool that had opened after the first round. Benny was fascinated by the statistics of the thing, explaining how odds had been set for each of the fighters advancing beyond round one. Cam had the lowest odds, as he quickly became the crowd favorite among the novice-level entrants. His odds were two-to-one to make the final four and five-to-one to win it all. Benny put down two silvers for Cam to be crowned the next champion. He also placed two silvers on Lars and two on Brock for them to each make the finals.

Benny seemed most excited about Brock advancing. When asked why, Benny explained that the odds-makers had originally only given Brock a one-in-sixteen chance of making the finals. A feeling of disbelief had pervaded about his easy win in round one. After winning his second bout easily, the odds shifted to four-to-one. However, Benny had placed his bet after the first match, which meant he would receive more than three gold Imperials if Brock survived the day.

With lunch finished and time to spare before the next round began, Brock went in search of Ashland.

Peeking into Master Varius' classroom, he found his girlfriend cleaning the remains of two meals. She was alone, so he slipped inside. Her face lit up, transforming as she saw him.

"I wanted to see you before the contest resumes," he said as he crossed the room.

She set the plates on a large tray. "Your timing is good. Varius just left, off to a meeting before everyone heads back to the Arena."

Brock wrapped his arms around her. "So, we're alone?"

Ashland's eyes locked on his. "Yes," she said, leaning in for a kiss.

She pulled away, wrinkling her nose. "You stink. You need a bath."

He laughed. "I'm sure I do, but that will have to wait until I'm done with today's rounds."

She stepped backward. "Well, if you ripen any further, they may forfeit just from the smell."

Brock laughed again before changing the subject. "Are you on healing detail again this afternoon?"

Ashland nodded. "Yes. I...I want to be there."

"I'm glad you're there. It gives me strength and confidence."

She smiled. "You're too kind."

"No, I'm serious. I feel something when you're there," Brock said before lightening his tone. "I mean, look at how gorgeous you are. How could I not feel better with you around?"

She shook her head. "You are so bad, Brock Talenz. I swear you could charm a charging bull."

He shrugged. "I do what I can."

Ashland grabbed the tray and walked toward the door. He followed along, reaching past her to open it. With his hand on the handle, she stopped him.

"Brock, you need to promise me something."

His eyes met hers. She was serious. "Okay."

"You need to promise you won't perform any more healing during the contest."

"Okay, but why?"

She looked him in the eyes as she spoke. "You may not realize it, but healing takes more energy than you think. Not all of it comes from your patient. You need to save everything for the duels. Let me and the others do the healing. That's why we're there."

Brock nodded. "Fair enough."

She smiled and stepped aside so he could open the door. He walked with her until reaching the Paladin Wing and turned toward the Arena.

42

Applause sounded throughout the Arena as Vandermark approached the center of the floor. He nodded to the audience before raising his arms. The spectators stilled as he made the next announcement.

"We now begin round three of today's duels. This is where the truly skilled matches occur. Thus, we will feature a single duel at a time, ensuring that you won't miss anything."

He glanced at the paper in his hand and made the next announcement.

"The first two combatants for this round are Brock Talenz and Jasmine Theel."

The crowd roared in applause. Brock grabbed his helmet and staff and strolled toward the center of the Arena, while glancing toward the girl walking alongside of him. Of the seven female contestants, she alone remained. Like Brock, she held her helmet in one arm and a quarterstaff in the other. She matched him in height but had a lither build.

When they reached Vandermark, he wished them luck and headed for the sidelines, passing Budakis on the way.

The master paladin addressed them. "You two know the rules. When you hear the signal, give it your best."

He stepped aside to give them space. With helmets on, they eyed each other.

Seeing her balanced stance and perfect form, Brock knew that she was good. He took a deep breath to clear his mind. The bell rang and the building shook with the noise of the crowd.

They both stepped forward and quickly closed the gap. Rapid left-right-left flicks of their staffs connecting sent a staccato of clacks echoing through the building. Neither swung hard, but instead tested the other with speed and precision. Without fail, the staffs met in rapid succession.

Changing tactics, Brock spun out of the exchange, sweeping low. His opponent leapt over the blow, landing lightly and slamming her staff downward. When he dodged the swing, her staff struck the floor. He swung his staff at her head, but she ducked and rolled away.

Brock realized that he had neither speed nor agility advantages over her. He needed a different route to victory.

They both leapt forward to close the gap. Again, they traded a flurry of left-right-left blows of staff hitting staff. *Clack, clack, clickity-clack,* the sound filled Brock's ears, numbing them with the rhythm. He began to advance, pushing her backward as she continued to match every strike with a block.

Brock altered the path of his stroke, looping the end of his staff behind hers as it came up for a block. With his staff locked behind hers, he pulled back hard, rolling onto his back and pulling her with him. He coiled his knees in tight and then thrust his feet into her mid-section. Jasmine lost her grip on her staff as she flew into the air.

Completing his roll onto his feet as she landed on her hands and tumbled forward, he positioned his body between her and her staff. She crouched, glanced at her weapon on the floor behind him, and turned toward Budakis as he called the match.

Applause shook the building as Brock lowered his staff and bent to grab hers. Still breathing hard from the exertion of the fight, he stepped toward Jasmine.

"Here's your staff. You put up a great fight. You're the fastest I've ever faced."

Jasmine accepted the staff. "Thanks."

He yanked his helmet off. "Are you okay? You landed pretty hard."

She pulled hers off, revealing a mess of black hair. "Yeah. But I have a major headache."

They walked toward the stairs as a healer came down to check on the girl.

Brock left her with the healer, returning to the bench between Cam and Lars. His tall roommate clapped a big hand on his shoulder.

Lars leaned over. "For a little guy, you sure fight good. That must've been the fastest display I've ever seen."

Brock snorted. "Thanks, Lars. She was tough. I'd hate to face her again. It could have gone either way."

The crowd quieted, and everyone turned toward the center of the room as Vandermark announced the next two names. Lars was one of them. He scooped up his helmet and huge sword as he headed across the floor.

Purely overpowering his foe, Lars won his duel. Cam went next and handily beat the squat, thick-muscled boy he faced.

The last battle was Corbin versus Ian, one of his own sycophants. From Brock's perspective, Ian made a pathetic effort of pretending to put up a fight. As expected, Corbin won easily. Also as expected, he played to the crowd, savoring the attention.

Following Corbin's victory, Vandermark announced a brief intermission before they resumed for the day's final round.

Corbin sat at the far end of the benches from where Brock sat. Lars chatted with Cam, but their words slid past Brock, whose attention was on Corbin. He found himself wishing for a chance to beat the irritating grin off the face of the arrogant, self-centered jerk. Feeling the heat of anger brewing in his gut, he glanced up to where Ashland was seated. When her eyes caught his, she gave him a nod. The anger seemed to melt, changing to firm resolve.

Vandermark coaxed the crowd to a hush and made the next announcement.

"We have reached our final round for today, with two bouts remaining. The winners of these two duels will advance to the finals, to be held two days from now, where they will vie for the title of Arena Champion." He paused, waiting for the applause to subside before continuing. "For the first of today's final matches, I call Cameron DeSanus and Lars Merling to the floor."

The two boys grabbed their helmets and weapons and trotted to the center of the floor. As Lars slid his helmet into place, Brock observed a resigned look on the massive boy's face. Cam's expression was as stoic as ever. The two listened to Budakis before he cleared the area. The bell rang, the crowd roared, and they sprang into action.

Brock glanced toward Corbin, who was staring back at him. Corbin made a gesture across his throat with his index finger. Brock's eyes narrowed as he glared at his rival. The exchange lasted a few minutes, interrupted when the crowd went wild.

His focus shifted to his two friends' duel to find Cam standing over Lars, who held his shoulder as he squirmed on the floor. Cam knelt beside his injured friend. A healer ran in and knelt to the other side of Lars. Less than a minute later, Cam reached out a hand and hauled Lars to his feet. The two clapped each other on the back, and the crowd went wild.

As his friends approached, Brock glanced toward Ashland and took a deep breath, finding that feeling of resolve.

Vandermark took the floor and announced the last two contestants.

Brock stood and slid his helmet down over his ears. Cam and Lars clapped him on the back as they wished him luck. Corbin was already halfway to the center, waving to the cheering crowd as he crossed the floor.

When they reached Vandermark, the headmaster nodded and retreated as Budakis approached.

"You boys know the rules. On the signal, give it your best." Budakis grinned. "This is it. Win this and you're fighting in the finals."

Brock nodded and took position. When Budakis stepped away, Corbin began his taunting.

"I've been waiting for this, wishing for a chance to crush you publicly."

"Be careful what you wish for."

"You're going to feel pain, you little snot," Corbin snarled.

"We'll see."

The bell rang, the crowd erupted, and the two rivals launched into action.

Corbin came in hard, swinging his longsword in a wide arc. Brock blocked the strike and then jabbed at the taller boy's leg. While Brock connected with Corbin's thigh, it had minimal effect since it was at the very end of the thrust. Corbin's long reach and long weapon created a greater reach advantage than anyone Brock had fought.

Winding back for a hard swing, Corbin's arm came down at an angle. Brock twisted and flicked his wrists to swat the strike, redirecting it so it swept past him. Brock swung his staff downward as he jumped back, the butt of the staff scraping Corbin's forearm and leaving an angry red streak.

Corbin's face contorted into anger. He lifted his sword high for a killing blow, chopping downward. Brock lifted his staff and braced both arms for the impact. The longsword struck the center of the staff. A loud *crack* and *clang* sounded as Brock staggered backward, white spots invading his vision.

He shook his head and blinked to clear the tears. His head pounded fiercely from the glancing blow to the helmet.

Brock looked up just in time to see Corbin's sword cutting through the air, aimed at his neck. He ducked and rolled away to get clear. When Brock came to his feet, he looked down at the staff, now in two pieces. *How did that happen?*

He reversed his grip on each of the staff halves, holding them like two short swords. Luckily, he had some training with the short sword and knew the basic forms.

Corbin's face was pulled into a twisted grin. "You're going down now, boy."

Rather than respond, Brock waited for his opponent to attack. He didn't have to wait long.

Corbin took a wide swing, going for another killing blow. Brock dove forward and ducked. As the swing flew over Brock's head, he stabbed upward, jamming the butt of his shortened staff into Corbin's groin before rolling to Corbin's shield side, away from the reach of his opponent's sword.

When he regained his footing and found Corbin doubled over, Brock released a flurry of left-right strikes with the two staff halves. Corbin held his shield up to block the blows but took a number of solid hits on the back before he scrambled away.

Corbin turned toward him with his face in a grimace of pain. After a couple breaths, Corbin's expression contorted in anger. With a roar, he lunged, driving the tip of his longsword at Brock's chest. Brock twisted and the sword scraped along the fabric of his sparring vest. With Corbin in close, Brock swung toward the boy's face with the butt of the half-staff leading. Corbin's head snapped back when the thrust smashed into his chin. Like a rag doll, he crumbled to the floor.

Brock stared down at Corbin, panting from the exchange. Time seemed to slow. Corbin didn't move as blood dripped from his mouth. The Arena fell eerily quiet. Brock glanced at Budakis, who stared at Corbin. Brock then looked toward the stairs to find Ashland in mid-descent.

Time lurched forward. Budakis jumped in and called the match while holding Brock's arm high. The crowd erupted, the noise deafening. Ashland ran in and knelt beside Corbin. She rolled him onto his side as he coughed, spraying blood onto the dirt floor. She looked up at Brock.

"He bit the tip of his tongue off. I can heal him, but I can't grow it back. He'll never be the same."

Brock shrugged. He thought he would feel satisfaction from beating his mean-spirited rival. Instead, he just felt numb.

Corbin's body shuddered when Ashland healed him, but he remained unconscious. Ashland patted his cheek to wake him. After a moment, Corbin stirred, sitting up slowly. Ashland offered to help him stand, but he pushed her away. Rising to his feet, he shoved Brock aside as he stumbled toward the changing room.

Budakis stepped before Brock. "Let me look at that." He grabbed the two pieces of the broken staff, inspecting the ends where it split. "I knew it. I've never seen a wooden sword snap a quarterstaff like that. Someone tampered with your staff, Brock." He held an end up for Brock to see. "See how the outer part of the break is straight and clean and only the core is splintered?"

Budakis handed the two halves back and walked away. Brock stared at the broken staff, not sure what to think. He looked toward the cheering crowd, still feeling detached from the moment.

Brock knew he was victorious. He had beaten Corbin, whom he detested. He was advancing to the finals, yet he felt no sense of accomplishment. Instead, he felt an overwhelming sense of dread, as if his future had grown dark.

43

B rock sat in the stands with his friends. Benny watched intently, trying to gauge how he should place his bets for today's contest. He had already won big with the money he had placed on Brock and Cam. His new goal was to pick all four finalists, so he watched the opening round closely to gauge the skill of each victor.

Brock's heart wasn't in it. He felt off, distracted since his duel with Corbin. Something was bothering him, but he had no idea what it was. Cam leaned close. "Who is she?"

Brock looked to where Cam pointed, seeing the red-haired apprentice paladin. While Brock had healed her opponents numerous times, he had never seen her get a scratch.

"Her name is Tegan," he replied. "She's good. Fast, agile, and strong."

Cam nodded as he watched her dance around her opponent. She landed numerous strikes that her foe tried in vain to counter. "She's amazing."

Tegan's opponent became frustrated, leveling a wide-arcing blow at her hip. The girl leapt into the air, flipped over the strike, and landed to face his open backside. She jammed one of her swords into his exposed armpit, and he fell to one knee. With the match called, a healer ran out, and the crowd leapt to its feet, clapping and cheering.

Cam stood, craning his neck to watch Tegan as she walked back to the bench. He appeared enthralled, watching her every move. The round completed with eight apprentice-level combatants remaining and the adept-level fighters up next. The round passed without Brock realizing it. At the following intermission, he decided to leave and get some air.

Brock made his way to the Main Hall and stepped outside, squinting in the bright light of the sun reflecting off the remaining snow. The snowbanks, which had been as tall as Brock only weeks earlier, didn't even reach his ankles. The air was cool but not cold. He strolled along a gravel path that crossed the lawn, lost in thought. After a bit, he headed back indoors, but he opted to head to his room rather than return to the Arena.

The translation of the mysterious book had been slow but steady. Brock and Benny now had the first two chapters translated. While they had to skip a few scattered words, the general message was clear.

Alone in his room, he focused on the book, translating one word at a time. The hours passed quickly as key details from the third chapter began to coalesce--details that changed everything.

When the door to the room opened, Brock's eyes lifted from the book to find Benny and Cam entering.

"What an awesome day!" Benny exclaimed, grinning from ear to ear. "You missed it, Brock. You totally missed it."

Benny sat on the end of his bed. Cam sat across from him, a bemused look on his face.

"I put the money I won yesterday on that red-haired girl, Tegan, and on an adept named Goren. Guess what happened?" Benny was grinning, bouncing up and down.

"Um…they won?" Brock guessed.

"Yes! They won!" Benny shouted. "Tegan paid four-to-one, and the other paid two-to-one. I now have more than ten gold Imperials! Ten!" He was so excited. "And, if the big lug over here," Benny nodded toward Cam, "comes through tomorrow, I can win more from the bet I put on him to win it all."

Brock smiled, finding Benny's enthusiasm contagious. His gaze shifted to Cam, who still had the odd look on his face.

"What do you think, Cam? You saw those two fight. Can you beat them?"

Cam blinked. "What? Um…well, Goren is good, classic longsword and shield fighter, about my size. His form is perfect. He knows what he's doing, so it'll be tough."

Brock nodded. "What about the girl?"

Cameron smiled. "You saw her. She's amazing. I don't know if I can beat her, but I love to watch her fight. It's like a beautiful song, so perfect that you don't want it to end."

Brock chuckled. "I think you have a crush, Cam." Cam grinned, shrugging.

Benny laughed. "So, you like this girl, and your first time meeting her is in a duel in front of the whole Academy?"

Cam shrugged again. "I have to get past Brock first, though."

Brock snorted. "I just hope I can give them a bit of a show and not get killed in the process. I doubt I'll get lucky enough to beat you, Cam."

Cam's response was another shrug. Benny changed the subject.

"Have you made any progress, Brock? Are you learning anything yet?" Benny gestured toward the book.

Brock nodded, pulling out his notes. "Yes. The third chapter gets into the actual application, explaining how Chaos works. As you had already determined, Chaos is a natural force that's all around, we just can't see it. In order to manipulate it, someone called an Arcanist gathers it and then channels it into a special rune. Apparently, the rune somehow gives the energy purpose, defining its effect."

Benny nodded. "Okay. That makes sense, but how does this person gather the force in the first place? How is it channeled into the rune? How long does it last? How strong is the effect?"

He shook his head. "I don't know. I haven't gotten that far. I hope we can get more answers from the book, though." Brock paused, considering his next words. "I want to tell you guys something. It needs to stay between us. I need your word that it remains a secret."

Benny glanced toward Cam, who spoke first. "I promise, Brock."

With a nod, Benny added, "Me, too. You can trust us, Brock."

Brock took a breath to ready himself. "I've done this before." His finger tapped on the book in his lap.

Benny glanced down at the book, then up at Brock. "What do you mean?"

"I mean that I've used Chaos before. I didn't know what I was doing or how I made it happen. But I've done it before, more than once."

Benny pushed his spectacles up, staring intensely. "What happened?"

Brock glanced at Cameron before responding. "You know our catapult? How it launched the ball ten times further than everyone else? I think I did that. I think it was Chaos that made it happen."

Benny was focused, his curiosity high. "What did you do, Brock? How do you think it happened?"

"I had carved a rune into the frame of the catapult." Brock bent over and opened his desk drawer. He reached in and grabbed a book, handing it to Benny. "The rune from the book cover. I carved it on a whim. The symbol caught my attention the first time I saw it. I knew it meant something. While I was alone with the catapult, I carved it. Then, after Corbin and Karl broke the record with their catapult launch, I did something. I was so…frustrated. You know that I loathe Corbin and how he hates me right back? I couldn't let him win. I…did something. I'm still not sure what it was. Anyway, the rune began to glow for a bit before returning to normal. When we launched the ball…boom." He made a motion with his hands flying up and apart.

Benny stared hard, nodding slowly. "Now, the engineers have tried and tried, but they can't reproduce the same result. That means there's a limit to how long the effect lasts."

Brock shrugged. "I guess. I don't know anything about that. I barely know what I described. I'm not even sure that I can do it again."

Benny waved the comment off. "Oh, we'll figure that out. We just need to experiment." He tapped on the cover of the second book. "Can you tell me what this symbol means?"

Brock nodded. "That was the first thing I tried to discover when this other information came to light. I found it right before you walked in." He glanced at Cam, then back to Benny. "That symbol means Power."

Brock ignored the raucous crowd and focused on Cam, who stood across the circle from him with sword in hand and shield ready. The bell rang and the crowd's noise filled the arena. The two roommates exchanged nods and stepped forward.

He let Cam take the offensive, swinging repeated strikes only to be blocked by Brock's new staff. The loud clacking of wood on wood sounded out in a steady beat. After a dozen of these exchanges, Cam changed tactics. A downward chop fell, which Brock dodged. Cam thrust his shield into Brock, knocking him back. Brock rolled with the hit and came to his feet a couple strides from his opponent. Cam took two quick steps, closing the gap and swinging hard. Rather than blocking it, Brock ducked low and swung his staff at Cam's legs. The larger boy leapt in the air, but Brock nicked one heel, causing Cam to stumble backward when he landed. Sensing an opening, Brock attacked before Cam could regain his balance. Cam blocked the series of strikes, the attack pushing him backward a few steps. When he realized that the opening had closed, Brock resumed a defensive stance.

Cam advanced, swinging a flurry of quick strokes that Brock blocked in rapid succession. He kicked his foot out to trip Brock, who spun away. They paused and measured each other. After sparring many times, each knew the other's tendencies.

They both leapt forward, clashing repeatedly as the exchange lasted far longer than either wanted. The effort left them exhausted, causing one of them to make a mistake.

Cam came in hard, trying to end the fight. Brock ducked and rolled away from the strike, sweeping his staff low while Cam was overextended. The staff struck hard behind Cam's knee, causing him to fall backward. Sensing his opportunity, Brock closed for a killing blow. Cam rolled backward, coming to his knees and raising his shield just in time to block the strike. The swing deflected off the shield and left Brock exposed. Cam's sword struck hard under Brock's arm and pain exploded in his side, causing him to arch his back and to fall to his knees.

With one hand on the ground, Brock fought for air, each breath feeling like a dozen knives thrusting into his ribs. Budakis called the match. Brock heard the crowd roar, but he didn't care. He just wanted to breathe and for it not to hurt so damn much.

Cam knelt beside him. "I think you broke some ribs. I hit you pretty hard."

Brock glanced up at Cam. "Thanks. I hadn't noticed."

Cam flashed a grin before stepping away.

Ashland slid into the spot Cam had just vacated.

"I'm here," she said as she placed her hand on his cheek.

He gave a small nod. "Ready."

A shock of ice cold made his body shake, driving the last of the wind from his lungs. Gasping to reclaim air, he thankfully realized it no longer hurt to breathe. A wave of immense hunger hit him.

"Thanks. What would I do without you?" Brock said between breaths.

Ashland smiled, pulling a hard roll from her pocket. "Most likely, you'd get yourself killed."

He accepted the roll and her assistance as she helped him to his feet. They walked to the side of the Arena as Vandermark quieted the crowd. He announced a short intermission before the next match, which would pit Cam against Tegan. Brock glanced toward his roommate, who sat on the bench with his helmet off as he stared at his opponent. The grin on Cam's face made Brock wonder who was in more trouble: Cam or Tegan.

The hot water felt wonderful, soothing Brock's sore muscles. Steam rising from the pool filled his nostrils as he closed his eyes in relaxation. That single bout with Cam wore on him more than his four bouts on the first day of the tournament.

The noise of the crowd carried through the changing room to the baths. Brock waited to see if Cam was advancing to the final round or was coming to join him. After a few minutes without Cam showing, he decided that his friend had won. Brock felt a twinge of guilt for not watching, but it soon passed. He was done with these senseless duels. Any bit of joy he used to get from sparring was now gone. All the same, he wished his friend the best of luck.

Soaking in the bath alone, he enjoyed the serenity of the moment. With closed eyes, his mind drifted until a roar from the Arena brought him back to reality. With a sigh, he waded to the stairs to grab his towel. Once dressed, he emerged from the changing room to see how his friend fared.

As Cam came into Brock's view, Goren swung a wide-sweeping strike. Cam's shield knocked it aside, and his sword came around low to hit his opponent hard behind the leg. Goren dropped to one knee, and Cam smashed him on top of the head with his shield. Brock cringed, knowing how that felt. Cam stood ready above Goren's prone body when Budakis jumped in to call the match. The applause grew to a crescendo as Budakis held Cam's hand high.

Brock smiled, feeling happy for his friend. If anyone deserved the recognition, it was Cam. Not only was he physically gifted, he also worked harder at perfecting his skills than anyone Brock knew.

While the crowd watched the victor receiving his medal, Brock climbed the stairs to join Ashland. She flashed him a smile and slipped her arm around his waist as he put his around her shoulder. Although it hurt when she squeezed him, he didn't care.

Soon after, the crowd began to filter through the doors to fill the halls outside. Brock and Ashland followed along, holding hands. He just wanted to spend some quiet time with her before joining his friends to celebrate Cam's victory.

44

"It's not working, Benny. I'm telling you, I don't feel it," Brock complained.

Benny shook his head. "I know we're close. I just know it."

Brock sat and opened his water skin. "I need a break. My head's still throbbing from last night."

Benny flashed a grin. "The wine was good, right?"

As Brock drank from the skin, he nodded. Swallowing, he replaced the cap. "Too good. That's the problem." He rubbed his eyes. "Where did you get a whole cask anyway?"

Benny held up his hands. "I'm sorry, but I cannot divulge my sources. I'd hate to give a secret up so easily."

"Well, it must have cost you plenty."

Benny nodded. "Oh, it was expensive, but I figured it was the least I could do after you and Cam helped me win all that gold."

Brock chuckled when he thought about the prior evening. Benny had been more animated than ever as he raved about how his bets had won big. After opening the cask, it wasn't long until half of their floor had joined them in the lounge for a cup or more. Brock still wasn't sure why he had let Benny drag him out to the quarry behind the Foundry yard this early. He would have gladly slept longer, since he still felt the lingering effects of too much wine. Thank Issal it was Seventh Day.

Taking a breath, Brock gathered the will to try again. He walked over to the solid steel pole wedged under the huge stone block. His fingers traced the rune of Power they had carved into it.

"Tell me how you expect this to work again," he said to Benny.

Benny walked over, patting the pole with one hand. "It's simple. From what I can tell, the way the rune worked with the catapult is that it somehow augmented the normal amount of energy released, resulting in an energy level many times higher than normal. Here, you have a strong lever wedged under an extremely heavy object. If you can somehow charge the symbol that's engraved in the pole, the energy applied to the lever will be multiplied many times, which will allow us to lift the stone block."

Brock nodded. "Okay. I think I got it that time. The last time, you spouted cryptic stuff like," Brock's voice took on a nasal quality, *"the applied effect caused the potential energy to increase exponentially blah, blah, blah."*

Benny laughed. "That was close. You almost had it, but the terms aren't important. What I need you to do now is make it happen."

"That's what I'm telling you. I'm not sure how it happened before." Brock shrugged. "It just kind of happened."

Benny shook his head. "Don't give up, Brock. Think back to the Catapult Challenge. Focus on what you did. Think about what you saw, what you heard, what you smelled, even what you felt."

Brock nodded, thinking back to the situation. Corbin had just launched his catapult, breaking the school record. This was after he had tried to sabotage their catapult. Wait. Sabotage. Brock thought about the Arena Championship, recalling how he had left his staff in the changing room before breaking for lunch. Corbin knew the staff would break when he had swung the heavy overhand blow because he had sabotaged it first.

Anger began boiling inside of Brock. He closed his eyes, imagining Corbin sneaking into the changing room and making deep cuts into the staff. Brock felt the heat of that anger and...he also felt an angry energy around him. He absorbed that energy, drawing it in until he felt like he would burst. Opening his eyes, he poured the frantic energy into the rune and it began to glow hot red.

"Whoa! Look at that!" Benny exclaimed.

A wave of exhaustion washed over Brock. The rune pulsed, slowly dissipating until it looked like a normal engraving.

Benny smiled. "Can I try it again?"

Brock shrugged. "Suit yourself."

Standing beside the pole, Benny showed a hopeful smile. The past six tries had yielded nothing except a lot of grunting.

Benny took a breath and pushed down on the pole. The huge stone block launched into the air. The solid steel pole screamed a high-pitched tone as it vibrated, causing Benny to let go. He fell onto his rear, rubbing his hands as he watched the stone block land in the snow thirty strides away.

Benny began to laugh, slapping his leg in glee. Brock squatted and asked, "Are you okay, Benny?" Nodding, Benny scrambled to his feet.

"That was the most amazing thing I've ever seen." Benny rubbed his hands together in excitement. "Let's do it again."

Spring rains started the next day. The remaining snow in the valley melted steadily, while the surrounding peaks remained white as the rain turned to snow at the higher elevation. After three weeks of steady rain, the sky cleared, and the sun began to dry away the pools of water that had formed.

The experiment with Chaos had provided interesting information on how long the magical effect lasted. The enhanced power of the lever had held steady for almost an hour before a rapid decline. By the time two hours had passed, it had returned to just a solid metal pole. After their successful and slightly scary experiment, Brock convinced Benny that they needed to learn more before somebody got hurt or killed. Disappointed, Benny shifted his focus back to his new invention.

Brock divided his free time between translating the book and spending it with Ashland. He preferred the latter, but much of her time was occupied by tasks set by Master Varius. When the rains relented, the two were able to leave the Academy for a night in Fallbrandt. Brock was happy to see Tipper and thrilled to spend time alone with Ashland. The couple relished every moment, not returning to the Academy until sunset the following evening.

In the weeks after the Arena Championship, Corbin changed, his usual boastful persona becoming withdrawn. Even in Hierarchist class, where he presided as Prelate of their imaginary government, Corbin was quiet and brooding. Brock assumed that it was related to the lisp that Corbin had developed after losing the tip of his tongue, though nobody dared to tease him. To Brock's surprise, he began to feel sorry for Corbin.

When the weather was dry, their Paladin class moved outdoors four days a week. While they still spent time on tactics and fitness training, ranged weapons replaced their wooden melee weapons. They were taught how to use the short bow, longbow, and crossbow. After spending two weeks introducing basic bow techniques, Budakis had them each select one that they were to master. Brock opted for the short bow, but when Budakis announced the Marksman Tournament coming in late spring, Brock had low expectations. He couldn't seem to grasp the nuances of the weapon.

While the bulk of the class practiced at the range, each day Budakis would send a group of fifteen students to spend time with Master Herron, the horsemaster. On those days, Brock learned the basics of horsemanship, from caring for the animal to riding one. He found that he could barely sit for two days after his first day of riding. Within three weeks, the soreness became little more than an annoyance.

In ecclesiastics, the focus on divining finally ended when Varius introduced the next talent they were to develop.

"We are now three quarters of the way through your novice year. I'm sure you feel that this class has been moving slowly, focusing too long on only a few concepts. That feeling is understandable. However, I cannot stress enough how valuable healing is to the Empire and to its citizens. If the extra effort spent on developing the skill produces just one more healer per year, it's worth it."

Varius surveyed the room before continuing. "Of course, the other talent we've covered thus far is divining. Though far more common, it also has value and is worth spending a couple months to develop." Pausing, she smiled. "I will now introduce a third ability that can manifest through Order. Prophecy."

She glided down the aisle as she spoke. "Prophecy is an ability relating to the prediction of future events. While it can appear in various forms, the most common form is often perceived as simple intuition. It's that little warning in the back of your mind that causes you to react to something about to happen, even before it occurs. I realize that this is a complex concept, so let me give you an example.

"Someone who has a strong connection with Order might enter a room but stop suddenly, not knowing why. A second later, the chandelier above falls to the floor right where the person would have been if he or she hadn't stopped. In this case, a subtle ability in prophecy becomes a sort of additional sense, catching the smallest glimpse into their own immediate future.

"You may wonder how this is possible. How could one see into the future? To understand, you need to think of Order as a force that exists not only in the present, but also in the past and in the future. I've explained that Order is within all living things as the life force that binds us. While we only experience time in this moment, always moving forward in a linear fashion, the Order existing within you has existed throughout your whole past and extends into your future, stretching forward like a thread through time. When connected to that force of Order, you may be able to extend that connection out just a bit into the future, giving you a glimpse of what is coming.

"There are two key items to note. First, it's far easier to see into your own future than the future of others, because it is tied to you. Second, the near future is much easier to determine than a more distant future. Your thread of Order extending into the past has been defined and is singular, but your future is an array of possibilities, fanning out wide from the present. The closer you are to now, the less variability there is to your future and the easier it is to foretell.

"There is also a far rarer manifestation of prophecy. This is true prophecy, where a person will experience a vision of some critical event in the future, possibly a distant future. In this form of prophecy, one must connect to the broader force of Order that exists in all living things. How this occurs is unknown, though many theories exist. In all documented cases throughout history, though there are few, this type of prophecy has served as a warning used to guide and prepare for some critical event.

"You won't find this in any books, for it is only handed down verbally." She paused, scanning the room. "Without a doubt, mankind would not have defeated The Banished Horde if the Ministry hadn't followed the guidance of such a prophecy. Ignoring that prophecy would have resulted in our utter defeat and in the extermination of mankind."

The class remained silent, considering the message she was sending.

"Now that you understand the basic concepts, it's time to begin some exercises designed to develop your skill in prophecy."

She turned and waved Ashland over. The girl handed a stack of cards to Varius, who held one of the cards up.

"These cards each have a common rune marked on them, which you will use to perform a simple task. Your partner will stand behind you, flipping a card up to face your back. Your job is to call out the rune on the card just before you spin around to see what it is."

She surveyed the room. "I see the looks on your faces. Yes, this is like a trick street performers might use to impress an unknowing crowd. The secret is that it's not a trick. They cannot read minds, and they don't have a mirror. This is something made possible by a close connection to their own force of Order. Through it, they can see a moment into the future, much like glancing around a corner just before you walk around the bend. They see what's on the card in their mind, then spin to see the same image with their eyes a moment later." Varius smiled. "It's quite simple."

She began handing cards to tables on one side of the room. Ashland followed, handing cards to tables on the other side. As she passed him, Brock whispered to her.

"Will you be my partner?" She smiled, giving a small nod.

With the cards distributed, Varius called for everyone to find a partner. Brock wasted no time seeking out Ashland. Seeing them together, Varius raised an eyebrow, but made no objection.

Brock shuffled his cards. "I'm assuming you've tried this before."

Ashland sighed. "Yes, but I'm not good at it. Healing and divining come easy. Prophecy has eluded me thus far."

He smiled. "Yeah, but this time, you have my support. Love conquers all. Right?"

She smiled back. "Right."

"I have the cards, so you go first. Turn around." He told her.

Ashland turned her back toward him. He stared at the back of her neck, past the stray curls hanging from her bun, and he resisted the urge to kiss that neck. Picking a card, he saw the rune of *artifex altus*. He flipped it so it faced Ashland's back and waited. He found himself thinking about the rune on the card, expecting her to say it.

"Artifex altus," she said, and then spun to see the card. A small squeal of excitement slipped out before she covered her mouth. She whispered. "It worked. I could see it. I knew what it was!"

Brock smiled. "I knew you could do it. Now, it's my turn."

He handed the cards to her and reversed direction. He sought his center, cleared his mind, and let it fill. Amazingly, it did.

"Laboris." When he spun to see that exact card facing him, a grin spread across his face, matching Ashland's expression. "That was amazing. It was so clear. I could see it in my head."

Ashland nodded. "Let's try again."

45

Benny spread the map-sized sheet of paper on the table. On it was a sketch of some crazy looking contraption.

"This is it, Brock. I'm going to be famous," Benny said, excited.

"Okay, but what is it?" Brock asked as he inspected the drawing.

"This is like a carriage but with only two wheels. It's smaller and lighter and doesn't need a horse to pull it. Instead, it uses a crank that is pedaled by your feet." Benny smiled proudly.

"Why would this be better than walking?" Brock asked.

Benny sighed. "See how the crank is smaller than the wheel? Each time the crank rotates, the big wheel turns a full revolution, which multiplies the result. Besides that, wheels roll. They roll, Brock!" Brock laughed. "Okay, Okay. What if you tip over?"

"Watch."

Benny drew a copper from his pocket and rolled the coin across the table, the coin continuing until it slowed and tipped over.

"If you're moving fast enough, you won't tip over, like the coin. If you stop, you can always take your feet off the crank pedals and put them on the ground. It's simple."

Brock smiled at Benny's energy and optimism. "Okay. I believe you. What's next?"

Benny smiled. "You guys will help me build it. I will be famous, of course. You two will be famous for helping me be famous."

Brock laughed at the serious way Benny made the ludicrous statement. "Yes, I'll help. Cam?"

Cam replied from the nearby sofa. "Sure. As long as there aren't any wine casks involved. I'm still recovering from the last one."

Benny grinned. "Great. We'll start in two days, right after dinner."

Brock nodded. "Sounds good, Benny."

Satisfied, Benny changed the subject. "What about the translation, Brock? Have you made any progress?"

Brock shrugged. "Yes and no. I've been trying to figure out a symbol. It's something that I…had some experience with in the past. But I'm not getting a clear translation."

Benny raised an eyebrow. "What have you found so far?"

"Well, this symbol means something like life or move or maybe alive. I can't tell for sure." Brock responded, "But I think…"

"Brock."

He turned to find Parker standing in the doorway to the lounge.

"Can I speak with you?"

Brock nodded. "Excuse me, guys."

Once in the hallway, Parker waved him into the room he shared with Benny. Brock slipped inside and Parker closed the door.

"Sorry for not spending time with you since the tower repair."

Brock shook his head. "Don't worry about it, Parker. I know you're caught up in politics that influence your situation."

Parker nodded. "Thanks for understanding." He paused briefly. "But that's not why I pulled you in here. I wanted to warn you."

Brock's brow furrowed. "Warn me? About what?"

"About Corbin," Parker said. "For some reason, he's hated you since his first day here. But since…since the Arena Championship, he's gotten worse. It used to be almost amusing, as if you were just a pawn he would attempt to manipulate. Now, it's as if he's possessed or something. He mentions things he wants to do to you. Bad things. I'm not the only one in the group who finds it disturbing. He isn't right in the head. I'm afraid he'll do something…something horrible."

Brock nodded. "Thanks for letting me know, Parker. I'll be sure to be careful."

Parker released a sigh. "I hope there's nothing to worry about, but I'm afraid that isn't the case. I thought I should let you know. You've always been a friend to me. In fact, you've been great to everyone anytime I've been around you. Who knows, maybe that's why Corbin hates you. Issal knows he hasn't treated others well."

Brock put his hand on Parker's shoulder. "Thanks again, Parker. You take care, too. If Corbin is becoming dangerous, you may want to keep a distance."

Parker pulled the door open. "Take care, Brock. Watch your back."

"Okay. This is good," Benny said, stopping at the side of the road.

Brock and Cam stopped pushing the contraption, holding it upright on the narrow road that wrapped around the Girls' Wing.

Benny smiled. "For the moment of truth. Get on and give it a try," he said, looking at Brock.

"Me? Why me?" Brock asked.

Benny pointed at Cam. "Well, he certainly isn't going to fit on it. We didn't make it for giants. As for me, I need to observe. Plus, you're more athletic and will likely fare better than I would."

"Benny, this is your invention. You should have the honor of the first ride," Brock argued.

Benny shook his head. "It may have been my idea, but it wouldn't exist without your help. You and Cam have spent just as much time building it as I have."

Brock rolled his eyes. "Fine. I'll test your crazy invention. But if I get injured, you have to run and find a healer."

With Cam holding it upright, Brock swung a leg over the top pipe and sat on the wooden seat.

Benny shuffled to the opposite side from Cam. "Put your feet on the crank pedals and hold onto the crossbar. It will allow you to turn. When I count to three, Cam and I will start pushing. You try to keep it from tipping over, and we'll let go once it's rolling. Once we let go, turn the crank hard to keep going."

Brock nodded and Benny counted down. "Three, two, one, go!" As they began pushing, Brock's feet began to rotate with the pedals. The faster they pushed, the faster his feet rotated. The thing wiggled and shook as he tried to keep his balance. When he rounded the corner toward the front lawn, Benny and Cam let go.

He turned the crank, pumping his legs and gaining speed. Thrilled, he began to laugh, drowning out whatever Benny shouted from behind him. As the slope increased, he went faster. However, he spotted a sharp bend ahead and realized that he was moving too fast. He attempted to slow but the wheel attached to the crank had too much momentum. Lifting his feet off the pedals, he held them up as the thing sped toward the bend without a means to slow or stop.

"I can't stop!" He shouted as he sped off the road onto the lawn.

His rear bounced violently on the wooden seat and his teeth chattered from the vibration as he headed toward a clump of trees, their branches filled with newly budded leaves. Leaning to one side, he turned the front wheel just enough to avoid a big tree. When the wheels ran over a large root near the trunk, he bounced in the air, landed hard on the seat, and one hand slipped off the crossbar. The front wheel turned sharp and violently grabbed the turf, stopping the contraption and launching Brock over the crossbar. The world spun as he flipped in the air, landed on his lower back, and rolled forward another rotation.

Brock lay on his back and stared up at the scattered clouds in the pale blue sky while long strands of grass tickled his cheeks in the light breeze. He heard the sound of footsteps rapidly approaching until Cam appeared in his field of vision, stopping to look down at him.

"Are you okay, Brock? Should I go get a healer?"

"How do I let Benny talk me into this stuff?" Brock replied, lifting one arm. "Help me up."

Cam grabbed his hand and yanked him to his feet.

Brock's fingers raked grass from his hair as Benny came running in, breathing heavily.

"Brock. I'm glad you're okay." Benny gasped for air. "What went wrong?"

Brock snorted. "Well, a few things actually." He raised one finger at a time as he recited his complaints. "First, there's no way to stop. Once I got going, I couldn't slow enough to make that sharp turn. Second, there's no place to put my feet if I take them off those spinning pedals. Third, the hard seat gave my rear a sound beating on every bump. Lastly, I made the mistake of letting you talk me into testing one of your crazy contraptions."

Benny nodded as Brock spoke until the last statement. "Don't worry, Brock. I'll make some changes, and it'll be better next time."

"Oh no," Brock replied, shaking his head. "I'm not riding this thing again until you can prove it's safe."

As he walked away, Brock shouted over his shoulder. "I'm going to find Ashland. I told her I'd spend the day with her when I was done here."

Benny and Cam stood beside the crashed contraption, watching Brock walk away with one hand rubbing his rear.

Brock and Ashland rested on the front lawn, not far from the site of his recent crash. The blanket they sat on offered little comfort for his sore backside. Ashland's laughter echoed through the area as he told his story.

"And so I lay on the lawn, not far from here, and stared up at the clouds thinking of how Benny almost killed me with his crazy contraption."

He reached into the basket, grabbed a hard roll, and popped a chunk into his mouth.

Ashland recovered from her laughter. "So you didn't break anything? You didn't need to be healed, right?"

Brock snorted. "Somehow, no. I have some bruises and it hurts to sit, but most of the damage was emotional."

He paused, distracted, when he noticed Corbin and his group walking down a nearby path. Corbin glared at Brock with hate smoldering in his eyes. Brock glared back until his rival passed behind a clump of trees. Ashland noticed Brock's change in demeanor and turned to see what had distracted him. Once Corbin was out of sight, she commented.

"He hates you, doesn't he?"

Brock nodded. "Yes. He has since my first day here."

She put her hand on his. "I can't see why. You're the most loveable person I know." She smiled.

He smiled back. "I wish everyone felt that way." His gaze shifted toward where he last saw Corbin. "I think he's gone through life with everyone kissing his feet, always bending to his will. I refuse to do those things for someone I don't respect. I believe it eats him up inside." He paused, reflecting on the issue. "Then I beat him in the Arena and... well...you know."

She nodded. "Yes. I know. His tongue will never heal. I suppose it reminds him on a daily basis, making it even worse."

Brock nodded. "Parker said that Corbin is now so bad that he's scaring the others. They're afraid of what he might do."

Ashland looped her arm around his, pulling him close as she leaned in for a kiss.

"Let's not worry about him for now. Let's enjoy this beautiful evening together," she said.

He smiled. "Any evening I spend with you is beautiful."

She smiled back. "Thank you, Brock." Her smile faded, her eyes glancing down. "School ends in a few weeks. Have you decided what you'll do during the break? Where you'll go?"

He shook his head. "No. I hadn't thought about it all."

Looking down at the blanket, she asked timidly, "Would you like to spend it with me? That is, if you don't have to go home or have other..."

He interrupted, "I'd love to spend it with you. I don't care where we are if we're together."

Smiling, Ashland leaned in for another kiss, pulled away, and gazed into his eyes. She reached up to put her hand on his forehead, closing her eyes.

For a moment, he didn't think anything of it, until panic struck when he realized what she was doing. He still hadn't figured out how to tell her he was Unchosen.

Her eyes flashed open. She yanked her hand back, recoiling from him. Her hands covered her mouth as horror reflected in her eyes.

"No!" she cried out. "No, it can't be!"

She scrambled to her feet and backed away from him.

"Ashland, I'm sorry. I...didn't know how to tell you," he said.

She turned and fled.

"Wait!" He stood to run after her. "Ashland, come back!"

He stopped, watching her run across the lawn toward the school. His heart felt as if it were in his throat. After everything he had gone through, being Unchosen was still ruining his life.

He slowly walked back, distracted as his mind scrambled for a way to fix things. Gathering up the remains from their evening picnic, he headed back to the school.

46

B rock needed to find Ashland – needed to show her that he was who she thought he was and that being Unchosen shouldn't matter. He checked her room but found the door locked with no response to his repeated knocks. Rapidly descending the stairs, he headed toward the training temple.

When he opened the temple door, he found it empty save for a single glowlamp illuminating the dais in the heart of the dark room. To be sure, he approached the dais in search of signs of Ashland. Oddly, the glowlamp was on the floor, tipped on its side. He lifted the lamp and set it on the altar.

Brock! He looked around the room for the source of the voice.

Brock! Help! There it was again. It sounded like Ashland, but the voice was in his head. He closed his eyes and shouted with his mind. *Where are you?*

After a moment, he heard it again. *The Foundry! Come quick!*

His eyes flashed open as he leapt off the dais and ran out the door. He sped down the dark corridor and yanked the Foundry door open before darting inside.

It was dark and appeared deserted. A scream sounded from across the long building. Brock sprinted toward the sound, his eyes desperately searching until he noticed a dark silhouette near a burning forge.

"So, peon," Corbin said as Brock came into view. "You've decided to join us for the show,"

Brock stopped, seeing Ashland strapped to a press with her head wedged beneath the press plate. Her hands were tied behind her back, her legs and chest strapped down.

"Corbin, you don't have to do this," Brock pleaded. "Let her go. She's done nothing to you."

Corbin laughed. It was a disturbing sound. "I don't think so. You see, killing her is the perfect way to get to you. You helplessly watching makes it even sweeter."

Brock took a step. Corbin turned the press crank and Ashland released a horrible scream.

"Come any closer, and I crush her head. It won't bother me to kill her. After all, it was easy for me to kill that whore, Amber." Corbin grinned. "She squirmed for a bit when I held her pillow over her face. When she stopped and I lifted it to see her blue lips and empty eyes, the satisfaction was glorious."

Brock was shocked. Not that Corbin had killed Amber, but that he had enjoyed it. He held his hands up.

"Okay. I'm staying here."

Corbin shook his head. "No, move over there," he said, pointing to Brock's left.

Brock moved as directed. "Corbin, please let her go. It's me you want."

Corbin laughed again. "Oh, that's true. Better yet, I now have you both." He reached out and flipped a release on the wall.

Hearing a noise above, Brock glanced up as a wooden beam crashed down on him. The world went black.

Blinking, Brock's vision regained focus. His head throbbed, scraped and bloody from a glancing blow. His chest hurt, and it was difficult to breathe. He realized he was pinned beneath a wooden beam. Shifting slightly, he was able to get his hands beneath the beam. He tried to lift it, but it barely moved. Trying again, he strained with all of his might, and it still would not budge.

Corbin laughed. "This is so sweet. You're trapped but still alive." He laughed again, the demented sound sending chills down Brock's spine.

"Not only am I going to kill your girlfriend, but you'll witness the whole thing before I kill you."

Brock was horrified. He couldn't let Ashland die. As his mind raced for a solution, an idea born from desperation formed. Squirming, he was able to slide one arm from beneath the beam, just far enough to touch the scrape above his temple. He held his finger up to see it red with blood. Using the finger, he traced a rune on the back of his other hand.

A scream of terrified pain came from Ashland as Corbin slowly crushed her skull with the press. Filled with anger and fear, Brock closed his eyes and drew in Chaos. The raging storm of energy made his body tremble, ready to explode. His eyes flashed open and he poured the energy into the Power rune he had drawn.

Brock's vision went white, his body filling up with an immense sense of strength. The vision cleared but remained unstable. He pushed against the beam with the hand still beneath it, and the beam flew into the air, spinning as it crashed into the far wall. Brock climbed to his feet.

Corbin turned to face him with rage in his eyes. He grabbed a solid metal rod standing nearby, grunting as he lifted the heavy bar over his shoulder.

"Why won't you just die?" Corbin screamed as he charged. "Die!"

Corbin drove the butt of the heavy rod at Brock's face. Brock's hand flashed up and caught the rod just before impact. With a super-powered push, he thrust the rod back at Corbin. The other end smashed through Corbin's eye, emerging out the back of his head as the force of the impact blasted him across the room.

Brock ran to the press that held Ashland. Rather than turning the crank, he tore the upper press plate off, and tossed the heavy metal plate aside.

Ashland lay still, her head turned to one side. Trails of blood ran from her eyes, nose, and ears. With his throat tight with fear, he gently put his shaking hand on her face. He closed his eyes and tried to calm himself. When he found his center, he reached out and searched for Order within her. Try as he might, he couldn't sense anything. She was a hollow, empty shell.

Brock opened his eyes and looked at her through tears of anguish. The back of his hand caressed her cheek, smearing the blood trails. He loved her so much. He couldn't lose her. He refused to lose her.

He closed his eyes again, finding his center. Still charged with the Power rune, he tapped into the Order within himself, drawing on it as hard as he could. He bent his will on his own source of Order and forced it into Ashland, demanding that it heal her back to life.

Her body convulsed, and she let out a horrifying scream, echoing the scream that came from Brock's own mouth as the world went black.

47

B rock blinked, but he only saw darkness. Fear struck. Fear that he had gone blind. Fear that he was dead. He sat up and noticed the dim glow of a lamp through a small window. His head swam, dizzy from the sudden movement. When he glanced around, he found that he was on a bed in a small room, the window cut within the only door.

He swung his legs off the bed and tried to recall what happened. Images of his encounter with Corbin flashed in his eyes. Ashland! She was hurt, maybe dead. He had to know that she was okay.

With weak and shaky legs, he tried to stand. Placing one hand on the bed to support himself, he inched toward the door. He tried the handle and found it locked.

Pounding on the door, he yelled. "Help! Get me out of here!"

After a moment, a man's face came into view. It was Master Eldarro, one of the academy enforcers.

"Back up and sit on the bed," Eldarro shouted through the glass.

Brock nodded, complying as instructed. The door opened, and Eldarro stepped inside with a glowlamp in one hand and a cudgel in the other.

"It's good that you're awake," Eldarro said. "Varius thought you'd wake soon."

"Where am I?"

"You're in the Infirmary. You've been here for four days, unconscious," Eldarro replied.

Brock's brow furrowed. *Four days?* "What about Ashland? Is she okay?"

Eldarro glanced toward the door before answering. "The girl? She's in the room next door, unconscious as well."

Brock breathed a sigh of relief. At least she was alive. "Can I see her?"

Eldarro shook his head. "Sorry. Maybe tomorrow, but I can't let you near her."

Brock was confused. "Why not?"

"That's up to the headmaster. He's still gathering information, trying to sort out what happened." Eldarro paused. "For all we know, you're the one who tried to kill her."

"Kill her? I love her. I'd never hurt her," he pleaded. "Corbin Ringholdt was the one trying to kill her, trying to kill me too."

"Perhaps." Eldarro stepped back to the door. "We'll see what Vandermark decides. All we know now is that one student is dead. How and why it happened is what they're attempting to uncover."

Eldarro grabbed the door handle. "The headmaster will speak with you tomorrow as part of the official inquiry. Until then, you'll remain here. Food and water will arrive shortly."

The door closed, leaving Brock alone in the dark room.

Vandermark visited the next morning. Brock described the events in the Foundry the best he could. Unable to answer some questions without revealing the use of Chaos, Brock claimed that his short coma had left holes in his memory. Vandermark finished his questions and departed, leaving Brock alone again.

When Eldarro delivered lunch, he informed Brock that he could go see Ashland, but only through the window in the door to her room. He waited impatiently as Eldarro shackled his wrists behind his back. Eldarro then grabbed his arm and escorted Brock from the room. A desk, a chair, and some cabinets occupied the room outside and only one of the other cell doors was closed. Eldarro escorted Brock to that cell, placing him before the small window.

Brock gazed into the dark room, waiting for his eyes to adjust. When the room coalesced, he saw Ashland laying on her back, as if she were simply sleeping. He smiled despite the tear tracking down his cheek. He longed to hold her – longed to tell her it would be okay.

His thoughts reflected on their last conversation, and he remembered that she had called out to him somehow, her voice in his head although she was far away. If she could do it, maybe he could do the same. Closing his eyes to find his center, he reached out to her.

Ashland. Please wake up. Come back to me. I love you. Please, Ashland, wake up.

Brock opened his eyes, hopeful as he stared into the dark room. The spark of hope began to dim when he saw no movement. Just before the last remnants of hope fled, her eyes opened. He stared harder to ensure it wasn't his imagination. Ashland lifted her head slightly, looked toward the window, and flashed him a weak smile. His heart soared.

"She's awake," Brock said with tears in his eyes. "Thank Issal, she's awake."

Eldarro pulled him from the window, glancing inside to see for himself. He then spun Brock around and dragged him back to his cell before unlocking his shackles.

"You'll need to wait in here. Vandermark will want to speak with her as soon as possible."

He closed the door, locking Brock in his dark prison.

The hours passed slowly. In an attempt to stave off depression, Brock practiced his meditation. Burying himself in the calm solace of Order, he was able to keep his mental state in check.

When dinner arrived, he broke from his meditation and quickly consumed the meal, since he was still recovering from days without food.

About an hour later, Eldarro opened the door.

"Okay, Talenz. You're free to go."

Brock squinted in the light from the glowlamp.

"Free? What happened?" Brock asked.

Eldarro shrugged. "Ask Vandermark. You are to meet with him first thing tomorrow."

Brock emerged from his cell and glanced at the room next door.

"Where is Ashland?" he asked, seeing her cell empty.

"I helped her to her room. She's there resting as she recovers her strength," Eldarro replied.

"Okay. Thanks, then."

Brock exited the infirmary and headed toward Ashland's room. When he arrived, he knocked softly. He bit his lip as he waited for a response, his stomach aflutter.

"Yes?" He heard Ashland's weary voice.

"It's me," he said through the door. "Can we talk?"

"Come in, Brock."

He opened the door and found her on the bed. He smiled, happy to see her. Even if she couldn't accept him being Unchosen, at least she was alive and well.

Brock sat on the chair beside her bed. "I'm so glad you're okay. I feared that I had lost you."

She smiled. "I heard you. You called me back."

Brock nodded. "I just tried to do what you did when you called for me to come to the Foundry. How is that possible?"

"Telepathy," she replied. "It's a rare ability involving Order. You don't learn about it until your second year. It requires two highly skilled ecclesiasts who also have a strong bond."

He nodded, thinking that it made sense. Order was in all living things, somehow connected. A strong connection between the two people must be what made it possible. Taking a breath, he readied himself for the next topic.

"I need to explain something. It's a secret I've shared only with Tipper, and that's because he knew me before I got this." He pointed to the rune on his forehead. "When you touched my head the other day, I'm sure you realized that I'm Unchosen. I wanted to tell you, but I didn't know how." He paused. "Being Unchosen leaves you with few options and no future. I just wanted to make a better life, to make a difference. I paid someone to mark me with the rune of Order and came here to become something better."

"Brock. You don't understand," Ashland said, sitting upright. "I don't care if you're Unchosen. In fact, I saw runes when I read you. I even saw the rune of Order." She shook her head. "But I also saw something else; something the Ministry labels as evil."

Chills climbed his spine, fearful of what she might say. "What did you see?"

Ashland stared into his eyes. "It was a rune that looked like a starburst with four large points."

A second wave of chills washed over Brock. "Chaos," he said. "That's the rune for Chaos."

48

Ashland stared into Brock's eyes. "How do you know what the rune is called? We were never taught what it meant, only that it was bad."

Brock shrugged. "Benny and I have...been doing some research. We found an old book with that rune on the cover and have been translating it, trying to understand what Chaos is and how it works."

She nodded, her eyes downcast. "Well, when I divined you and saw that rune, I wasn't prepared for it." Her eyes lifted to meet his. "But I know you, and I love you. If it's part of you, I've decided it can't be evil. You're too good of a person."

He smiled. "I love you, too. I'm sorry I never told you I was Unchosen. No more secrets, I promise."

He leaned in for a tender kiss. Pulling away, he said, "But if I am Unchosen, then why can you divine runes within me?"

She nodded. "That's because any ecclesiast skilled in divining is supposed to look for that mark during the Choosing ceremony. If the symbol you call Chaos is present, the person is to remain Unchosen. It's one of the first things we learn in apprentice-level training."

Brock thought about what she said. It seemed to make sense. That's why he was skilled in Order, despite being Unchosen. He was born with the talent, but they didn't mark him because they saw Chaos within him as well.

"There's something else, Brock." Ashland looked down at the floor. "I also am Unchosen."

He was surprised, never imagining that he wasn't the only one at the school under false pretenses.

She continued. "When I was ten summers, my parents used everything they had to pay for me to be marked. They then sent me off to live with a distant uncle to train for the Academy."

Curious, Brock leaned in and placed his hand on her forehead. When he drew upon her, he saw symbols appear. The first was Order, but Chaos and four others followed.

His eyes opened to see her staring at him, fear reflecting in her expression. When he nodded, she looked down to stare at the floor.

Softly, she said, "It's...what I've feared since I first learned about the rune they call evil. That I was Unchosen because it is part of me."

He put his fingers under her chin, lifting it until their eyes met. "Ashland, I refuse to believe a rune marking some ability within you is evil. You said it yourself about me."

She nodded, smiling. "How do you always know how to make me feel better?"

He shrugged. "Maybe I read a book that told me what to say."

It was late when Brock stepped into the boys' lounge. Benny, Cam, and a dozen others were in the room, talking in small groups. One by one, they noticed him standing in the doorway, their conversations stopping as they stared in his direction. Benny was the last to notice.

Benny stood and exclaimed, "Brock! You're free! Are you okay?"

To the room, Brock announced, "I've been cleared of any charges. I don't have details yet, but I'm to meet with Vandermark in the morning. And, yes, I'm fine."

The boys gathered around him, patting him on the back and stating that they were glad to see him. Some asked about the incident with Corbin, but he explained that he couldn't discuss it until meeting with Vandermark. When they dispersed, Parker pulled him aside.

"I'm glad to see you're free, Brock. When I heard that Corbin was dead, I went to Vandermark and told him about Corbin's obsession with you. I convinced most of the others to do the same, hoping it would help your case."

"Thanks, Parker," Brock replied. "I appreciate the support. I just pray they let me stay and put the whole thing behind me."

Parker nodded. "By the way, you missed the archery contest while you were out."

Brock had forgotten about that. "That's right. I'm sure I wouldn't have qualified anyway. At best, I'm average with a bow. How did you do?"

Parker smiled, pulling a medal from inside his tunic. "First place with the longbow," he said, proudly displaying his prize.

Brock nodded, grinning. "Good show, Parker. I heard you were skilled, but I guess I didn't realize how well you handled a bow."

"Effects of a misspent youth," Parker grinned. "I've been competing with a bow since I was ten summers, winning the Sol Polis Tournament two of the past three years."

"That explains it," Brock said. "Congratulations."

Brock patted Parker on the shoulder and left to join Cam and Benny.

"Hi, Benny. Have you made any progress?"

Benny smiled proudly. "I finished the book on the Wailing War."

Brock raised a brow. "What did you find?"

Benny sat forward eager to share his findings. "Well, you know how The Banished Horde was an unstoppable force, destroying any army it opposed until the final battle?" Brock nodded.

Benny smiled. "When the Ministry got involved, things changed." "Okay. Spit it out," Brock said.

"In order to combat the might of The Horde, the Ministry unleashed a secret weapon. They don't ever name it in the book, but there are hints and clues. Apparently, the use of Chaos turned the tide. The armies of man defeated The Horde and returned to Fallbrandt, where they agreed to form what is now the Empire."

Brock nodded. "Interesting. That makes sense. According to Byland Hedgewick's note, the Ministry decided to erase any mention of Chaos from the histories. But what happened to the Chaos users who helped to defeat The Horde?"

Benny shrugged. "The book doesn't say and that was hundreds of years ago."

Brock sighed. "Well, we aren't going to solve this tonight. I'm heading to bed. I'm exhausted, and I have to meet with Vandermark in the morning."

~

Vandermark finished reading the report, set the paper down, and leaned back in his chair. He stared at Brock, his gaze lingering for an uncomfortably long moment before he leaned forward and broke the awkward silence.

"I'm sure you're aware that this will be a delicate situation for the Academy. I've been put in a position where I must inform the leader of the Empire that his son is dead–dead at the hands of one of our own students, no less."

Vandermark paused, exhaling. "However, after a thorough investigation, I have determined that Corbin was at fault in this matter. Why he was on a mission to destroy you is still unclear. Perhaps that's something you can shed some light upon?"

Brock nodded, steadying himself. "On our first day at the Academy, he and I got into an altercation. He was forcing himself on a female student, and I stopped him. He...took offense to my standing up to him. That was the first of a series of confrontations. After I defeated him in the Arena Championship, it became even worse. He was aware that I am...very close to Ashland, and he wanted to hurt me by hurting her. When I came to her defense, he attacked me."

Vandermark nodded. "That story makes sense, based on the information I've gathered. What I still don't understand is how the solid metal rod was driven through his skull. You're a fit lad, but not nearly strong enough for that."

Afraid the conversation might lead in this direction, Brock had prepared the best story he could concoct.

"Sir, as you know, I was rendered unconscious for days following the event. Other than grappling with Corbin to release Ashland, I don't remember much at all. I recall that somehow, the press broke, and a huge wooden beam went flying. Perhaps one of those events caused the rod to impale Corbin. If not, then I have no idea."

He stared back at the headmaster, trying to appear as innocent as possible. His armpits were damp with cold sweat, but he maintained a calm exterior.

"Very well," Vandermark replied. "Before you're dismissed, you must understand that any details of Corbin's death are to remain private. I am sure other students will ask about it, but you will tell them that you are not allowed to discuss the death of another student. Do you understand?"

Brock nodded. "Yes, sir."

"Please resume your classes as scheduled. The year ends soon, and you have little time remaining to prove you have what it takes to continue at the Academy. You are excused."

Brock stood. "Thank you, sir. You won't be disappointed."

He stepped to the door, pulled it open, and left to resume his career at the Academy.

49

"W hen Brock came around the corner on the Hedgewick Roller, the whole class gasped, even Karl Jarlish," Benny said, trying to not spill his glass of wine. "Brock sped in, looking as if he might run right into the crowd until he pulled the brake and the roller slowed to a stop, just inches from where Nindlerod stood.

"The old man began clapping and hopping around, giddy with excitement. I was so happy at his reaction that I jumped in, grabbed his arm, and danced a jig with the old coot." Benny laughed and everyone else joined in.

"And that's why we celebrate today. My invention, the Hedgewick Roller, has earned the top prize for this year's Invention Challenge." Benny held his glass high. "I hope that in years to come, people throughout the Empire can benefit from this affordable form of transportation." He climbed down from the chair and clinked glasses with others standing nearby.

Brock felt happy for Benny. The boy had some crazy ideas, but they usually turned out to be genius. He put an arm around Ashland's shoulders and sipped his wine with the other.

"I'm surprised you agreed to ride that thing after the last episode," she said to him.

He nodded. "Yeah, I know. I have to give Benny credit, though. He took my complaints to heart and made some changes. Now that there's a way to stop the thing, it's actually fun to ride."

Brock glanced around the room, estimating that over two hundred students had gathered in the lounge, including many girls. Once word spread that three casks of wine were part of Benny's celebration, students swarmed to join the party. Even Parker was there, laughing with Benny as they chatted. Without Corbin in the picture, Parker appeared to be a new person, free from Corbin's influence. In fact, most of the boys who had followed Corbin had befriended Brock and the others in the weeks since his death.

Benny patted Parker on the back and strolled over to where Brock sat with Ashland. "How do you like my little party?" he asked.

Brock lifted his glass to tap Benny's. "I've never heard of anyone throwing a party for themselves, but I like it. I bet the wine cost you plenty, though."

Benny shrugged. "It wasn't that bad. I paid for it with some of the coin I was awarded for my invention, so it evens out."

"You still haven't told me how you've been able to get the casks here anyway." Brock remarked.

Benny smiled. "Take a guess."

"I bet Dory helped you get them."

Benny frowned. "You spoiled the secret. It's not as fun now." Brock laughed.

Cam approached, nodding to the group. "There's one week left of school. What are you doing for summer break?"

Benny responded, "I plan to go see my father in Selbin."

Brock shrugged, glancing at Ashland. "We haven't decided except that Ashland and I plan to go somewhere together. What are you planning, Cam?"

"I'm traveling to Nor Torin to see my family. Maybe you guys could come with me?"

Benny jumped in. "Hey, Selbin is on the way to Nor Torin. We could travel together."

Lars approached the group. "What are you going on about now?"

Brock replied, "Hi Lars. We're talking about summer break."

"Oh, that. I'm going to see my mom and pops at their farm just past Selbin," Lars said before downing his wine.

"I'm from Selbin," Benny said. "In fact, these guys are going to Nor Torin, so we thought we'd travel together." Benny reached up and patted Lars' thick shoulder. "Would you like join us, Lars?"

A wide grin broke out on Lars' face. "If you guys will have me, I'd like that a lot."

"Of course we'll have you, Lars. You're one of us, too," Brock replied.

Benny called out. "Parker, come here."

Parker walked over. "What's up, guys?"

"We're talking about what we're doing for summer break," Benny replied. "We're all going the same direction, so we're traveling together."

"What are you planning, Parker?" Brock asked.

"I'm heading to Sol Polis, which is pretty much the opposite direction from you guys," Parker replied. "I'm traveling with the others down to Wayport, and we're taking a ship the rest of the way to save time."

Brock nodded. "That's what I expected. I guess we'll see you when break is over then."

"If we all make it," Parker said. "We haven't been raised to apprentice yet."

Brock hadn't thought about that. *What if I'm not raised?* After the incident with Corbin, he hoped that the Academy didn't decide it was more trouble to keep him around than he was worth.

Grouped by level, students filled the heart of the massive temple. A narrow section of masters divided each of the three groups like a purple spoked wheel of blue. The dais at the center of the wheel included Headmaster Vandermark and Master Ackerson, who assisted in running the proceedings.

After an initial welcome speech, Vandermark began calling the names of adept-level students who were being promoted to master. One by one, they approached the dais to accept a master's cloak and a signed writ, proclaiming their newfound status. Beginning with the loremasters, the ceremony continued one discipline at a time until all of the new masters had been announced.

Next came the apprentice-level students who were being raised to adept. As it was with the previous group, the ecclesiastic students were the last names announced. Brock waited anxiously until Ashland's name was called. He clapped and cheered as she approached the dais to claim the pin she would add to her cloak, marking her as adept. He was happy to see her continue toward her dream to become a master.

Finally, the advancing novice-level students took their turn. Vandermark began with those who would specialize in Lore before moving on to the Engineers. As expected, Benny's name was one of the first called. He held his new cloak up for everyone to see before reclaiming his seat.

Vandermark proceeded by announcing the Hierarchists, with Parker's name as one of those advancing to the apprentice ranks.

When he began announcing future Paladins, both Lars and Cameron sat up in anticipation. Neither had to wait long. Already among the best fighters at the school, it was obvious to Brock that they would advance.

To complete the ceremony, the headmaster began calling the names of those being promoted to apprentice ecclesiast. As the names were announced and Master Varius handed new cloaks to proud recipients, Brock grew increasingly more nervous. With one cloak remaining, Vandermark announced the last name.

"And our final novice to advance is Brock Talenz."

A wave of relief washed over him. As he stood and made the trek to claim his prize, he found himself reflecting on the incredible odds of his accomplishment. From an Unchosen nobody, he was one of only fourteen ecclesiast students raised to apprentice and was just two years from becoming a master.

He accepted the cloak from Varius, clutching it to his face to kiss it. As he returned to his seat, he wiped the tears of joy from his eyes with the precious new cloak.

EPILOGUE

A single glowlamp on the altar lit the center of the dark training temple. Master Varius turned in Brock's direction upon hearing him enter.

"Ahh, Brock," she said from across the room. "Thank you for coming. Please join me."

He descended to the center of the room and climbed the steps of the dais before Varius addressed him.

"You're probably wondering why I asked you to meet me here tonight. I wanted to speak with you before you left for summer break." Her expression appeared serious as she looked him in the eye. "I'm sure you've realized that you're more skilled with Order than your classmates. What you may not realize is that you may be the most powerful ecclesiast we've seen in generations. Ironically, the only student I've seen who's even close is Ashland.

"You have the ability to be something special, Brock. I saw a glimmer of that the first time we met. Since then, I have watched you blossom, your skill and power growing steadily. It will be years yet before we know your limits. Perhaps you'll uncover abilities we haven't seen in centuries."

She glanced toward the door, then back to Brock. "You might be wondering why I'm telling you this. Others among the Ministry fought hard to have you expelled after Corbin's death. I fought to keep you, informing Vandermark of your potential. I convinced him that unless he found proof of your guilt, it was worth the risk of upsetting the Archon."

"Thank you." He nodded. "I appreciate your support."

Varius nodded. "It was for the benefit of the Academy and the Empire, but you're welcome."

She continued, "I've requested to instruct the upper-level ecclesiast classes next year. I plan to guide your development, Brock. You've become a bit of a private project for me, and I don't intend to let another take over now."

"Thanks." He didn't know what else to say.

"Have a good break, Brock. I'll see you in a month," she said, before turning toward the altar.

He left the temple, walking down the quiet hallway as he considered the exchange with Varius and the message she was sending. She had bet on him and expected a return on that investment.

Seeking a moment alone, he stepped out into the dark summer night. A cool mountain breeze was chasing the heat of the day away. He looked up at the stars, inhaling the clean air.

A noise caught his attention and he realized that someone was out on the lawn, not far from the building. He descended the stairs and followed the path to where the person stood. As he approached, the person jumped.

"Who's there?" Croaked an old voice, one that Brock knew well.

"It's Brock, Master Nindlerod."

"Brock? Oh, Brock," the master engineer replied. "You startled me. You shouldn't sneak up on an old man in the dark. This old ticker could blow, you know," he said, tapping his chest.

Brock smiled. He liked Nindlerod. "Sorry sir. I'll be sure to make more noise next time."

Nindlerod nodded. "Okay, then."

The old man then bent to look at some odd device consisting of large tubes mounted to a tripod.

"If you don't mind my asking, what are you doing?" Brock asked.

"Well, come over here and see for yourself." The master stepped away from the device.

Brock stepped closer and bent to look into the tube. Closing one eye to see better, an image appeared. It was a bright circle with swirling lines.

"What is it?" Brock asked.

"That's a planet, my boy," Nindlerod said.

Brock looked into the sky where the tube pointed and saw what looked like a large star, flickering in the night sky.

"I don't remember that one," Brock said.

"Exactly. That's the problem," Nindlerod replied.

Brock looked at him. "What do you mean?"

"Boy, I've been charting stars and planets for five decades."

Nindlerod pointed at the sky. "I've never seen this one before, either." "That's odd," Brock said.

"Yes. Very odd indeed," the old man replied. "The oddest part is that it continues to get larger."

"You mean it's growing?" Brock asked.

The master shook his head. "No, boy. I mean that the image keeps getting larger. That's because it's getting closer to us, to our planet."

Brock's gaze drifted toward the sky. The revelation left him unsettled, feeling as if a long shadow had darkened his future.

The story continues in The Emblem Throne, Runes of Issalia Book Two.

NOTE FROM THE AUTHOR

I hope you enjoyed The Buried Symbol. If so, Brock's adventures continue in *The Emblem Throne* and *An Empire in Runes*, books 2 and 3 of the series.

Best Wishes,
Jeffrey L. Kohanek

For my latest book news, sign up for my author newsletter at www.jeffreylkohanek.com

ALSO BY JEFFREY L. KOHANEK

Fate of Wizardoms

Book One: Eye of Obscurance

Book Two: Balance of Magic

Book Three: Temple of the Oracle

Book Four: Objects of Power

Book Five: TBD

Book Six: TBD

* * *

Prequel: Legend of Shadowmar

Runes of Issalia

The Buried Symbol: Runes of Issalia 1

The Emblem Throne: Runes of Issalia 2

An Empire in Runes: Runes of Issalia 3

Rogue Legacy: Runes of Issalia Prequel

* * *

Runes of Issalia Boxed Set

Heroes of Issalia: Runes Series+Rogue Legacy

Wardens of Issalia

A Warden's Purpose: Wardens of Issalia 1

The Arcane Ward: Wardens of Issalia 2

An Imperial Gambit: Wardens of Issalia 3

A Kingdom Under Siege: Wardens of Issalia 4

ICON: A Wardens of Issalia Companion Tale

* * *

Wardens of Issalia Boxed Set

Made in the USA
Columbia, SC
12 October 2021